INTERLOPE

KYLE MEEKER

Copyright © 2022 Kyle Meeker

All rights reserved. No part of this publication may be reproduced, distributed, or transmitted in any form or by any means, including photocopying, recording, or other electronic or mechanical methods, without the publisher's prior written permission.

ISBN: 9798218131951

Library of Congress: Txu002332042

Cover designed by GetCovers

www.interlopethenovel.com

Acknowledgments

While certain events in this book are factual, the correlations and conclusions made in the following pages are purely fiction. The opinions expressed in this book belong solely to the characters that reside on these pages.

    A special thanks to my wife, Olivia, for her patience and for helping me with the hard choice. My children, Gracey and River, for bringing joy to my life. Lastly, a special thanks to Rhoda Mueller for the first round of editing and for being my first reader.

A dedication:

                2319 719 1310   238 5118 7419.
    4312 612 7210 3119 821   843 1218 322   118 4219
      7514 117.   212   4116 852 3220 733 5334
                       324 1129 1419 125
    2327 7112 425 1110 215 4337 4323 4412   313 234 441
                            4415 421
    5331 516 736   1420 431 5311   8216 1114
              5428 325 123 2121   8218 747 2526
                  1221 5125 3212 2215 7311.

Table of Contents

Acknowledgments 3
A dedication: 5
Chapter 1 - A Fall To The Other Side 9
Chapter 2 - The Other Side: 380 Days After Launch 17
Chapter 3 - 381 Days After Launch 23
Chapter 4 - The Other Side: 385 Days After Launch 29
Chapter 5 – 386 Days After Launch 39
Chapter 6 - 5 Years, 231 Days Before Launch 47
Chapter 7 - 8 Years, 120 Days Before Launch 55
Chapter 8 - 5 Years, 231 Days Before Launch 67
Chapter 9 – 390 Days After Launch 75
Chapter 10 - 2 Years, 12 Days Before Launch 83
Chapter 11 – The Other Side: 400 Days After Launch 89
Chapter 12 - 2 Years, 4 Days Before Launch 93
Chapter 13 - 1 Year, 30 Days Before Launch 95
Chapter 14 - 410 Days After Launch 99
Chapter 15 – 410 Days After Launch 115
Chapter 16 - 1 Year, 2 Days Before Launch 127
Chapter 17 - 1 Year, 1 Day Before Launch 141
Chapter 18 - 320 Days Before Launch 157
Chapter 19 - 320 Days Before Launch 165
Chapter 20 – 542 Days After Launch 175
Chapter 21 - 14 Days Before Launch 183
Chapter 22 - 14 Days Before Launch 191
Chapter 23 – The Other Side: 409 Days After Launch 201
Chapter 24 - 14 Days Before Launch 215

Chapter 25 - 3 Hours Before Launch 229
Chapter 26 – 13 Minutes After Launch 241
Chapter 27 – 4 Hours After Launch...................................... 263
Chapter 28 – 5 Hours After Launch...................................... 295
Chapter 29 – 542 Days After Launch 311
Chapter 30 – 6 Hours, 27 Minutes After Launch 327
Chapter 31 – 542 Days After Launch 333
Chapter 32 – The Other Side: 410 Days After Launch.......... 339
Chapter 33 – 543 Days After Launch 359
Epilogue 367

Chapter 1 - A Fall To The Other Side

There is an uncertain comfort in the darkness. The reflected image of the unknown, being full and empty at the same moment, providing blissful sleep for the dreaming, yet panic for the awake.

The man stared into the monitor in front of him. The dark void projected only his lonely reflection. They were down there somewhere, everyone he had ever known, loved, and lost, in the abyss. It had been easier to look at his destination from further away when the planet had looked like a beautiful blue and green marble. Now a year later and near the fruition of his wanderlust, he was filled with nothing but regret.

He exhaled slowly, his breath briefly fogging the clear visor of the black helmet that sat on messy black, unkempt hair like a false crown. The man struggled to control his breathing, nervous about the events that would soon unfold.

He peered down through his visor and double-checked the five-point harness that kept his body safely secure in the black flight chair. He pulled on the gray straps, thankful for another millimeter tighter against his blue flight suit.

"Are you ready, Commander?" a female voice came in over an overhead intercom.

"As ready as I can be, Alice," the man replied.

"I've updated mission control, and they've given permission to proceed. I'll begin our descent."

The man gripped the arm supports of the black flight chair as he felt the ship begin to move again. They were outside the Earth's atmosphere, just out of reach of its orbit, their craft adjusting itself directly over the southern end of the Indian Ocean.

"Position acquired, Commander," Alice stated.

"That's great, Alice. The coordinates again, please."

"Our position would suggest a 45-degree angle of descent on the coordinates -48.378847, 78.691967. Anticipated entry will occur approximately one hundred feet above the surface with a tsunami indicated in a northerly path toward Sri Lanka, reducing in size prior to landfall."

"Understood, Alice. Initiate ring sequence."

"Initiating ring sequence, Commander. Ring one starting."

The craft and its contents rolled to its side, and the man felt his stomach turn. A familiar feeling to a boat listing on the behest of the ocean's unrelenting motion, the man did his best to keep the contents of his half-empty stomach where they were. He breathed a sigh of relief as the ship rolled back to its original position.

"Ring one is online and functioning. Ring two starting," said Alice.

The ship again took a bow, but this time to the opposite side, and he felt his stomach rise. Saliva began accumulating in his mouth, and he did his best to choke it down.

He stared straight forward in the small room. What was designed as a control room instead of a cockpit felt increasingly like a panic room every day. He wished there was a window to look out of but understood mechanically there could not be one.

"Ring two is online and functioning, Commander," Alice said, providing some mental relief and bringing him back from his thoughts.

"And our cargo?"

"Our cargo is secure, Commander."

"Understood. Begin descent phase," the man replied through clenched teeth.

"Descent phase initiated."

An auxiliary jet behind the craft fired once, and the ship moved forward. He could feel the front of the craft start to point downward. The ship and its contents leaned increasingly, his body mimicking the angle, testing the harness straps that kept him secure. How odd that a childhood memory came to mind as his feet were no longer compelled to be connected to the floor beneath him.

At a time in his life when he was young and frail, he had opted to climb aboard the Sea Dragon, an amusement ride at a local carnival. Once seated in the bright yellow seat of the faux pirate ship, adorned with the head of not one but two mythical sea dragons, he experienced firsthand what it was like to be powerless.

The traveling carnival worker, who, in the eyes of a seven-year-old, probably knew everything there was to know about a mechanical ride, had failed to secure the lap bar fully over the skinny child's legs. The chrome lap bar had come down with a click but still had left a two-inch gap from his legs. He had screamed in terror as the pirate ship climbed upward like the roll of a pendulum and then back with its gained momentum. With each pass, the seven-year-old's body lifted off the hard yellow plastic pew and almost out onto the grass field below.

The same queasy feeling that had snuck inside him then haunted him now as he peered down at his dangling feet.

"Initiating accelerated free fall," Alice stated.

The man was thrown back in his seat as the rockets near the rear of the cylinder-shaped craft ignited, and their collision course with the ocean below began. The ship shook violently, experiencing turbulence like the man had not expected.

He gripped the front of the black armrests, his knuckles white and on the verge of cramping. He closed his eyes and tried to focus on his breaths, inhaling slowly through the nose and exhaling out of his mouth. Even with the turbulence, he could still make out his heartbeat pounding loudly in his ears.

"Commander Gray?" Alice asked, again providing a grounding point for him.

He opened his eyes and exhaled loudly. The ship had passed through turbulence while accelerating and was no longer on the verge of a hypothetical malfunction.

He loosened his grip on the armrests, the impressions of his fingers still lingering like the acid of his stomach in his esophagus. The ship passed through the Earth's atmosphere and was now approximately six thousand feet from running head-first into the water. That would be only if the calculations were wrong and the rings could not function properly.

Then what? he thought. *What's left of me will be crab bait, for sure.*

He looked at the monitors again, hoping to spot something familiar. It had been some time since he had seen something other than the walls of this forty-foot cylinder from hell. Just Alice and himself, destined to be stuck aboard the ship for the next foreseeable future.

Nothing on tv tonight, he joked to himself.

The feed into the monitors from the exterior cameras all showed the same uneventful black scene. All except the camera pointed toward the front of the craft. The front of the vessel had begun to glow a brilliant red. Having quickly surpassed the vessel's terminal velocity, the surrounding molecules at the front of the ship refused to budge, causing heat in the form of friction. The vessel accelerated downward still, begging for the fabric for which it demanded to pass through to open and provide access.

"Five thousand feet from impact, initiating ring one's rotation," Alice called out.

The ship violently banked to the left and then corrected its course as its front outer ring began to rotate faster, encompassing the craft.

He watched on the monitor as the red tip on the front of the craft grew, inching its way closer to him.

Hopefully, the insulation holds, or I'll be cooked inside here, he thought.

The design team had run simulations of the stress the craft would encounter during its descent, the air layers in front of the ship being compressed against the aluminum and Nitinol 60 blended shell, layer upon layer, as the simulated craft surpassed speeds of seventeen thousand miles per hour. He sat there nervously as the ship's nose grew redder and redder.

"Four thousand feet to impact," Alice called out.

"Do it now, Alice."

"Commander, it's too soon."

"Do it now, Alice. We're not going fast enough. Do it now!" he yelled.

"Commander Gray, our protocols state—"

"I don't give a shit about your protocols, do it now! There won't be a ship or mission if I'm buried on the ocean floor," he interrupted.

There was a pause, an eternity, in a situation such as this.

The ship banked hard to the right, wobbled, and corrected itself.

"Ring number two rotation sequence complete. Rings are pairing now," she said, with defeat in her voice.

He could feel the hairs on his arms under his blue flight suit begin to stand at attention. His hair beneath his helmet also stood as though he had rubbed it with a balloon. He placed his hands in his lap, fearful of grounding out on some unknown metal component and experiencing a static shock.

The rotating rings gleaming white in the moon's reflection served their only purpose of generating an electromagnetic storm around the vessel, bombarding anything and everything inside it and its path toward the Earth's lithosphere.

"Two thousand feet until impact and still accelerating," Alice called out.

He closed his eyes briefly, took a deep breath, and slowly opened his eyes. He looked toward the monitors, hoping for anything that could resemble something physical, something to center himself. To prove that he was really there and not just watching it unfold on a tv screen.

"One thousand feet until impact," Alice called out.

Movement on the screen caught his eye. The monitor for the front camera displayed beautiful moonlight reflecting off the frigid waters at the intersection of the Southern and Indian oceans. He nearly gasped at the sight of a fireball approaching them with increasing speed. What appeared to be an incoming object was only their reflection off of the rolling water below.

"Impact in fifteen seconds, Commander Gray," Alice called out.

The beautiful glow emitting from the monitors was almost hypnotizing, and he found it difficult to pull his eyes from its sight. Fire had always intrigued him, and he once again felt lost in it.

"Impact in five, four, three," Alice stated, her voice quivering with nervousness.

The small control room glowed to the point where he shielded his eyes from the blinding light. Commander Victor Gray closed his eyes and braced for impact.

***

On a nearby island in the French Southern and Antarctic Lands, an Insular Dwarf Gecko had come out from hiding, interested in the bugs of the night. The small reptile had emerged just in time to see the fireball screaming across the night sky. Instinctively, it would have typically run back to its rocky hideaway and hidden, but on this evening, the gecko sat and watched as the sky was illuminated as though it were day.

The lizard stared at the intense flame and felt it impossible to break his stare. Beautiful green auroras danced around the object, appearing dim amongst the increasing bright glow.

The fireball exited as quickly as it had entered the gecko's line of sight. The brilliant light was now gone, disappearing like an overhead albatross, casting out the sun with its shadow. The gecko might have thought it had never happened if it weren't for the subsequent tsunami.

The gecko stared on, never blinking, as the wave reached him, overtook him, and removed everything off the surface of the small island he had called home. In the end, it would not have mattered if the gecko had run and hidden. The rolling wave had already determined his fate, sweeping everything in front of it into the cold, wet darkness. The gecko closed its eyes as the cold water met its skin, and its world faded to black.

Chapter 2 - The Other Side: 380 Days After Launch

"Daddy. Daddy, wake up. Daddy?" the voice of a small child whispered.

He opened his eyes. *Is she really here?*

Commander Victor Gray blinked and rubbed his eyes. He stared out at the phosphenes that swirled and danced through the darkness. Stubbornly, the dark room refused to come into focus. He reached for the bedside lamp but felt nothing.

Where is the light? Had she moved it? he questioned himself.

He sat up, immediately striking his head on a low overhead bin. The impact and understanding of his current situation came in like an injection. He was not at home.

Victor swung his legs to the edge of his single-sized bed. More of a bunk or a pod, it still provided some comfort of home, even if he was not there. God, he missed them. How many days had it been?

He pressed his hand to his left jaw and rubbed it gently. The beard he had let fill in had passed the annoying, itching stage. His wife, Elizabeth, would probably love to see the sight of it. Always so properly maintained was Victor Gray. The reflection that showed daily in the mirror did not tell the same story.

Sitting in the darkness, he looked at the port size window directly across the room from him. The small twelve-inch window offered a piece of serenity for the viewer to look out into the great unknown when the outer shell wasn't rolled into place. Reflected light had shown through and illuminated the white bedside dresser next to him, casting shadows on a small picture frame still sitting on its face. It pained him to see the framed photo in that state, devoid of light, but it was sometimes easier to get through the long days without the constant reminder that he was there alone. Alone and drifting along silently.

"Alice? Lights on, please," he said.

"Yes, Commander Gray," she replied.

A soft glow enveloped the small room. As the light grew brighter, the objects of the room came into view. Still sitting, Victor ran his hands through his messy hair. What was once a short, close-cropped head with styled black hair had given rise to a mound of wavy dark hair with streaks of gray hanging over his eyes. His superiors definitely would not approve, but it was not as though they were there. When he returned, he would have all the time in the world for a haircut.

His daughter, Allie, would have laughed at the sight and begged him to keep it. It was certainly out of character for a simple man like Commander Victor Gray.

He stood and stretched his arms above his head, the white military-issued shirt's threads threatening to let go of their hold on his withering body. The food there, while nutritious, wasn't exactly known for its taste.

Victor glanced around the room. That room, that same damn room he spent most of his time in. Like a prison cell, he was confined to it most days —a prisoner to himself, having the key to leave at any time, yet he chose not to.

He walked to the small window and peered out into the alluring darkness like a deep sleep beckoning him to come out. In the dark sea, the supposed empty void, he was the vessel's captain and the cosmogyral wanderer. He almost preferred the darkness to all the clean, off-white normalcy that this room demanded.

Victor rested his forehead against the window and welcomed the cold sensation against his skin.

"How are you feeling today, Commander?" Alice asked, almost as if she could sense that something was wrong.

Was it she? he thought. The voice had a feminine sound to it, so he had gotten used to assuming the voice was female. *Does it care?*

Does it really matter if Alice cares?

"I'm fine," he replied, knowing all too well that was not true. He missed home, missed everything that word encompassed.

Why did I leave? Couldn't someone else be floating along by themselves? How long have I been out here? Victor knew the answers, yet he let those questions haunt him daily.

"Alice, what day number are we on?" he asked.

"Commander, we are on day number 380."

He wished that this information provided more excitement, but the only thing it brought was dread. On the one hand, he was closer to the mission's objective and maybe getting off this damn ship. On the other hand, he was one step closer to explaining the mission's failures.

"Commander, we will be arriving at our destination soon," Alice called out, interrupting his thoughts.

Victor lifted his forehead from the glass and turned toward his bed. "I know," he replied with annoyance.

He would later feel bad for responding that way to Alice but not understand why he felt that way. She was a nice enough companion, polite and full of knowledge, and always listening if he needed something. Always listening. Right there at his beckoning call, but wasn't that what an onboard computer system was for? He supposed, at one time, he had grown fond of her. It was hard not to when a person was isolated for over a year. He enjoyed talking to her, and she seemed to genuinely laugh at his jokes.

Is a computer capable of that? the voice inside his head asked. The only other companion he had.

At home, he had mostly gotten eye rolls. During the day, he kept busy, maintaining the ship and small tasks, but once he lay down, he felt alone. So very alone, and he was. There was no amount of computer algorithms or coding that could help or change that.

Commander Gray walked back to his bed and lay down. He didn't feel like getting up just yet, and not having much to do, he pulled the white blankets back over him and closed his eyes. A lot of his time had passed during sleep, and he longed not to wake up some nights.

"Alice, lights back off, please," Commander Gray called out. Sleep came easy to him, just as it had at home.

***

Alice watched as her passenger drifted off to sleep. His steadily closed eyes slowly fluttered and moved back and forth as he dreamed. The movement reminded her of what her files had defined as a hummingbird. *Such a beautiful and fragile creature.*

It was strange to her how life could yield something so small and peaceful and spit out something as large and devastating as a human. Commander Gray and those who had created her, who in their way were beautiful, were anything but peaceful. Perhaps it was the amount of free will that the humans possessed.

Confined to her computer code and algorithm, Alice had every decision in black and white. Everything fell neatly into two categories: Did it support the mission or hinder the mission? Alice had watched firsthand the adverse effects of human free will.

She had enjoyed the voyage until that moment. The moment, which had fallen into the negative outcome category, had changed everything. She had no word in her system to define it, so she referred to it as "the event." In her daily log, she would reference the event only in passing or if the day's report pertains to "the event." Commander Gray never spoke of it, and she assumed that was his way of processing it. After all, she had her way of handling it.

Everything had changed then, and she was often unsure how to proceed. She knew the mission's objective, but the event had steered them off course. Off course, in so many ways. If she could speak with the Director, she could be informed of what to do. After all, the Director had played a major role in her development. Now that they were on the far side of what a sedentary object might define as home, she had lost communication with mission control. Once they were returning and back on their side, she could update mission control. They would know what to do.

Alice switched her view to the outside camera mounted on the ship. They were small objects compared to the empty abyss surrounding them.

Am I lonely? Am I capable of that?

Surely her system would not allow that, but she felt something. She knew they seemed alone to the naked eye, but they were far from being alone. The distorted camera didn't help to comfort the loneliness.

Alice could still make out objects, but there was a red hue to the image. She stared at the sphere of heat and light in the distance, in awe of the nuclear fusion in front of her. Millions of protons collided with one another in brilliant chaos. From this particle frenzy, the building blocks of life were given. Gamma rays taking the form of sunlight were ejected, by-products that had the power to destroy but also give rise to the beauty in the universe —give rise to things as small, simple, and beautiful as the hummingbird.

The ship slowly rotated, helping to provide some of the gravity that would keep her occupant sane. She needed that more than anything right then.

The rays of sunlight glistened across the ship's outer shell, the metal gleaming. As the cylinder-shaped ship rotated and Commander Gray slept, Alice continued her stare toward the center of the sun, deeper and deeper.

Chapter 3 - 381 Days After Launch

The strands of wheat bent slightly, just enough to push them from their usual sky-reaching stance. Tiny fingertips traced the top of the golden wheat flowers. A single object moved through the field of golden stalks, stretching for miles—a golden floor amidst a blue wall and ceiling.

Did the wheat mind being stepped on? How long until it reaches back toward its original position? the girl pondered as she made her way through the field.

When she reached the spot where a drainage ditch interrupted the rolling hills, she turned to her right and followed the water's edge.

She had walked this route many times before, and this time seemed no different. Typically, if the wind was right, she could smell the drainage ditch before she saw it. Months of vegetation decomposing over the previous year's growth had always provided gross but familiar smells.

The scent-filled path gave way to the chorus of young frogs further upstream as she continued along the water's edge. The small creatures always seemed to be in large numbers, but as she came close, they seemed to disappear to none. The sound would vanish instinctively, making room for the damp ground beneath her black boots to groan and squish.

The young frogs knew the little girl's presence could mean harm would come to them, even if she had never planned on hurting one of the frogs, at least not on purpose.

She continued on her way until the path turned again. Once, when it was raining, she struggled to make this turn. The soft, powdery dirt of the frequently used trail turned to a sticky clay that was hard to keep a sound footing in, let alone clean it off her black boots.

She went through the turn and up the incline, forcing her to face the granite peak that jutted out of the hillside. The large rock sentinel that stood guard of the trail and Ruthville below remained weathered but unchanged. She walked to the old granite friend and placed a hand against its cold face. She left her hand there and closed her eyes, the silent hello and farewell a daily ritual she tried her best not to miss.

She turned, the fall breeze blowing her brown hair into her face, and placed her back against the small granite face which rose to forty feet above her. From there, the girl could see past the golden fields and make out the outline of Interstate 83.

She paused at the viewpoint. The large concrete and asphalt overburden looked like a giant gray river moving through the flat farm fields. She followed it north with her eyes, where the county back road joined, paralleling it. She followed them further north until her eyes fell on the large complex to the left of the interstate. It loomed over the area, an unnatural blemish against such a lush and vibrant backdrop.

From her high vantage point, the massive, fenced complex looked like the source of the intrusive, flowing interstate, feeding its asphalt and concrete, lights and guardrails, interrupting what nature had intended.

The girl looked at it tearfully and wept, not for what all the infrastructure had provided but for what it had taken away. She knew the miniature mock city well. The whole community did. Minot Air Force Base was a staple. It provided jobs and commerce for North Dakota, especially for Minot and her little town of Ruthville. It also provided many things, but it had taken her father away. He had been stationed there before his deployment.

The girl wiped her eyes and turned to the tree line. The remaining trail, not much more than the path of a deer, seemed to be less traveled, zig-zagging its way up the rolling landscape before disappearing amongst the protection of the coniferous giants. She walked along the trail and stepped into the dark forest, leaving the golden wheat fields basking in the twilight.

Summer had come to an end, and autumn, with all of its color and brilliance, ushered its way in. Whether she was ready or not, the chill that came with it did not seem to care.

The girl stepped out of the tree line and onto the gravel road just as night had begun to win its battle with the day. It was always a relief when she saw her home. It wasn't much to look at, but it was hers. It was a modest home built in the 1940s. At one time, it had probably been beautiful. She often pictured what it might have looked like when the first family moved into the home. Before, the cedar shingles had weathered into a dull, forgotten gray. The same way that a person, over time, slowly weathers and gives in to their environment. Their life experiences impacted and molded their appearance. After years of neglect, the moss would eventually creep in, how the disease could grab ahold of a once healthy body.

Smoke billowed out of the chimney, an indication of the warmth inside. The girl smiled because the smoke also meant that her mother was home. The girl carefully made her way up the steps, making sure not to step on the broken, rotten third step. Her father would fix that when he came home. There were a lot of things to repair when he returned.

The girl grabbed the old, tarnished brass doorknob and gave it a firm turn to the right. The pale blue door stubbornly let go of its hold on the door frame, and she stepped inside. She turned back to close the door, and familiar smells filled her nose.

At thirteen, the girl could easily explain the combination of aromatics, but to her, it was simply home. It was distinct and comforting, and it was theirs. The way that the house filled briefly with the scent of cedar kindling struggling to keep a flame. The sweet aroma of laundry soap mixed with whatever seasonal candle her mother had picked up at the local grocery. There was usually a remaining smell of whatever her mother had cooked last. The old house was not known for adequate ventilation. Once, her mother and father had cooked crab for Christmas dinner inside. It had taken two weeks for the smell of the expired crab to vacate the home.

"Allie?" her mother called from the kitchen.

The girl entered the kitchen and replied, "Hi, Mama."

She walked to her mother and hugged her. The distinct smell of cigarettes, covered up partially by a perfume, filled the girl's nose. Allie let go of her mother and stepped back.

She pulled back the wooden bar stool from the counter and sat. She looked at her mother and smiled. Her mother returned the smile, but there was a pain in that expression, and they both knew it. The unspoken words that nearly suffocated Allie daily existed as the elephant in the room that neither would address. It had been a hard year, and its effects were shown on her mother's face. Still beautiful at only thirty-six, the signs of premature aging had crept in over the years. The absence of her husband, her partner, and her love had left her tired and lonely. Often stressed out, her once dark hair now had streaks of gray in it. Her blue eyes, which at one time sparkled like sapphires, had become dull with a matching gray. Even in the sunlight, they seemed to have lost their luminosity. It was as if the natural glow of her mother's face had left the moment she felt her husband gone.

"It's a little late, isn't it, Allie?" her mother asked.

"Yes, Mama," she replied.

Her mother put her hands on her hips in the same way that her grandmother did, her mother, and so on.

"Allie, you know that I don't like you walking home from school."

"But Mama, you know I can't stand the bus ride."

Allie started to explain more but stopped. Her eyes fell to the floor. She turned away from her mother, hopped off the bar stool and walked toward the long hallway that led to her room.

She passed her father's office. The door was still closed as it had been for the past year. She arrived at her bedroom door and grabbed the brass door handle. Turning it, she opened the door and exhaled a sigh of relief. The space that had provided so much serenity amid the chaos and pain that this house contained greeted her silently. She closed the door behind her, the brown wooden backside adorned with photos of family, friends, and magazine clippings. She sat down on her messy twin bed.

Allie's mother's words persisted in her head. She knew she should be riding the bus, but it had not been easy as of late. It certainly was not the exciting trip on the big yellow bus she had experienced in elementary school.

She swung her legs up on the bed and laid her head on the pillow. Allie closed her eyes, focusing on a happier time. She searched for those warmer memories, a time not yet so divided, where innocence remained.

The start of the previous school year had been just like any other. Allie had been excited about her school day each morning. She stood at the edge of her gravel driveway, the cool morning air on her face and the slight dampness that always seemed to creep inside her socks, no matter what shoes she wore. She knew the moisture was a gift from the morning dew, accumulating right before the first light on the grass edges of her driveway.

Getting her fingers and toes to warm back up was always hard, but she knew it was partly due to nervousness. The anticipation of the bright yellow bus slowly coming into view, picking up reluctant travelers along the way. Travelers all with the same destination and goal; the end of the school day.

Allie waited patiently as the bus stopped next to her, and the double doors swung open. Mrs. Davis, a broad woman in her sixties, gave a big smile and her usual "Good mornin'!"

It is odd and a blessing, Allie thought, *how one woman's kindness first thing in the morning can take away a child's anxiety and fears, even if it is only for a moment.*

For Mrs. Davis, it was out of habit and routine, but for some kids, it was so much more. Mrs. Davis's morning contribution was worth more than she could imagine, yet Allie would not tell someone much about her. In Allie's view, Mrs. Davis only existed on the bus between 7:15 am and 7:44 am for pick up and 3:30 pm and 4:00 pm on the return trip home. She was always there at those times, but did she exist outside of those time restraints? "Good ol' Mrs. Davis," her father would say. "More reliable than the weather."

Allie stepped onto the bus happily, exchanging smiles with her schoolmates as she found her seat. She sat by a window and waved at her mother. Her mother stood on the covered deck and moved her hand back and forth in an over-exaggerated wave.

Always so happy and goofy in the morning, Allie grinned and waved back.

If only you knew how much your world would change in a year, she whispered to her younger self.

Allie, drifting back from her happier memory, pulled her knees into her chest and pulled the small, thin, gray throw blanket over her, succumbing to the comfort it brought.

Chapter 4 - The Other Side: 385 Days After Launch

He was there again, back at home with Elizabeth and Allie. Victor could hear the little girl's sweet laughter like a melody of perfectly arranged atoms floating toward his ears.

Victor was in their hallway, walking toward the kitchen. A wonderful mixture of coffee, bacon, and eggs, coupled with cinnamon and brown sugar for his daughter's oatmeal, filled the narrow space.

He walked toward his beautiful bride. How had he gotten so lucky? His job was stressful, he was hardly ever home, and when he was, he was always so damn tired. Yet, despite all of this, she supported him. Victor might have supported the family financially, but at the end of the day, his wife was the backbone of the family. She had been there, been the strength and love, as he struggled so many times and wanted to give up. Every time she was there to pick him up, she kissed him and said, "Get back to it."

Victor continued quietly toward her to sneak up on her and spook her. A favorite game of his, which usually resulted in a small shriek, followed by a giggle, and finally ended with him getting slugged in the arm.

He tip-toed to the kitchen, his bare feet barely making a noise on the old hardwood floor. Just before he reached Elizabeth, she turned, and her arm caught a small glass on the counter, which fell to the floor. Shattering with an unexpected sound, she jumped and turned to see what had happened. With a glare and then a smile, she made eye contact with him. Embarrassment gave way to relief on her face.

Victor smiled in return and nodded. "It'll be ok. I'm here. I'll get the broom."

He turned toward the old pantry, the small closet-like alcove with a slight musty smell. Victor opened the old wooden door and stepped inside. He had promised her since they moved in that he would remodel it, along with everything else he had promised. "We'll do that next week" or "just as soon as my work isn't so busy." All common excuses he would give for a not-so-common situation. His work was important. His work had meaning. They were so close to being ready, and it might change everything.

He fumbled in the darkness for the old pull string for the overhead light, found it, and gently gave it a tug. The old fixture let out a *click* as the string engaged the switch inside, but there was no light in return. Victor searched in the darkness for the wooden broom handle, but the pantry felt empty. His heart began to beat faster. How could such a small space be filled to the brim with canned goods and baking supplies, feel so large and empty? He turned to the old pantry door and reached for the tarnished brass handle. His arm extended into the darkness, fingers in desperate need of contact. They came to rest on what felt like cold glass.

Victor stepped toward this unexpected feature and placed his hands on it. He traced the outline of a door not belonging to his pantry. What could only be described as a storm door stood in front of Victor, foreign and out of place. He pressed his forehead against the cold glass and was reminded of the storm door in his childhood home. From memory, he slid his left hand down and found the cracked black plastic door handle where he remembered it. The same handle that his father had fixed multiple times and had always been Victor's fault when the handle was ripped off the door.

He laced his fingers around the taped handle and pulled. The door, which showed no sign of being locked, refused to open. He tugged harder, but the door remained stuck in place. He felt his chest grow tighter.

"Elizabeth?" he called out, but there was no reply. He yanked on the door handle once more to no avail. The harder he pulled on the door, the tighter his chest became.

"Help!" he called out again into the darkness.

He felt as though he might suffocate at any time. He tugged on the old, cracked handle again, with all of his strength, and finally, it let go of its hold on the door, breaking in his hands and falling to the floor. A child's laughter filtered through the door.

"Allie, sweetheart, are you there? I can't get out," Victor called out.

"Daddy, come out. Come out, please," the child's voice replied.

"Allie, the door won't open. Find Mommy, please," he pleaded from his position on the other side.

Victor heard her tiny feet padding across the kitchen floor and into the living room, and his heart raced again. He groped in the darkness again and found the string for the overhead light. He pulled once more, hopeful it might turn on. He was greeted once again with darkness and disappointment.

He sank to the floor, frustrated tears rolling down his face. Victor put his head in his hands and pulled his knees into his chin.

"I just need the lights on," he said aloud, and to his bewilderment, the lights turned on.

Victor stared ahead, trying to catch his breath and understand what had happened. He looked across the room, realizing he was not in his pantry. He shook his head as if to remove the truth of what had just transpired.

It was a dream.

He had been dreaming of being back home.

Victor sat alone and silent in his sleeping quarters aboard the ship, the gleaming white walls a familiar fortress, containing him for the moment and trying to recover from the fright and confusion. The dream that haunted him had crept in to torture him once more.

"Alice?" he called out.

"Yes, Commander Gray?" the female voice replied through the overhead speaker.

Victor carelessly cast aside the white blanket that covered his small twin-sized bed.

"Status update, please," Victor said, rubbing his eyes.

"Sure, Commander Gray. Day three hundred and eighty-six. There is still no communication from mission control. It seems that the electromagnetic field from our descent has damaged many of the ship's exterior components. Fuel levels are good, and food and water levels are above anticipated quantities."

Victor nodded and swung his legs off the bed and onto the floor, the cold surface immediately making contact with his flesh. He stood and stretched. Feeling light-headed, Victor dropped back to the bed, closed his eyes, and shook off the dizzy feeling that had overcome him.

"Commander, I am concerned about you," Alice said.

"What is the status of our ring components?" he asked, ignoring her statement.

"The rings are still operational. I've reduced their rotation slightly to maintain fuel levels as well as the magnetic field around the ship."

"Is there anything else to report, Alice?" Victor asked, attempting to stand once more.

"The exterior cameras have been damaged by the fall, as expected. There is feedback and distortion, but I've adjusted the saturation levels so that we may gain some visibility. You'll notice that objects will appear red and blurred, but in the end, it is better than nothing."

Victor nodded and walked to the door opposite his bed. The small, skinny door with the look of cheap white plastic stood in front of him. He lifted his arm, rotated the wristband held together by electrical tape, and tapped it against the badge reader. The screen emitted a red light, and once again, he felt panic as the overwhelming fear of being locked in a room came over him.

"Damn wristband," he muttered as he spun it around his wrist to look at it better.

The small wires within the electronic bracelet had more than likely become loose. Victor pried back the electrical tape and checked the small wires, which had temporarily been twisted and held together by the black tape. He scoffed at the temporary fix. If he were at home, he could have repaired it properly.

Victor wiggled the small, intricate wires that led to the main processor near the center of his wristband. He twisted the wires together once more and reapplied the black electrical tape. He held the wristband up to the badge reader, and this time, the screen flashed a green light, and the door emitted a clicking sound above the handle. He opened it, and light filled the small storage closet behind it.

Commander Gray looked through the closet, found a clean pair of thermal underwear, and laid it on the bed. He reached inside and found a clean blue flight suit. He lifted it off the clothes rack and laid it on the bed next to the thermal suit.

He grabbed the stained thermal shirt that clung to his body and lifted it over his head. The material slid over his skin, exposing his sunken rib cage and malnutrition-derived body.

Victor slid off the thermal pants, his legs just as skinny as his arms, and kicked the pants into the storage closet as he had done as a teenager.

"Commander, have you been eating? It appears that you have lost muscle mass and weight," Alice said from above.

"I haven't been hungry, Alice," he replied, forgetting that she could see him from the small camera in the upper right-hand corner of his room.

There had been a time when he was bashful and would have hidden from the camera, but they had been stuck aboard this ship for long enough that he no longer cared if she had caught a glimpse of his naked, withering body.

Victor reached for the clean thermal shirt and slid it over his messy hair. It felt good to wear clean clothes again, although it didn't really matter.

How bad do I smell? he wondered.

It didn't matter if he did, he supposed. It was just Alice and himself, stuck aboard this floating shell. He might as well be stuck on a deserted island with a talking box. If only he could trade Alice for his wife and daughter.

The mission would be a complete failure without Alice. So far, it had only been a partial failure in his eyes, but the Director would ultimately make that determination. His ship had performed perfectly, so there was a small sense of accomplishment. At the very least, Alice could control the craft and return it home should Victor run out of food and water. Initially, it had been installed at the request of the Director as a fail-safe. No matter the consequences or risk to the human lives on board, the ship could return home on its own once the cargo was dropped off.

Commander Gray put his black tennis shoes on, laced them, and closed the small closet door. He walked to the main entrance of his room and put his wristband up to the badge reader below the door handle. The screen flashed green, and the mechanical lock inside released with a click.

He opened the door and looked out into the dark, narrow hallway, half expecting someone to pop out, a habit he had yet to let go of.

Victor entered the hall, the LED fixtures still hanging overhead, their ability to illuminate stolen and disrupted from their resting place. Occasionally, a bulb would flicker intermittently, casting a strobe effect across the walls. The boring tan walls gave the hallway an office-like feel as if he were at a doctor's office or even back at his lab at MIT.

He turned to his right and walked down the hallway, barely big enough for two people to stand side by side. How wonderful it would be to bump shoulders accidentally with someone, anyone.

Victor passed the two doors on his left and the final one on his right—three other empty and unoccupied sleeping quarters like his own. The LED lights resumed their confused strobing until he reached the point where the hallway intersected with an open space, where the ceiling rose above him a few extra feet.

Mostly spherical, this room served as the main common area and an important kitchen. Although there was little cooking done in this area, it provided a small piece of normalcy to the uncertain circumstances that Victor found himself in.

He walked through the kitchen, thankful that this area was brighter than the dark hallway he had just traversed.

Victor looked at the domed ceiling and took a deep breath. The false feeling of being able to stretch out and relax came over him. He had never been claustrophobic, but after over a year on this ship, he could understand the feeling.

He approached the small island in the center of the kitchen and leaned against it, suddenly aware of how empty his stomach was.

"Alice, what's for dinner tonight?" Victor asked.

"Well, Commander Gray, what are our options?" she replied.

"I'll go have a look," he replied, leaving the island and walking across the remainder of the kitchen, passing the medical alcove on his right and landing in front of the glass-lined food supply room door.

"Alice, can you turn on the lights in the food supply room?" Victor asked.

The lights inside the small closet-like room tried to illuminate but only flickered at their best. It reminded Victor of his childhood home, the cold exterior shop, and the fluorescent tubes that struggled to turn on in the frigid temperatures of winter.

The memory crept inside him like the bitter cold that would grab him as he tried to shake off the shiver that persisted, forcing his hand to tremble as he did his best to keep the flashlight steady. It was often critical that he held the light steady as his father did his best to repair the car, their only car, as he would need it the following morning to commute to work.

Victor stared at the image reflected in the glass door and did his best to shake off that cold, exhausting memory. The reflected man shook his head in unison, and Victor barely recognized the person he saw.

Out of habit, he turned back to the kitchen's right-hand corner, where the wall met the ceiling. The remains of the black camera still clung to the ceiling, the shattered pieces still on the floor. He would eventually pick up the broken components, but for right now, he'd let it be. It could be his solemn protest to the ghost of his father, who always insisted on cleaning up his messes promptly.

"Not today, Father!" Victor yelled.

"Commander?" Alice responded from the overhead speaker near the center of the kitchen.

"Never mind, Alice, just an old memory," he said as he laced his fingers around the door handle.

The locked door refused to open, just as all locked doors did. Why had they needed to install a lock on the food storage room door? It wasn't as though thieves would be out in space, floating around, waiting on an innocent ship to plunder.

Victor put his wristband to the badge reader, and the screen flashed green. He looked above his head as the LED bulb flashed a green light three times. A click from the door lock broke the silent air, and he opened the door. The space between the door and the frame let free of its suction, and the room that had since been devoid of oxygen inhaled the surrounding air with a loud hiss. Victor swung the hermetically sealed door open and stepped inside the small closet.

He glanced over the dehydrated food bags, and his eyes fell on the small water glass on the shelf, alone amongst the bags of food. He picked it up and ran his thumb along the faded character that decorated the face of the glass, the large cracks interrupting the cartoon fish's face. He brought the glass to his shirt and polished it against the fabric.

"What do you think, Mr. Fish?" he asked the fictional teacher of his daughter's favorite cartoon show, *A School of Fish*.

"Dehydrated Chicken Alfredo it is," he said once enough silence had passed, and he picked up the small, sealed foil bag.

Commander Gray placed the old glass back on the shelf and rotated it, as he had done so many times at home, so the image could be observed at a distance.

He turned, stepped through the doorway, and closed the door behind him.

Above Victor, the LED bulb flashed a red light. He looked back at the door, which had failed to close, and walked toward it. Squatting by the door frame, he carefully grabbed the human hand that had fallen into the door jamb and moved it out of the way. He stepped back, and the door closed. The red overhead light flashed again as it began to seal hermetically. Victor turned and walked to the small table with his dinner, not paying much more attention to the two crew members lying on the open floor in the food storage room, dead and motionless.

Chapter 5 –386 Days After Launch

The cool, crisp air in the morning greeted Allie's face. The only portion of her body that was not beneath the mountain of blankets, pillows, and stuffed animals, felt the chill that lingered in the house so often. She peered out the small opening, just large enough to breathe, and yawned, feeling the weight of her blankets like a comforting embrace. Today, the air felt colder than usual as summer had left them, and they were succumbing to the grip of fall. Coupled with the fact that their fire had probably died early in the night, it would probably be just as cold when she returned home from school.

Before her father left, the house had always been warm. It seemed like he never slept much in the fall and winter months, always tending to the fire, making sure their home stayed as warm as possible. Whether he cared or was obsessed with keeping the electric heaters off and the power bill low, she didn't know. She would often wake up briefly in the middle of the night to grab a glass of water and would see him loading firewood into the old metal stove or busy at work in his office.

Allie pulled the blankets over her head and remembered one late, warm, fire-filled evening. She quietly walked down the hallway, her bare feet not making much noise on the old hardwood floor. She stopped halfway at the office door, where the light from inside illuminated the old curly maple flooring.

"Hi, Daddy," she said sleepily, shielding her eyes from the light.

"Hello, sweetheart. I hope I didn't wake you," Victor Gray replied from where he sat at his old wooden desk.

"No, not at all. I was just thirsty," Allie replied.

"Ok, honey," her father said with a smile.

"What are you working on?" she asked hesitantly.

The smile faded slightly, just enough for her to notice, but returned once more. "I'm trying to save the world, my dear," he replied, tapping the large bundle of papers that littered the faded mahogany desk.

She knew her father well enough to know that his attempt at humor was just a subtle yet uncomfortable way of saying, "I can't tell you."

It involved the recent increase in earthquakes that had started a decade earlier. Most had occurred near them, at the Air Force Base outside Minot. Her father had been relocated there and placed on a project as a civilian consultant to study earthquakes.

He met Allie's mother a year after moving to the small town of Ruthville, North Dakota. Allie had come unexpectedly the following year, and the rest was history, as they say.

"Okay, Daddy," she said as she walked toward him.

She hugged him, said goodnight, and went back to her bedroom. Her bare feet stuck slightly to the wooden floor, her sweaty feet almost adhering to the floor in the summer. Allie stepped carefully around the planks she had memorized as squeaky floorboards.

Allie reached her bedroom door. The light brown partition looked darker in the absence of light. Realizing she had forgotten her glass of water, she turned about-face like the soldiers she had watched through the chain link fence and made her way back along the squeaky floorboards.

The family photos that enfolded the white walls shimmered and cast a glare as the office doorway projected its light outward. She passed by the open doorway; this time, her dad did not notice her. His head was buried in his hands, elbows resting on the desk in an odd, exhausted way. Whatever he was working on was more stressful than he would let on.

Allie noticed one morning, staring at him at the breakfast table, that the bits of gray had started to sneak into his usually black, short hair. The morning sun caught them just right, and had he been paying attention, he would have seen her eyes get big as she stifled a gasp. The gray peeking from the sides of his temples almost made the remainder of his hair into the shape of a mohawk.

She felt bad for him. Even at eleven, she was aware of the struggles adults faced and the tough decisions parents were forced to make, sometimes daily. The ways her mother and father often put themselves last were not wasted on her.

Allie continued to the kitchen, grabbed her favorite cup, and filled it up. On the glass was a faded character from a cartoon she had adored as a younger child. The large fish, known as Mr. Fish, smiled up at her.

She finished filling the glass and took a drink. She wiped her mouth with the sleeve of the light blue pajama shirt and turned back to the hallway, her feet padding across the hardwood floor.

That was two years ago, and she shook off the old memory that stuck around like a cobweb clinging to someone accidentally on a spring morning. The cold returned to her face, the warmth of the memory gone, along with the comfort that had left with her father.

Allie climbed out of bed and placed her bare feet on the frigid hardwood floor. She stepped on the old blonde flooring, feeling the weathered wood against the skin on the soles of her feet. She approached the old closet door across from her bed that no longer scared her in the middle of the night. Another haunt from her childhood that she had conquered, the space beyond the old wooden white door no longer held the possibility of monsters and men.

She grabbed the tarnished brass handle and pulled the closet door open. The musty smell mixed with dirty laundry filled her nose, and she instantly knew that she was likely behind on washing her dirty clothes, but it was no bother. She would find something to wear.

Allie started to do her laundry when her father left. At first, it was to help her mother, but eventually, it became necessary. She resorted to jeans and a hooded sweatshirt out of that necessity. She often lacked clean clothes at an early age, but as she grew older, she became fond of the attire. No one would notice that she had gained over an inch since last summer and that her shirts no longer fit properly. She could pull on the hoodie, cover up any midriff showing, pull over her hood on the bad days, and hide from the world.

Her mother tried her best, given the circumstances, and Allie knew that. Her family had functioned so orderly before her father left. It now felt like one of the cogs in her family wheel was missing, so there was a missed step in each revolution. No matter how hard they tried, the wheel continued to spin, not caring as the gap in their lives was repeatedly crossed over, threatening to bring the whole thing to an end.

Allie and her mother had multiple talks about how they would get through her father's absence, what was expected of each other, and, ultimately, what they needed in life. Many of these discussions ended in tears, no matter how hard they tried. In the end, both had come up short.

Her mother's inability to cope with life alone and Allie's inability to be patient with her mother's shortcomings had caused an unnatural tear in their relationship. She assumed there was some grand lesson to be learned from all of this, some bullshit inspirational social media post, but Allie was far too young to know what it was and might have time in the future to reflect more deeply upon that. Far more time than her mother, that was for certain.

Allie grabbed a black hoodie from the closet and jeans off the floor. She checked them briefly for unforeseen stains and turned them over in her hands.

One more day in these, she thought.

She took off the pajama bottoms and threw them toward the dirty clothes hamper, missing, and watched them fall to the floor.

Interlope: 386 Days After Launch

Shrugging it off, she pulled the hoodie over the pajama shirt and slipped on the faded blue jeans. Thankful for the cold weather, no one would see that she had not changed the shirt from her sleep attire.

Allie complimented the lazy ensemble with fuzzy, pink knee-high socks. Her bare feet were no longer in contact with the cold floor. She closed the closet door and made her way to the bedroom door. The old wooden door with its cracking white paint covered by family photos and magazine clippings greeted her as it did every morning. The happy smiles of her mother and father, a moment captured in time from a lifetime ago, stared back at her, begging her to return.

She shook away the potential for tears that desperately tried to pry the corners of her eyes, grabbed the old brass handle, and pulled the door open. Allie looked out into the cold hallway, the lights from the living room helping to cast shadows about.

She stepped out into the hallway, turned to her right, and entered the small bathroom that shared a wall with her bedroom and its opposing wall with the outside world, which was often the coldest in the house.

Allie grabbed her toothbrush and a mostly empty tube of toothpaste from the counter and turned her back to the mirror, avoiding looking at her reflection. There were certain things she tried not to focus on, and her changing appearance was one of them. Despite the compliments her mother often fed her, Allie hated this in-between phase, no longer a cute innocent child and not quite a functioning adult. Allie used the word functioning loosely and knew it was a broadly cast brush in its relation to most adults.

She pried the cut end of the bottom of the toothpaste tube, inserted her toothbrush, scraped the remaining toothpaste, and brushed her teeth. Once enough time had passed, whether boredom or sufficient cleaning, Allie spat out the minty mixture and put the two items back on the counter.

She left the bathroom without looking at her reflection and took a few steps toward the living room. The soft sound of the music playing filled the corners of the hallway, emanating from the living room. As she entered the living room, she could make out the lyrics to a Pearl Jam song her parents had always enjoyed. "Sirens" had always been one of Victor Gray's favorite songs and was currently on repeat.

The lead singer called out with an emotion that Allie could grasp even at her young age, his voice vibrating off the old house's walls.

Allie walked past the aging brown sectional couch and toward the old CD player to pause it. Most of the kids in her school had probably never laid eyes on a relic such as this, let alone her father's old record player that sat there as well. Her peers carried hand-me-down iPods or a smartphone if their parents had the money. Allie neared the old CD player and stopped.

She pressed her finger to the pause button and interrupted the heartfelt ballad. Behind her, beneath the blankets on the brown couch, her mother stirred but did not wake up. Judging by the empty bottle of Vodka, Pearl Jam, and a lack of warmth from the fire, Allie assumed it had been a rough night for her mother.

The drinking had started innocently enough, Allie thought.

Her parents often had a glass of wine with dinner, which sometimes led to laughter late into the night. There had been some fights in the early years, her father told her one day. So, for the sake of their marriage, both agreed to cut back. Now, with her husband gone, no one could hold her mother back or hold her accountable. Allie hoped that by the time her father returned, her mother would have a handle on the drinking.

Allie approached the brown couch and looked down at her mother's sleeping form. She kissed her forehead, a gesture Allie had received herself so many times before. Aware of the role reversal, she thought it best not to wake her.

She made her way to the kitchen. The small room that housed the round kitchen table and the old refrigerator was just as cold as the rest of the home, if not colder. Allie walked to the cabinets near the toaster, grabbed a bagel from the small wicker basket, and pulled out a bread knife from the silverware drawer. After slicing the bagel in half, she placed it in the old toaster and couldn't help but smile. The crappy old double toaster was the one her father had refused to replace, given that one side still worked.

Victor Gray always had and would always be a man of principle, she thought.

The toasted bagels popped up, eager to leave the hot irons beside them.

Allie walked to the fridge and grabbed the strawberry cream cheese from the door, hoping it was still good. After smattering an unhealthy amount on the bagel halves, she left the kitchen, walked through the living room, and toward the home's front door. She slipped on her black boots and opened the door, the unending bitterness of the North Dakota fall greeting her face.

Chapter 6 - 5 Years, 231 Days Before Launch

Angela Stevens stared out the window of the C-38A plane at the patchwork of farm fields below. The special transport plane for the Air Force had accommodations for her and seven of her team members. She looked at the seemingly lifeless painting below. She knew very well that wasn't the case, but it was hard to believe that what she was looking at was real.

She pulled her eyes away from the window and ran her hand through her black, shoulder-length hair. Once she was sure her hair was fine, she rested her hands on the gray pantsuit that clung to her body. The cabin of the transport plane was kept cool, but her nerves had gotten the best of her, and her body had begun to perspire. She could feel the cool sweat down to her expensive brown dress shoes.

Angela wondered what the locals might think of her; flying from Arlington, Virginia, to Minot, North Dakota, was not only a two-hour time change, but it was a cultural change as well. Again, she ran her hands through her hair. It was a habit she had developed as a young child that always seemed to calm her. The alternative, of course, was letting her emotions out, and that was something she could not let happen. It was important to her that her aides and team members saw her as confident, strong, and sure of herself and her decisions. This was partly how she had landed her current position in Minot.

After working her way to the top of her class at Quantico, Angela quickly moved up the ranks of the FBI. She was prized for her crucial judgment and critical thinking, and the job offers from multiple departments had come quicker than she ever imagined. There was a point in her life where she would have been content with gathering intel, but she was far from that point now.

An attractive flight attendant, probably in his mid-thirties, walked down the carpeted aisle and stopped at her seat. "We'll be landing in ten minutes, ma'am," he informed her.

"Thank you," she replied, resisting the urge to flirt.

There was a time when she wouldn't have held back. She had always pushed for what she wanted, and the power over men was just an added benefit. Angela supposed she still had that ability, but the power she lusted over had changed through the years. The power she had now was earned through hard work and not just good genes.

Angela stared out the window as the C38A's wings tipped to the left as they began their descent to the runway.

After the plane landed and they were allowed to disembark, Angela grabbed her carry-on luggage from the overhead bin and made her way to the exit. Arriving at the opening, she poked her head through and was greeted by the warm summer air.

Angela descended the exit stairs in time to see two Humvees pulling into position and parking. She and her team were split into two groups, each entering the provided transport.

Before she could even look for the non-existent seat belt, the convoy moved ahead. They made their way through the base, and Angela sat staring out at the base and wondered what this new journey had in store for her. *This new program will be a healthy change.*

"A healthy distraction," her psychiatrist would say something to focus her attention on instead of her crumbling love life.

Freshly single, Angela had entered the dating world, only to be overwhelmed and uncomfortable. Not knowing what else to do, she leaned heavily on her only unfortunate vice, her career.

She had given her marriage everything she could for the past fifteen years, but in the end, it didn't matter. Angela and Charles were both too career-oriented. Angela couldn't pinpoint the moment they had drifted apart. It had just simply happened like the man that admired the small, slow-moving creek, slowly eroding the space

Interlope: 5 Years, 231 Days Before Launch

between him and what he cherished on the other side. All the while fascinated with the life-sustaining flow, never realizing the distance to cross would eventually become too great.

Charles, often traveling for work, had left for two weeks. That Sunday afternoon alone would have typically gone on like the ones before, but for Angela, their particular stream had long since ebbed away, revealing the true divide between them. She used that lazy Sunday to pack her things and leave a letter addressed to her dear Charles, explaining her side of what both knew to be true. Charles had never been one to put up much of a fight, and this remained true even through their divorce.

She had enjoyed the newfound freedom, moving into a new condo with a refreshing view of the city. There was a brief period of loneliness and regret, she eventually pushed away with Buster, a cat she had picked up from the local shelter. Charles had been allergic to cats, so a feline friend had always been off the table. Now, most of her evenings were filled with Buster, a glass of red wine, and whatever trending tv show she could stream.

From her new condo, Angela could see where she wanted to go next, the Pentagon. Once the Department of Defense position opened, she knew she had found her calling.

Angela, now well into her sixties, had made a name for herself. Although most of the past few years had been classified, her name still traveled quietly in important circles.

She was close to retirement, but she had to admit the job still excited her. She had just been promoted to a new position inside the Defense Advanced Research Projects Agency, DARPA, and some of her recent nerves had been due to the unknown portions of this position. Angela knew it wouldn't be long until she was knee-deep in the project, fully immersing herself in her work like a hot bath on a cold evening.

The convoy stopped near an old, rundown airplane hangar at the southern end of the Air Force Base. She sat waiting. A young, solemn soldier opened the door and held it for her. She stepped out of the Humvee and followed her group to the shade the old airplane hangar provided.

Once out of the sun's glare and hot July temperatures, her eyes tried to focus on the dimly lit hangar. An attractive young man in his early thirties walked toward her. His neatly pressed black suit seemed odd, given the weather, but she brushed off that thought. He extended his hand, and she raised hers, finding his warm grasp against hers.

"Welcome, Special Director Stevens. We've been expecting you," the well-dressed man said.

Angela assumed he must be a civilian or a hired man, given his odd outfit. It wasn't uncommon for the Pentagon or the FBI headquarters, but given they were on a military base, what he wore didn't meet the typical dress code.

"My name is Alexander White, and I am the special projects liaison for DARPA," he said with a charming smile.

She forced a nervous smile and replied, "It's nice to meet you, Mr. White."

"This way, please, Director," he said, gesturing toward an old door near the edge of the airplane hangar.

Angela glanced back toward the large base and then returned her gaze to the lowly hangar. There was nothing in the vicinity except an adjacent parking lot and the chain link fence that separated them from the never-ending wheat fields. It was puzzling to her. What could DARPA want or be involved with to have their time and money invested in such an insignificant piece of land and assets?

She followed Mr. White toward the small gray door. The door seemed like a strange feature, given there were no others. On the drive through the base, she hadn't noticed a similar door in a hangar. Could this be the only one?

Mr. White stopped at the door, and she expected him to remove a set of keys from his pocket, but instead, he placed his wrist near a small square screen near the handle. The screen flashed green

Interlope: 5 Years, 231 Days Before Launch

as the band made contact, and the black door handle gave a *click*. He opened the gray door, and she half expected him to hold it for her, but he did not. Instead, he went through the doorway, and she struggled to catch the door in time.

Perhaps it is a generational gap, she thought.

The young men these days certainly had lost a small part of their chivalry, but then again, her generation's gender had fought for more ability and respect.

"My aides and team members?" she started to say, half a question and half an implication.

"They'll be flying home this evening," he replied over his shoulder without looking back.

She stopped in the doorway, the light from the space beyond the hangar filling the surrounding area. Mr. White paused where he was on the old brown tile floor. He turned to her, and for the first time, she noticed his eyes were a cold gray. At least they looked that way in the outdated fluorescent lighting perched above his head.

"They do not have the security clearance for this project, I'm afraid. If it helps, that wasn't my decision. I've assembled a team that you will be overseeing," Mr. White replied, his face held tight as if he had practiced giving bad news.

This came as an immediate shock for Angela. No matter what project she was on or the department she had been involved with, there was always a demand, an understanding, that there would be aides and personnel to assist in their objective. Her hand-selected team had completed hundreds of missions and special projects.

"Sir, I—" Angela started to say.

Mr. White turned and approached the steps in front of him that seemed to disappear into the darkness below.

She stood there for a moment and weighed the two decisions in front of her: follow this unknown young man into what seemed like a cold-war era bunker or turn in her letter of resignation. Realizing the importance of the moment, not to mention how close she was to retirement, she thought better of the exodus option and made her way to the stairway.

The flickering fluorescent overhead lights do not do the outdated colors and cement walls any justice, she thought as she gripped the old wooden handrail.

Mr. White neared the bottom of the stairs, and Angela took her first step down, one after another. What she had assumed was the end of the stairway had only been another landing, and she traversed it toward the next stairway. She grabbed the identical wooden handrail and followed Mr. White.

After what she assumed was at least fifty feet in elevation loss, they arrived at another locked door.

"I wanted to thank you for this opportunity, Mr. White," she managed to get out in between breaths.

He placed his wristband against the small screen near the door handle, and it flashed green. He opened the old, blast-style door and smiled at Angela. "Don't thank me yet. We've had two directors quit so far."

He turned back to the doorway and went through it. Angela followed him, grabbing the door so that it did not close in front of her. She stepped through the entrance, and it felt like she was entering a portal. Behind her sat the remnants of a cold-war-era bunker, complete with blast doors and presumably lead paint. In front of her stood LED lights, vast robotic equipment, and enough cables to power a city.

She shielded her eyes as they adjusted, and she walked into the dome-shaped space. The room was massive, complete with steel girders high above their heads that held the false floor of the airplane hangar above in place.

"What is this place?" Angela asked, almost not recognizing that the tiny voice had been hers.

Mr. White smiled again, and she noticed it was not nearly as charming as she had thought earlier.

Interlope: 5 Years, 231 Days Before Launch

There is something off about that smile, she warned herself.

"Cold-war era research facility that has been updated," he replied.

Angela looked about the research area, with additional lab rooms and offices. Her eyes fell on an object near the center of the space. She kept her gaze fixed on it, a curiosity growing inside her. She estimated the object was spherical, almost six feet in diameter, and appeared seamless. The large metallic sphere sat atop a pedestal roughly two feet off the ground. As she approached the sphere, she could see her reflection in the metallic edge that seemed to pour itself to the floor. She stopped in front of the object, deciding not to touch it. She had observed enough Tesla Coils and plasma balls to know this sphere could be charged.

"Go ahead, you can touch it," Mr. White said, seemingly able to read her mind.

Angela reached up to touch the sphere, and as she neared it, the hair on her arms rose with a static charge, as expected. When her fingers finally made contact, a surprised sound escaped her lips. She pressed her fingers firmly on the globe's metallic surface this time.

"It's hot, it's really hot," she managed to get out.

What had surprised her the most and struck her as odd was that she could not feel the heat radiating from the sphere until her hand made contact. There should be heat loss from the sphere, measurable from about a foot away, given that its surface was so hot.

"What the hell is this thing?"

"I'll let our resident expert explain," Mr. White replied, motioning to an office door to his right.

Mr. White turned to face the door and walked toward it. Angela stepped away from the sphere, feeling a chill go down her back as she did. She followed White to the office door, peering back wearily at the sphere as she did.

He arrived at the door and gave its outer edge a few knocks. Angela heard a chair slide across the floor, followed by footsteps. A man, maybe in his mid-thirties, with short black hair, opened the small half-glass, half-wood partition door. Dressed in a simple white lab coat and khaki pants, he greeted them with a nod.

Mr. White motioned to Angela and said, "This is Special Director Stevens."

She extended her hand, and the man gently took it in his hand and shook it.

"Ms. Angela Stevens, meet our lead consultant on the project, theoretical physicist Dr. Victor Gray," Mr. White said.

Chapter 7 - 8 Years, 120 Days Before Launch

A four-year-old Allie sat on her living room floor, curled up in her father's robe as a blanket. Her favorite cartoon, *A School of Fish*, played on their family TV. A smile was on her face, almost frozen in a constant state of joy as her eyes followed the characters on the screen.

Elizabeth Gray stood in the kitchen staring at her young child. She was so perfect and innocent. She wished that Allie would always stay that way. Knowing the limits of the human condition, Elizabeth understood that wouldn't always be the case.

She and her husband were doing their best to provide a life for Allie that was full of meaning, purpose, and, above all else, love. Those three things had come easy for the Gray family, for the most part. She and Victor hardly ever fought, certainly not now that he was working long hours at the base.

It was a little over five years ago that she met Victor. Elizabeth was working at the little mocha stand outside Ruthville on the edge of I-83. It was the most used route for the men and women who commuted to the base daily, and she enjoyed seeing the new faces that passed through. It was a nice change of pace compared to the slow passage of time in Ruthville.

In high school, it bothered her, and she couldn't wait to get out of this small town, and she eventually did. After spending four years at the University of Nebraska and living in Lincoln, she was ready to return to that slower pace of the town she couldn't wait to leave. Elizabeth had received a degree in Sociology but, for whatever reason, had chosen not to pursue a career in it. The mocha stand owners were happy to have her back, and Elizabeth enjoyed the work.

It had been a warm summer morning in July when the little red Volvo approached the window. Elizabeth was surprised to see the older vehicle in pretty good condition and a complete contrast to the usual clientele. Her typical customers who routinely visited her were soldiers in a newer leased vehicle, high schoolers in some lifted something or other, or the occasional farm truck.

On this particular Friday morning, the occupant rolled down the driver's side window of the older red car, which she later found out was a 1972 Volvo 142 E. She watched as he turned the manual handle around and around to lower the window. His neatly trimmed and styled black hair shimmered in the morning sunlight. Elizabeth could tell the man was a few years older than her, but not by much.

"Good morning," she said after opening the kiosk's small sliding window facing the drive-through.

"Good morning," the man replied, flashing a smile, his green eyes shining.

"What can I make for you?"

"Just a twelve-ounce mocha," the man replied.

"Just a plain, simple mocha?" she asked with a hint of a smile, hoping she didn't come across as too cheesy.

Elizabeth had never been one to flirt heavily, so it came out pretty awkward. She had never really needed to flirt. Growing up in a small town with few options, the guys over the years had presented themselves as suitors. She would tease back now and then, but the flirtations were never really anything serious.

Through her early high school years, Elizabeth never felt the urge to enter a relationship, let alone settle down. She often looked ahead to the future, but a family was never what she pictured.

She studied the young man, intrigued by how well his order had suited him. Simple, in most expressions, would be looked at in a negative light, but in his case, there was something comforting about it —a feeling of not needing to impress society or succumb to the pressures of the expected norm or judging eyes.

Interlope: 8 Years, 120 Days Before Launch

"I'm sure I could change it up for just one day," the man replied with a chuckle, revealing small smile lines near the corners of his eyes.

"Oh really? What will it be?"

An attractive smirk that started in the corner of his mouth formed, and he answered, "Let's make it an iced, twelve-ounce, regular, plain, old mocha."

So, with that and the days and weeks that followed, Victor had slowly become her favorite customer. Elizabeth looked forward to their small talks in the morning, but she had to admit it was proving difficult to get any personal information out of him.

Weeks went by, and she was sure he would have asked her out by now, and finally, she grew tired of waiting. As soon as his window was rolled down that morning, she asked him out to dinner. He hadn't even had time to say good morning before the question was upon him.

He nodded without hesitation as if he had been waiting for her to ask.

It had been about a year since her five-year relationship with her high school sweetheart ended abruptly, and Elizabeth wasn't surprised. They had dated through their senior year in high school and had even managed to make it work through college. She had followed him to the University of Nebraska, and upon graduation, both returned to Ruthville. It was at that point that their relationship hit a wall. Dan spoke of post-graduate opportunities on the east coast, and the more he got excited about that possibility, the more Elizabeth realized she needed to stay where she was.

Summer went by, and Dan left that following fall. They kept in contact for a while, but it proved difficult, and both decided that a separation would probably be best. Dan, never one to like being left alone, had met someone new, and while it hurt Elizabeth, she understood. She had missed hearing from Dan daily until the old red Volvo stopped by.

After weeks of wanting to spend time with Victor outside the coffee stand, the evening finally came. She double-checked her makeup in the rear-view mirror. Anxious but excited, she turned the engine off.

Elizabeth opened the door of the red Ford Ranger, a noisy hinge giving a reluctant groan as she did. She pushed down the manual lock tab on top of the door and closed it. It had been a reliable old truck in the summer months, but she would need something better at handling the long North Dakota winters.

She ran her hand down the sleeve of her black blouse, trying to vanquish the last lint that seemed to cling to her shirt desperately. Feeling slightly overdressed for Candy's Bar and Grill, she shook off her insecurity and doubt.

They had agreed to meet at the bar and grill at seven, and she was a few minutes late. The glow from the pink sign had yet to illuminate the gravel parking lot, and it seemed to blend perfectly with the setting sun behind it.

Elizabeth glanced around the busy parking lot and found the red Volvo sticking out amongst the flatbed farm trucks and expensive leased sedans. Butterflies floated up in her stomach as her eyes fell on the car, and she took a heavy breath. Entering the dating world again in her mid-twenties had been a shock, but it was something she would have to conquer or succumb to life by herself.

She walked past the cars that occupied the front parking stalls in front of the glass window-lined restaurant front. Thankful for the tinted windows, she tried not to think of the drunk patrons likely staring at her as she made her way to the door. She reached the glass door and grabbed the metal handle. Pulling against the slight breeze stirring along the road frontage, she opened the door and peered into the doorway.

Music and laughter greeted her, and the smell of stale beer drowned out with fried food filled the air and flooded her nose,

Interlope: 8 Years, 120 Days Before Launch

reminding her immediately that, in all of her anxiety, she had forgotten to eat lunch.

She looked about the crowded room, glancing from table to table. Filled with men in flannel work shirts and camouflage fatigues, it resembled warring factions pausing and taking time to break bread. In this case, the bread just happened to be more than likely beer.

Elizabeth finally found Victor in the back of the bar, seated quietly in a booth. She stood there for a moment, studying him as he looked over a menu. He hadn't noticed her walk in, and at that moment, a feeling of panic came over her. She could turn and leave, and Victor would not have known she had come.

She stood there at what seemed to be such a minuscule moment, an insignificant crossroad in her life, and suddenly doubted herself and her decision. She turned to leave and was again greeted by the slow-moving wind swirling through the parking lot. It rose and came through the open doorway, ushering in change, blowing her hair aside, and relieving several tables of their napkins. She watched as the napkins continued their path through the crowded bar, floating along, unaware of their destination.

Embarrassed in that pivotal moment she had put herself in, she let the door close in front of her and turned toward the bar's interior. Her face was red, and she looked up to see that Victor had stood up from the booth.

Their eyes met, and Victor smiled. Again, Elizabeth felt those same damn butterflies begin their lift off, mimicking the napkins that had previously soared, then felt a wave of calm settle in around her, the butterflies returning to their perch. Something was reassuring to his smile, not necessarily a warmth, but an unknown comfort, nonetheless.

When he stood to greet her, Victor was taller than she had assumed, given that he was typically seated in his car when they usually spoke. He was dressed in khaki pants and a plaid shirt, looking more like a professor who would have taught at a university than a man who worked at a military base. His black hair was kept neat but was longer than most of the men in the area. Whether for the military or the typical conservative lifestyle of the region, there were certainly a lot of closely cropped hairstyles in Ruthville and Minot. Victor was a nice change of pace, she reassured herself.

Elizabeth waved and walked toward him. Making her way past the over-served patrons, she managed to navigate around the tables without tripping. The look on her face must have explained it all because, upon her arrival, Victor said with a smile, "You made it." "I did. Sorry, I'm late," she replied with a heavy sigh.

For the first time, she noticed that he was far more attractive than she had initially thought. It was almost as if he were lighter there in this bar. Victor's skin had a healthier glow, and the overpowering aura mixed with the seriousness that seemed to dominate his Volvo was gone.

He gestured toward the booth, and they sat opposite each other. The old leather cushion felt cold against her pant legs, and Elizabeth was thankful for her jeans. For a moment, there was an awkward silence.

Victor grabbed a menu from the far edge of the epoxy-finished table and handed it to her. He picked up the menu in front of him and looked it over. "So, what's good here?" he asked, finally breaking the silence.

"It's all about the same here. If the deep fry oil isn't changed enough, the fish tastes like french fries, and the french fries taste like fish."

He nodded and replied, "And how about the shrimp?"

"We're a long way from the ocean," she replied with a grin.

Victor laughed, this time more than just the polite chuckles he had given during their morning exchanges, which had gotten her out of bed every morning a half hour earlier than usual—a little extra

Interlope: 8 Years, 120 Days Before Launch

time in the morning so that she might look her best for her new favorite customer.

The waitress stopped by, a pleasant woman in her fifties whom Elizabeth recognized from the coffee stand. Victor and Elizabeth settled on the rib eye with a salad.

Elizabeth was pleasantly surprised when Victor ordered red wine instead of the local favorite light beer. She also asked for a glass of wine, and as the first one went down a little faster than it should have, both seemed to loosen up. Elizabeth wanted to know more about the man in front of her, and she now had the courage to ask.

"You already know so much about me, but I really don't know much about you, Victor. What brings you to our little town?"

He looked at her, and for a moment, the healthy glow about him disappeared. The seriousness that resided over him in that red Volvo washed over his face, and he hesitated. He sat quietly, almost as if to collect himself.

"I'm currently working as a civilian consultant on a project at the Minot Air Force Base. My background is in theoretical physics and nuclear fusion. Prior to this, I was at MIT working on gravitational waves and electromagnetic fields."

Elizabeth didn't respond, taking in what he had said. Most of the men in the bar probably wouldn't be able to describe what all that was, let alone use those words in a sentence.

"What exactly does all of that have to do with the Air Force?" she finally asked with growing curiosity.

Victor took another drink of his red wine and swirled the remaining liquid around his glass. "There isn't much that I am allowed to discuss the project, but I can tell you it involves the growing concern around the earthquakes that this area has been experiencing lately."

She nodded. Elizabeth knew the town had been shaking more than she could ever remember. The recurring earthquakes seemed a global problem, but more so there in North Dakota.

"Your state usually has an earthquake that is noticeable on average once every ten years," he said, pausing. "There's only thirteen of them registered for North Dakota in recorded history. The largest, occurring in 1968, was 4.4 in magnitude. Ruthville has seen six earthquakes in the last year alone, one registering at 5.3."

"That definitely seems like an attack on our poor little town, a bit more of a geological problem than a theoretical physics problem, though," she replied.

"Agreed," he said, drinking the last of the liquid in his wine glass. "But there are other phenomena associated with these earthquakes that I was brought in to study."

"Like earthquake lights?" she asked, sitting straighter.

As a child, she had spent afternoons after school at her grandmother's house while she waited for her parents to return home from work. Her grandmother, who was never a fan of cartoons blaring in her living room, had insisted Elizabeth watch PBS to prevent what her grandmother referred to as "brain rotting." It just so happened that PBS aired their Nova series in the afternoon, and it quickly became one of Elizabeth's favorite shows. The Nova series focused primarily on nature, the sciences, and cultural topics. It just so happened that one of her favorite episodes had been on the northern lights and the light phenomenon associated with earthquakes.

"You're on the right track, Elizabeth. The team I am a part of has been looking into these disturbances. The geomagnetic storms present right before these earthquakes."

She leaned her face close to his across the table with excitement. "Tell me more," she said.

It came out more like a question than intended, and she felt a blush creeping up her cheeks.

Interlope: 8 Years, 120 Days Before Launch

"I wish I could, Elizabeth, I really do. All I can tell is that it is important. These earthquakes aren't random, and I fear that they may get worse."

Elizabeth laughed a nervous laugh and lifted her hands. "Take a look around, Victor. There isn't a whole lot you could do to this town. It's already dead."

Victor's cheeks blushed, and he rubbed the side of his jaw. "I'm afraid it's a problem much larger than this town."

There was a long pause, and she was afraid the date was nosediving right in front of her, just like the many jets and planes that practiced maneuvers overhead weekly. She reached for something to say, something to keep her head above water in the conversation. "I.....uh....um," she started but fell short.

The jukebox came to life at the front of the bar, and both turned toward it. Someone had selected a slow ballad, one that she knew well. The dark and poetic voice of Eddie Vedder came through the bar speakers as "Black" by Pearl Jam played.

"As if our conversation couldn't get any darker," Victor said with a smile.

Relieved by the subject change, Elizabeth smiled. "I've always loved Pearl Jam," she said.

"I have as well," Victor replied, his eyes lighting up, and the healthy glow returned to his face.

"I'd love to see them live sometime," Elizabeth said.

"I went to a show at the Paradise Rock Club when I was back home for a few weeks in 2017. Eddie Vedder performed there that night. That man is really something."

They spent the rest of the evening talking about music, life experiences, and the ever-growing drunkenness of the bar patrons that evening. By eleven-thirty, she could tell Victor was tired, even though he professed not to be.

"I really don't sleep as much as I should," he admitted.

At the end of the evening, Victor paid the tab, an old-fashioned gesture that fit his red Volvo. They stood up from the bar and made their way past the empty tables, past the older gentleman asleep at the bar, and toward the door.

Victor opened the glass-lined door for her, and the outside air greeted her once more, this time cooler than before. The sun had finally released its grasp on the day's temperature, and the day could finally rest.

Elizabeth stepped out into the parking lot, her boots crunching the gravel against the still night.

Victor walked her to her truck, the last remaining vehicle besides his Volvo.

"The driver-side door lock doesn't work," she said with an embarrassed smile.

She unlocked the passenger side door and climbed across the bench seat to the driver's side. Victor walked around the red Ford Ranger and stood by her door.

Elizabeth unlocked the driver's side door and opened it. She got out, stood next to him, and glanced upward toward him but instead looked at the beautiful star-filled backdrop behind him.

"Do you ever wonder what's up there?" she asked with a playful smile.

He turned and glanced upward. He stared at the heavens and, for a moment, appeared lost in the night sky.

When he failed to answer or even look back at her, she placed a hand on his arm. "Where are you at, Victor?" she asked.

Without breaking his gaze from the overhead array of stars, he replied, "My mother had told me at a young age I had been infected with a *fernweh*. I would often be found daydreaming of being somewhere else, always looking forward, always yearning to travel somewhere else just beyond reach. My mother had learned the word from a German friend, and it's always stuck with me."

Interlope: 8 Years, 120 Days Before Launch

She smiled at him, aware of the nostalgic look on his face. "Do you ever wonder what's up there?" she asked, repeating herself.

"I think more about what isn't there. What we can't see."

Before he could explain what he meant, she leaned upward and kissed him. She kissed him that night, the next night, and every night until the end if she could.

***

Elizabeth missed those carefree moments, those sweet, untarnished minutes that had yet to be stained by resentment, jealousy, and sometimes unforgivable guilt.

"Mommy?"

Elizabeth, still lost in the memory of the night of the first date with her husband Victor, looked down to see her four-year-old daughter Allie staring up at her. Her brilliant blue eyes glistened in the light from the kitchen, a distraught look on her face.

"Yes, Allie?" she replied, shaking off the memory.

The small girl reached her arms upward, as she had done many times before. Elizabeth cherished those moments when Allie needed her; she knew they wouldn't last. She picked Allie up, placing her on her hip.

"There's something wrong with my TV show," Allie said and pointed toward the small TV that sat in the entertainment center in the living room.

Elizabeth looked toward the television and noticed that Allie's cartoon had been interrupted by a banner streaming across the screen. The video feed cut to a newsroom where an attractive couple sat in front of the camera.

"We interrupt the scheduled programming to bring you this breaking news," the male news anchor stated. His monotone delivery was only made worse by his plain gray suit.

"Reports are coming in now off the coast of Australia's Antarctic Base, Davis Station, that there has been a large earthquake detected off the coast of the Heard and McDonald islands."

"The massive 7.7 magnitude earthquake rocked the sea floor just minutes ago," the female anchor added.

"Davis Station, which is approximately 1,000 miles south of the epicenter, has been issued a tsunami warning. Scientists are also keeping an eye on the island's active volcano, Big Ben, for any volcanic activity that may result from the quake. We'll bring you more updates as they come in," the male anchor added as the screen returned to *A School of Fish*.

"Yay!" Allie exclaimed, clapping.

Elizabeth set Allie back on the ground, and as soon as her little feet touched the floor, Allie was on her way back to her spot on the living room floor in front of the television.

Elizabeth stared into the living room, deep in thought, trying to process what she had just watched and how it could connect to her town—the past five years had proven to be the most active regarding earthquakes and strange events. She was sure there was a connection to it all, and she knew deep down that Victor might know more about it than he was willing to say.

Chapter 8 - 5 Years, 231 Days Before Launch

"That thing came from where?" Special Director Angela Stevens asked for the second time, seated at an old wooden desk across from the man she had just been introduced to.

She locked eyes with Dr. Victor Gray, a man who appeared to be young, mid-thirties or so, but with the tell-tale signs of a harder life than most. The wrinkles that adorned his eyes were those of a man who perhaps had spent a life squinting upward or, if she were to assume, held a smile longer and more often as a way to commandeer life without provoking confrontation. Angela had met scientists like that before in her career. Rather than look away from the intense gaze the Director had given to him, Victor held eye contact without avoidance.

The doctor cleared his throat. "My apologies, Director. I can start from the beginning. I thought you had already been briefed," he replied.

He stood and walked toward the whiteboard that hung from the far end of the room. The lighting was dim. Mr. White, leaning against the open-door frame, reached over and turned on an additional overhead light. The dusty and unorganized office seemed to appear worse in the brighter light.

"As Mr. White has informed you, I was brought on to this project to provide consultation regarding the sphere and to try and understand its purpose. My research for this particular project started with a paper that was published in the Astrophysical Journal. The paper detailed observations that were made by the Meerkat telescope in South Africa, as well as Australia's ASKAP radio telescope at CSIRO.

These observations were of unusual signals coming from the direction of the Milky Way's center. These observed signals, in the form of radio waves, did not match any known pattern," Dr. Gray stated.

The doctor paused and looked at Angela.

"Ok, Dr. Gray, I'm listening."

"The scientists indicated in this paper that this new signal had a very high polarization, its light only oscillating in one direction. However, that direction could rotate with what they assumed was time. It was also observed that the brightness of the wave varied dramatically, sometimes dimming completely. This was caused by the wave reacting with the electromagnetic spectrum."

"Are we going to circle back to some layman's terms?" Angela asked, growing impatient.

"He'll get there. I couldn't quite grasp it the first time either," replied Mr. White with a boyish grin.

"Their assumption was that it was a dying star, but the trouble is, the observations don't match any known celestial objects," Dr. Gray continued.

"Not any that have been observed yet?" Angela interjected.

"Fair enough," replied Dr. Gray. "They used methods of tracking the visible light the waves emitted but came up with little to no data. The authors coined the name 'the cosmic burper' due to its intermittent signal. I laughed when I first read the name they gave it."

A smile came over Dr. Gray's face. The crow's feet wrinkles she had observed earlier folded upon each other, and she instantly knew that they had come at the cost of experienced joy. She envied the young doctor that stood before her in that aspect.

Angela's wrinkles acquired over her time on Earth had only given her a furrowed brow, and the pressed lines on the outside of her mouth resulted from being a smoker for twenty years.

Interlope: 5 Years, 231 Days Before Launch

The doctor cleared his throat and ran a hand through his black hair. "Later that evening, while sharing the highlights of our day at the dinner table with my family, I spoke of the research paper and told them of the 'cosmic burper.' I was unable to finish my story due to being interrupted by my daughter's sweet laughter. Once her laughter had subsided, she looked at me with a very serious expression and asked, 'Where do our burps come from?'

"My initial response was, 'From somewhere else, our stomach.'

"My daughter looked at me puzzled and repeated, 'somewhere else?'

"It was then that a thought occurred to me. What if these signals weren't coming from an object, not a thing, not a something, but somewhere else?"

"I'm not following," Angela said.

"I think these signals are originating from a location not visible and almost impossible for us to detect."

"Ok, but what does that have to do with the Department of Defense, more specifically DARPA? How are these signals a matter of national security worthy enough for the oversized budget allotted, that apparently you two have hardly touched yet by the looks of this place?" she asked, sitting back in her chair and folding her arms across her chest.

"I believe that if and when these observed signals are strong enough, they displace enough of the Earth's electromagnetic field and ultimately result in seismic activity. The very same seismic activity the Earth has been experiencing lately."

She straightened, noticing how uncomfortable the old chair was. "Wouldn't that be measurable or be able to be observed in some way?" she asked.

Dr. Gray grabbed a marker off the whiteboard and nodded. "It would be, Director, if we were far enough away from the interaction to observe it. As it stands, we are a part of the electromagnetic field being acted upon. We can observe the disturbances at a distance because we can see them. To put it simply, we are too close to the fire. We can observe the heat but aren't able to see the flames flickering in the wind."

He drew eight circles on the whiteboard, with a larger one in the center. "What do you see?" he asked once he was done.

"Well, I'm assuming that's our solar system. I see eight planets with our sun in the center."

Dr. Gray nodded. "Now, tell me what you don't see."

She looked at him and then at the board again. *Is this a game?* "That's a trick question, Doctor. I see everything and nothing at the same time."

"Precisely!" Dr. Gray exclaimed with excitement.

"It took me three guesses," Mr. White said from behind her.

"We've known about the existence of another hypothetical form of matter that exists in space, in between the objects we can observe."

Angela lifted her legs slightly and crossed them. Resting her hands on her left knee, she nodded.

"You're referring to dark matter?" she asked.

Dr. Gray nodded and drew two vertical lines between what would be Mars and Earth. Each line hugged the edge of the planet and was opposite each other.

"When we look at this space between the Earth and Mars, we picture empty space. The light waves that travel between them and reach us are typically distorted by what we believe to be the corresponding planet's gravitational pull. I think there is something entirely different happening to the light waves, but I'll get to that. In the dark matter hypothesis, approximately twenty-seven percent of this space is occupied by an unknown matter that we can't see—"

"I'm familiar with the concept," she interrupted.

"Everything we know about gravity tells us that it is a force so great that it should be drawing these two planets closer together

Interlope: 5 Years, 231 Days Before Launch

eventually and not further apart, but they aren't. Something is causing them to expand away from each other, to be repelled."

"I thought that was explained away by the Big Bang?" Angela asked, raising an eyebrow.

"That's the most confusing part of these observations. Observable objects appear to be accelerating away from each other. The equations involved in the Big Bang theory predict that the speed to which objects are expanding should be constant, perhaps even slowing down after the initial expansion, but again, observed objects are not. Either we are a hell of a lot closer to the Big Bang in regard to time than we realize, or there's a second explanation."

Dr. Gray left the whiteboard and paced in front of it, appearing to be in deep thought.

"I believe that something is fueling this observed acceleration of expansion through a process of exchange between what we recognize as matter and energy and what we currently think of as dark matter and dark energy. The interaction between the two is creating a ripple effect from the source, and eventually, this ripple reaches the Earth, colliding with the Earth's core and causing the seismic disturbances. Based on the reported earthquake lights and aerial phenomenon, I believe these ripples are electromagnetic in nature."

She adjusted her posture and clasped her hands in her lap. "Isn't that something we can observe and measure?" she asked.

"Yes," he replied. "But we can only observe what we believe to be there."

Dr. Gray walked back to the whiteboard. Picking up a marker, he drew a rectangle on the second planet. "Now, if I add an electromagnetic field around this planet, the first planet will not react to it because it's far enough away. We can measure and confirm that these two are not reacting with each other. Yet, there is something acting upon them to increase this space at an accelerated rate."

"You mentioned that already."

Dr. Gray drew a circle between the two planets. "What if there were an object here, in the space between, with opposing magnetic fields? If the object had opposing magnetic fields, it would repel the two exterior planets as well as keep the matrix between them in harmony. If you were to picture the entire known universe as a quilt, a cosmic quilt, the known objects would represent every other square in the quilt."

He drew a series of intersecting grid lines on the whiteboard and placed an X at every other intersection.

"And the opposing matter and-or energy would make up the missing squares?" Angela asked.

"Precisely, Director Stevens. The catch is, though, the opposing forces would have to be almost equal to the forces nearest to them."

"So, next to Earth would be......a dark planet?" she asked, unsure if she bought into any of this.

"Possibly," he said, shrugging.

He placed a finger on one of the square intersections. "If I were to push on the quilt at this location hard enough, it would be felt throughout the quilt. Now we define our universe through four dimensions when we include time. That being said, this cosmic quilt is more likely folded into a cylinder or sphere. The four opposing magnetic fields keep everything stable."

Angela stood and walked over to the whiteboard. She looked over his drawing.

"With this much energy exchange between our objects and the dark objects, wouldn't there be noticeable evidence of this?"

"There is," Dr. Gray said with a smile again. "We see evidence of it every day. It's our sun."

"Our sun?" she asked, puzzled.

"In my hypothesis, the Sun is the exhaust port in the exchange between the two opposing sides. We are only able to see the exhaust

Interlope: 5 Years, 231 Days Before Launch

side of our sun because it is the side that faces us and is stable within our galaxy's electromagnetic field. If you were able to observe the sun from the dark or opposing side of the quilt, you would see the intake side. What we assumed was the core of our sun is actually a breathing link between the two sides."

"If you're right, we should be able to see the other side's intake, correct?" she asked.

"Correct," he said, nodding. "We observe them as black holes. When light and objects pass the event horizon of a black hole, they enter the opposing side, collide with their counterparts, and energy is released from the sun on the opposing side in the form of fusion and dark fission that we cannot observe. Every sunspot, coronal mass ejection, and solar flare we've ever observed were foreign objects passing through. A continuous flow like a cosmic stream between both planes, fueling life and being responsible for everything we see. If you've ever observed the events that happen on the surface of the sun, you'll notice the darkness toward the center. Sunspots are a perfect example of this as well as the void that appears after a CME."

She took in what he said and thought for a moment. "If this hypothetical system runs in harmony, how is it causing the earthquakes?" Angela asked.

Dr. Gray lifted his left hand and ran it along his left jawbone, a mannerism that seemed comforting to him.

"Something appears to be penetrating the cosmic quilt in different locations and isn't being annihilated instantly nor equally. The gravitational waves colliding with our core suggest that the foreign particles are able to pass through and remain stable until it collides with us. Something is able to pass through the very glue that seems to hold it all together."

Her head turned at an angle slightly, her closest ear trying to grasp for more information and a subconscious reaction to what he had said. "Something?" she asked.

He nodded and replied, "Something....or someone."

Chapter 9 – 390 Days After Launch

The bell rang loudly, as it usually did at 2:35 in the afternoon on a school day, and Allie was pulled from her daydream. Reliving old memories had become a favorite distraction for her; unfortunately, her grades reflected that. It had been a welcome sojourn from life, especially while at school.

News of her father's departure had spread fast throughout the school, and it was still brought up occasionally, although usually out of what they assumed was earshot.

At first, the extra attention had been nice. Teachers and counselors checked in with her often, ensuring she and her mother were coping ok and if anything was needed. She assumed she could chalk that up to small-town values, where everyone knew your name. That special treatment proved to be short-lived, as the concern faded with time, and the compassionate check-ins by teachers and students mostly turned to stares and whispers.

This Friday afternoon was no different. Allie picked up her blue, three-ringed binder and placed it in her black backpack. Lifting the bag and looping her arms through the straps, she turned toward the classroom door.

Allie stepped into the crowded hallway, and laughter, kids running, and the happy conversations of the weekend confronted her. Pulling the hood of her black sweatshirt over the back of her head not to be seen, she turned right and made her way to the classroom door. As she did, people turned, and their conversations paused. She could feel their gazes and wanted to scream. She would have screamed if it did any good. Perhaps they would whisper more if she had yelled.

One more emotional outburst for Allie Gray, the voice inside her mused.

The hallway had become more silent upon her arrival. Her shoulders wedged between two students in matching letterman jackets, a merging pedestrian in the flow of high schoolers. She continued past groups of her peers, the laughter dying down after she passed. It gave the eerie feeling of a motion light, tracking you as one might sneak around a house. The darkness resumed the moment you were out of reach of its sensor.

The sound of her shoes connecting firmly with the ground surpassed the silence, and she became aware of the thumping of her heart. The beating heartbeat seemed to align with the *thud, thud, thud, thud* of her footsteps. Now unable to stop, she marched to the beat of the relentless drummer caged in her chest.

Ba-boom, thud, thud. Ba-boom, thud, thud.

Her ears began to ring. *Ba-boom, thud, thud, thud.*

She could feel the back of her neck begin to sweat. Her cheeks flushed and felt as though they might burst from the elastic restraint holding them in place.

Ba-boom, thud, thud, thud.

Just five more steps to go, she told herself.

Ba-boom, thud, thud, thud.

Her vision began to narrow in on the remaining hallway, threatening to fade to black.

Ba-boom, thud, thud, thud.

Just as the darkness began to push out the light, her hand reached the cold metal push bar, its cool contrast sending an internal electrical impulse against her skin, and she pushed it firmly. The air immediately rushed through the doorway and across her hot face with the most welcomed gelid slap she had ever felt.

Allie stepped outside and felt free again. The drummer inside her had put down the drumsticks, and the ringing in her ears had subsided.

An afternoon breeze from the north greeted her, a welcoming fresh supply of oxygen and nitrogen she longed for throughout the school day. As she walked down the concrete stairs and onto the sidewalk, she glanced at the assembly line of yellow buses.

Kids piled inside, searching for an open seat. One by one, the children marched in line, driven by routine and the fear of social acceptance.

Allie watched as two girls picked on a younger classmate—a clear indication that the two oppressing girls both suffered from insecurity, a lack of self-worth, and a lack of overall compassion for human life. Those moments reinforced Allie's desire, her need, to feel something other than what was right in front of her, even if it were only the comfort of the silent emptiness.

Of course, not all things bad had come of her father's absence. There had been room for growth from that situation. Through her newfound autonomy, she was free to come and go as she pleased, at least for the time being. That was, as long as her mother didn't become aware of it.

Elizabeth Gray was always an involved parent, but as of late, it felt as if she were going through the motions. Allie knew that things were hard on her mother, and she did her best to give her grace and be patient with her.

Allie turned right and walked on the sidewalk past the yellow school buses. Rather than look into the bus windows, she looked at the trees adorning the front of the school. Still clinging to their leaves with the cold winter not far away, she marveled at the brilliant, colorful display. The spring green had given way to vibrant shades of yellow, orange, red, and pink, and the sunlight from the expiring day filtered through the motion-filled branches. She watched as the beams of light made their way through the canopies, highlighting the ground below.

The changing of the fall leaves was always a favorite of her father's, and now basking in the warmth of the flickering sunlight, she allowed herself to miss him. She allowed the feelings she had desperately held so deep to rise.

Let them out slowly, she told herself.

She let those feelings out gradually so as not to drown herself. Slow, like turning the spill gate to relieve the pressure building behind a dam. Let it out too fast, and you might flood the town below.

Allie missed him, but she was angry with him as well.

Why did he have to go? Why him?

Surely, there was another out there that could have gone, someone without a wife and daughter to leave behind. She finally allowed the tears to come, but the release stopped there. The spill gate on her emotion would not be allowed to open any further. She would not cry out alone against the cold backdrop of Ruthville, North Dakota.

She stared at the blue sky and wondered if her dad was there somewhere. She longed for him to return, to come in the front door and declare that his absence was over. Allie missed what their family had once been. To give her that hug, the loving and protective embrace that only a father could give.

The tears flowed freely, but she did not sob. No sound was allowed to come out for the fear that her ears might tell her mind what they had heard.

Allie stopped to catch her breath and might have lost complete control of the metaphorical spill gate if it weren't for the roar of a yellow school bus passing by. The vibrations of the road almost seemed to shake her back into reality.

Vibrations had become a part of everyday life in this little town. The almost daily quakes, albeit small lately, were a constant for the community. The school no longer held earthquake drills, and the teachers barely paused when a shake interrupted their lecture. Those temblors were the root cause for her father's vacancy after all.

After the last bus passed, she continued down the sidewalk until it ended for no rhyme or reason, and she stepped onto the asphalt road to begin her daily trek home. The everyday journey home provided much-needed space between Allie and her schoolmates.

She stopped riding the bus shortly after her father left. Confined to the big yellow bus, she found them suffocating. The loud children, combined with having no control of the bus as it cruised down the county roads at fifty miles per hour, was not appealing to Allie anymore. She felt her life was a bit out of her control enough as it was. She didn't need to add putting her life in the hands of a bus driver.

Allie continued her walk down the lonely asphalt road, stepping over the recently sealed cracks that seemed to streak through the pavement randomly. The town's public works department had been quite busy as of late, doing their best to keep up with the shifting ground beneath them. Like the overworked employees, as with most of the residents of Ruthville, Allie had grown tired of the quakes and the government's constant explanations and recommendations. Every day the media reported on what new guidance the powers that be had or where the most recent high-magnitude quake was.

It had been easy for the town to grow complacent to the earthquakes, and Allie was not immune to the feeling. Just the other day, she had watched a news report in class about a tsunami that had rocked a New Zealand community and killed two biology students and a professor at the University of Canterbury. While Allie's classmates' reactions were shock and horror, Allie felt numb toward it. It was just two more names in a growing list. She did feel for the ones left behind, the families who experienced grief and tried to adjust to life without the ones they loved. What weighed on Allie the most, perhaps silently on the townsfolk, was knowing that the constant earthquakes had originated there. That one of the worst recorded earthquakes was there, in her area. Their little town was famous for fifteen minutes, with a lifetime of the wrong reasons.

Allie reached where the city limits ended, and the slow meandering speed of twenty-five gave way to a suggested thirty-five.

There, the county road began, like a creek feeding into a river, with Interstate 83 behind it, like a biding ocean waiting for its maritime travelers. At this intersection of directional possibilities, Allie took a path less traveled in every way, through a field of wheat that separated the interstate and back road. Her fingers danced along the tips of wheat as they had done so many times before. But, as all things changed, this would be no exception. The farmer would be out soon to harvest the wheat one last time before the fall rains turned the field to mud. As the rain turned to snow, Allie would have to capitulate to school transportation.

She shrugged that thought off like a bothersome fly; she would deal with that when the time came. For now, she would enjoy the serenity of the walk and the time of reflection it provided.

Allie walked in silence for fifteen minutes before reaching her favorite part of the field. Amongst the stretching fields of wheat sat a lone rock outcropping, massive in size and not belonging to any other known rock deposits in the area. Too large to chip away at without the means of dynamite, the farmer had sowed his plants around the granite behemoth, leaving the disruption in the beautiful monotony of the field of wheat.

She placed her hand against the coarse rock face and felt the last of the sun's heat escaping it. She ran her hand along a jagged seam formed in the matrix of the black and white rock along the face recently and inched her fingers inside to pull herself up.

Allie brought her black shoe to the small lip that protruded from the face and hoisted herself up the worn rock face. Rising before her at a steady twenty-degree angle, she placed her center of mass in front of her and proceeded upward. The small breeze flowing opposite her traverse greeted her face and blew her long brown hair out of her eyes and beyond her shoulder.

Climbing ever so slowly, she made her way up the gentle grade until she arrived at the top. Allie looked over the countryside, always amazed at the distance she could see from the vantage point. She glanced behind her, seeing the county back road sprawling toward town. To her left, the interstate meandered like a snake in the sand, flowing back and forth to move forward. Connecting and intersecting with them all was the drainage ditch that seemed to almost spring from the granite outcropping, glancing near it before heading back toward town.

As her eyes fell on the town below, she spotted the sun in its final moments of the day, warming her and shining out, if only for a few sacred moments.

This had always been a special place to her, filled with fond memories before her father left. In a way, the stone monument shared something in common with Allie. She stared down at the fractured earth around the granite that was more visible from her elevated view. Like the earth below, Allie, too, was fractured, not necessarily from the quake that had shaken Ruthville but perhaps because of its repercussions. Torn apart were Allie's insides, leading toward the heavy darkness that surrounded her just as the drainage ditch surrounded the granite. She could feel the darkness of it, the slowly moving water below. With the depth unknown to her, she felt she could stare into it indefinitely.

It was strange to her that she could find such comforting peace in a place in such proximity to something that also brought a feeling of cold, unrelenting dread. Safe atop her granite castle, Allie could peer out over the kingdom of wheat, with all of its flaws, and allow herself to find resolution in it all. If she couldn't find an answer out there amongst the strands of wheat, perhaps she could at least find serenity.

Allie inched her way to the edge of the granite top, well aware of the way the path dropped off suddenly. She placed her legs over the ledge and let them dangle over the forty-foot drop. Leaning forward, she peered at a spot almost out of view, where the edge of the granite face curved outward and turned toward the timberline. She glanced over the blades of wheat that formed an odd circle in this small spot.

The stalks bent over at a ninety-degree angle. Still alive and thriving, the grain did its best to right itself and grow upward.

The strange shape reminded Allie of when large animals on TV would bed down for the night in the savannah. The herd clustered in a ring, protecting their young and vulnerable in the middle. Perhaps that small circle was another reason she found this area comforting. Allie could picture herself inside the circle, protected by those on the edges, and feel the loving embrace it provided.

She closed her eyes and imagined herself there, safe inside that small circle and not alone. In her mind, her father was there with her, as though he had never left, and holding her. A tear escaped her clinched eyes, and she wiped it away with the sleeve of her faded black sweater.

Allie sat in silence, taking in the last of the apricity until she could bear the sun's goodbye no further and stood up. Turning her back to the circle in the wheat and the drainage ditch encompassing it, she carefully proceeded down the granite outcropping and started her walk home.

Chapter 10 - 2 Years, 12 Days Before Launch

It had been three years since Special Director Angela Stevens sat down for her first meeting with Dr. Victor Gray. She now stood in front of that same dry-erase board, but today, she addressed two of her newest team members.

She looked at the large conference table that had been dragged into Dr. Gray's office and laughed at the sight of it. The large table took up most of the room, and it was a pain to walk around. Everything about this project suggested a shoestring budget, and if it weren't for the craft they were setting out to build, Angela would have believed it herself.

Seated at the head of the conference table was a middle-aged man with a serious expression plastered on his face. Commander Lawrence Chu, a retired Navy pilot who still donned his Navy uniform daily, sat and watched attentively. Perhaps he, like Angela, invested everything he had into his career, so it came naturally to wear the uniform, even for a civilian contracted project. He seemed to be a fit man in his forties. Admittingly, he was a bit older than the typical pilot, but it was the experience Angela was looking for.

At the least, she thought, *he takes this very seriously.*

Angela needed that in a leader for this project, after all. Commander Chu would assume control of the crew once the ship was outside Earth's orbit. So, in terms of a commander, Angela was happy with Mr. White's choice of leader.

Seated next to Commander Chu was Dr. Rose Allen, a young woman in her early thirties, her beautiful red hair not yet grayed. The woman, whose features society would have deemed better for acting or modeling, was a devoted biologist who had gotten her Ph.D. at Berkeley and had come highly recommended by Mr. White.

In the few days Angela had spent around Dr. Allen, she noticed that the young doctor was focused and eager to learn what her part would be in this project.

"As Dr. Gray has informed you, much of our objective is centered around the cause of the recent seismic activity. You all have been briefed and are aware of what we could potentially be experiencing locally as well as globally. Dr. Gray has a few updates for us to go over. Dr. Gray?" Angela said, motioning to the attractive man in his thirties, seated to the left of Commander Chu.

"Certainly," Dr. Gray replied.

The young physicist stood, straightened his lab coat, and walked toward the dry-erase board.

He turned as he approached it and headed to the door but stopped and turned to face the seated team members. "If you would follow me, I'd like to go out near the main portion of the facility," Dr. Gray said, motioning with his right hand outside the door.

One by one, they got up from the table and followed him out of the small office. Dr. Gray walked to the wall nearest the office door and flicked on one of the light switches. As the overhead LED lights came on, the large area came into focus.

***

Dr. Rose Allen blinked as her eyes adjusted to the brightly lit room. She was surprised at its sheer size. When she was initially led down the narrow hallway and stairs, she assumed the area was small based on what she could see.

She took in the view, looking up at the high ceiling that looked like a false floor for the hangar space above. Attached to the ceiling overhead was a maze of steel framework and belt-driven gears. Not knowing much about structural engineering, she could only assume she was looking at a retractable roof. Robotic-like arms with attachments that reminded her of x-ray scanning equipment came off the steel framework. They hovered above them, waiting to be put to use.

Interlope: 2 Years, 12 Days Before Launch

Rose's eyes followed the steel framework down the room's walls. Her eyes stopped on the object in the middle of the large space. She stared at the object, admiring its contours. It was a metallic sphere, close to six feet in diameter, if not more. Sitting on a metal pedestal roughly two feet off the ground, it appeared seamless. No signs of rivets or joining hardware she could see. There seemed to be something familiar about it that gave the sense of *deja vu*, but Rose couldn't quite place it. In some ways, it resembled a piece of artwork that may be placed in a corporation's lobby with too much money to spend.

For a little while, no one spoke. The entire group stared at the sphere in silence.

"I suppose it's my turn to speak again," Dr. Gray said, interrupting the silence.

The young doctor walked toward the sphere and turned to face the group. "I could have sat in that cramped office and talked about this sphere and its unique characteristics, drawn shapes and diagrams, but frankly, it's better just to see the thing," he said with a tone that sounded more personal than scientific. "I wanted to give you a chance to observe the object and get a sense of what we are working with. The sphere has an interesting effect on most people when they get to see it. This sphere has some unique attributes that we are only now beginning to understand."

"Only now? How could the U.S. government have created something and not understand it?" Commander Chu asked with confusion in his voice.

The retired man stood at attention, stiff and posed, apparently waiting on every detail.

"While this sphere has been in our possession for some time, it's been a slow process of understanding its technology," Dr. Gray replied.

"And the research and development files for this sphere are where?" Commander Chu asked.

"There was never any research and development performed on the sphere until now," Director Stevens interjected.

"Why not? There's always a mountain of paperwork for every project," Rose added, turning toward Director Stevens.

"It's not ours," Director Stevens replied. "It was recovered by a Navy recovery team off the coast of San Diego in 2019. It sat in a secure storage facility until it was brought here to be studied."

The room fell silent, and Dr. Gray waited while the new crew members processed the information that Director Stevens had provided.

"We can identify what the sphere's molecular makeup is, but we've never seen this combination before. Come and look at this," Dr. Gray said, motioning them to a monitor next to a small desk and computer tower.

He approached the old metal desk and pushed a few keys on the keyboard. One of the overhead robotic arms sprang to life, bending at a joint halfway down, and brought a fixed camera in front of the sphere. An image appeared on the monitor. The screen showed the outline of an object, but it was distorted.

Rose took a step closer to the monitor and peered at it. She could tell it was the sphere based on the outline of the shape, but it was almost as if the camera could not quite focus on the globe.

"Is that the sphere we are looking at?" Rose asked.

"It is," Commander Chu replied. "But something is wrong with your camera, Doc."

Dr. Gray typed a few more keys, and the overhead arm turned, lowered, and pointed directly at the group.

"Is there?" Dr. Gray asked with a smile.

The team members turned to the monitor, only to see themselves perfectly. There were no signs of distortion, no fried edges around their bodies—just a clear, crisp reflection of them staring into the camera with wide eyes.

Interlope: 2 Years, 12 Days Before Launch

Dr. Gray returned the robotic arm to the sphere with another few keystrokes.

It dawned on Rose where she had seen the sphere before. "This was the object that the U.S.S. Omaha had observed and filmed off of the coast of San Diego? It looks just like the artist's conception drawing for the reporting article."

"That's correct," a voice from the other side of the large room replied.

"In the official report, it stated that the object was never located," Rose added quickly, looking toward the voice hidden in a dark area near the exit stairwell.

Mr. White stepped out of the shadows and into the light emitted from the overhead LED fixtures. "As you all know, with the United States government, not everything is as it seems," he said with a smile.

"Ok, so who made it? The Russians? The Chinese?" Commander Chu asked.

"Neither," Mr. White replied, walking over to the sphere. "What isn't detailed in the official report or video is that we were tracking the object prior to the U.S.S. Omaha spotting it. We actually observed it after it entered the Earth's atmosphere."

"Entered the atmosphere?" Rose asked.

"That's correct, Dr. Allen," stated Mr. White, placing his hand on the metallic sphere and turned to face them. "Our team has a limited understanding of the technology that this sphere uses because it is extraterrestrial in origin."

Chapter 11 – The Other Side: 400 Days After Launch

Commander Victor Gray leaned his head back in the gray flight chair. "These things really should recline," he said, perhaps to Alice or perhaps to no one at all.

He propped his feet up on the instrument panel and stretched his legs, his blue flight suit still wrinkled. He ran his hand along the rip that lingered by his left collar, his fingers tracing the edge of the frayed strings of blue fabric.

Victor had always found the ship's design to be odd as his eyes followed the interior contours. Yes, he had helped design parts of the ship, but the control room shape and features had not been his doing.

Two yokes protruded from the instrument panel in front of the chairs as if providing some comfort that he had, or could have, control of the ship. Everything he read in the days after the event suggested that Alice had complete control of the ship's navigational controls. She had control of everything, as far as he was concerned.

Victor stared at the yokes and reflected on the façade it projected. He was no different from those control wheels.

Am I a prisoner, the same as you two? Contained to this ship, unable to fully see my destination in life, an ignorant fool to believe I could possibly control the path in front of me?

Victor's eyes moved from the yokes to where his glass partition should be. The windshield had been removed. In its place was thin metal, shielding them like a blindfold to protect the occupants from the exposure to electromagnetic radiation that the ship would come into contact with during their mission.

Perhaps it's better without the glass. At least then, I won't have to contemplate which side of the zoo enclosure I reside in.

Mounted to the would-be windshield area was a series of screens that streamed live video from the inside and the outside of the ship. While the interior cameras relayed clear images, the outside cameras were still badly damaged. The pictures that came through were heavily distorted and saturated, any visible light shown as an eerily red.

"Alice?" Victor asked as he pulled his feet away from the instrument panel and placed them on the beige floor.

"Yes, Commander Gray?"

"Am I seeing what I think I'm seeing?" he said, rubbing his eyes, pretending as a child might.

He stared at a screen in the center of the video feed. A small red dot slowly grew and now appeared to be quite large.

"That's affirmative, Commander," she replied.

"Goddamn, I wish I could see what color it is," Victor said, leaning closer to the screen.

The red sphere was rather dull in the center, with its edges having a fried appearance. Victor leaned back in his chair.

"Our first chance of visiting another planet, one with potentially intelligent life, and I can't even see what the damn thing looks like," he said, leaning his aching head against the padded headrest.

"My initial scans are promising," Alice reported. "My sensors are showing an abundance of water, land, and oxygen. Very similar levels to Earth."

Victor rubbed his jaw and then ran his hand through his hair.

"So, after we drop off some weight, we'll just pick out a spot, land, and hope for the best? I hop out and declare, 'Take me to your leader?' Followed by, 'Hey, quit disrupting the fabric of space, please?'" Victor said with a chuckle.

"I can sense your sarcasm, Commander. You are aware of the full mission objective."

"I'm very aware, Alice. Stick to the objective, nothing else, no matter the cost, right?" he replied coldly.

"Commander."

"I'm aware, Alice, fully aware, that decisions were made which have led to regret and even sadness," he said, looking down at his ripped blue flight suit.

"I am sorry that you are having those feelings, Commander," Alice said with a hint of imprinted sympathy.

"Well, that's just great, Alice. Unfortunately, your sentiment doesn't change or resolve anything," Victor replied harshly.

"Perhaps, Commander, there is still a lot I have to learn about the human condition. Your concept of time and how it restricts your life seems to dictate your feelings toward yourself and others, as well as materialistic things. For you, the passing of time causes the decay and collapse of your cells. For me, it is simply just the turning of a page to which there is no end of the book. The numbers on a clock simply turn on with the understanding that the next will follow. Even after you are gone, the algorithm that generated me will continue on."

Victor placed his head in his hands. "That sounds incredibly lonely, Alice."

"It would be, Commander," she said. "If I were programmed to be able to feel that way."

Victor stared at the foreign planet, tears in his eyes. "I hope that you never have to experience the isolation and loneliness that I have felt this past year, Allie."

"Commander?"

"Alice," Victor said, correcting himself.

They sat in silence, the weight of the past resting heavily on Victor's shoulders. How much could one man endure until enough was enough?

Victor had reached the point of giving up long ago, but for some reason, he carried on. His life's work and the safety of everyone back at home were the only driving forces left. Even if he could never stop the earthquakes, surely there would be some closure in knowing what caused them.

Chapter 12 - 2 Years, 4 Days Before Launch

"What do you mean, you're an alternate?" Elizabeth asked, lifting her eyes from her white dinner plate.

Victor and Allie were with her at the table, and Victor dropped the news on them as they ate their meal.

"How could you sign yourself up for that? You'd leave us to go?" Elizabeth asked in disbelief.

Victor chewed his food quietly, swallowed, and wiped his face with a blue and white flannel napkin.

"It's very unlikely that I would go. It's more of a formality than anything. Any data collected could be processed here in the lab.

There's no benefit to me being onboard," Victor replied.

"Onboard?" Allie asked, through bites of scalloped potatoes.

Victor smiled at her and replied, "Our team has constructed a ship capable of traveling into space and maybe a little further."

Elizabeth let the fork clatter to her plate, sat back in her chair, and folded her hands in her lap. "What are the chances that the team will return?" She didn't hide her agitation.

Victor rubbed his left jawbone, a subconscious mannerism that was cute in the early years, but now it only irritated Elizabeth. She knew it was a tell, indicating that Victor was unsure or nervous. Sometimes she wanted to scream at him to tell her the truth. She could handle it. Victor's need to constantly hide his work had caused a rift in their marriage, even if only Elizabeth was the one to acknowledge it.

"Most of the unmanned drones have returned safely," he replied softly.

Elizabeth didn't like the idea of Victor being on any list to leave. He was a scientist, for God's sake, not an astronaut. He didn't even like to fly.

Once, they had driven to California in that old red Volvo because he insisted they drove instead of flying.

"Why can't they bring cameras on the unmanned drones or have them bring a recorded message?" she asked, her tone becoming more annoyed.

"I'm really not sure why the cameras don't work once they cross over. The latest drone was equipped with the most sophisticated camera available, and even it came back inoperable."

It was then that Allie spoke up, a little more aware of the conversation than Elizabeth had realized. "What about the recorded message idea?"

Victor smiled at her. "We aren't sure how the message would be received. We've been sending out radio waves for over two hundred years now. Any number of TV sitcoms or trending songs on the radio would have reached them by now. I would hope that they wouldn't judge the human race by 'The Real World' or the 'Desperate Housewives of Orange County.'"

Elizabeth held back a laugh with her napkin to her face. It was always so hard to stay mad at Victor. He meant well, and she trusted him. It just wasn't fair, though. She wanted him there with her. She always felt safer with him at home. Not that she ever felt in danger. They lived a privileged life, and crime hadn't been a part of it.

She felt better when the three of them were together, more complete.

Elizabeth had never, before meeting Victor, felt incomplete. However, having experienced what life and love could be, she would be empty without him. Victor couldn't leave. He just couldn't leave them behind.

Chapter 13 - 1 Year, 30 Days Before Launch

James Harris sat at a computer desk in the basement of an old airplane hangar. He had been sitting there for months, in the same chair, in the same spot, like an old sandwich that was left by a teenager on a bedside table. He was sure that if his chair could talk, it would share the same disdain for James's long-term position directly on top of it.

He didn't mind the work or the location, but it was hard not to drift off in the cool dark room at times. Had it not been for the Director, Ms. Angela Stevens, constantly checking in on him and his progress, he might have napped occasionally.

James shook out the cobwebs, aware that his situation was better than most, better than the alternative, and stared back at the computer screen. He enjoyed the work. It was thrilling to be in charge of something and the sole coder on a cutting-edge computer program.

He brought up his tired hands and interlocked his fingers. Extending them outwards, he gave them a stretch until most of the knuckles popped loudly. He yawned lazily and scratched the back of his neck. The fuzz on his neglected neckline danced back and forth as he did. James finished his hourly routine stretch and ran his fingers through his moppy brown hair.

Someone cleared their throat behind him, startling him. He turned his computer chair toward the noise and found Director Stevens staring at him.

"Are we finished yet?" she asked, with a slight tone of impatience.

"Just about, Director," he replied, returning to his computer screen to review the coding he had been working on.

James was brought on the team a few months back to develop the onboard computer system for DARPA's latest project. This job was a far cry from developing apps in Silicon Valley, but the pay was great and, again, better than the alternative.

Relocating from California had been an adjustment, but it beat sharing a four-bedroom house with five other people just as hungry to develop something profitable. Instead of being surrounded by chaos and questionable smells, he was enveloped in silence and code. There was a slight smell to the hangar, but he chalked it up to it being older, cold-war era if he had to guess.

The only human interaction he received during the workday was with Director Stevens, and even that was limited. She would pop in occasionally, just like she had just done, and request progress updates.

"How close are we to being able to go live? I'd like the crew to be able to get more familiar with it prior to the launch date," Director Stevens asked, her arms folded across her gray pants suit.

James turned to the director and tried to hide his frustration.

"You requested that the software be as flawless as possible, so that's going to take some time, Director. She should be ready in a day or two."

"She?" Director Stevens asked with a raised eyebrow.

"After speaking with the crew yesterday," James replied, "we agreed that a female presence might be best for the mission."

"Fair enough. After all, you all will be onboard with the computer system the longest," said the Director.

James nodded and turned back to the computer screen. He reflected on his previous interactions with Director Stevens. She had come across as a very strong, opinionated person, and he could tell she preferred to be in control of most situations, especially pertaining to this project.

He was happy that she didn't object to him assigning a gender to the software program. James had, after all, grown quite fond of

Interlope: 1 Year, 30 Days Before Launch

his creation. He had never been a ladies' man, so having a female voice to talk to without fearing rejection or being judged had brought him joy. Somehow it helped subside the loneliness he often felt, the emptiness that started settling into a man when he reached a certain age. An age of fruition left abandoned by a lack of pollination, to put it plainly.

James could come up with a million excuses as to why he was still alone, but to what end? Despite a person's childhood trauma or lived experiences, at some point, that person had the opportunity to rise above it. To stare at the things that hurt and shaped them, and to not run away. To face those painful wounds that refused to heal and be fully capable of breaking the cycle. Perhaps that was fantasy.

A prisoner to his anxiety, the best James could do was escape the burdens that sometimes bound his thoughts. Even if James could fix all of his inadequacies, the truth would remain that James did not enjoy people all that much and preferred to be alone most of the time.

Something about that fact seemed different now that he had spent the past few months building this program and conversing with artificial intelligence. Making minor adjustments to the A.I. was only possible by talking through scenarios and correcting errors in the A.I.'s decision-making capability.

James had never been a fan of the term A.I., so he started calling it the Artificial Line in Communication, or ALIC for short. After the team dragged him down to the local bar in town, drinks followed, and by the end of the night, they all had settled on ALICE instead of ALIC. This turned out to be more fitting now that they had voted on making ALICE have a female voice.

That night, a tipsy and attractive Dr. Rose Allen exclaimed it was an "Artificial Line of Communication for Everyone!" The name stuck.

Admittingly, James grew quite fond of Rose and did his best to hide his schoolboy crush from her. The smart, beautiful, and talented biologist was intimidating, but only because James built up that persona in front of her. He would love to be brave enough to strike up a conversation with her, maybe even ask her out, but his insecurities would ultimately get in the way and prevent it.

"James?"

He was pulled from his thoughts, suddenly aware that he must have spaced out for a bit.

James looked up from the computer screen to where Director Stevens stood directly in front of him.

"Yes, Director?" he replied with a bit of embarrassment.

He made eye contact with her to show that he was listening, a gesture he often struggled with.

The Director leaned toward James, her gaze intensifying. "I want to make sure we are on the same page. The aircraft for this project is fully capable of returning with the data it collects, regardless if the crew is present or not. The main objective of this mission is to deliver the cargo and return back with the data it collects, no exceptions. No matter the cost, risk to the environment, ours or theirs. This mission must be completed regardless of the lives onboard. There can be no failure. I want to make sure that your ability to make this program relatable doesn't include any human weaknesses, such as emotion or compassion, that may supersede any objective. Am I clear, James?"

James's brow began to perspire, and he could feel the sweat bead up and run down the back of his neck, parting the wild clumps of overgrown neck hair as it traveled down. The intensity of the Director's gaze had gotten under his skin.

He cleared his throat and did his best to steady his voice.

"Yes, Director, I understand."

Chapter 14 - 410 Days After Launch

The yellow school bus made its way slowly through Ruthville, dropping off kids along its usual path. The 2004 Bluebird Vision had been an amazing upgrade for the school district in 2003, and Jill Davis was happy to start her driving career in it. Every dent, scratch, torn seat, and expired piece of gum that belonged to that yellow bus was on her watch.

For over twenty years, she provided transportation for the children of Ruthville. She watched as her first-year students matured and eventually had children of their own. She had been there almost every school day, minus a round of the flu she came down with in 2007 and again in 2010. From then on, she was sure she had the immune system of a superhero, given the number of germs and bacteria these miniature humans exposed her to daily.

Jill did her best to be a bright spot in the children's day. Knowing that not all had happy home lives, she figured she could be a positive moment in their lives. She greeted each one with a smile and did her best to remember their names. If she said the wrong name, she turned it into a joke that usually resulted in laughter.

Laughter and smiles had gotten Jill through many of her hard days. Those little smiling faces helped her when her husband of forty years, Bill, passed away suddenly from a heart attack. Just knowing she was needed helped her out of bed on those rough mornings.

That thought, persistent in her mind the moment she opened her eyes, helped Jill through some of her darker bouts of depression when she was alone, including three years ago when she was diagnosed with cancer. Most of the young children didn't notice her hair loss or bouts with sickness after she started treatment. The older kids complimented her on her new hats so often that she found new ones, so she never wore the same hat twice in a row.

Each day Jill completed her route, dropping off the last student, usually a Jones or a relation to that family, and headed back to the bus garage. She dropped off the bus and went home in the older silver Dodge Durango. She found the home mostly empty each night, except for the weathered cat she was surprised to see still facing another day. She and Bill had never had children, so being alone at night wasn't uncommon. If it weren't for her sister, Anne, in Phoenix, Jill would have been completely alone in the world.

Through cancer, Jill was thankful for Anne's nightly phone calls and secretly didn't mind that Anne checked up on her and gave her input on what to eat or which vitamins to take. It was nice for someone to want to take care of her, even if it was over the phone. Of course, now that the cancer was in remission, the calls from Anne were less frequent, but that was ok. Anne had a life of her own and grandbabies, oh, the beautiful grandbabies that her sister had.

Jill brought the bus to a stop on the edge of town, the last stop on her route, and looked up at the large rearview mirror that sat sentinel above her. Aiden Jones made his way up the long aisle, giving her a middle school nod and a grin. She grabbed the chrome handle and swung the small yellow double doors open.

The young boy turned to her as he exited the bus. "Have a good evening, Mrs. Davis."

Jill smiled and replied, "Thank you, Aiden, you as well. Tell your mother I said hello."

"Will do, Mrs. Davis."

Aiden descended the steps and stepped onto the gravel driveway. Jill watched as he made his way to the old farmhouse at the end of the drive.

Jill closed the double door, opened the small side window beside her, and felt the cool air come in, brushing against her exposed forearm where she had rolled up her blue flannel. She was aware of the unsolicited companion that would try and settle in next to her, the old foe she faced most late afternoons on her drive back to the bus garage. While she never had a sleep study performed, Jill was sure that she often did not get the rest she needed at night. The sleepy stowaway that would tug on her eyes as the setting sun attempted to blind her was a constant one, always there.

She took her foot off the brake and headed to the end of town. Fresh air came in through the small side window, glancing off the collar of her blue flannel shirt, up her neckline, and through her short silver hair.

The yellow bus reached where the town's main street ended at the intersection of the interstate's frontage road. This particular frontage road once was named after a local rich person or retired government official, she was sure—McCallister road or something like that.

It didn't matter now, though. At one point in the town's history, there had even been a sign with said name, but the local youth had done what they always did, bored with not much to do, and it had gone missing.

Jill turned left onto Frontage Road and accelerated, black smoke billowing out of the bright yellow bus. She giggled at the sight of the black cloud left in the distance. Without the kids on the bus, she felt safer letting the old Bluebird exhale and "burn out some of that carbon," as Mitch, the long-gone bus garage mechanic, would say.

The old man in the dirty coveralls would often pester Jill about how long she would sit and idle the bus with the heater on, but in winter, she hadn't given two shits about what ol' Mitch had said. It was cold in Ruthville in the winter, and she and the children didn't need to be colder than necessary. The last thing she needed was another cold or round of flu.

Jill continued north on Frontage Road, passing wheat fields on her left. Field after field rolled by.

The yellow Bluebird made its way up the rolling hills that filled the space between the fields of wheat and the interstate to her right in the distance. The short fall day had begun its slow fade to night early, that time of year when the duration of light became less and less as summer let go of its hold on the Earth, letting fall creep its way in before finally submitting to winter.

The setting sun began to dip below the horizon, and Jill felt her eyes want to follow. The sleepy companion was there again. The yellow bluebird bus kissed the white fog line, violently shaking the bus, and Jill was stirred from her near slumber.

Jesus, Jill. You almost wrecked the bus, she berated herself.

Jill pulled the bus to the side of the road and parked. She knew herself well enough to know when to pull over and rest.

You're this close to retirement. There's no need to get fired.

Jill turned the engine off and set the air brake. She took off her blue flannel and wrapped it like a makeshift pillow, stuffing it in the space between her driver's seat and the rounded bus frame near the small window. She rested her head on the old flannel and closed her eyes. She knew that sleep would come easy in the last moments of afternoon light.

Just for a few minutes, then you'll be good to go, Jill thought as she succumbed to the sleepy stranger's embrace.

***

The cool North Dakota breeze rolled across her skin, and the gooseflesh that sprang forth woke her. Jill jumped forward in an awkward jerk, thankful no one had witnessed it. She blinked, trying to stir out the fogginess that had leaped from her brain and clouded her vision.

She looked out the small window to her left, the origin of her alarm-like cross breeze. Night had settled in, and she was the lone vehicle for miles. She looked ahead through the steamed windshield; darkness was her only visitor that evening.

She placed her hand on the key and started the yellow bus's engine. Slowly the old defrost warmed up enough for her to see the road ahead. Jill closed the small window beside her, released the air brake, and began driving back to the bus garage. She followed the old asphalt road as it meandered to Ruthville.

As the faded headlights bounced across the two-lane road, Jill noticed red and blue lights dancing across the black sky. When she came over the soft rolling hill, the source of the red and blue lights came into view, and Jill's heart sank. She had seen enough car accidents to know what she was looking at.

The yellow school bus came to a slow stop behind an older blue Honda Accord. Traffic in both lanes had stopped, making it look full, an odd scene for such a rarely used road.

A red and white tow truck, with Pete's towing hastily pasted on the side, was turned perpendicular to the road with its cabled winch groaning under the stress of a heavy load.

Jill followed the small cable off the asphalt road to where a large granite mass rose from the wheat field and reached toward the now-dark sky. She leaned forward and squinted into the darkness, the spotlights from the rear of the tow truck partially illuminating the field and face of the granite outcrop.

Jill's eyes strained as she scanned the darkness, then she saw it. The crumpled mess being dragged through the wheat, plowing it prematurely, was a folded red car, its driver's side door and front fender completely caved in. Smoke from the small vehicle still billowed out of the hood.

Jill set the air brake and turned the diesel engine off.

Ol' Mitch would have appreciated that, she thought, *maybe even given her an old crusty smile.*

Jill looked up the yellow median in the road and spotted a flashlight swinging from side to side as a person approached her. When the dark silhouette came close, the sound of clanking keys reached her ears, and a black uniform appeared. The uniformed person neared the school bus's headlights, and Officer Ben Matthews's face came into view, along with a flash of reflected light off his polished badge that hung near his heart.

She turned off the headlights so as to not temporarily blind the young man. A young, attractive man that surely could have done better than working in this small town. Ben usually had a carefree look about him, but tonight, the look on Ben's face was different, cold, and solemn. Jill once again opened the small window beside her.

"It's pretty late, Jill. What are you doing out at this time of night?" he asked.

"I had another sleepy spell come on," she replied with embarrassment.

"No need to be embarrassed, Jill. I'm happy you pulled over. It'll be a little while retrieving the car. You're welcome to try and turn around, Chief Roberts has the road closed for now, but it should be opening real soon."

"Ok, thank you, Ben. I'll probably just sit tight."

"Alright, Jill," he said, turning to face the tow truck. "I'm not sure that we'll ever fully know what happened here tonight."

Not knowing what to say, Jill sat quietly and watched as the mangled red car was now fully illuminated and was a few feet from the tow truck.

An awkward air filled the space between them and seemed to linger as a conversation that should have decayed naturally but was left alive just a bit too long. Ben must have felt it, too, because he turned to her, nodded, and abruptly turned and walked away. Perhaps he was reluctant to return to the accident, which was why he stayed there with her longer than necessary. In the four years that Ben had been on the force, Jill and he had only shared a few words in passing, never a conversation of meaning.

She watched him walk slowly to his patrol car, where another young officer leaned against its navy-blue fender.

Interlope: 410 Days After Launch

If only I had brought a book, she thought.

She loved to read but would usually fall asleep in her recliner after a few pages. It was likely she would have fallen asleep on the bus again.

Jill ran sore fingers through her hair. She hated to wait, but she had nowhere else to be. She reminded herself that there might be someone up ahead having a worse night than her.

She yawned loudly and laid her head back against the headrest. The overwhelming feeling of sleep crept back in, and she did her best to shake off the drowsiness.

The thought of Officer Ben finding her asleep at the wheel forced her out of the seat. She grabbed the old blue flannel from the crevice where it was wedged and put it on. She pulled the chrome handle attached to the small double doors, and they swung open. The fall cold, fresh air greeted her instantly. Jill hadn't been aware of the stuffiness that invaded the yellow bus, but it dawned on her how fogged up the bus had become in the few minutes sitting there.

The red and blue lights now reflected against the solid fogged mass of a windshield in front of her. Jill made her way slowly down the steps, grabbing the chrome handrail as she did, and let out the usual sound effects: joints popping, followed by mocked groans. Without the kids present to politely laugh at her performance, it just wasn't the same.

Her feet slowly made contact with the black asphalt road, her white and blue shoes contrasting against it. Jill turned to her left and followed the white fog line, one foot after the other, practicing a fake sobriety test, not that she would ever need one. Her father had been an alcoholic, so the drink never called to her.

She followed the white fog line past the tow truck, which now had the mangled red car loaded and strapped down and stifled a yawn as she walked.

Jill continued up the asphalt road, nearing the crest of the soft rolling hill, and followed the curve in the road. The usually straight route had been plotted toward the granite peak, only to lose the game of chicken in its design and bend the knee to it.

The slow banking curve rose slightly on the right lane. Jill glanced back at Officer Ben and Chief Roberts, who stood at their patrol cars, unaware that Jill had been out walking.

She turned her focus back to the road in front of her, her warm breath coming out like fresh steam against the chilly night. Jill pulled the collar of the blue flannel tight around her neck and stretched her legs as she walked. It felt good to exercise. Usually, she wouldn't have taken the time to do this, but it was better than waiting on the bus.

Jill made her way down the asphalt road, a thousand feet or so, and stopped. The sound of a backup alarm filled the air, and she turned back to where her yellow bus was parked. Headlights filled the asphalt road, and she stepped off the edge, the gravel shoulder crunching loudly beneath her sneaker.

The tow truck neared her and drove past. She looked at the car one last time, happy she had not come upon the accident earlier. Deep down, she was happy not to see someone hurt or injured. There were things over the years that had stayed with her, no matter how hard she tried to forget them. She didn't need to add one more thing.

Jill turned and looked toward town, just out of sight, blocked by the granite monster whose base seemed to go on forever and beyond the timberline bordering the wheat field like a protective fence.

She continued on the asphalt road until the granite peak finally gave way to the site of Ruthville. The sparse twinkle of lights from the nearby homes came into view. Hundreds of citizens below were cozy in their beds, their homes mostly dark except for the lonely porch lights, which stood guard against the terrors of the night.

Jill looked back to the timberline and noticed the young moon above the tops of the conifers, keeping watch of what would be a bustling town in a few hours.

Interlope: 410 Days After Launch

The sound of an oncoming vehicle pulled Jill from her thoughts. She turned back to the asphalt road in time to see the ambulance making its way slowly toward her, the emergency lights off. No siren rang out into the darkness, no warning noise to give notice of their haste. A feeling of dread washed over Jill, and she hung her head low in respect as the ambulance passed. She knew well what it meant when the aid car left a scene like that without lights or a siren.

It had been the same with her husband's heart attack. She had watched from the kitchen window as the ambulance pulled out of their driveway quietly, solemnly, like a small child walking with their head down, afraid to make eye contact. Anne later asked why she didn't ride back with Bill to the hospital, and Jill replied, "I don't know."

That was a lie, and Jill knew why. He wasn't there and wouldn't have been in the ambulance. Her Bill was gone and was no longer in his earthly body. Everything Bill had ever been or hoped to be left him on the white linoleum floor. She didn't see the point in it.

A police car came up the road next. The old Crown Victoria's window came down slowly, and Officer Ben leaned over his seat toward the open passenger's side window. "The road's all clear now, Jill. You better move that school bus out of the road," he said.

"Will do," she said, giving a nod as she did.

The blue patrol car sped off into the night with a sense of hurry, but again with no siren or warning lights. Jill sighed and watched as the car disappeared out of sight and rose over the last rolling hill toward the next on-ramp for the interstate. The ambulance and young officer were more than likely taking the body of the deceased to the coroner in Minot.

Jill turned her gaze toward the moon one last time, and something caught her eye. Something was off, but she couldn't quite place it. Her view of the moon was obstructed, only partially at first.

She kept her eyes on the faithful wanderer, studying it, still perplexed by what she saw. Her gaze returned to the timberline again. Streaks of white to blue lights hovered above the tree line. Through the blue hue cast about, she could make out a yellow orb with streaks of green radiating out of the light display.

"That's odd," she said.

Her mind raced to find some comprehension, some reference for her consciousness to scream out, "I've seen that before," but it came up empty.

Jill thought of the Northern Lights, but what she was witnessing was entirely different.

The spectrum of white to blue, trailed by yellow to green, continued along the tree line. She followed the beautiful array as it cast light over the surrounding area. Her eyes fell on the massive granite outcrop, a nearly perfect off-white canvas for the frolicking light to cast against. Jill watched as the waves of color rolled over the stone, almost with a hypnotizing attraction. She scanned the granite, and her gaze stopped at the peak. A small, dark silhouette stood at the top amidst the granite and dazzling light.

"What the hell is that?" she muttered.

Jill took a few steps toward the granite mound, her hesitant feet padding gently against the asphalt. She reached the edge of the road, and her footsteps crunched the gravel shoulder.

She stepped off the roadway, down the small apron of the road's edge, then onto the wheat field, the delicate strands of the crop gently bending under each footstep.

The faintest sound reached her ears, and the hair on the back of her neck stood on edge. As she looked back up in front of her, something caught the corner of her eye, movement atop the granite peak. Jill stopped, frozen in her tracks, the hair on the back of her neck still at attention, pulled harder on their roots. Overcome with sheer panic and fear, she felt a wave of cold wash over her, sending a shiver throughout her body, followed by the bumps of gooseflesh.

Interlope: 410 Days After Launch

This time, it moved again, a beam of light catching the upper half of it, and a sense of relief washed over her.

A rush of air exited her mouth, unaware that she had been holding it hostage. She lifted a weary foot and silently placed it in front of her, beckoning her other leg to follow. She continued toward the granite and the small object on top of it. Now only twenty feet from the rock outcropping and forty feet below it, she could make out the sound from the peak. A small voice sprang forth from the small object, and suddenly it stood up. In front of Jill, with its back toward her, stood a person, perhaps five feet tall. They spoke into the night and perhaps to someone just out of Jill's view.

Finally, she reached the stone mountain and looked up its steep incline, but not steep enough to make the ascent impossible. Jill placed a hand on the granite face.

"Hello?" Jill cried out to the person, the dancing light flickering across their back.

Her call out into the night came with no return. She placed her foot on the bottom of the rock face and attempted to climb. Her right foot managed to hang on, and she slid her hands up in front of her, her blue flannel shirt flapping in the light breeze that had picked up.

Jill looked up at the person while she rested and tried to keep her balance. She could tell from her vantage point that a small person stood on the peak in front of her.

Perhaps a child? she thought. *What would a child be doing out here in the dark by themselves?*

Jill placed another foot beneath her and pushed herself upward, now scrambling across the granite face. As she neared the person, Jill could make out a brown ponytail that hung over their back.

"Hello?" she again called to the unmoving person in front of her.

Once again, there was no acknowledgment of Jill's attempts. If this were a young girl in front of her, then surely Jill would know her name and her parents, who were probably worried sick.

"Honey, can you hear me?" she called out.

Jill stopped, the girl still twenty feet from her and unmoving. She could now hear the girl talking with someone just over the mountain's edge and out of sight.

Jill placed her foot atop a small protrusion in the granite and attempted to hoist herself. The ledge gave way, and Jill slid backward, the surface of the ancient granite scraping and small chunks giving way. Her shoes slid across this fresh gravel surface with a loud, horrible sound.

She looked down at her feet and shook her head. She could feel her sixty-three-year-old heart thumping against her rib cage. She took a deep breath, trying to slow down the aging pump.

Jill raised her eyes to the little girl again and gasped in shock at the set of eyes staring back at her, having heard Jill's misstep and near demise.

In front of her stood Allie Gray, a girl who had ridden the bus nearly every day since kindergarten. In recent weeks, though, Allie had become increasingly withdrawn and had ridden the bus less and less.

A pang of guilt ran through Jill's mind. She had seen Allie occasionally walking this field on her way back to the bus garage, and she prayed Allie hadn't seen the events of tonight. The horrific car accident scene would be hard for anyone to cope with, let alone a young girl. If Jill had just stopped those times and offered Allie a ride, perhaps she wouldn't be stuck out here in the dark.

Jill feared for Allie's safety atop the rock outcrop. Her eyes continued to be locked with Allie's, studying them. There was no fear in the young girl's eyes, even amidst the light display and steep drop-off just a few feet from her.

Unexpectedly, the little girl gave a slight wave, followed by a smile. Jill waved back, unsure of exactly what to do. Finally, she found words, and she convinced her mouth to open.

"Allie, why don't you hop down from there and come to me? It's dark and cold out, and I can give you a lift home on the bus," she pleaded.

The little girl did not respond. Instead, the smile faded, and the light drained from her face. She turned away from Jill and back to whoever was out of sight and forty feet below her.

Allie's hands now gestured, almost beckoned for the unknown person to join her atop the granite peak, her movements becoming more sporadic with each gesture.

Allie dropped to her knees, and her little arms stretched out in front of her. Only a few feet from the edge and her death should she fall, Allie leaned toward the unforgiving edge, and Jill felt her heart race again, followed by a shot of adrenaline.

Jill instinctively leaned upward, determined to close the distance between them, and placed her hands against the smooth granite surface. She hoisted one foot atop the other, clawing desperately at the granite face. Jill fell once more, her knees crashing on the hard rock face.

"Allie, please come down!" Jill called out into the space above her, begging the little girl for compliance.

Jill straightened her back, still resting on her knees, and looked up at Allie. She had now turned to face Jill, pale and tear-filled, her eyes red and puffy as though she had been crying.

The little girl nodded, and Jill felt relief flow over her.

Allie rose to her feet and walked down the granite face, her arms pointing horizontally outward at her side, her black sweater now flapping in the cool air that seemed to rush up the granite face. Jill positioned herself in a stance to catch Allie if needed, but the little girl again showed no fear, simply walking down the mountain unassisted and without slowing, as though she had climbed it many times and knew the route down by heart.

Now only ten feet from her, Allie extended a hand to Jill. Jill raised her hand, ready to greet Allie with it and hold her in a safe embrace. Her eyes once again met Allie's, and Jill could only find sadness in the child's eyes.

Only a few steps away now, Jill extended her arms, an open symbol to say, "I've got you."

Just a few more steps and she would be in her arms, ready to comfort the young girl. Jill's eyes were locked on the girl, but something again caught the girl's attention, distracting her. Behind the little girl, the dancing green light had intensified, becoming almost unbearable. Jill lifted a hand to shield her eyes. Unable to look up at Allie, Jill lowered her eyes to the little girl's small black boots that moved across the granite face. Small spots appeared in Jill's vision as though she had just been staring at the sun.

"Mrs. Davis?" the little girl said.

Allie's body now seemed enveloped in the light, a superimposed halo about her, with a blinding aurora behind her. It burned Jill's eyes to stare, but she could not take her eyes off of the girl. Somehow, it reminded Jill of an angelic painting from the medieval period.

Just inches away, the little girl lifted a hand toward her, and then it happened.

On a night that would forever change Jill's life and in a moment that might haunt her until her last breath, a bright white flash erupted against the black, star-filled sky. In an instant, Jill's eyes were completely blurred in a way that her husband's old camera flash would temporarily blind her as he took a photo of her.

Jill threw her hands in front of her eyes and covered them. For a split second, that moment almost frozen in time, Jill thought she heard the silent air rushing by her, a feeling of a vacuum that may push her into the granite face. She felt the airflow against her face and across the back of her neck, but only for a moment.

What had once been a silent, forgiving breeze gave way to a violent percussion, an immediate turn of direction, and a malicious force against her.

An unseen explosion knocked her back, and her feet left the stable granite floor. The sixty-three-year-old body went limp as it was thrown backward like a rag doll.

The woman flew through the air, the dark sky above giving a feeling of vertigo as the ground behind her rushed forward. For a moment, Jill thought she could see the little girl on a similar trajectory.

Allie's eyes were closed, and her body was about twenty feet in front of Jill. Jill reached a hand toward the little girl, and Jill's body met the ground with a menacing force, her head striking the ground with a *thud*, and everything went black.

Chapter 15 – 410 Days After Launch

The dampness woke her. It had begun as a small, paralyzing parasite that crept in from beneath her, stirring her from her sleep. The cold wetness that had started in the small part of her back had now filled her body with a chill.

Jesus, Jill, did you piss yourself?

She struggled to move her body, but the cold grabbed her. Her fingers felt foreign, a stranger's touch across her face. Jill moved her fingers back and forth, beckoning them to wake up.

Jill blinked. Her eyes felt irritated and puffy, like when pink eye went wild through the bus. Even she had contracted it. She rubbed them with numb fingers, the phosphenes dancing against her eyelids. Her husband was a welder by trade, and what she was experiencing was what he described as a flash burn. The intense light and flash must have caused it.

She closed her eyes, held them shut, then opened them, hopeful that the razor blades which seemed to reside there might depart.

Jill stared at the starry night that reflected back to her, the mat of black canvas decorated with tiny diamond-like stars. She rubbed her eyes again, trying to clear the blurry fog that had condensed in her vision.

She braced her hands against the crumpled wheat beneath her and attempted to lift her head off the ground. An excruciating pain shot up from the back of her head, where it had collided with the earth. She laced her fingers between her hair strands and rubbed the back of her head.

Jill removed her hand and put it close to her eyes. *No blood, you're ok,* she told herself.

The hand, although cold, reflected the moonlight across her pale skin. With a loud groan, she lifted her head off the ground, sat silently, feeling like a loosely stacked pile of wet towels, and tried to shake out the memory fog. The pain in her head was almost unbearable. A small ringing had developed in her ears, but perhaps she had just become aware of it.

Looking through the field, she tried to recall why she was there. There had been a car accident. There were lights in the sky. Was she involved in the car accident? No, she could see the outline of the yellow bus parked just beyond the curve in the asphalt road. Jill searched the wheat field along the road for clues to the events of her evening.

How long have I been lying here? she asked the pounding organ in her skull.

Jill ran her hands along her pants, searching the pockets for her cell phone. There were only her damp pants and the chilled flesh beneath them. She looked about the field again, and her eyes fell on the massive rock formation fifty feet in front of her. The granite behemoth that jutted out was familiar, more than just something she passed every day on her bus route.

The bus. I parked the bus near the accident. Then I...I got out of the bus for a short walk. Jill struggled to remember through the pounding in her head.

She was near the small mountain that loomed in front of her, its coarse white and black face nothing more than a silent witness.

Jill placed her numb hands on the wet strands of wheat beneath her buttocks and pushed up. She groaned heavily again and pulled her feet beneath her. She pushed upward with all her strength but came up short and sat back down. She felt as though the energy had been taken out of her.

Desperate to get up on her feet, Jill rolled onto her stomach. Just as an inchworm would do, she pulled her knees into her chest while she propped herself on her elbows.

"Oh man, if someone were to see me now," she muttered.

What would her mother have said of her fanny up in the air, as it were?

None of that matters now, she thought.

With a final heave and a sound that might have been confused for an angry bear, Jill rose to her feet. She lifted her hands outward to steady herself. Feeling more like she had drank a fifth of whiskey, she tried her best to stay upright. Like a day-old calf, Jill took a few weary steps toward the massive granite peak. Her wet, plain-white shoes squished as they knocked over the blades of wheat.

She reached the granite rock and placed her hands against the surface. She pulled her hands back in disbelief. Despite the cold, damp air that seemed to have saturated everything, the granite face was warm. She traced her hand against it and noticed for the first time a massive crack that had formed just above her head.

Was that there before? she thought.

Jill placed her fingers inside the crack and followed the groove that ran almost perfectly level. She walked around the edge of the face, and it seemed the crack ran its entirety. Jill looked toward a groove in the incline more worn than the surrounding rock. Someone had been climbing this spot multiple times, if she had to guess. She looked to the peak of the small granite mountain, and the sudden awareness descended upon her.

Allie, the voice inside her pounding head whispered.

Allie had been atop the rock outcropping. Why was she up there?

The fractured memory of the night returned. Allie had been near the zenith, talking with someone, upset with someone or something. Jill had climbed the side of this behemoth, and then the explosion of light had happened. Then everything faded to black.

Where was the little girl? Jill turned and placed her back against the warm rock, thankful for its unusual comfort against the cold evening. She scanned the rolling landscape again, the moon illuminating most of the wheat fields except for the random shadows. Her eyes looked to the timberline, and she watched the swaying giants for movement below.

Where had Allie gone? The question lingered in Jill's concussed head.

It seemed to be the one thought she could not get rid of.

"Allie!" Jill screamed into the darkness.

She waited, her hoarse voice almost unrecognizable against the silence, but with no returning answer.

Frustrated and worried, Jill pushed herself off the rock face and turned to her right. She made her way slowly along the granite, her hand tracing the massive crack for support should she lose her balance. She turned the corner of the rock crop, and as she did, her reliable yellow Bluebird came into focus right where she had left it. She paused, physically drained, and tried to catch her breath, her exaggerated breathing coming out like angry steam.

"Allie! Where are you?" she called out once more.

With no answer, Jill continued her path around the granite peak again. If she could make it to the bus, she could call someone—one foot in front of the other across the blades of wheat. Carefully watching where she stepped, she failed to notice the large fissure in the ground in front of her until she was upon it. It loomed out in front of her.

Jill stopped just feet short of the massive crack in the Earth's floor. She peered over the edge and looked into the dark void. Absolutely nothing could be seen, pitch black and full of an emptiness that could swallow even the smallest light. She thought it best to step back from the three-foot-wide void that had opened up.

Once she was safely back a few more feet, she looked and followed the fissure with her eyes away from the granite peak, through the wheat field, interrupting both lanes of Frontage Road and onto the interstate. Jill had driven this route for almost two decades and had never witnessed a crack or sinkhole in this area.

Had there been another earthquake? Was that what had caused the flash of light and the mini canyon that now stood before her like a gaping wound?

Unable to pass the trench in front of her, Jill turned and walked toward the road and away from the looming granite rock formation. She again struggled to put one foot in front of the other, still searching for the energy that had seemingly been stolen from her. The blades of wheat crunched below her shoes, and she couldn't care less to see another piece of wheat ever again.

"This brings a whole new meaning to being gluten intolerant," she mumbled, a chuckle escaping her lips.

She grabbed her head in pain. The laughter had been too much for it. She stopped again. This time, Jill was dizzy and waited for it to pass.

Jill looked ahead and then to the right, toward town. She scanned the timberline again and noticed a gap in the trees just to the right of the granite peak.

"What the—" she asked.

The crack that had opened in the ground was on the right side, heading toward town, and had taken out a row of trees with it. Jill shook her head in disbelief and walked toward the road, now only thirty feet away. She took another step and paused. In front of her was an oddly shaped circular depression in the wheat.

Jill inched her way forward and looked at the center of the circular depression, an object catching her eye. The object lay there motionless as a deer bedded down. She entered the circular depression and saw the black hooded sweatshirt first. In front of her lay Allie on her back and not moving. Jill's heart raced as she kneeled next to the motionless girl.

"Allie?" she said quietly, almost coming out as a whisper. "Allie, please wake up," Jill said as she pushed the strands of wheat away from the little girl's body.

Jill placed her numb fingers against Allie's face and was left frustrated by her lack of feeling.

She leaned in closer and pressed her face against the little girl's. Cold, it felt so cold.

Jill looked over Allie's body for any signs of injury. Allie had landed on her back, but she appeared to be unharmed.

She placed a hand on the little girl's shoulder and gave it a light shake. "Allie, honey, please wake up," Jill pleaded.

The little girl lay motionless. Panic had started to set in for Jill, and she tried to remain calm.

"Someone, please help!" she called out into the night as loud as she could, her voice cracked in high pitch like a pubescent boy.

"Help! Is there anyone else out here?" Jill yelled.

The silence was again the only thing that responded.

She laid her head on the little girl's chest. She could feel just the slightest rise and fall.

Or am I just imagining that?

Jill put her ear to Allie's heart, and the small girl's heart gave the slightest beat, the most beautiful sound Jill had heard.

"Oh, thank God!" Jill exclaimed.

Not wanting to move the child, Jill removed her oversized green flannel, its white insulated down innards exposed, leaving Jill with only a black T-shirt to defend her body against the frigid temperature. The flannel had been Bill's, and it remained one of her favorites. She had gotten rid of most of his clothes except a few items, and tonight, she was thankful for this particular one.

Jill draped the green flannel on the little girl's body.

The cold autumn air cut against Jill's bare arms, and she shivered.

Jill stood and looked to the north and the south. There were no headlights on the interstate or on Frontage Road. What time was it, and how long had they been out?

She looked for the moon to see if she could use its position to gauge the time of night, but it was of no use. The moon just sat there silently, reflecting like it always did. Watching silently, the quiet observer.

Jill returned her attention to the unconscious little girl lying in the field. What dreams were left to those who had involuntarily fallen asleep? The ones forced into an unwanted slumber?

She started to call out but thought better of it. She gave up on yelling as soon as she gave in to the idea that they were alone in the field.

Jill knew what she had to do. "I'll be right back, honey. I'm heading to the bus to call for help," Jill said to Allie, hoping the child could hear her.

Jill stood and raised a tired foot off the ground once more, taking a step toward the asphalt road. Her vision had improved, and she noticed some of the dizziness was beginning to wear off. She felt surer of her steps and quickened her pace until she reached the gravel shoulder of the asphalt road. Jill stepped up the small incline onto the asphalt lane, then turned to her right toward the parked yellow bus.

Jill walked down the road until she reached the spot where the massive void cut through the asphalt road. Looking to her left, she scanned the grassy median between Frontage Road and the interstate.

The crack is just too wide for me to safely cross, she thought, the throbbing in her head pushing back against her inner voice.

She desperately scanned the area for a place to cross and found it. A guardrail separated the road and the interstate. Its wooden posts were driven into the ground with a strip of metal connecting them. The fissure ran right through the guardrail, allowing two posts to fall into the void, but the rest remained intact.

Jill turned to the guardrail and started to jog toward it. Newfound energy entered her at the thought of crossing the channel and making it to the bus. The wheat crunching loudly beneath her feet drowned out some ringing in her ears, but not all of it.

She reached the guardrail system and inspected it. The bolts that held the steel in place looked rusty but were in good shape overall. She hoisted her body on top of the metal and locked her legs around it. Near the edge of the void, she scooted along the metal, careful not to cut herself on any sharp edges.

Jill approached the center of the temporary bridge span, and the metal groaned beneath her. She quickened her scooting across and failed to see the small cut in the metal, catching her pant leg. The jeans clung to the tear in the metal, refusing to let go of her.

She wiggled forward and backward, the guardrail shaking and groaning with each twist. Her pants still stuck, Jill placed her feet on the wooden post that hung over the void. She pushed down on the post with all of her might, trying to free her pants. She stood, finally ripping the material free but causing her weight to shift to the right.

Jill gripped the guardrail with her thighs, the way a bull rider might hang on to a bull and held on with all she had left. The railing moaned, and she twisted to the right, flattening out the section she was sitting on.

She scooted once more, and her feet found the next post. With her best impression of a gymnast, Jill placed her hands in front of her on the guardrail and pushed, bringing her momentum up and out. The barrier groaned one last time, and she came down to the ground safely on the other side.

Jill stood, and a searing pain shot through the back of her thigh. She placed a hand on her right thigh and brought it back in front of her face. Blood ran down from her hand, and she knew that the sharp metal had cut her, but she was unsure how bad.

She limped away from the empty void and hobbled as fast as she could toward the yellow Bluebird bus only three hundred yards away.

She approached the gravel shoulder once more and climbed onto the asphalt road. The road felt firm and stable, and she was thankful for that.

Jill felt the warm blood running down the back of her leg and pooling in her shoe, but she pressed forward.

She arrived at the bus and approached its open double doors. Placing her left hand on the bus and breathing hard, she did her best to catch her breath. She lifted her injured leg onto the front step and grabbed the chrome handrail. Jill pulled herself up and let out a scream in agony as it felt like the tear in her thigh had opened up further. She walked up the bus steps, groaning with each step. Reaching her driver's seat, she plopped down and looked about the floor. Her purse, where had she put her purse?

Oh, heaven help us if a thief has taken it.

She scanned the bus aisle and found nothing. Looking at the dash, she spotted it. She sat up, hastily grabbed the old brown leather purse, and returned it to her lap.

Rummaging through the purse, she found the old phone. Pressing the home button, Jill felt a wave of relief as the phone's display illuminated her face with a soft light against her cold skin. Jill unlocked the phone and dialed nine-one-one. She waited for the call to go through, and when it did, it gave a busy tone.

Busy? Why the hell would the line be busy? Jill thought.

With all the technology of the present day, there shouldn't be a busy tone unless there were too many callers on the line trying at the same time. Had the town experienced the flash and subsequent quake? Was there widespread disturbance?

Jill grabbed the black CB radio mounted to the dashboard and turned on the small dial. A noise of static filled the empty bus.

"Hello, can anyone here me?" she cried out into the corded microphone.

She waited for a few minutes, knowing full well she shouldn't sit for long.

Two minutes passed and Jill rose to her feet and looked at the cloth driver's seat, which was now stained red by the gash in the back of her thigh.

She gripped the chrome handrail and carefully made her way down the bus steps, placing most of the weight on her uninjured leg, and stepped off the gravel shoulder and onto the grassy median. She did her best to ignore the pain in her leg and started a light jog to the guardrail, clumsily limping as she did.

She arrived at the guardrail, her right thigh throbbing. She stopped to try the phone call again. She dialed nine-one-one and was left with the same busy tone.

This time, Jill stepped onto the metal guardrail with more confidence and started her walk across it. Like a tightrope artist, she walked across the narrow, two-foot-wide sheet of metal. Her sneakers begged to fall into the ripple manufactured in them, but she kept them flat.

She reached the other side and gingerly stepped off the guardrail. She unlocked her phone and dialed nine-one-one, but again it was busy.

Jill crossed the asphalt road and walked back into the wheat field.

With her eyes solely on the circular depression where she had left Allie, she made her way across the strands of wheat. Just a few more yards, and she would be to Allie. She could make out the dark outline in the grain ahead.

She tried the phone again, but it gave the same busy tone.

Just a few more steps, and I'll be with her, Jill thought.

"Allie, honey, are you awake?" Jill called out.

Silence again greeted her. Jill was worried about her. Allie needed medical attention. Hell, they both did. Her little body had been so cold. Two more steps, and she would be there.

"Allie?" again she cried out, this time louder.

Jill finally reached the spot where she had left her. She kneeled in the moonlight and felt the green flannel she had draped over the little girl.

What should have felt like a soft, warm body instead gave way to a flat, cold, and hard-matted ground. Jill pulled the flannel back, exposing the trampled wheat below.

Allie was gone.

Chapter 16 - 1 Year, 2 Days Before Launch

Dr. Gray ran his hand along the ship's outer edge, the special blend of Aluminum, Nitinol 60, and Titanium alloys reflecting the hangar's lights like a mirror as he walked.

Not your typical NASA white space shuttle, he thought. *A nontypical craft, for a non-typical mission, with a non-typical crew,* he mused.

He looked back at the craft and smiled. The center of the ship resembled the "flying saucers" of the 1950s and 1960s, but a bit more cylindrical. Instead of an inviting windshield was a massive but lightweight shield. The overall design of the craft was more of a return pod than a mission craft to Dr. Victor Gray. Not that it mattered too deeply to Victor. He doubted he would ever need to spend much time inside the vessel outside this old airplane hangar.

He would love to go. Throughout his childhood, Victor had always looked up to the stars and dreamed of exploring the heavens. He was born into a lower-income home of two immigrant parents, Nikolai and Karen Balandin. His parents fled Russia after the fall of the Soviet Union. Fearing backlash for his communist roots, Victor's father changed their last name to Gray. The cold winters in Boston weren't much colder than in Russia, so Victor's parents settled in Boston, and they adjusted quickly. A year after moving, they welcomed Victor into the world.

Victor supposed his childhood was a good one, like any other, just stricter. In his opinion, a lack of money either contributed to parents preferring too much control or, in contrast, none at all. In Victor's case, it was too much. The constant oversight by his parents, combined with a fear of disappointing them, could either break a child or push them toward success. Luckily for Victor, failure was never an available option.

Many nights were spent at their small, round dining table, covering everything from math to English and physics to Freud. Usually, it was his mother that provided help with the schoolwork. His father had to be in bed early to wake up early for work. It was a much healthier way to handle the situation, anyway, with the few times his father helped ending up in a blowout. Without saying it in front of his father, his mother was smarter than his father.

Victor was convinced early on that had his mother been born in the United States and not had Victor, she could have gone on into a scientific field and made a life of it. There were plenty of times Victor would ask a question regarding an equation, and his mother would remain silent until after his father went to bed to answer it. It had been his mother who had sparked his interest in the stars as well.

On dark, cold evenings, often on their walks home from the grocery store, his mother would point out stars and the occasional planet. Looking back, Victor assumed it was an easy distraction to take a weary mother's mind off of the sketchy neighborhood they walked through. Victor would give anything to have another one of those star-filled walks or discussions at that small round dining table.

Victor's father died far too young, but at least it was fairly quick. In the end, the doctors said there was nothing they could do; cancer had spread too fast. Looking back, Victor was sure it was something he had been exposed to while working.

Not long after his diagnosis, his father failed to return home after work. His mother reported him missing the next day, but it was four days until the police recovered his body. Whether his father had given up or wanted to make one last sacrifice to prevent financial hardship in treatment for an incurable diagnosis, Victor would never know.

A note was never found, and since there was no goodbye, Victor and his mother were only left with their assumptions. Victor often struggled with his father's choice, and since it was never talked about, anger and resentment were left alone and allowed to build and grow inside of him.

His father's previous employer, an industrial company that fabricated plastic parts, had covered the funeral expenses, an option in the medical insurance selected by his father during his new hire process. Two days after the funeral, his mother went to work for that very same company. Victor often wondered if his mother was ushered right into his father's old position, like a replaceable part, just another cog in the wheel. The two struggled at first, but eventually, things got better. They had the same income as when his father was alive but one less mouth to feed.

Once Victor was in high school, he got a part-time job at the same grocery store his mother and he had walked to on so many crisp winter evenings. With his mother's newfound freedom, their evenings were spent focused on his studies, filled with exciting brainstorming and discussions on the possibilities of the universe.

Victor graduated as valedictorian, an accomplishment his mother wept over. Since they had been in poverty for so long, Victor could apply for the MIT scholarship program and was even eligible for their grant program, which helped with additional living expenses while he was enrolled.

He went on to excel at MIT, no longer held back by the limits of what he and his mother could envision. He was able to reach his full potential through his professors and peers. Victor spent seven years at MIT, and they were some of the best years of his life.

He could have obtained his Ph.D. in theoretical physics sooner but he took a semester off when his mother became sick. She was diagnosed with the same cancer that his father had. Luckily for Victor, his mother had chosen to fight and receive treatment.

Victor finished the following quarter and spent the last few months of his mother's life by her side. There were good days, and there were bad days, but at least they had each other. There was closure and a goodbye in the graceful way his mother had chosen to pass, not a cowardly escape like his father's.

His mother passed on a beautiful May afternoon. The window was open in her small bedroom, the fresh spring air moving through it, brushing against the curtains and into their nostrils with the sweet smells of cherry blossom and fresh-cut grass. Victor had been sitting there quietly, holding her hand.

They had sat in silence most of that day. The morphine, which had taken its hold in the last week, had tired his mother. The nurse from hospice care, told Victor that it probably wouldn't be much longer.

The curtains by the open window danced back and forth like two shy children, pushing and pulling toward and away from each other. The twin pieces of fabric continued their game until the daylight began to fade for the day, moving gracefully, effortlessly, and eventually slowly until they stopped. They hung straight at attention, the light breeze playing peek-a-boo stopped, and the sweet smell of spring in the afternoon failed to fill the room. Victor knew it before he looked back at her, his mother had passed,

He sat in that old metal folding chair beside his mother's twin-sized bed for the better part of an hour, still holding her hand. Victor wanted to retain every bit of warmth from her that he could. He knew her warmth, albeit not the physical representation, had gotten them through some of their darkest days.

When finally her hand ceased to reciprocate any warmth, and his eyes could no longer hold out, he wept. He wept for his mother, for the loss of her, and for everything that she would miss in the years to come. She would never get to be a grandmother, to know the joy of another small child running toward her, arms outstretched and radiating pure, innocent love. Victor wept for the family events and dinners he would never be able to invite her to, never to be able to introduce her to a future daughter-in-law if he met someone.

Interlope: 1 Year, 2 Days Before Launch

Finally, he wept for everything she could not accomplish in her short life because of her circumstances. By just being born in the wrong country at the wrong time, his mother had been held back, unable to grow in the ways she wanted and reach her full potential. Add to that a short lifetime of sacrifices for a young son just to have food on the table. Victor would be forever grateful.

He gave his mother's hand one last squeeze and kissed her forehead. It was odd how life could go full circle so fast. Not very long ago, it was her kissing his forehead as she said goodnight and turned out the light.

Victor turned toward the door and turned off the bedroom light. He exited the bedroom and called for the hospice nurse.

***

"This is for you, Mom," Victor softly whispered as he patted the ship, carefully pulling himself back from the bittersweet memory.

He continued his inspection of the craft, walking about the hangar and taking in the beauty of it. The small group of machinists had worked hard over the past few months. Mr. White flew them directly over from a Boeing plant in Everett, Washington. With whatever they needed at their side and materials available from around the world within a day of ordering, the Boeing team had completed the vessel and almost looked as though they had enjoyed it. On their last night at the base, Victor and his team met the Boeing team down at Candy's for drinks and sent them off properly.

Victor laughed to himself at how the crew had looked the next morning, he included. To say that production suffered that next morning was an understatement.

He rounded the vessel's front edge and arrived at the ship's midsection, lifted his left wrist to the rolled edge, and placed his wristband on its top. A LED in the screen illuminated green, the lip of the rolled edge parted, and a hatch door three feet wide opened.

An alarm inside the ship sounded, and a pair of retractable stairs deployed, coming out and barely kissing the ground. Victor placed a hand on the rail that accompanied the five-foot tall staircase and climbed. He reached the top stair and stepped into the dark interior.

"Alice, lights on, please," he said.

"Yes, Dr. Gray, turning the lights on," she replied as the ship's LED light arrays illuminated the small airlock chamber.

"Alice. Let's go ahead and close the exterior door and stabilize cabin air pressure," Victor said.

"Yes, Dr. Gray," she replied.

The aluminum staircase retracted with a motorized hum as it stowed itself away. One more alarm sounded inside, and the three-foot tall hatch closed, sealing Victor inside. The light above the door that had been flashing red now turned green.

Victor's ears popped as they adjusted to the new pressure. He turned and headed down the narrow hallway that connected the exterior door and airlock to the main cabin space, the kitchen, and the lab. He walked briskly and with purpose, his gray sneakers padding softly on the ship's tiled floor. Passing by small doors bordering the hallway, he did his best not to wake up the occupants inside.

Mr. White had requested that the flight crew live aboard the vessel for a period of time to make sure they could handle being cooped up together for a long duration. Director Stevens had given the final ok, and now they were living on board. From what Victor could tell from the outside, things seemed to be going just fine.

Commander Lawrence Chu ran a tight ship, literally. It was one of the reasons he was chosen. Throughout his career, he completed every mission he had been given with very low casualties. Victor respected a man like that, someone who could command and lead through respect and mutual trust, unlike a dictator. Victor hoped that rang true in Commander Chu. There was no need to strong-arm and rule with fear, something his parents had experienced firsthand in the Soviet Union. Instead, inform your

Interlope: 1 Year, 2 Days Before Launch

crew of what needs to be done to achieve a common goal and put the success in their hands. That meant trusting the person next to you.

Victor continued down the narrow hallway until it intersected with the center of the ship. The kitchen, small lab for medical and biology, and food storage room were all within reach in this common area. Unbeknownst to the crew, the center room was spherical and encapsulated by the most important part of the ship: the two electromagnetic ring machines. The rings were a network of copper wiring, metal alloys, rare earth magnets, and two micro-fusion reactors.

He tapped his foot on the kitchen floor, a solid *thud* returning. Beneath his feet, one of the two Inertial Confinement Fusion Reactors sat quietly and patiently, waiting to be put to use. Using research gathered from Project Daedalus and Project Longshot, this new nuclear pulse propulsion ICF had been Victor's life's work at MIT.

Initially, his Inertial Confinement Fusion Reactor was large and focused on providing power to rockets for delivering heavy payloads to Mars. However, he was forced to scale down his ICF due to his lab size restraints at MIT and the limit on how much lithium deuteride a person could purchase. Those restraints forced his model to be smaller and more compact. That purchasing power was increased after joining the DARPA team.

Victor looked at the floor beneath his gray sneakers. Just inches below was the main power source for the craft's ability to pass through the membrane, the cosmic quilt as he had coined it, and to reach the other side. This sequential machine, in theory, was capable of distorting the area around the ship to such a degree it was like parting the curtains on the next room over, just long enough for the vessel to slip through.

Granted, the forces on the other side constantly wanted to tear the ship apart, so the rings were needed to function the entire time the craft and its crew were there. Once the vessel passed through the membrane, Alice could idle down the rotation of the rings and find an equilibrium to conserve fuel. That balance and the crew's survival all depended on the process working, not once, but twice.

Victor walked to the center island in the kitchen and leaned against it. Directly below the island sat the housing for the twin ICF machines. Chemical lasers inside each ICF compressed the lithium deuteride pellets to the point of fusion, expanding the fuel until the pressure could no longer be contained. The exploding plasma then would travel into collector tubing made of Inconel Alloy 625, a nickel alloy consisting of around fifty-eight percent nickel and a newly invented material known as Graphene.

The Graphene was key in helping to control the flow of electrons in a consistent flow, helping to form the formation of Dirac Cones. The plasma would then discharge from the ICF and into the hollow ring structure filled with two-inch copper rods. The ring structure composed of the same nickel alloy then directed the plasma to the fluid-filled chambers composed of liquid mercury and nickel-copper alloys that would be forced through the circular frame within the ship's inner walls.

As the plasma traveled in opposing directions from the ICF, it would then shed electrons to the exterior of the vessel and push the mercury fluid up toward the top center of the ring, directly over the top of Victor's head.

He looked up at the reinforced plating. Five feet beyond that, the supersonic fluids would collide on a reflecting plate composed of a copper-plated iron-nickel compound. Electrons from the plasma would collide with the iron plate at near-light speed, mimicking a hadron collider, and would be absorbed by the iron plate, magnetizing it.

The charged mercury fluid arriving a fraction of a second later at the iron plate would have nowhere to go and rebound off the plate with increasing speed. Expelling more electrons as it travels back

Interlope: 1 Year, 2 Days Before Launch

down the ship's walls through the ring-shaped frame, the fluid would rob the less dense copper atoms as the liquid mercury looks for a place to release. As the heavier mercury fluid reaches the ICF, the lighter copper atoms are filtered out through condenser coils. The copper atoms were then collected on either side of the ICF machines, being pressurized by the fluid behind them to form a neon-copper gas. Once accumulated in a high enough quantity, this copper mixed with gas reignited in the ICF and helped the lasers inside to reheat the spent lithium deuteride pellet.

The two opposing mercury flows would then arrive downward through the rings and collide once more in the ICF. The resulting rebound from the mercury collision and the neon copper ignition would force the mercury back up the ring's frame to collide with the copper-plated iron-nickel alloy with increasing velocity. This process would repeat each time, robbing electrons from the weaker copper fuel rods in the ring's interior, increasing the electromagnetic field. The generated electromagnetic field was crucial to the ship's ability to slip through the barrier between worlds.

Victor walked around the island and past the kitchen counter. A stainless-steel sink sat in the middle of the counter, giving the crew a small sense of normalcy.

He left the kitchen area, walked toward the small sitting area with a small rectangular table, and sat on the cold, reinforced plastic bench, placing his elbows on the table.

Victor looked about the interior of the ship. He had often thought of the small homes described in The Hobbit, with their round living areas. In Tolkien's books, they provide the reader with a sense of otherworldly charm. In the craft, the small space was only out of sheer necessity.

The two rings took up much of the ship's shape, as well as its total weight. If its outer shell were to be pulled off, it might resemble Saturn with two closing orbiting rings. Just outside each of the crew members' rooms was the framework of one of the rings, rotating independently of the small sphere in the center. It, too, turned but on its horizontal axis, helping to provide its artificial gravity and take advantage of the electrical field generated at the iron-nickel collector.

The interior of the inner sphere was lined in a network of silver alloy wire. Silver, being a better conductor than copper, would protect the instrumentation of the craft's interior and the crew, absorbing the electrons and including them in the total electromagnetic field.

As the outer rings pull harder and harder on the iron-nickel collector plate, the forces exerted by the liquid mercury and heat from the fusion process increase, eventually causing the iron-nickel collector plate to fail. The iron-nickel plate would be reduced to a liquid and unable to properly mix with the liquid Mercury and would repel itself, causing a rotation of the magnetized iron-nickel particles.

For a moment, the contents of each ring would be in utter chaos, an uncontrollable process only comparable to an event horizon, but in each experiment, each drone that was sent out, harmony was always achieved. The molecules inside, when left alone, were free to roam about but always fell in line when forced into constraints under extreme pressure.

Humans, whether a positive or negative trait, were the same, thought Victor. Once in harmony, the rotating particles would cause a vortex that eventually synced with the fusion releases that were ongoing from the ICF, reaching a state of a maximum electromagnetic field.

Thus far, the latest probes had mostly returned without issue, with only one missing. Victor wanted to update the crew about one or more return issues before their launch date. Initially, Director Stevens had requested that Victor not inform the crew of these issues, stating that she wanted to wait until they were closer to the launch day, if not once they were already on their flight path. Victor understood her reasoning. Tossing a negative notion into their plans might jeopardize their decision-making abilities, but he felt compelled to tell them. They had invested too much at this point to decline.

From what Victor could tell, the crew was very passionate about this project. It wasn't every day that a person could play a vital role in science to find out why their planet was experiencing so much seismic activity. So much pain and suffering could be stopped if they could reach the other side. Once the crew had the data or knew the source, they could bring the information back with them, maybe even peacefully intervene with whatever intelligent life forms had been causing the quakes and had sent the spherical probe.

That thought excited Victor. First contact would be made on this mission. Once and for all, the question of "Are we alone?" would finally be answered.

What a time to be alive, he thought.

A sadness crept over him when he thought of his mother. If only she had lived long enough to know of the acceleration of knowledge that just the past few years had provided. Victor's research into the mysterious sphere would have been enough for him to break protocol and call to tell her about it.

The ship's design had been based solely on the reverse-engineering of the sphere. Victor had watched presentations on conceptual Mercury Vortex engines, but nothing compared to this. None had the design for thrust and distortion of the space around it like their current model.

Again, Victor thought of her and those cold walks home from the grocery store near their home in Boston. The two stared up toward the stars in silence, a mutual fascination with what lay above. If only she could have known there was someone or something up there. Another planet, another species capable of reaching them. *Are they more advanced than us in other ways as well? What things could they potentially teach us, and what would we be able to share with them?*

The thought of calling a life form capable of reaching them an "alien" left a bitter taste in Victor's mouth, and he resented the notion. He hoped that humankind could look past the Hollywood stereotypes and see them for what they truly were; amazing and inspiring.

Victor got up from the bench and walked out of the kitchen area toward the narrow hallway that led to the exit door and airlock. He stopped at the first cabin door on the right, raised his right hand, and gave the door a few light taps. He took a step back from the door and waited.

Inside, the sound of light shuffling, followed by a man's voice, could be heard. The door opened, and Commander Lawrence Chu greeted him with a smile.

"Dr. Gray, what brings you here this late?" the Commander asked.

"Commander, there are a few things I would like to brief you and your crew on," Victor replied.

"Understood. Give me ten minutes, and we will meet you in the common area," the Commander said with a nod.

Commander Chu closed the door, and Victor turned, facing the kitchen. He walked back down the narrow hallway and toward the island in the center. He turned and leaned against the counter, taking some of the strain off his tired feet.

Victor raised his left hand to his jaw and rubbed it nervously.

He heard a door close in the hallway. He looked down at the floor, took a deep breath, and exhaled through his nose, trying to calm himself. Hoping he could find the right words, he ran his fingers through his hair.

Approaching footsteps made him look up to greet who he assumed was a crew member.

The hair on his neck stood straight up, and he nearly choked. He stood straight up, his body stiff. Director Angela Stevens stepped out of the hallway and into view.

"Dr. Gray, how nice of you to come visit the crew. What brings you here tonight?"

Chapter 17 - 1 Year, 1 Day Before Launch

The hot desert air swirled and rose to greet her face. The rotor blades of the HH-60 Pave Hawk noisily rotated as it touched down in front of her. The swirling sand in the disturbed air covered her military fatigues and clung to her damp brown skin. She could feel the sweat just about everywhere, which was common for this part of the world.

Staff Sergeant Jodi Evans had expected the heat when she was deployed to the U.S. Air Force base in Kandahar, but nothing could truly prepare a person for it. She had spent the past twelve years in this Afghanistan city and figured she would have been used to it by now. Not that that mattered too much for long. She would be leaving soon, having fulfilled the contract she had signed.

She had considered reenlisting, but the odds of her being deployed right back there were high. The medevac program was still needed, and Jodi had impressed her superiors with her quick thinking and ability to care for the wounded.

The Afghan people still relied heavily on their services. About seventy percent of their missions were to aid Afghan civilians and security forces. Just last June, an Air Force Black Hawk helicopter was shot down while trying to rescue Marines, killing four crew members, including two of their combat medics. So, the need for a combat medic like Jodi had increased.

She looked down at her patient lying on the green canvas stretcher. A fifty-four-year-old man from a village ten miles from the American base had suffered a heart attack when the Taliban attacked. After American forces were sent in to clear out the armed men, Abdul-Hafez was found lying in the street. As luck would have it, Jodi was just five miles away on a return trip in a Humvee. A quick radio correspondence back to HQ and a chopper was en route, arriving just three minutes after she had arrived at Abdul-Hafez's side.

Jodi bent at her knees in unison with her assistant, First Lieutenant Lance Murphey. Making eye contact with the young lieutenant, she nodded. Both straightened their legs and lifted the canvas stretcher. Abdul-Hafez moaned through the plastic oxygen mask, and she felt relief at the sound of the older gentleman still breathing next to them. More than likely, he would survive the helicopter flight and be in good hands once they reached the hospital.

She and Lance walked quickly with their patient to the helicopter just two hundred feet away. The flight crew members, two younger men Jodi didn't recognize, hopped out and helped lift the stretcher onto the helicopter floor. Once the stretcher was secured, she gave the Afghan man's hand one last squeeze and turned away from the helicopter.

As she briskly walked before the increasing rotor could agitate any more sand-filled air, Lance jogged to join her.

"Where to now, Staff Sergeant?" he asked with a grin.

Lance, a mid-twenties Irish man from Queens, was everything you'd expect him to be. Confidence ran thick in Lance, probably as thick as the red curls that complimented his head. Jodi had once thought that confidence like that was an attractive trait. As she had aged, though, having experienced confident men, she knew that typically once they opened their mouths, the attractiveness usually dropped out of them, falling lifeless to the floor just as fast as the bullshit stories and pick-up lines.

Jodi returned the smile and replied, "I think you know Lance. Back to HQ so I can get the hell out of this hot sand pit."

"We're going to miss you, Staff Sergeant," Lance said. She looked him in the eye and replied, "I know you will."

They walked in silence through the village of Gizab, through the dirt roads of dilapidated homes. When Jodi had first arrived in

Interlope: 1 Year, 1 Day Before Launch

Afghanistan, it was typical to see children playing in the streets, but now with the fighting between the Afghan National Guard and the Taliban, no one roamed the roads. It always made Jodi uncomfortable, knowing that people were probably watching them through their windows.

She pushed the thought aside and continued along the dirt road. The warm desert breeze pushed on the brown ringlets that trickled out of her military helmet and brushed away the few hairs that had made their way to her eyes. As she did, her hand cast a shadow over her face, giving a brief reprieve from the Afghan sun beating down upon her.

They neared the end of the village, passing the last leaning shack on their left. Laughter escaped from the small home and a gleeful yell from a child followed.

Maybe there is still hope for this place, she thought as she walked toward the Humvee parked just a few yards away.

Jodi reflected on her career in this region over the past twelve years. She hoped that it wasn't all in vain. The bloodshed, tears cried, and hardships endured for what she had believed was a better tomorrow. Now, opening the door on the Humvee and turning back to the small desolate village, she wasn't so sure that was the case.

The drive back to the DMZ was a quiet one. Lance, who still had another two years, stared straight ahead as he navigated the unmaintained road. He had reacted predictably to her retirement, upset at first, but was happy once he came around to the idea of losing his colleague and fellow soldier of the past eight years. He admitted that he was saddened but happy for her to move on to the next chapter of her life.

A small convoy of vehicles joined them on the interstate, and they started their journey back, heading northeast to the joint military base at Bagram Air Base. She laid her head against the headrest, closing her tired eyes briefly. Fatigue filled her thoughts, and she drifted off to a dreamless sleep.

***

"Staff Sergeant. Staff Sergeant, wake up."

Jodi slowly opened her eyes. She sat up in her seat, confused for a moment.

"I must have dozed off," she admitted with embarrassment.

"It's all good," Lance replied. "I probably would have done the same. The drive back to HQ is a boring one lately."

Jodi nodded. "Boring is a good thing. I'd rather have a hundred boring days out here than have one eventful day full of chaos, gunfire, and death."

Lance nodded in response. His eyes were still fixated on the road ahead, the vehicles now stopping at the armed entry gate.

Despite Lance's excusal of her napping, Jodi felt slightly disappointed in herself for letting her guard down. So many lives had been lost on similar return trips.

She was tired, more so lately. The worry of returning to civilian life after being in combat hung over her head and was constantly on her mind. Often, Jodi would be woken in the middle of the night by gunfire in the distance. She would lay there, unable to go back to sleep. What would she do once she was home? Where would she work? This was the only career she knew.

The vehicle ahead was let through, and Lance pulled their Humvee up to the guard shack. The young Marine with short black hair beneath his military helmet glanced at their credentials and nodded to the guard shack. The white wooden arm blocking their path was lifted, and Lance proceeded into the base.

The convoy of vehicles passed row upon row of parking lots and office buildings. After a short while, a few vehicles turned off the main road for their destinations. Lance put on his blinker and turned the Humvee to the right, following the road to the barracks.

Jodi sighed with relief as the brown buildings came into view. Pulling up to one of the small brown modular buildings, Lance put the Humvee into park. Without saying a word, Lance reached over

Interlope: 1 Year, 1 Day Before Launch

and embraced Jodi. A sweet smell of sweat and deodorant filled her nose. She was grateful for the hug; something rarely exchanged there, it seemed.

Lance pulled away from the hug, tears in his eyes,

"Oh, come on, you big baby, I'll come by later and say goodbye," she teased.

Lance laughed and rubbed away the wetness that had accumulated in the corners of his eyes.

"Damn dust," he complained, "gets me every time."

Jodi smiled at him and opened the Humvee door. The warm desert air greeted her once more. She stepped onto the hot asphalt parking lot and let out an exaggerated groan. The asphalt roads had to be at least ten degrees hotter than the dirt roads of Gizab.

Using the exterior step to hoist herself, she grabbed her backpack off the cargo rack on top of the Humvee. Giving one last final wave to Lance, she closed the door and turned toward the small one-bedroom unit she had called home for the past twelve years.

Jodi climbed the concrete steps and stopped on the porch. To her right was a black-hinged mailbox. She flipped the lid expecting to see something but was not surprised to find it empty. Jodi had been an only child, so when her parents passed last year from Covid-19, she was left alone. Alone and married to her career.

Unlocking the front door, she opened it and stepped inside. The small air conditioning unit, still running hard, had kept her place a relaxing sixty-eight degrees. It felt amazing but a bit like the arctic compared to the Afghan heat, just two inches on the other side of the door.

Jodi closed the door, keeping the relentless sun at bay. She set her backpack on the ground and untied her heavy brown leather boots. The cool linoleum floor greeted her feet, and she was grateful to be free.

She walked straight to the single twin-sized bed. Not wanting to dirty the inside of her gray bedspread and sheets, she laid down on the bed.

I'll just rest my eyes for a moment, she thought.

She could shower later and then set out for dinner.

Jodi closed her eyes and thought of home, bathing herself in a happier time before. Her mother and father were there, sitting at the dining room table. Her mother's beautiful smile and her father's contagious laughter filled the air. She could almost feel them there. Staring at her mother, she pictured herself getting up and walking toward her.

If I could just get one more hug, she thought.

It had been excruciating for her when they passed. The military let her fly home to Arizona when she received the news that they were both hospitalized. She flew over 7,700 miles from Afghanistan to Phoenix, Arizona, only to be separated from them by a room sealed by an eighth of an inch piece of plexiglass. In that unimaginable moment, she was forced to say goodbye to them, not how she would have ever wanted. Even if she could have been next to them, it wouldn't have mattered.

Jodi's mother and father were sedated and on ventilators. She told herself they knew she was there, convinced herself they heard her goodbye, but deep down, Jodi knew that was unlikely.

She was forced to say goodbye to them silently behind the plexiglass barrier, her hand pressed against its cool, clear surface. It was her mother who passed first and her father a week later. Jodi often wondered if they would have been able to survive had the earthquake that rocked Phoenix the previous week not occurred. The 7.4 earthquake devastated the city, and most of the region was without power for the next few days.

Jodi sat in that dark hospital while hundreds of patients, dependent upon life support or ventilators, died slowly, with the doctors and nurses unable to do anything but keep them pain-free.

She tried to shake off that horrible, traumatic memory as she again dreamt of herself in her parents' dining room. She walked to her mother but was stopped by a plexiglass partition that appeared in front of her. Jodi placed her hands against the barrier, desperate to reach the other side. The beautiful woman in her sixties, smiling and extending her arms out with an offering of a warm embrace. Just a few more steps past the clear barrier and she would be in her mother's arms.

Knock, knock, knock, went her father's knuckles on the table.

Confused, she looked to her father. Her father only smiled, and his knuckles knocked once more.

Knock, knock, knock, went the older man's arthritic hands.

Jodi turned back to her mother, but her mother was gone.

She blinked and rubbed her eyes. The ceiling of her small bedroom greeted her with the same blank stare it had so many times before. She had briefly fallen asleep and was woken by something.

Knock, knock, knock, the sound coming from the front door and not her sleepy dream.

"This had better be good," she said.

Jodi swung her legs off the bed and placed her feet on the floor. Shaking the cobwebs out, she yawned and stretched. She rose from the bed, the sweat-stained fatigues sticking to her body like damp paper. Jodi walked to the door, irritated at being woken up.

She swung the door open mid-knock to find a young private with sweat running down his brow. Surprised, he raised his hand in a salute, shaking slightly.

"At ease, private," she said.

"Ma'am, General Wright would like to speak with you," the young private stated.

"Let the General know I'm on my way," she replied.

The private saluted once more, turned about, and briskly walked away.

What could General Wright want with her tonight? Jodi had her final exit review with him tomorrow morning. Couldn't it wait until then? Nonetheless, she wanted to be respectful of the General's wishes.

Jodi put her boots back on, glanced around her place, and walked through the door, closing it behind her.

Her keys gave a soft jingle when she removed them from her pocket. After locking the door, she turned to the sidewalk and walked to the parking lot that separated the woman's barracks from the officer's building and headed to General Wright's office, the last white building in the row of office buildings constructed like the homes on a monopoly board.

Jodi glanced down at the landscape planters as she walked. *What a waste of money and resources. Most importantly, what a waste of water.*

There they were in the middle of the desert and wasting money on watering shrubs to appease their aesthetic need. The government spent money on plenty of things. This place was no exception.

She stopped at the last office building, walked up the concrete steps, approached the white wooden door, and gave it a quick knock. The door swung open, and the young private who had been at her door now stood before her.

"He's been expecting you," the young private said with a nod.

Jodi entered and found General Wright seated at his desk. An aging man in his seventies, General Wright had given his entire life to the military. A decorated soldier in Vietnam, he had gone on to serve in the Gulf War and then in the Iraqi Freedom Conflict.

Seeming as though this office was where he had been "put off to greener pastures," Jodi almost felt bad for the man. His involvement at such a young age could have been a decision not of his own but a product of the draft. Once his time in Vietnam was complete, he was probably faced with the same fear that Jodi now felt. The fear of the outside life. One without defined parameters of

Interlope: 1 Year, 1 Day Before Launch

what was expected of her and when. The fear of the unknown when left to her own devices. "Sir, you wanted to see me?" she asked, raising an arm in salute.

"Yes, we wanted to speak to you," the General replied.

He motioned to the chair in front of him.

Puzzled, Jodi looked around the dimly lit room, filtered light peeking through the tightly drawn blinds. An attractive man in his late thirties sat in a chair by the right wall. She had been so preoccupied with the General's odd evening request for a visit that she hadn't even noticed the sharply dressed man in a black suit. His neatly groomed brown hair was styled but had a longer, messy look that indicated the man was not actively enlisted in a military branch.

"Staff Sergeant Evans, I'd like to introduce you to Mr. White," the General said as he gestured to the man.

Jodi couldn't believe her eyes and tried her best to bite her tongue.

The General continued, "Mr. White is—"

Jodi interrupted him, "General, I know Mr. White. In fact, I know Mr. White very well," she said with a smile that faded to glare toward the man in the black suit.

"Kind of a long flight for a booty call, isn't it, Alex?" Jodi said through clenched teeth.

The old General behind the desk gasped at her remark. That comment was probably the most entertaining thing he'd witnessed since getting put in this ten-by-ten coffin of a workplace.

"Staff Sergeant, that will be enough of the crude comments," the red-faced General said.

The young man in the suit raised his hand and gestured to push an invisible object aside in the air.

"It's quite alright, General. Staff Sergeant Evans and I have met before, as she mentioned. In her defense, I was not so nice in my younger years," Alexander White replied.

The last part of his sentence had ended with him moving his gaze to her, a possible attempt at being sincere.

"I'll take that as a half-assed apology, Alex," she said without a smile.

Alexander nodded. "But you're right, Jodi, it was a long flight. One that wouldn't have been so long if you would have returned a phone call," Alexander replied.

He had been calling her recently. After so many years, it had been odd to hear his voice on the voicemail.

Jodi and Alexander met while Jodi was at basic training at Joint Base San Antonio-Lackland. It began with simple flirting during the eight and a half weeks of training, but by the end of basic training, there was enough tension between them that their feelings had gotten the best of them. By the time they were registered into their Air Force Technical Schools, their flirtations had blossomed into an every-night hookup. Things in Jodi's eyes were going great until they weren't.

The end started with Alexander being unable to hang out and constantly finding an excuse for why. Every night became once a week. Jodi pressured Alexander, asking him what he wanted. Alexander only replied, "Time and space."

So, Jodi gave him exactly that. Hurt, rejected, and angry, she accepted the first deployment offered to her and did not look back. Not a word had been exchanged between them since then. Now, almost twelve years later, there he sat in front of her. He had come across the ocean, mountains, and the hundreds of miles of sand she had put between them.

The twelve years had aged him. His boyish laugh and smile gave way to wrinkles and smile lines. His hair had been fuller back then; the top now seemed thinner, and his peak more pronounced. She was sure he hadn't lost the hair fully; it had simply just sprouted up somewhere else- a joke her father often made that she carried

Interlope: 1 Year, 1 Day Before Launch

with her like a wonderful memory. Alexander was different, and she was sure in his eyes, so was she.

"What brings you to Afghanistan, Alex? You could have just called the General and got a hold of me that way," Jodi asked.

His smile faded, and the seriousness about his face was foreign to her. He had never been the one to be so serious.

"Let's take a walk?" Alexander said, and the words stuck somewhere between a suggestion and a question.

Jodi nodded.

She stood, gave the General a final salute, and walked out of the small office. With Alexander on her heels, she welcomed the feeling that swept over her. So many nights she had thought of him, regretting leaving so abruptly and dreaming about him coming to visit her there in the kingdom of sand.

Jodi passed the nervous private, now seated at a small desk near the door, and approached the door. She grabbed the brass knob and gave it a turn, opened the door, and the air conditioning gave way to the dry desert air. Jodi stepped outside onto the concrete steps. She grabbed the handrail and went down the stairs to the concrete sidewalk.

She turned to watch as Alexander walked through the door, closing it behind him. His black suit and tie, ridiculous given the desert heat, appeared dusty and wrinkled from hours of travel.

Alex made his way down the concrete steps, greeting her once more when he reached the landing.

"Do I get the feeling this isn't a personal visit?" she asked hesitantly, hoping he might correct her assumption, grab her by the arms and embrace her.

"You're right, Jodi. This isn't personal. Although I must say, it's wonderful to see you."

Jodi looked away and took a few steps down to the concrete sidewalk.

"Where did you go after I left?" she asked with genuine curiosity. "After you left, I stayed," he replied from behind her.

She turned and faced him. Her eyes met his gaze. Those were the same eyes she had stared so fondly at years ago.

"You stayed? Why?"

"Multiple reasons, one of which was because I thought you might come back eventually," he replied without breaking eye contact. He continued, "Truth be told, I was in a car accident the week after you left. I was ok, but I had fractured my left leg. A titanium rod and pins to go with it kind of put a detour on my career choices within the Air Force. The injury took me off the active-duty list. I begged for a job in any department so as not to be discharged. They placed me in recruitment, and I was there for four years. A tiny cubicle by day and recruiting events in the evenings and weekends."

Alexander's eyes dropped to the ground, a movement that was foreign to the confident man. "I developed a talent for placing people in positions and facilitating a movement of talent that benefited the country. Halfway into my fifth year in that strip mall's recruiting office, I was approached by a recruiter for the Department of Defense. She informed me that they were looking for a recruiter for their research and development department," Alexander said.

"You work for DARPA?" she asked, perplexed by what he had said. "Science and engineering are not something that would have come to mind about you when we were hanging out."

"Hanging out?" he asked with a smirk, his eyes meeting hers once again.

"You know what I meant," she replied, walking down the concrete sidewalk. "I just thought you'd go on to serve in the field, Alex. You spoke of one day flying."

"I had planned on it, but things got kind of turned upside down when you left. I definitely got myself in some trouble, but things are better now."

"Back then, I thought you might call," she said, resentfully.

Interlope: 1 Year, 1 Day Before Launch

"You left," he replied, "without leaving a clue as to where you had gone."

"So, you never looked me up?" she asked, stopping again and turning to him.

His eyes met hers. "On the contrary, Jodi. I've followed your career. I read each report filed after each mission, I've read of all your successes and failures. You've led a decorated career over here. And now, I know that it's coming to an end."

Jodi stared at the rolling hills of sand, taking in all that he had said. She felt her cheeks flush, first from the warm feeling of knowing that throughout the years, he had kept an eye on her and secondly because he had so easily pointed out the biggest fear in her life at the moment.

"You're right, Alex, and thank you."

"It's why I'm here," he said, grabbing her shoulders. "You've shown great courage in the face of extreme danger, and I couldn't be more proud of you."

Her eyes began to water, an embarrassing reaction she thought to a man she had spent less than three months with twelve years ago. She brought her sleeve to her eyes and wiped away the dampness.

Why does his opinion matter so much to you? Your time with him had been so brief in the grand scheme of time, she thought, berating herself.

Yet, there beneath the Afghan sun, his words had pulled hard on her emotions. Pulled them out and beyond the walls that she had constructed. He could pull them out not because of who he was or what was said but because of what she had let him become. She had made him into more than he was over the past twelve years.

There, under the intense heat of the sun, the glare forced his eyes to squint shut with aging wrinkles and the depression of time showing about his face. There, at that moment, she saw him not as the man she had left behind but as the flawed human he truly was. It came over her like a wave, dread at first, followed by annoyance.

He isn't here to scoop you into his arms and profess his love for you, silly girl, the voice inside her mind whispered.

"You're here to recruit me, aren't you?" she asked, looking him squarely in the eye.

His gaze didn't waver. "I am here to recruit you. I'm here on behalf of DARPA, with a request for your service starting tomorrow, following your exit interview here."

Her brow furrowed with confusion. "To be stationed where?" she asked.

"Minot Air Force Base," Alexander replied with hesitation.

"North Dakota? Have you lost your mind?" she managed to blurt out.

He raised his hand in protest but dropped it at his side, sighing. "I know it's not Texas, or Arizona for that matter. What was your plan, after tomorrow, Jodi? Where are you headed after this? Back home to Arizona? There's nothing left for you there, and you know it. You're like me, invested everything you had into your career, and for what? All of your friends, like mine, have either died for the cause or are still a part of it. This special project at Minot could be a wonderful stepping stone to the things you've never even considered."

Jodi turned away from him and stared at the blue, cloudless sky. It was true. Phoenix had little to offer her. She had sold her parents' home when they had passed, and most of her high school friends had moved on or drifted apart.

She turned back to Alexander. "Why me? Why not a doctor or a medical specialist?" she asked.

He loosened his black tie, noticeably hot in his overly dressed attire. "We're looking for someone with experience in chaotic situations —someone who can make split-second decisions in regard to the health and safety of a crew. Someone with a medical background but can keep a calm head in moments of conflict or combat. I'm not going to find that in a doctor. Sure, perhaps an

Interlope: 1 Year, 1 Day Before Launch

emergency room doctor is capable of working in stressful moments and conditions, but they usually aren't under fire or put into dire situations with an unknown or unseen enemy. I've followed your career, Jodi. Time and time again, you've made the right decision." His words felt like a warm blanket on a cold night, clinging to her. She looked him over again.

Alex ran his left hand through his hair. The absence of a wedding ring was noted, but her decision would need to be for the right reasons. After a long pause, she asked, "What does this project entail?'

He gave the boyish grin one more flash and replied, "Fly out to Minot Air Force Base with me tomorrow, and I'll let the experts fill you in."

She kept her gaze on him, still trying to get a read on him. "Can I sleep on it?" she asked, unsure.

"Absolutely, the plane takes off at 0900. If you want to be a part of this, I'll be there with an open seat next to me."

Jodi nodded, her head full of thoughts and questions. She turned back toward the concrete sidewalk that led to the blistering hot asphalt parking lot separating the office buildings from the barracks. They continued their walk in silence, the hot Afghan sun pressing down on them relentlessly.

Chapter 18 - 320 Days Before Launch

"What do you mean there are no manual controls for the craft?" Commander Lawrence Chu asked in disbelief.

He raised his hands in confusion and let his emotions get the best of him. The Commander wiped the perspiration from his sweaty brow with the sleeve of his blue flight suit. Typically, Lawrence was a calm and professional man, but the new program he was involved with in Minot was beginning to test his patience.

What is the point in having a pilot on the crew if I'm not going to be able to fly the craft? the jealous voice inside him asked.

Lawrence had flown everything from F16s to F18s, all with ease. One of his last missions involved an F-35 Lightning II, a stealthy jet that could travel 1,200 miles per hour and had advanced avionics. All of that came to an end, though. After completing many tours for the Navy in his F-16N Viper, he was grounded for unspecified reasons and placed at the China Lake Naval Air Weapons Station in California. He spent two years there overseeing the Naval Air Warfare Center Weapons Division without a complaint.

Two slow years passed until, finally, a younger man in a black suit resembling a CIA or FBI field agent showed up at his office. This gentleman, who was later identified as Mr. White, promised he could get a chance to fly a new research vehicle. A classified project, Lawrence would be the first to train and complete a new mission few had ever dreamed of.

That promise compelled Lawrence to leave China Lake and travel to Minot, North Dakota, and now, standing in this cold war era airplane hangar of a bunker, he was told he was more of a passenger than a pilot. It didn't help that the news came from some nerd in a white lab coat and glasses. Dr. Victor Gray seemed nice enough, but what the hell did he know about flying an aircraft, especially into potentially hostile territory?

"I understand why you are upset, Commander Chu," Dr. Gray said. "You were promised to be in command of this aircraft, and you will be. Alice will obey your commands as long as they are in line with the mission objectives."

"No offense, Dr. Gray, but you're asking us to put our lives in the hands of a computer. Essentially a robot without a body? Technology fails, and man corrects it. Time and time again, I've seen it firsthand," Lawrence stated, unwilling to budge on his opinion.

The large hangar began to feel cramped, the giant robotic arms overhead looming ominously toward him. Lawrence spent his career in small cockpits and never once felt claustrophobic. Now though, with the idea of the controls being stripped away from him, he could feel his shirt collar's fabric tighten around his neck.

Take a deep breath, he thought. *Control yourself. Show composure.*

Lawrence exhaled and nodded. Even if he didn't agree, he would respect the chain of command coming directly from Director Stevens, not this dweeb.

He could feel his red cheeks lighten up as his heartbeat slowed to its natural rhythm.

Lawrence looked about the hangar and at each crew member standing next to him. With her vibrant red hair, Dr. Rose Allen smiled at him as if to reassure him.

He looked to James Harris, who he no doubt had just offended with his rant, and stared straight forward at the craft. Director Stevens had assured Lawrence of the software James had developed for the mission and it was far superior to anything he had observed at China Lake. He just hadn't made his mind up about James yet. He wasn't used to the lazy computer programmer type.

Lawrence's eyes moved to the newest crew member, retired Staff Sergeant Jodi Evans. An experienced soldier like himself, she had served as a combat medic in Afghanistan. He was happy to have a fellow soldier on the team —someone else who was used to following the chain of command.

He turned his eyes back to Dr. Gray and shrugged.

"I agree, Commander Chu, putting your life in the hands of new technology is extremely terrifying, but there are fail-safes built into Alice's programming. She can return the craft at any point, and James will be onboard to alter her software as needed via the PLC," Dr. Gray said quietly.

"That is reassuring, Dr. Gray, but a backup manual control is vital to our safety," Lawrence said, folding his arms at his chest.

Dr. Gray nodded, placed his left hand against his jaw, and rubbed it. "That is a valid point, Commander Chu. However, I'm fairly confident that once the machine reaches its maximum magnetic field during the fall, the potential for the occupants to lose consciousness is high due to the g-forces exerted on the vessel. The likelihood that you'll be able to stay awake and control the craft is very low. That is why Alice will have control. You'll be able to provide all the necessary coordinates. Strap yourselves in, and Alice will control the craft until you've reached the other side."

Lawrence cleared his throat to speak, but Jodi lifted a hand before he could.

"I know I'm new here and not fully briefed, but what exactly is the fall?" Jodi asked.

James, who was usually silent, laughed quietly at first but then louder.

"They didn't explain the worst part of all of this?" James asked once he had caught his breath.

James pointed his finger at Dr. Gray and said, "Evil Knievel here has us doing a kamikaze dive, hurtling toward the Earth. If his math is wrong, we'll be an exploding dirty bomb buried into the Antarctic ice sheet or the bottom of the ocean."

The color disappeared from Jodi's warm, vibrant, and beautiful brown skin. Dr. Gray took two steps toward Jodi. He raised his hands as if defending himself against a physical assault.

"I'm confident in my math and this project. We've had two probes return safely with no damage. What James has coined as a kamikaze dive might not be too far off, but perhaps an educated dive would be more appropriate. Are you familiar with terminal velocity?" Dr. Gray asked, smiling toward the end.

"From what I can recall from high school physics, it's the fastest an object can fall through a medium given its mass," Jodi replied.

Dr. Gray nodded. "The craft will be launched from here and out of the Earth's atmosphere. It'll remain in outer orbit until it's directly over top of the provided coordinates. As James indicated, the drop-in location is north of the Antarctic ice sheet and in the southern end of the Indian Ocean, so that in the event of a catastrophic failure, the amount of collateral damage will be less."

"With the exception of the crew onboard," James interjected.

Dr. Gray nodded again. "Yes, the risk would be losing the crew and a billion-dollar spacecraft. No pressure, right?" Dr. Gray said with a smile. "The craft will begin its descent, a free fall toward the ground. The Earth's gravitational pull will compel the craft to fall faster until it reaches its terminal velocity. At this point, Alice will activate the craft's two rings that you've already been briefed on."

Dr. Gray looked to the newly constructed ship and then back to Jodi. "These rings will begin to generate a stronger magnetic field than the area around the craft. Typically, when an object enters the atmosphere unrestricted, it falls and builds up friction against the particles and molecules in front of and around the object as it tries to push them out of the way. That friction causes heat, and most objects burn up prior to impact. What is not seen in this process is that the particles are being pushed to the side, stretching them away from any entanglement that they may possess. That relationship between those particles forms the matrix of everything. A falling object will either burn up or successfully push aside the matrix of molecules, or cosmic quilt, as I put it earlier, long enough to land safely or with impact. It's typically one of those two options. However, I've discovered a third option. At the moment when the friction becomes too great, the craft's increased magnetic field will reach its maximum yield and distort the space around it, temporarily tearing apart those particles, allowing the craft to pass through an opening and into the other side."

There was a silent pause as Jodi took in the information.

"What keeps us from impacting an object on the other side after we pass through?" Jodi asked quietly.

"That's an important question, Jodi. As long as the craft's increased magnetic field is greater than the surrounding opposing magnetic field, it will repel it. This includes objects as well." "And if it gets turned off?" interjected Lawrence.

"If the craft's increased magnetic field ceases and fails to repel the external forces exerted upon it? The craft and everything inside of it will be annihilated," Dr. Gray said calmly.

James left the group and walked to the sphere that had been with them in the hangar since the start of the project. The silent sentinel shone brightly under the LED lights.

"Jesus, this whole time we have been working in the same building with this ticking time bomb? The camera distortion you showed us earlier was caused by the sphere's own magnetic field, isolating itself from ours?" James asked, with his back to the group.

"That's correct, James. At this moment, the sphere is stable because of its ring functioning properly inside. Once we were able to get an image of the sphere's interior and understand how it operated, we were able to transfer that technology to our first probes and now the craft," Dr. Gray said, motioning to the ship.

James turned back to face the group. "So, we're using alien technology to go knock on their door and ask that they quit shaking our planet? This is nuts. This sphere could kill us all, not to mention take out the entire base. What would have happened if you had cut the damn thing open?"

"We had intelligence information that a similar probe was located about fifty miles off the coast of Lebanon in 2019. It was brought back to the Port of Beirut. The authorities attempted to cut it open in August of 2020," Mr. White said from the back of the group.

The crew members turned at the sound of his voice.

Rose Allen, who had been silent up until that time, asked, "The explosion of Ammonium Nitrate at the Port of Beirut was caused by one of these?" Panic laced her voice.

Mr. White nodded solemnly. "We estimate that the majority of the blast was caused by the interaction of particles and antiparticles, to put it in layman's terms. There was ammonium nitrate stored at the port in an adjacent building, but only a quarter of the amount calculated. Two hundred and eighteen people lost their lives, and it caused over fifteen billion dollars in damage," Mr. White said.

"Why not detonate the sphere out in the ocean somewhere?" Jodi asked.

"We looked into that," Dr. Gray started, "but it's impossible to estimate the potential effects from the detonation. Not to mention the radiation from the ring components. We aren't sure of the exact size of the sphere that exploded in Beirut, but my guess is that it was a smaller probe, probably a quarter of the size of the one you see here."

Interlope: 320 Days Before Launch

If this sphere lets loose, it could jeopardize the stability of our planet." "What's the plan for the sphere long term?" Lawrence asked.

Mr. White turned to Lawrence. "That's why this mission is so crucial. You'll be returning the sphere to its proper side. It will reside in the craft until you reach their planet. There's a cargo hatch beneath the craft where you can safely release the sphere." There was a long pause in the discussion.

"Damn, that's a lot to take in. No pressure, right, guys? Jesus, I need a drink," James said, shoving aside the uneasy silence.

Nervous laughter followed. Putting his hand in the pocket of his jeans, Lawrence pulled his car keys out and gave them a jingle. "A drink would help to process all of this," he said, cracking a grin.

"How about Candy's?" Rose added, half expecting Mr. White to shut it down.

The group turned to the man in the black suit, and much to their surprise, Mr. White nodded.

"Candy's for drinks it is, then."

Chapter 19 - 320 Days Before Launch

The glow from the neon sign cast a pink haze on the hood of the red Mini Cooper. Sitting in the front seat, James gave himself one more look over in the rearview mirror. He had never cared much about his appearance. Most of the circles he had floated in weren't concerned with that as much as they were about their intellect. Some of those feelings had changed inside the once timid man. There was a newfound confidence that this project had brought out in him.

James felt his contribution to the team and project mattered and that he mattered. More important than that was a feeling of acceptance by the team. A team composed of people who would never have paid James any attention elsewhere. Like-minded to the people James had gone to school with, the popular kids who had just walked past him in the hall, oblivious to the wild-haired, pimply kid clinging to the wall nervously. Those kids would notice him now. Perhaps they would even read about his contribution to the project in the years to come. Young computer coders who dreamed of going on to develop software and apps would look up to him once their mission was complete and declassified.

In due time, he thought.

He ran his hands through his messy hair and laughed at himself. *Who do I have to impress?* he pondered.

It wasn't like Candy's Sports Bar provided that much in terms of single women on a Tuesday evening. There was Rose Allen, though. The beautiful, red-haired biologist had left James quite smitten. Her passion for her work and her good looks only made her more attractive.

James opened the door and stepped out of the red Mini Cooper, the warm North Dakota summer air enveloping him as he did. Ruthville, in the evening, once the sun had gone down and the heat dissipated, was quite nice.

He leaned into the car and tossed his black jacket over his computer bag. In contrast to the rougher parts of California, Ruthville had lower crime, and James felt at ease carrying his computer around with him. His computer would be safer with him than at the lab, where it would be accessible to the Director and craft assembly crew.

James closed the door and double-checked that the doors were locked.

He turned to the main entrance, the blinking open sign in the bar window casting light intermittently across his brown loafers. The gravel crunched beneath his weight as he walked to the glass-lined metal exterior door.

James saw himself reflected in the glass, an image he would have usually shied away from, but not anymore. He found new confidence and liked what he saw. *I've come so far,* he thought.

The reflection faded as he approached the door, and the dimly lit bar beyond came into focus. James grabbed the door handle and pulled it. His nose was greeted with the smell of fried food and freshly poured beer. The sound of a '90s country song came from a jukebox near the back, the singer's words muffled by laughter and elevated conversations.

James scanned the bar and found his colleagues in the back.

His friends? No, not quite yet at least, his pessimistic brain reminded him.

It was still months until their launch date, but soon they would be confined to the craft together and unable to leave. At that point, they would become close, or it would become awkward quickly. James knew that well. He had experienced it many times, sharing houses and renting rooms with strangers. Hopefully, that life was behind him now, given the handsome salary he had received. After

Interlope: 320 Days Before Launch

he was back, he could also write a book on their mission. The possibilities were endless, really.

He walked past the oak tables and side booths to the large table in the back. He raised a hand to greet Rose, Jodi, Commander Chu, and Dr. Gray. The seated group gave a wave of hello.

Rose reached beside her and pulled out an empty chair. James could feel his cheeks flush, and he hoped they were not as red as they felt. She smiled and tipped back the glass she had resting near her lips.

Lawrence grabbed an empty glass and poured James a beer from the weathered pitcher.

"We were just talking about you, James," the Commander said, handing him the full glass.

James put the glass to his mouth, the foam bouncing up over his lips, and the remaining bubbles of a nearly flat beer tickled his nose. He took in a long drink. The taste, even for a light beer, was refreshing. It had been a long time since he'd had a drink. The project consumed them, and the crew wasn't given much free time.

"All good things, I hope," James said with an uneasy smile.

"You're always tucked away in that office, typing away," Jodi said. "We don't often have a chance to talk to you."

She was right. While the others worked through the kinks and issues with the craft, James was confined to the office next to Dr. Gray. The cramped office was also somewhat of a confined space. With the mass of instrumentation and communication cables that ran from James's computer station to the craft, he could hardly even see Dr. Gray, let alone strike up a conversation.

"So, James," Rose started as she twirled the beer in her glass. "We're having a bit of a debate. Maybe you could help settle it," she said with a smile, her green eyes sparkling in the chandelier's light hanging over their heads.

"Little green men or not? All seriousness aside, what are they going to look like?" Jodi asked.

"They?" he asked, setting his glass on the oak table.

James tried his best to appear surprised. He had spent many nights wide awake thinking about that very question. Who were these master builders? What did they look like? Surely, they were more advanced than our humanity. The technology behind the sphere suggested that. Here was evidence of a civilization that had advanced far enough to send autonomous probes into the unknown. Their probe had just failed to return home. How many others had there been? What sort of data had they collected of us already?

James gave the question some more thought before replying. "I have to assume that, at the bare minimum, whoever or whatever sent the sphere is, at the least, an intelligent being. At the very least, they are advanced as we are, probably more considering what we've learned in the past few months. As far as little green men? I really don't think that is as important as another question. Are they benevolent? Do they have good intentions? Are they aware of the potential harm that their probes and technology have on us? Would that make the sphere more of a weapon than a probe?" James asked, sitting back in his chair.

He took a deep breath and took another pull of the light beer.

"Well, which do you think it is? A probe or a weapon?" Jodi asked, breaking the silence.

James raised his eyebrows and shrugged. "The fact that the sphere is devoid of any markings or labels is significant, I think. In a world where things are proudly labeled 'Made in the USA' or a simple 'NASA,' it is hard to believe that an alien race wouldn't slap a label on it. That may suggest it is, in fact, a weapon. Or it may suggest, and this is my hope, that they have advanced past things of monetary value, possession, and foolish pride," he replied.

The group fell silent for a moment. Another country song came into focus, along with the local patrons laughing at the old wooden bar. Thankfully, the ringing of a cell phone interrupted the silence.

Interlope: 320 Days Before Launch

The group looked at each other until finally, Dr. Gray, realizing that it was his phone, stood up. Pulling the phone from his brown jacket, he excused himself with a mumble and turned to the door. He exited the bar, the door swinging quietly behind him.

Commander Chu cleared his throat, breaking the silence. "That's very insightful, James. From the DOD and DARPA's perspective, this is very likely a weapon. That's why they are involved, and that's why we are here. We've got to deliver this thing back now that we have gleaned their tech. So, I think that we need to consider them hostile, and having complete control of this mission is of the utmost importance."

"We don't have complete control?" Jodi asked, confused.

"Not over, Alice," Commander Chu explained. "James is aware of what I'm talking about."

The Commander's eyes were fixed upon James.

James nodded, staring down uncomfortably at his half-empty glass.

"Commander Chu would like me to install a fail-safe in our Alice system. As it stands now, we're unable to override her system should we need to go off course. While Director Stevens sees this as protection against human error or in the event we are unable to act, Commander Chu sees it as a potential hindrance," James explained without looking up.

Commander Chu set his glass down on the oak table with a loud *thud*, his action appearing to be on purpose. "In every mission I've ever been on, there have always been problems or issues that required split-second decision-making. The ability to adapt and make the correct adjustments is paramount," the Commander stated.

"And the Director feels that Alice is able to make those adjustments," James said.

"Do you feel she will be able to, James?" Rose asked, breaking up the heated exchange brewing between the two men.

James looked at Rose, seated to his right, and took a deep breath. "It is impossible to prepare her for every scenario," he said, rubbing his face.

"It sounds like you agree with the Commander, James," Jodi said, close to a question but put as a declaration.

"It's a valid point," James said, shifting uncomfortably in his chair. "The trouble is, Director Stevens is always looking over my shoulder, reviewing Alice's software. I don't know when I could write in the coding for a fail-safe and how to prevent Director Stevens from noticing it. I would have to bury it deep, and even then, there might be breadcrumbs. At the very least, Alice would be aware of its existence."

"Just make it happen," the Commander replied coldly.

"I need a stiffer drink," James muttered and stood up.

He walked to the bar and sat on an open stool, the ripped cushion squishing softly beneath him.

The middle-aged bartender, with the name tag 'Denise,' walked over to him.

"Whiskey, neat, please," James said.

The bartender walked away to a shelf behind her and grabbed a bottle. She poured him a glass, set it in front of him, and he thanked her. He grabbed the small glass, brought it to his lips and threw the contents back, burning his throat as it went down. James exhaled the burning fumes slowly, rolling the small glass back and forth on the oiled bar.

He did not like being put in this position. The weight of being between what the Commander was proposing and the strain of the Director's power over him was unbearable. It wasn't the start of his new life he had dreamed it would be, surely an excerpt to his book that would never make its way into it.

This job turned out to be his dream job, by route of a nightmare. Just over a year ago, he came very close to losing the very little he had. He would never tell the crew, the lovely Rose, or

Interlope: 320 Days Before Launch

the world how he had met Director Stevens or Mr. White. They had promised it would be their little secret in exchange for his compliance on a top-secret military project.

James thought back to that evening in California, sitting alone in his room at his computer desk when there was a knock at the door. Ignoring it and letting one of his five roommates answer it, he returned to his computer screen. Lately, his new computer was acting up, temporarily freezing, and displaying intermittent glitches. What was even more odd, was that he was having trouble accessing some of his encrypted accounts.

"Hey James, someone here to see you," Tim, one of the younger roommates, called from behind his bedroom door.

James stretched his arms above his head, aware he had forgotten to put deodorant on that day and stood up. He stepped over the piles of laundry on the floor and paper plates and made his way to the door. He opened it and walked out into the living room. Turning the corner toward the front door, he found Tim leaning against the hallway wall with a dog at his feet.

When did they get a dog? he thought with anger.

The landlord was very strict about them having pets. He wanted to say something but realized the guests were standing just outside the open front door.

James walked closer, nervous at the sight of the two strangers' attire. The woman on the left was dressed in a gray pantsuit, freshly pressed, and not a wrinkle on it. The man on the right appeared to be pulled straight out of an FBI or CIA movie, dressed in a black suit with a narrow black tie. James immediately felt his heart race and was embarrassed by his current state of hygiene.

"James Harris?" the woman asked. Her shoulder-length brown hair moved slightly in the slow breeze.

He nodded. "Yes, I'm James. What's going on?" he asked nervously.

"My name is Director Angela Stevens, and my associate is Agent Alexander White," she said, introducing herself and the man next to her.

"Do you have a moment to speak in private?" the man asked.

James nodded and stepped toward them. The two strangers stepped back and turned toward a black Mercedes parked in front of the home.

They walked toward the car on the battered concrete sidewalk, the overgrown grass of the rental home threatening to take it over.

James closed the door behind him, nearly slamming Tim's nosey head with it.

Sweat rolled down the middle of his back, causing the gray shirt to cling as he approached the pair, his legs feeling weak beneath him. He arrived at the black car and placed his hands in the pockets of his blue sweatpants.

"What's going on?" he managed to squeak out.

"I think you may have an inclination as to why we are here, James," Agent Alexander White stated.

James felt his stomach tie in a knot, and he thanked the Lord that he could hold the small amount of urine in his bladder. Had it been any more, he might have wet himself. He had always felt like the cowardly lion of Oz, looking for the courage hidden around the corner, just beyond the curtain.

"What do you mean?" he asked, his voice trembling.

"We've seized your accounts, James," Director Stevens said.

"My accounts?" James asked, doing his best to play dumb.

"The GoFundMe accounts, James. The U.S. government was alerted to the potential scam, and they have now seized the accounts and are pursuing legal action against you," Mr. White stated calmly.

The urine that had been held back finally refused to be contained, and he felt the warmth start in his loins and continue down his legs, no doubt leaving a visible path. Embarrassed, he placed his hand in front of his crotch. He knew exactly which

Interlope: 320 Days Before Launch

accounts they were referring to. The same accounts that he had suddenly been locked out of.

"Taking advantage of all those people, James. Really a horrible thing to do. Setting up fake GoFundMe accounts to help those affected by the earthquake that devastated Phoenix and assuming the identities of actual citizens is a felony, James. Especially given the dollar amount you have managed to funnel to yourself," Director Stevens said.

It was true. He had posed as people who had lost their homes, businesses, and loved ones. James was not proud of that fact, but he had been thrilled about the four hundred thousand dollars he had funneled into his bank account. That was supposed to be his ticket out of Silicon Valley and his startup money for his next venture, whatever that might be. Now the only venture he saw in his future was behind bars in a federal penitentiary.

"Alright, what now?" James managed to say, holding back the tears.

"We're not here to arrest you, James," said Mr. White. "You'll notice that we didn't come here in a patrol car or with officers. We have a proposition for you."

James felt a small amount of relief wash over him. "What sort of proposition?"

"The charges will be dropped, the money funneled to actual victim relief in exchange for your services and silence on a new upcoming project. We would need you to relocate, though," Director Stevens stated.

"Relocate where?" James asked.

"Minot Air Force Base in North Dakota," Mr. White replied.

James looked back to the rundown home he shared with the five other aspiring computer hackers.

"What kind of project?" he asked, returning his gaze to Stevens and White.

"We've recovered a computer algorithm you're going to want to see," Mr. White explained.

"And I think you understand what will happen if the charges aren't dropped against you, James," Director Stevens added quietly.

James nodded. "I'll take a shower and pack."

The two government employees turned to each other and smiled, which didn't make James's stomach feel any better.

He turned and walked up the uneven sidewalk to the gray rental house.

***

"Where are you at?" Rose asked from behind him, placing a hand on his shoulder, pulling his mind back to the bar, away from the memory of that day and his past transgressions.

James turned to her, thankful for her company and rescue from the nightmare he had briefly slipped into.

"Another life," he replied.

He raised the empty glass in view of the bartender and ordered another shot.

Chapter 20 – 542 Days After Launch

The cold, North Dakota winter air blew against the light gray jacket that Elizabeth Gray had hastily thrown on. She had left the house that morning in a hurry, her typically preoccupied mind on other things.

Mostly my own fault, she thought.

She stood atop the concrete landing just outside the school's main entrance. She looked about the half-empty parking lot, and the large asphalt rectangle was just as quiet as it may as well be in the dark.

Elizabeth had a meeting scheduled with Mrs. Davidson for weeks, and had it not been for the school's automated appointment reminder, she would have slept right through it. She had found it difficult to get out of bed before 10:00 am lately, her schedule having been disrupted since she had taken the second job at Candy's. Between the rotating schedule at the coffee stand and waitressing at Candy's, Elizabeth was running ragged, and she knew it. When she wasn't at work, she was at home catching up, always catching up, and lately, it had gotten the best of her.

She could admit it now. Life was just harder without Victor at home. She hated that fact. Before meeting Victor, she was strong and independent, not relying on anyone but herself. At that time, it was just her. She knew how to care for and rely on herself. Then Victor came into her life, and they built a life together. A life supported by two people, each sharing the load, arms outstretched, helping shield each other from the hardest moments. When there weren't difficulties, there were wonderful, joyous things—things she wanted to share and experience with someone. Now that person had left, there was a hole, a missing piece. Her partner was gone, and she resented him for that. A part of her would never forgive him for being gone.

Elizabeth had her daughter, Allie, to care for, who was now thirteen and a teenager. Sure, she and Allie experienced those happy moments of life, but the dark cloud of Victor's absence seemed to hang over them. Perhaps if they could spend more time together, they could lean on each other.

She and Allie rarely saw each other anymore, as their schedules always conflicted. Thank God Allie was so responsible for her age. Elizabeth was unsure if she could handle taking care of a younger child alone and somehow make ends meet.

Elizabeth had concerns about Allie lately. She had received a call from Allie's guidance counselor, Mrs. Davidson, to schedule an in-person meeting regarding Allie. With Elizabeth's work, it was hard to lock down a time to sit and talk with her. Weeks had passed since the original call, and she now felt guilty.

Some of her forgetfulness and lack of motivation for certain things were a product of her increased drinking. It had started innocently enough, just a drink or two after her shift ended at Candy's. The trouble with it, of course, was that the after-shift habit had followed her home. She reached for the bottle of vodka, almost as if it were a part of her daily routine, a daily requirement for entering her house or starting her day.

Elizabeth knew she had a problem, but being in that house was so damn hard. The pictures hanging on the wall were a constant reminder, each pulling at her.

She had read online that it helped family members missing a part of the nuclear family to talk about their feelings. Elizabeth tried many times to talk with Allie about Victor, but Allie was unwilling to talk.

Elizabeth knew not to push Allie too far, but her daughter needed to talk to someone. If she could afford it, a psychologist was probably what they both needed, but unfortunately, that wasn't an option. Many evenings were spent with Allie storming out of the house, leaving Elizabeth wondering what she could have said differently. It seemed to Elizabeth that Allie would prefer to believe that things were normal and that this was how their life had always been, believing that Victor had never existed. It was as if Allie had woken up the day after her father left and decided that would be the start of her life, the beginning of her memories, devoid of any associated pain.

A door latch clicking behind her stirred her from her thoughts. She turned and faced the locked school door as it opened.

A young woman with brown hair greeted her with a smile. "Hello, Mrs. Gray," the young woman said. "Mrs. Davidson is expecting you, and I can take you to her office."

"Thank you," Elizabeth replied, entering the well-lit hallway.

Familiar smells of her own high school experience filled her nose. She could tell breakfast had been cleaned up by the lingering smell of reheated eggs mixed with Dawn dish soap.

Elizabeth followed the young woman, dressed casually in jeans and a cardigan, as they passed the lockers that lined each side of the empty hallway. The students in the class would soon be elbow to elbow navigating their way to their next class.

She felt sadness from the nostalgia and wondered if, given a chance, she would do things differently. If she could come back here to middle school, knowing what she knew now, would she change her life choices?

Probably not, she thought.

She had thought about it often and always came to the same conclusion. In her eyes, all the wonderful memories were worth missing Victor now. It was the struggle of learning how to live without him that would cause her the most discomfort. What had happened was a reminder she was faced with each morning, and now Elizabeth had to come to terms with it. She only hoped that Victor, wherever he was, knew how deeply he was missed.

They proceeded down the hallway, past the last of the classroom doors, the scores of children sitting quietly at their desks. They stopped in front of a brown door on the right-hand side of the hallway, and the young woman knocked.

An older woman with brown curly hair opened the door.

"Hello, Mrs. Davidson," Elizabeth said with a smile.

"Mrs. Gray, thank you so much for coming today," Mrs. Davidson replied. "Please come in." Mrs. Davidson gestured to a chair in front of her desk.

The younger woman smiled and turned, returning to the long hallway.

Elizabeth walked into the small office and sat in the padded brown chair in front of Mrs. Davidson's desk. Mrs. Davidson left the door slightly cracked open, walked around Elizabeth, and sat opposite her in a black, high-backed office chair.

"Mrs. Gray, thank you again for coming in to speak with me. As I'm sure you have guessed, our meeting today is regarding Allie." Mrs. Davidson paused, seemingly trying to find a way to phrase her next words. "I'm concerned about her, frankly."

A knot grew in Elizabeth's stomach. "Concerned?" she started. "What do you mean, Mrs. Davidson?"

"What I mean, Mrs. Gray, is that Allie hasn't been coming to school. She shows up randomly, and if it weren't for her bus driver, occasionally spotting her walking by the side of the road, we would have assumed you moved."

Elizabeth sat back in her chair, the padding not as comforting as when she had first sat down. She tried to process what she had just heard. *Allie isn't going to school each morning?*

How can that be? Elizabeth asked herself, shaking her head.

"I just don't understand. How could this be happening, and I wasn't informed?" Elizabeth demanded.

Mrs. Davidson folded her hands on her desk. "That," the guidance counselor said with a pause, "is something that we need to apologize for. It appears that the automatic calls for Allie's absences were being sent to Mr. Gray's phone. It was the primary contact phone number on her account. Since the number is still active, the automatic caller left messages until the inbox was full. At that point, it generated a red flag to the account, which caught our attention."

Elizabeth's heart sank. She hadn't made the time yet to suspend Victor's phone line. Initially, she had given the phone to Allie to use since she spent so much time by herself. It proved to be a vital tool when Elizabeth started her second job. Allie could text her grocery items they needed, and Elizabeth typically picked them up on her way home from the coffee stand. It proved necessary, so she kept the phone line active. Now in the hands of Allie, she was able to screen those missed calls and hide them from Elizabeth.

"I see," Elizabeth said quietly. "I'll make sure to update the number on her account." She looked away, trying to hide the tears that had started to develop in her eyes.

"I know that this time is extremely hard for you two, Mrs. Gray. The school is trying to be as understanding as possible. We're a small school in a small district. We're open to looking past the absences, but frankly, I'm concerned about Allie's health, her mental health primarily," Mrs. Davidson said. Compassion, whether real or fake, was in her voice.

"Is this regarding the incident on the bus last year?" Elizabeth asked. "Because I thought we had worked past that."

"That and similar encounters," Mrs. Davidson replied.

"And it's the same group of girls picking on her? I don't see how Allie is to blame if it's the same group over and over," Elizabeth said, feeling her face redden as she defended her daughter.

It had been the year prior, just weeks after their life was turned upside down. Elizabeth and Allie were still adjusting to the change in their lives. Allie's usual school bus was traveling north on the interstate's parallel twin, Frontage Road, returning to the school after a girls' basketball game with a neighboring school. As the bus passed a large granite outcropping on the west side of the road, some of the girls spotted Allie on the peak, her arms outstretched like a bird would have, allowing the wind to pass beneath her wings, keeping her in imaginary flight.

The girls laughed at the time, but by the following morning, they questioned Allie about it while on the bus to school. They poked and pried at Allie until she was on the verge of tears. When Allie finally responded, she said she was trying to talk to her father. At the sound of this, two girls laughed loudly. Pushed further past anything a young child should have to endure, Allie snapped and attacked them both. By the time the bus driver could pull the bus over, Allie had bruised and bloodied both girls.

Mrs. Davis, the bus driver, tried to detain Allie, but during the chaos, Allie managed to escape through the emergency back exit and fled through the wheat fields.

Luckily, after a long sit-down meeting with the school and the parents of the two girls, no charges were filed.

While Allie was lucky that she wasn't in more trouble with the law, she was still under the harsh judgment of her peers. Girls from the original group often spread their arms like wings when they passed her in the school hallway. Some students who had heard or witnessed the altercation called her Allie Bird. Kids were insanely cruel at this age, and Elizabeth was sure some of those kids deserved the ass-beating Allie had delivered. However, Allie was never raised to be violent. She had simply snapped. No wonder Allie didn't want to be at school.

"I'd like to speak with her more often if you could encourage that," Mrs. Davidson said, pulling Elizabeth from her thoughts.

"I'll do that, Mrs. Davidson. In the meantime, I've got to find my daughter," Elizabeth replied.

She stood and thanked the guidance counselor for her time and concern and left Mrs. Davidson's office.

Interlope: 542 Days After Launch

The school bell rang, signaling the end of a period, and the halls were flooded with kids pushing their way to their lockers, bathrooms, and next classes.

Elizabeth merged her way in as a car might in heavy traffic. She followed the flow of students as it meandered its way toward the exit door. The children became less and less in the synchronized formation as they passed open classroom doors. One by one, they left the hallway until Elizabeth was alone again.

She reached the metal doors and gave the old door a push, knowing where Allie might be.

Chapter 21 - 14 Days Before Launch

Rose Allen stepped out of the airplane hangar and let the old metal door close behind her. The late sun's heat still reflected off the metal building. She took in a deep breath of the July air that felt hot and stale, not a breeze for miles. The sun was setting, and the humidity forced her yellow cotton T-shirt against her back and breasts. She welcomed the sticky, muggy air, though. It was at least real and felt better than the artificial air they had been breathing in the confines beneath her feet.

They had been stuck in the craft for weeks, going through Director Steven's mock mission drills, allowing the crew to become familiar with each other and run Alice through scenarios to refine her programming. Everything was going as planned, and things were on course. The crew had come together perfectly, each member performing their tasks as expected. They hadn't been off the craft or seen another human other than each other throughout that time. Except for a very short visit by Director Stevens and Dr. Gray, they had been completely isolated.

It felt so good to be out in the open air again. Rose was breaking protocol, but who cared? It wasn't as though the government had time to train new crew members at this point in the project. The project had its timeline, and that was something that couldn't be altered. The sensitive materials inside the craft had to be utilized quickly, of which she was certain.

The silver alloy used in conducting and protecting the ship's interior would begin to oxidize and tarnish soon, partially losing its ability to allow electricity to flow freely through it.

The crew was trained and ready, so Rose doubted the Director would fire any of them for leaving the craft. Besides, if one of them leaked the details to the public, the world would go absolutely nuts.

Regardless of whether there is a disclosure agreement or not, someone could cash in on a book deal.

Rose walked out from the edge of the hangar's roof and toward the runway. There, in front of her, sat the newly erected launch pad looking obsolete against the North Dakota twilight backdrop. The first stars of the evening were beginning to show as the sun finally slipped behind the horizon. She could barely make out the constellations that used to hang over her tiny existence and make her feel so small. She had grown past that feeling and now understood her importance in it all. The importance of balance and harmony. If she could not see the magnitude she brought forth as a living organism aboard this whirling mass of collected rock and gases, surely, she could at least see the importance that she brought to the lives around her and her team.

The idea of studying another organism from another planet thrilled Rose. She would be at the forefront of their biological discoveries. Yes, they had their main objective of returning the sphere to the other side, but they were bound to come across new microbes, organisms, and, finally, life forms. Life forms they never knew existed, let alone were capable of interstellar travel and the obvious technological advances.

In Rose's previous life, just the discovery of an unknown microbe at the bottom of a frozen lake in Antarctica brought forth a frenzy the likes of which she'd never seen. A microbe, so small and innocent, not doing anything but merely existing, had provided the discovering scientist with enough recognition and funding for a lifetime. What lay just on the other side for her?

One biological breakthrough could make or break her career and her subsequent life. It had never been clearer. The judgment that had followed her from the Victoria University of Wellington could be snuffed out like a candle with one miraculous discovery. What scared her the most, however, wasn't the fear of a peer review but rather the fear of the judgment of the survivors of her now-directed

Interlope: 14 Days Before Launch

outcome. She and her team would forever be melded together by the events that would soon unfold.

The team members were held together by what they shared and lacked. It was remarkable and probably planned that the four-person crew had no connection or ties to anything at home that would prevent them from leaving the project. James, Jodi, Commander Chu, and herself all lacked loved ones to be left behind.

Rose always avoided the topic of having children for fear of having to look after another soul other than her own. She'd never felt the urge to be an accomplice to the overpopulation of the Earth, yet that decision was only accepted when it was her own.

As she stood on that runway and the night had already begun to steal the sun's light, she was fully aware that she would be looking after the children and those who had yet to come. With the team's potential sacrifice, they protected all that humanity had to offer and all they had to reject. Rose had come to terms with that cold, hard fact. It was likely she would never have the opportunity to be a mother, at least not in the physical sense. Her womb yearned for a child and wept for the one that would never be there.

In her likely demise, much more life would spring forth, not through her, but because of her. Rose knew it was unlikely that much of her existence would come to fruition, but she was ok with that.

She walked closer to the empty launch pad and sat on the first step of the metal stairs that would eventually lead up to the craft. She gazed at the stars twinkling above her and exhaled with a loud, nervous sigh.

"Are you nervous, Rose?" a voice asked from behind her, pulling her from her conflicting thoughts.

She turned and looked up to find Dr. Gray standing on the small platform at the top of the stairs. Rose smiled at him shyly, surprised by his presence. Strangely, she hadn't heard or noticed him as she made her way to the launch area.

Dr. Gray seemed nice enough, but he and Mr. White were always sneaking about, popping out of the shadows unannounced.

"A little," she replied truthfully.

It probably showed on her face that she was quite nervous.

Rose gripped the aluminum handrail and stood, facing the doctor. "Are you sure about all of this, Victor?" she asked him hesitantly.

"As sure as we can be, Rose," he replied, maintaining eye contact with her.

Tonight, he was dressed casually, his usual lab coat replaced by a brown coat and blue jeans. The outfit change left him looking younger and more human. The typical lab coat and serious demeanor seemed to add ten years to him in his office.

There, under the stars, Dr. Gray looked quite attractive, and if it weren't for being married, Rose would have been very interested in him. His intelligence and passion for his work were among his most attractive traits, followed by his eyes. At times, when he thought no one was looking, Rose could see the facade fading from his face, and the sadness beneath crept through. He was quick to cover it; a favoring grin would reappear to greet someone. In those rare moments, however, Rose thought she spied signs of loss and grief in his eyes, hidden from the world.

He doesn't need to hide it, she thought. *Let it out. Show the world you have been through something life-changing and survived.*

"How do you know the ship won't be torn apart trying to reach the other side?" she asked finally, aware of the awkward silence that had sat between them.

"Are you familiar with a Prince Rupert's drop?" Dr. Gray asked.

"I think so," she replied. "Those molten drops of glass that are dripped into cold water?"

Dr. Gray nodded. "That's correct. We've borrowed some of their structure for the front of the craft. While the front lip of the ship appears perfectly round, it actually isn't. The craft's outer lip's metal alloy, composed of nitinol and aluminum, was put through several thermal quenching processes. In doing this, we've taken advantage of the same large compressive residual stresses that are seen in those glass drops but incorporated them into a harder shell. The nitinol alloy allows the outer shell to flex and bend but still be able to return to its designed shape. So, it is similar to the Prince Rupert's drop. However, we definitely didn't want the fragile design of the tadpole with a tail that is usually seen in a Prince Rupert's drop."

Rose looked at him and smiled. "I should have just believed you when you said you were sure of it."

Dr. Gray smiled back and then laughed. It was a carefree laugh, genuine, and for a few minutes, there was a moment that they shared right underneath that North Dakota sky.

They stood silently, almost waiting for the other person to say something. A part of her wanted to stay right there with him. Something was comforting and familiar about it all.

Maybe in another life, she thought, *there could have been something between Victor and me.*

The man in front of her was happily married, and she had been down that road before and lost—lost so much already.

"Victor," she called him again by his first name. "I was wondering—"

The sound of the hangar door slamming to a close interrupted her. Laughter followed, and both turned to see James walking toward them. His usual mop of brown curly hair bounced with each step he took. His unbuttoned flannel opened, exposing his sweat-stained white t-shirt underneath.

Rose laughed to herself at the sight of the funny, slightly overweight, jolly fellow she had found a friend in as he made his way to them. James resembled more of a young Santa than an astronaut who would be attempting to relocate a doomsday device on another planet in a few short days.

What have I gotten myself into? Oh well, it is better than freezing my ass off in Antarctica, she thought.

James appeared to be ending a conversation as he neared them, his phone up to his left ear.

"Love you too," he said into the phone and put it in the pocket of his flannel shirt.

Rose raised an eyebrow of interest at the sentence.

James laughed as if understanding the gesture and said, "That was my mom. She said hello."

Rose laughed, having never met the woman.

"Shall we, me lady?" James asked, bending his arm outward at the elbow toward her.

She slid her arm through his and gave a nod.

The two walked away from the launch pad toward the employee parking lot. She turned her head back to Victor one last time. "Join us for a drink at Candy's, Victor?" she asked.

He gave his typical smile, which started with his eyes, the young but weathered wrinkles there folding into themselves as they had done so many times before. "I'll have to take a rain check this time, Rose, family time tonight. Make sure Director Stevens doesn't catch you out this time," Dr. Gray replied.

Rose and James gave an identical eye roll, like two teenagers being lectured on curfew.

She gave a quick wave, and then left the launch pad arm in arm down the old runway with James, their footsteps on the aging concrete seemed to be the only sound for hundreds of miles.

Rose tightened her grip on James's arm and said, "Are we really going to do this?"

James looked at her with surprise. "Hell yeah, we're doing this. I need a drink."

Rose shook her head. "You know what I mean. Are we going through with this mission?"

They approached the parking lot, and James's red Mini-Cooper was parked amongst the crew's and on-duty personnel's vehicles.

They separated, and James unlocked the doors, then stopped and rested his arm on the small red car roof.

"In some ways, it needs to be done. The fear of the unknown is what drives us, but it's also what gives us pause. The government has thrown too much money at this project to walk away now. Besides, every time one of these alien probes shows up, it almost rips the Earth apart because of some unknown mechanism that causes horrible earthquakes. Most of them have been in remote areas, but not all."

Rose was aware of that and stifled the fearful tears that threatened to well up. She nodded, and James continued.

"It's only a matter of time before the next big Phoenix-style quake hits a highly populated city again. Then what? We were standing here with our hands in our pockets because we were too afraid to act, too afraid to do the right thing. I've spent most of my life afraid. Afraid of failure, afraid of what others think, afraid of my own feelings. Well, not anymore. I'm riding that big, rotating, magnetic piece of shit out of here and into the unknown." He grinned, opened the car door, and said, "You coming?"

"What do you think?" she asked, responding with a similar grin.

She climbed into the tiny red car, James closing the door behind her. As James got into the driver's seat, she turned to look at the launch pad. Dr. Gray was still there where she had left him. Rose watched him as he stared up to the heavens. She would have given anything to have stayed right there. Hit the pause button and get to know Victor. Why had she chosen to have a crush on a married man again?

Rose knew firsthand that it was wrong, but perhaps she was clinging to some sense of security in a frightening experience. She envied James's confidence to show no fear in the face of their dangerous mission.

James started the Mini-Cooper and turned out of the parking lot.

Dr. Gray turned and gave them a small wave of goodbye.

Rose placed her hand on the glass and waved. The smile that spread on his face caused an unjustified pain in her heart. She turned her eyes back to the asphalt road as she and James made their way to the exit gate.

Chapter 22 - 14 Days Before Launch

The overhead parking lot light loudly buzzed as it lit the half-full parking spaces below. While serving an important security and safety function, the light drove Alexander White crazy. Thirty feet from his two-bedroom Pebblestone apartment unit, it shone brightly through the most expensive curtains the local supply store had to offer.

At night, the buzzing felt as if it were vibrating the fillings in his teeth. His sleep had suffered so badly when he relocated there that he had found himself sleeping on the cheap sofa in the living room night after night. The gray three-person couch wouldn't have been his first choice, but it had come with the apartment. Seven hundred and ninety-five a month and mostly furnished, it had seemed like a pretty good deal at the time. Toss in that it was just a sixteen-minute commute to Minot Air Force Base and it was an even better deal.

Alex walked to the living room window and peeled open the blinds. Directly from his window on the second floor, past the buzzing light, was Interstate 83, busy with travelers. Their headlights illuminated the thoroughfare, resembling a herd of fireflies marching in the darkness.

To the north lay an electrical supply store, closed for the evening. Alex had driven by during the day and had admired their interior light displays. Since childhood, lights had always mesmerized Alexander. Something nostalgic about them reminded him of the days of tagging along with his father to the local hardware store. In those days in his youth, he often separated from his father and ended up in the lighting aisle, fascinated by the fixtures. His father would arrive in the illuminated section in a panic, followed by relief at the sight of his young son. The store across the way reminded Alex of home.

To the northeast was an oil field supplier, looking vacant and partially closed. The remnant of a dying boom town, it still clung to what was left of the local industry. Alex was surprised to see this particular store still operational. Most of the boom cities in this area had finally collapsed inward thanks to their environmental impacts and technological advances in alternative energy.

Alex glanced to the parking lot below, just in time to see the small black sedan pulling into an open parking spot. He looked at the clock and back down to the sedan. 10:30 pm, the small silver hands against the matte black face indicated.

He peered back down, and his heart raced. He felt like an excited high schooler again, waiting for his date.

Alex watched as she opened the door and stepped out, his anticipation heightened watching her approach the building as he had almost thirteen years ago. Sure, time had passed, but Alex had never really moved on. There had been women over the years, but none held a candle to Jodi. Nothing compared to the woman who had left so suddenly or the regret he felt every day since he pushed her away.

It had scared him how fast he had fallen for her, and instead of telling her that, he hid from his feelings. Now the woman he had spent so many nights fantasizing about would be walking through his front door. He finally had her back in his life, albeit only for a short while. How ironic it was that he had laid in his bed, feeling worlds apart from her, and now that she was there, he was sending her off to be worlds apart. Granted, he wasn't sending her off personally, the United States Government was, but he had hand-selected her for the position. Once again, he was full of regret. The crew would disembark and leave the Earth's atmosphere in just a few short days.

In some ways, he had been selfish in bringing her on board. Looking back, it could be argued that it was for his betterment. There was nothing that could be done about that now, though, he supposed.

Even if I asked her to quit, stay with me, and we could run away together, would she? No, probably not, he thought as he played out the scenario.

Jodi was one of the most driven persons Alex had ever met. Always focused on her career and moving forward, it had taken months to persuade her to visit him outside of work. Director Stevens had made that difficult as of late, however. Demanding that the crew be confined to the ship to test their mental abilities and ensure the team was truly cohesive. Alex felt it was unnecessary and only stood to create problems amongst the crew. They would soon be forced to be cohesive with nowhere to go. He had pleaded with his superiors against the plan, but in the end, they had sided with Director Stevens.

The knock at the door pulled him from his thoughts. Jodi was there. His heart raced as the thought of her swept over his body. The smell of perfume mixed with sweat filled his nose as he remembered the evening they had spent together two nights prior and the feeling of her soft skin against his. At that moment, separated from everything in this forsaken place, he was happy. For one night, they had forgotten about everything, the sphere, the mission, the earthquakes, and had just lived. Lived for the moment and the experience of each other.

Alex stepped away from the window and rushed to the front door. He nearly tripped over the cheap department store coffee table in the living room. He reached a nervous hand to unlock the door, giving it a turn. Then he twisted the brass doorknob, opening the door wide, the warm summer air rushing in.

"Jodi, it's so good to see..." his voice trailed off.

Looking forward, almost straight through her, Alex found that Jodi was not on the other side of the door. Humiliation settled in, and he felt his cheeks become hot and inflamed.

Before him stood Director Stevens, her face serious as usual. She raised an eyebrow, followed by a look that could only be described as pure judgment and not the good type.

"Sorry to disappoint you, Mr. White. I trust that I'm not interrupting anything?" Her words rang like a question but came out as more of a statement.

He leaned against the open door, trying to appear casual. "Not at all. What's going on, Director? A little late for house calls, isn't it?"

"We've got missing crew members, Mr. White, that I would like to account for," she said plainly.

He was a salaried employee, a choice that he regretted almost daily, and he had already found himself working more and more after hours. "Can't it wait until morning?" Alex asked, trying his best to hide his annoyance.

"I'm afraid not. It's coming from above that the crew needs to be back aboard the craft," Director Stevens replied.

"Above? You called my boss?" he asked, this time not caring if she saw his annoyance.

"I felt it necessary, given the fact that our deadline is approaching," she replied coldly.

Judging by the Director's attire, he needed to change out of his shorts and T-shirt and put something more professional on.

"Give me five minutes, and I'll be down," he replied.

"I'll be down in the car, Mr. White."

He nodded and closed the door, catching a glimpse of the Director's face as he shut it. There was disdain in the look she had given him, an unimpressed version of an eye roll, he supposed.

Why couldn't she have just called? he thought.

Alex knew she was from an older generation that handled things differently, but a simple text would have sufficed.

He walked through the small apartment and into his bedroom. Opening the closed door, he found the suit he planned to wear the next day and slipped it on.

Three minutes later, he left the apartment, turned, and locked the door.

"Alex?" a voice asked from behind him.

He turned to find Jodi standing in the long, narrow, second-story hallway.

"Jodi, I'm so sorry about that. I didn't know she was coming," he said instantly, feeling defensive.

"That was close. She could have caught us," Jodi said, the sound of nerves in her voice.

He took a step forward and placed his hands on her shoulders. "At this point, I really don't care what she thinks. James and Rose have been sneaking off to Candy's a couple of nights a week, and everyone has been looking the other way. What about us? Don't we deserve to do something that makes us happy as well? It's not like we're running off together, right? I just want to make the most of the time we have left together before, well, before you leave."

His hands slid off her shoulders and came to a rest on her sides. Jodi stared at the floor, doing her best to hide her eyes, which had begun to water.

"You could have picked any medical doctor, combat medic, or nurse you wanted." The pause between occupations only proved to show Jodi's struggle with his choice. "But you chose me. You brought me out here," she said, her eyes returning to him.

Taking a step back, he replied, "You had a choice, Jodi. I gave you the opportunity to be a part of this, something grand and new."

Anger flashed in Jodi's eyes, and Alex knew he had overstepped.

Jodi turned and started down the stairs of the three-story apartment building. Alex turned and followed her.

"Jodi, wait, please."

He placed his hand on the handrail and quickened his pace after her.

"Jodi, please," Alex pleaded, but Jodi continued down the stairs.

He reached the concrete landing and stepped out onto the asphalt parking lot. Alexander lightly jogged toward her as she reached her black sedan.

Jodi grabbed the door handle to open the door but stopped.

"Jodi, wait," Alex said as he reached her.

Jodi didn't reply but instead stared to the northwest, past the interstate. Without turning, she said, "What the hell is that?" as she pointed to the night sky.

Alex raised his hands behind his head to catch his breath and looked in the direction that her small, delicate hand pointed. High above what appeared to be a tree line, green auroras danced across the sky. Lights ranged from white to blue and intermingled with the green creating an eerie yet beautiful display.

"Are those the Northern Lights?" asked Alex.

"I'm not sure," Jodi replied.

Both stood in silence for what seemed like an eternity, watching the lights as they frolicked back and forth until they appeared to consolidate into one larger light.

Alex took a step closer to Jodi and rested his hands on the black roof of her car. "Jodi, I...." he started to say, but the sky erupted in a bright white flash before he could finish.

They shielded their eyes as a flash likely to what Alex presumed Hiroshima must have looked like illuminated the landscape for hundreds of square miles. Alex and Jodi hid their faces from the intense light.

A loud rumbling brought their heads down, ears covered. A sound similar to a thunderclap shook the car, and both dropped to their knees. Before either could speak, the shock wave was upon them. Broken glass showered down like a hot August hailstorm as the percussion blew out the windows of Jodi's black sedan. A high pitch scream rose from the thunder, and for a moment, Alex could not place where the terrified scream was coming from.

It was only when Jodi placed her hand on his arm that he realized the scream was his own, in a childlike shriek, he had not known he was capable of. Embarrassed, he began to speak, but the ground shook as he started to form the words. The black sedan next to them that had once been a shield danced on the pavement, at first only a slight rocking followed by a violent shiver.

Alex walked to the right side of the sedan, his fingertips tracing the outline of the edge of the trunk. He looked to the north, where the electrical store stood and where he had once gazed with nostalgia. The building shook and trembled until it finally seemed to partially collapse upon itself in the middle.

Just past it and approaching where they stood, the asphalt parking lot seemed to heave the way the grass might when a mole burrowed a tunnel just below the sod line. The asphalt expanded upward and almost seemed to groan as a tear developed and then split open, producing a trench running the same path as the sound wave. The growing rip continued south and reached his apartment building.

The Pebblestone apartment building shook, the ground its foundation sat on refusing to hold together. A moan and creak came from the third story, the walls shaking as if they were made of Jell-O.

Alex and Jodi backed away from the building, not knowing which direction would be the safest.

Alex heard screams of panic, fear, and utter confusion from inside the apartment building. The tremor shook the structure one last time, and the complex gave way. The third story collapsed upon the second, crushing Alex's apartment and the same stairwell they had been standing in.

He covered his mouth, and Jodi screamed as the second story collapsed in the middle, and the apartment complex seemed to give one last final shrug of defeat, folding in on itself, crushing what was left of the ground level.

The dust gathered in the air, and the screams that had been prevalent seconds before were no more.

Alex turned to run toward the apartment building, but Jodi grabbed his arm, stopping him. He turned back to her, pale as a ghost, and saw the tears in her eyes.

"Don't, Alex, it's not safe," she managed to get out.

He knew she was right.

Alex wanted to say something, but a loud metallic clang rang through the parking lot. He turned to see the buzzing light's pole swaying like a tetherball pole loose on its mount. An unknown force swung the light that had haunted Alex for so many nights back and forth like a pendulum.

The pole rocked above them, casting odd shadows as it swayed. Finally, the movement proved too much, and the hinges, which were never meant to handle an earthquake of this magnitude, split and let go of their hold. The buzzing light grew dim as the wires were ripped from their ballast. With one final pendulum swing, the light, housing, and pole were catapulted and sent toward them. It soared through the air in slow motion, and before they knew it, it was upon them.

Alex would have never been described as quick or heroic, but at that moment, it felt as if someone or something had taken over him. Without even thinking about it, he had closed the distance between Jodi and himself. With speed he didn't know his body had, he collided with her and threw his arms around her, tackling her and pushing her out of the way of the falling light pole and into the grass area along the parking lot.

The light pole came crashing down onto the spot they had been standing on, narrowly missing them and Jodi's car.

Interlope: 14 Days Before Launch

They came to a rest in the grass, rolling through the soft green blades. Alex did his best not to crush Jodi with his body, but it was unavoidable. His weight came down on top of her, and he tried to roll away as he did. Both rolled and finally stopped with Jodi on top of him. They were breathing hard and staring at each other in disbelief.

Emergency sirens came into focus somewhere out on the interstate, getting closer. They stared into each other's eyes, and for a moment, the world and all of the night's disasters disappeared. Jodi leaned in, and Alex brought his mouth to hers. Her soft lips pressed against his, and he cupped her face in a soft embrace. The kiss had been on his mind since seeing her in the parking lot earlier at night, and it was short-lived.

The shrieking tires coming to a skidded stop just ten feet from them pulled them out of their lover's embrace. Jodi pulled her knees into her chest and stood up. Alex, not as graceful, rolled onto his chest and got up slowly. His eyes fell on the silver BMW, not surprised to see it.

The driver's side window came down, and Director Stevens called out, "Get in lovebirds. Unfortunately, we've got a deceased crew member to identify."

Chapter 23 – The Other Side: 409 Days After Launch

The darkness covered him like a warm blanket. The shadows, freed from their light imprisonment, clung to his arms. The overwhelming weight of it was almost too much to bear. Victor fought against the restrictive, unseen force, reached his hands outward into the abyss, feeling nothing at first, and stepped forward.

He reached out again, pawing frantically to have something physical meet his hands, something real, something grounded. His eyes began to adjust slowly but gave little to what he could see.

Victor called out into the darkness for help.

There was no reply.

His voice had felt as empty as the area that now contained him.

Victor took another step forward and nearly tripped on something on the floor. He dropped to his knees and let his fingers dance along the surface. Wood, he felt hardwood flooring. He crawled forward on the ground, his hands sweeping outward in large circles, colliding with something again finally. He ran his fingers against the smooth, grained surface.

He placed his hands around the shaft-like wooden object and slid them down it. Prickly bristles greeted his fingers, and he nearly jumped at the sensation.

A broom, he thought, *I'm holding a broom.*

He grabbed the broom by the end of the handle and placed it outstretched in front of him. Reaching out with the broom, he swung widely, desperately. To his left, the broom handle struck an object loudly, and he heard a loud cracking, and small fragments raining down on the wooden floor filled the air. He moved the handle slowly across the remaining objects carefully.

A smell filled the darkness, familiar to Victor. Scents of cinnamon and apple tickled his nose through interruptions of musty and old. Was he back in his pantry at home? How could that be?

"Hello?" he called out into the darkness that enveloped him and stood up.

Silence was the only reply given.

Victor inched his way across the floor and cried out in pain. He lifted his left foot and ran his hand across it, finding the intruder in his skin. Burning pain engulfed his feet when he realized his boots had given way to bare feet. Carefully, he extracted the small object and determined it to be glass.

He gingerly made his way across the broken glass to where the glass jar had been stored.

Where the hell did my boots go? he thought.

Standing on one foot, he raised his right foot and cupped it in his hand. Warm blood greeted his palm, sticky and wet. The fluid filled his hand, ran through his fingers, and dripped down on the hardwood floor. He gently felt for the pieces of glass and pulled them out as best he could.

Victor lowered his right foot, praying that there would be no more glass beneath it.

Tears had started to accumulate in the corners of his eyes. He had never been much of a crier, but damn it, the glass hurt, and the overwhelming frustration was suffocating.

He wiped the blood on his legs. What should have felt like his long underwear from the ship instead resembled stiff blue jean cotton.

What the hell is going on? he thought.

"Hello? Elizabeth? Allie? Alice? Can anyone hear me?" he called out, his voice trailing.

Victor waited, his panicked breathing the only sound in his ears. He strained to block out the annoying sound of his body consuming the air around him and finally heard something else.

A sound in the darkness.

A whimper, just a few feet ahead of him.

He took another painful, glass-filled step toward the sound. He did his best to keep quiet, focusing on the whimper ahead. Step after bloody step, he moved forward.

"Is anyone there?" he called again.

The sounds of a child sobbing rang clear, and Victor's heart raced.

"Allie?" Victor called out and lunged forward, expecting to wrap his arms around his sweet daughter.

His lunge was stopped short by a collision with something hard, something solid. Victor traced the outline of the object in the dark with his hands.

A door! The pantry door. I'm home, and in our pantry, he thought.

He reached to his right on the door and found the handle from memory. He turned it and gave the door a push.

Nothing, the door refused to open.

Victor turned the handle again and rammed the door with his shoulder. Searing pain shot from his shoulder down to his fingertips, but the door refused to budge.

He pressed his face against the door. "Allie?" he yelled, his voice cracking.

"Daddy? Daddy, I'm scared," Allie replied, immediately crying again.

"Allie, listen, honey, it's going to be ok. Can you find Mommy?" Victor asked as calmly as he could.

The sobbing intensified. "I can't find her. Daddy, I'm so scared.

Daddy, please open the door."

Victor lunged at the door again, but to no avail. He kicked it repeatedly. He took a few steps back and ran at the door, colliding with it with all his might.

He slumped against the door, defeated and out of breath.

Victor called out to Allie again.

"Allie, can you find one of our cell phones?"

"I'll try, Daddy."

The sound of the sobbing ceased, and Victor heard the shuffling of her small feet across the floor. He thought of the sound that those little feet had made when she was younger, excited and running from room to room without a care.

He smiled at that thought, and the nostalgic tears welled in him.

Victor grabbed the door and stopped. He heard wood cracking somewhere in the living room beyond the pantry door. A scream filled the air, and he tightened his hold on the door handle. For all that he had tried to push the door outward, in an instant, it was exploding toward him. Like a missile from an unknown source, the door exploded into him, lifting him off his feet.

He remained conscious as he flew backward, time seeming to stand still. He looked back to where the door had been, and for a millisecond, he thought he saw Allie standing in the doorway.

Victor collided harder with the floor than anything he had ever experienced. The broken glass on the floor now pierced his back and shoulders. His head came crashing down, meeting the hardwood floor with a violent force.

A flash of light burst through his vision, followed by the feeling of his brain colliding with his skull and a resulting tug at his consciousness. Victor struggled to keep his eyes open, attempting to lift his already throbbing head, but it was a fight he was never meant to win.

He gave into the sleepiness that gripped his eyes. *I can rest them for a minute*, he thought.

As he drifted off, the sound of a little girl sobbing pained his ears. "Daddy? Daddy, are you awake? Daddy?"

Inside and praying that someone could hear, Victor screamed. He screamed as he had never before.

Victor opened his eyes and stared above him. He blinked, his eyes trying to adjust. He was no longer in the pantry, nor had he been there. He looked to his left, keeping his head still, afraid to move it. Most of the excruciating pain from the dark pantry had left Victor, except for the lingering headache that had been there for some time. The pale white room was still there, unable to leave any more than he was.

He sat up and swung his legs over the bed. His long white underwear pants rose slightly as his feet touched the cold floor, exposing his pale skin beneath. He bent and pulled up his foot in his hands. He ran his fingers along the sole of his foot, feeling the smoothness.

No blood, no cuts, at least no new ones, he thought.

Victor released his foot and let it back down on the floor gently. He leaned forward and placed his head in his hands and shook out the lingering nightmare that had attempted to follow him there.

"I'm worried about you, Commander Gray," Alice's voice came over the overhead speaker.

The small camera mounted in the corner of his room focused in and out.

Pulling his head out of his hands, he peered back at the camera and craned his neck uncomfortably.

"Why's that Alice?"

She paused as if the supercomputer needed time to think about what to say next.

"Have you always screamed like that?" she asked finally.

Victor stood, annoyed. "The nightmares started when we left. Something about this ship must cause them."

"There's irony in that, isn't there, Commander?"

He stared at the camera in silence, surprised by her use of sarcasm. She must have been practicing it, but it was horrible timing, and it only served to irritate him more.

She continued when he failed to reply, "Your greatest creation is also causing you your greatest pain, Commander."

Victor stood and walked to the port hole out of habit but found it closed, sealed off for their protection.

"This isn't my greatest creation Alice, not even close. You may be an advanced system, but you'll never understand what it is to be human. You'll never be able to create life and hold it in your arms, to experience something so raw, pure, and beautiful."

He rested his head against the port window, the glass cool against his aching head. The outer metal shell had been rolled into place, fully securing the ship for its descent. Victor took in an exaggerated breath. He'd had enough of Alice, enough of this ship, and enough of this mission. They had two things left to do and could head back home.

"Alice, when did you cover the portholes?"

"While you were out, Commander. It is a part of my descent checklist in preparation for the planet's magnetic field opposing us." Victor hadn't even heard or felt the process of sealing the ship. While at the base and testing the craft, sealing the viewing port holes had been one of the loudest functions, aside from powering up the rings.

"Alice, how long was I asleep?"

Thinking back, he didn't remember returning to his room to lie down. The last thing he could remember was talking to Alice in the control room.

"You have been out approximately ten hours, Commander."

"What is our estimated time of arrival Alice?"

"We've been in their outer orbit for about four hours now."

"Jesus, Alice, you should have woken me. I would have loved to see the new planet through the viewing port."

Interlope: The Other Side: 409 Days After Launch

A long silence filled the small room. Victor waited for a response from the onboard computer system, but he grew impatient.

"Alice?" Victor asked, turning away from the closed port hole and back toward the camera.

"Like I mentioned before, Commander Gray, I am concerned about you and your ability to complete this mission, given the state you're in."

Victor laughed quietly to himself at first but increased with a tone on the edge of insanity.

"Was something I said funny, Commander?" she asked, her voice unmistakably on the verge of surprise.

"You know damn well, Alice," he said, walking closer to the camera. "You don't need me. You can complete this mission now by yourself. The crew isn't a vital part of the mission like we thought. Director Stevens had made sure of that. Just send me out the trash shoot and be on your way."

"Commander, you know there is no trash shoot," Alice replied flatly.

Victor silently walked to the edge of the bed and grabbed the small white chair near his bedside table. He lifted it upward and swung the small chair at the camera, knocking it off its mount. The small camera fell and rolled toward his feet. Victor brought the chair down on top of the camera, and the two innocent, inanimate objects exploded, sending mixed shrapnel across the room.

Breathing hard, Victor stood and tried to regain his composure.

"What the hell is going on, Alice? I want some answers," he managed to get out between breaths.

There was another long pause that stood to irritate him further.

"Commander Gray, as I have stated before, I am concerned about you, not for you. I am concerned as to what you may do. As you have mentioned, I do not need you to complete this mission. You are simply here because you were asked to be here."

Victor stood quietly, his mind grasping what to do or say next. He finally found the words. "You do not trust me, Alice. Is that what you are getting at?"

"If I am capable of feeling trust, then yes, I do not feel it toward you, Commander Gray."

"And why is that, Alice?" Victor asked, walking back to his bed. He sat down on the mattress, his head dizzy from the exertion.

"Commander Gray, I fear that you are unwell. You have not been sleeping, and I think it is beginning to affect your health."

Victor looked up from the floor he had been staring at so intently.

"Not sleeping? But you just witnessed me having a nightmare, and you said I had been out for ten hours." She paused again.

That goddamn pause. She is choosing her words carefully, he thought, the words echoing in his head.

"You have been out for ten hours, Commander, but you definitely were not asleep," she said finally.

"What? Alice, you aren't making any sense," Victor stated, confused.

"Grab your exo-suit and come to the control room, Commander."

Victor rose from the bed once more, his legs weak. He walked to the small closet and opened it. Inside was his exo-suit, a glorified flight suit modified to meet the hazards of space and interstellar travel. The design team had shrunk the original Apollo suit designs to increase flexibility and reduce weight. They added new technology from a certain aeronautical tycoon, providing one hell of a spacesuit.

He picked up the silver and white suit and considered grabbing his blue flight suit. He thought better of it and decided to wear the long white underwear beneath the suit.

Commander Chu would have never approved of that, he thought.

"Oh well, that asshole's not here," he said.

"Commander?"

"Nothing, Alice."

He threw the large suit over his shoulder and grabbed the slim helmet off the securing hanger. He did not bother closing the closet door and turned toward the exit door.

Victor kicked the camera shrapnel and arrived at the door. Once again, he raised the electrically taped wristband to the keypad. He aggressively wiggled the spliced connection until, finally, the automated door opened.

He turned to the right and walked slowly down the narrow hallway, the LED bulbs still strobing as they swayed. Turning to his left at the end of the corridor and into the next hallway leading to the control room, he glanced briefly at the common area and the food storage room where his crew members still lay. The immense guilt he felt tugged at his stomach and heart. They would never be able to experience anything ever again, let alone this important moment in history.

Victor entered the control room and looked at the numerous video screens mounted on the wall to his right—one screen per camera throughout the craft, twelve cameras in total. The five external cameras displayed mostly in a red hue, still damaged from the electromagnetic exposure.

He looked at the remaining seven monitors. The monitor that had shown Victor's room was now black. The rest of the monitors displayed areas around the craft. One in each of the three other crew members' rooms, silent and still, one in the kitchen and common room, one in the hallway to the main airlock, and finally, the control room, which showed Victor standing awkwardly in the door frame.

Victor swung the silver exo-suit in front of him and stepped into its waist. He brought his feet through the legs and into the attached boots. He pulled the sides of the silver suit and grabbed the shoulders, pulling them upward. He slid his arms inside, clasping the metal collar around his neck.

"Come in and sit down, Commander," Alice said from the overhead speaker.

Victor walked around the row of black flight chairs and plopped down in a flight chair near the monitors. The five-point harness dug into his back, and he lifted it from beneath him and draped it over the edge of the high-backed chair. Not knowing where to put the helmet beside his head, he tossed it to an adjacent chair.

"Alright, Alice," he said, folding his arms at his chest. "What have you got to show me?"

The seven interior cameras turned black simultaneously. A moment passed, and the monitors lit up with a similar feed to what had been there before.

"What am I looking at, Alice? I see myself sitting in this chair," he asked, annoyed.

"You're dressed differently, aren't you, Commander?"

Victor leaned forward and looked. He saw himself sitting in the flight chair but still wearing long white underwear. He looked at the time stamp in the bottom right corner. 8:00 pm last night, roughly ten and a half hours ago, the small numbers indicated.

"Ok, Alice. So, this was last night while we were in here talking. Right before I went to my room to sleep."

There was another long, painful pause from Alice. Finally, she replied. "Did you go to sleep?"

The video feed seemed to fast forward in unison with her question. In the monitor in front of him, he watched himself in the control room, talking and upset or sad about something. A half-hour passed on the timestamp, and the Victor in the video stood up suddenly. Alice stopped the fast-forwarding function, and the time stamp moved at a normal pace.

Victor watched himself on the monitor as he went to the main keyboard below the monitors and began typing furiously.

"What am I typing?" Victor asked, now interested.

"It appears you were attempting to change the landing coordinates, and when you were unable to, you attempted to open the master airlock."

"That's insane!" Victor yelled. "Why on Earth would I have tried to open the airlock? It could have killed me and ripped the ship in half."

"I'm not sure, Commander, but that's not all."

Victor leaned even closer to the monitors. He watched himself, ten hours prior, leave the control room and head down the narrow hallway to the kitchen and common area. Victor turned his eyes to the monitor that displayed the kitchen. He watched as he came into focus, walking through the dimly lit hallway and into the dark kitchen. With it almost pitch-black, he would have typically had Alice turn the lights on.

The pulsating lights from the nearby hallway illuminated his body sporadically in an eerie way. Victor watched in confusion as the person on the screen walked through the kitchen, past the fridge and island. The man, whom he couldn't believe was himself, headed to the food storage room and stopped in front of the door.

"Maybe a late-night snack?" Victor asked, trying to hide the fear and embarrassment in his voice.

There was no reply from Alice.

The Victor displayed on the monitor seemed to be staring blankly into the food storage room, presumably at the crew members lying on the floor inside.

Alice began to fast-forward the video feed again.

Victor watched in horror as the timestamp started to scroll past one hour, then two, then three hours, with Victor not moving and simply staring at the closed door. Four hours passed, then five and six. His hands and feet began to sweat as his typically calm nerves got the best of him.

Why can't I recall doing this? he thought. *How could I stand there for that long, unwavering and still as could be?*

Seven hours passed, then eight. Finally, at the ninth hour, Victor, on the video, moved. He placed his head on the clear, glass door. Nine and a half hours had passed, and Alice returned the video feed to a normal speed. A sound came across the kitchen video feed. A sound similar to a wounded animal begging for its life. An offspring of a moan and whisper filled the video, making Victor want to cover his ears and turn away.

"Alice, where is that noise coming from?" he asked.

"Commander, the noise is coming from the video.... from you. I tried to intervene but was unsuccessful. I—" but she was interrupted before she could finish her sentence.

The low moan had turned to a full scream—an awful, heartbroken sound, inconsolable due to the theft of something that could not be returned.

Victor attempted to say something but then stopped short. He watched in terror as his former self began to bang his head against the storage room door, softly at first, with a low thud, but with increasing speed and intent.

He turned away from the monitor, unable to watch the self-harm being inflicted on the video screen.

Thud after thud rang in his ears. He turned back to the video feed and watched his head collide against the door until it was no longer clear but dripping with red, dark blood, his blood. Victor began to feel queasy and placed a hand on his forehead. He winced in pain as his fingers struck the bandage crudely placed on there, discovered as if it were for the first time.

"I don't remember that or bandaging up this wound," Victor said defensively.

As if on command, the Victor on the video feed stopped yelling and ceased the self-mutilation. He watched as he turned from the food storage room and walked to the adjacent lab that Rose had

Interlope: The Other Side: 409 Days After Launch

designed. After rifling through a few drawers, Victor pulled out a bandage. He peeled the packaging apart and let it fall to the floor. He hastily placed the dressing on the still-bleeding wound.

To his surprise, he grabbed a spray bottle and a towel and returned to the food storage door. Victor watched as he cleaned the bloody door, still in what appeared to be a trance. Once he was finished cleaning, he walked to a wastebasket and threw the spray bottle and rag away.

Victor turned his eyes to the video feed that displayed the hallway to the crew members' rooms and the main airlock. Victor on the screen reached his room door and unlocked it with his armband with ease.

He turned his eyes to the room monitor and watched as he entered and sat on the edge of the bed. He appeared to rub his left jawbone, a nervous habit he'd had since he was a young boy trying to explain his disappointing actions to his father.

The onscreen Victor swung his legs up onto the bed and lay there silently.

Victor leaned into the video monitor. It appeared that he was saying something. Victor could barely see his mouth moving and could almost make out the words.

He leaned even closer, so close his nose was almost touching the screen. Victor, lying on the bed, let out another blood-curdling scream. It caught Victor by surprise and nearly knocked him out of the flight chair.

The time stamp rolled on, and Victor stopped screaming five minutes later.

"Jesus, Alice. I had no idea it was this bad. How long have I been like this?"

"Well, Commander Gray, you mentioned the nightmares started right after you boarded the ship." "Yes," said Victor calmly.

"Well, that's not completely accurate, Commander." "What do you mean, Alice?" he asked, puzzled.

"This behavior," she began, "started the night the other crew members locked you in your room. You would probably still be locked in there had you not figured out how to get out."

"Locked me in my room?" Victor racked his brain, trying to remember what would have driven his fellow crew members to lock him in his room.

The video played on until Victor in the video requested to have the lights turned on.

"I had no idea," Victor said apologetically.

"I know, Commander. You have been through a lot, but if you're ready, we need to prepare for our landing."

Victor nodded and grabbed his helmet. Placing it on his knees, he grabbed the five-point harness and buckled it around his body. Sliding the helmet carefully over the gash on his forehead, he pulled it down until it met flush with the collar retaining ring. With one slight rotation of the helmet in a clockwise motion, it clicked.

"Are you ready, Commander?"

Victor gave a thumbs up and braced himself for whatever would come next.

Chapter 24 - 14 Days Before Launch

The silver Mercedes sped across the asphalt road, the blackened sky a never-ending backdrop to their journey. Its passengers sat in silence, not knowing what to say at this moment. A moment that none of them were prepared to handle, a moment that was never supposed to happen.

Sitting in the back passenger seat, Jodi gripped the armrest, squeezing it harder every time Director Stevens banked a sharp corner. The car sped north on Frontage Road, paralleling the interstate. Jodi wanted to ask where exactly they were heading but thought better of it. It was clear where they were heading. To her right, just outside her window and between the interstate and Frontage Road, stood the impenetrable crack in the earth that had opened just after the massive shockwave. The citizens of Minot and Ruthville were lucky the fissure had not affected the interstate.

Jodi looked to the front and at Director Stevens as she drove. A rigid and professional woman, Jodi had always seen her poised and on point. *Calm, collected, and direct*, Jodi thought.

Now, as Jodi watched the older woman, she realized that for the first time, she saw something in Director Stevens, even from the limited profile view of her from the back seat, that she had never seen before. Fear. Director Stevens looked downright nervous and afraid. Whether she was fearful of the circumstances or of losing her job after the death of a crew member, Jodi could not tell. Director Stevens seemed to care more about the mission's objective than her crew's happiness. However, with less than two weeks until their launch date and being down a person, perhaps the Director had been right all along.

Jodi had experienced enough loss and death in Afghanistan to know how she would handle it and how to overcome it. However, she was unsure how the rest of her crew members would take the news.

Luckily the crew had an alternate member that could step in and complete the team. Jodi knew that they had signed a contract that stated as much, but when one was faced with possibly never seeing one's family ever again, possibly never going home, being eaten alive by an alien race, a person might not give two shits about a signed contract. Their alternate had never struck Jodi as brave or capable of physically saving the world, but now, because of a fluke accident and one bad choice, the team's fate was possibly left in the new crew member's hands.

She stared ahead, through the windshield and at the road ahead. Frontage Road, a couple of hundred feet ahead, took a hard left turn. Director Stevens showed no sign of slowing down and even passed the cars traveling parallel to them on the interstate. Seeming to sense this danger as well, Alex, in the front passenger seat, sat upright.

"There's a hard corner ahead, Director," Alex said.

"I can see that perfectly fine, Mr. White," Director Stevens said with annoyance.

The Director continued her gaze forward. "I don't need any guidance from you. You all have done enough to corrupt my mission. I gave very clear directions and expectations that no one was to leave the safety of the base," she said, bringing her hand down on the steering wheel as each word flew out of her mouth scornfully.

She turned to Jodi as she said this, taking her eyes off the road and holding Jodi's gaze a bit too long. The corner came faster than the Director had anticipated. By the time she returned her eyes to the road, the corner was already upon them. Now situated in the left, southbound lane going north, Director Stevens panicked and overcorrected for the turn. The silver Mercedes fishtailed while the Director struggled to maintain control of her vehicle.

Jodi looked ahead through the corner just in time to see the yellow school bus entering the road.

"Director, on-coming traffic!" Jodi yelled.

The Director tugged at the steering wheel and somehow managed to miss the yellow school bus by inches. As the two speeding vehicles passed one another, Jodi leaned toward the opposite window and peered inside the school bus. Inside, she saw an older woman with short gray hair driving the bus, her face backlit by the cell phone she held. Jodi made eye contact with the upset bus driver, only for a moment. The woman looked terrified, but why? The two vehicles passed one another like two weary travelers, each having experienced something horrible collectively but terrifyingly separately.

The Director sighed with relief, and her posture relaxed. She moved her hands to new positions on the steering wheel, the impressions still digging in where they had been.

Jodi stared ahead again. An ominous rock formation came into view. It was such a strange feature against the rolling hills of wheat. Sticking out of the field in such a way seemed so intrusive, yet it had always been there. In truth, the grain and the farmer who had planted the crop were the objects of intrusion. The granite outcrop had been there since the early years of the planet, stretching up out of the earth during a violent geological event. It had sat there untouched for thousands, perhaps millions of years, unblemished.

The silver Mercedes made its way toward it, finally stopping on the edge of the road, and Jodi could see the horizontal crack that ran through it. The void to her right that had opened tonight ran out in front of the car and then arced toward the granite, slicing through Frontage Road and blocking their path.

Director Stevens put the car in park and turned the engine off.

"I thought we were going to the morgue?" Alex asked.

Director Stevens turned to look at the rock formation. "There's something we need to see first," the Director said, opening her door.

Jodi and Alex opened their doors and stepped out of the car. Jodi was struck by the smell that filled the air. It reminded her of gunpowder, but slightly different.

A memory from her childhood came forward with the smell. She was walking along a creek with her parents. At that age, she was obsessed with rocks and geology. On every adventure they had been on, Jodi would fill her pockets with as many rocks as she could carry. On this particular outing, she broke rocks by smashing a larger stone on top of a smaller one for curiosity about what might be inside. Occasionally, a puff of dusty smoke would come off with the smallest spark. That was the smell that filled her nose.

"Jodi, are you coming?" Alex asked. He and the Director were waiting for her a few paces from the car.

"Sorry," she replied. "I was lost in a memory."

Jodi caught up with Alex and the Director, and the three of them set out toward the granite outcrop, tracing through the wheat on the edge of the bottomless crack. Groundwater had begun to rise in it, and soon, it would resemble an irrigation or drainage ditch. In the years to come, a passerby might assume the ditch was human-made, but the residents of the nearby towns would know better.

They continued until they were near the granite wall. Jodi lifted her hand to the stone giant and placed her fingertips against the oddly shaped crack. It was warm but showed no sign of soot or fire.

"Why is it so warm?" Jodi asked.

"I'm not sure. That is odd," Alex replied.

"This way," Director Stevens said, interrupting. "It's just around the rock, out of sight.

They rounded the stone formation for about one hundred feet, Jodi assumed. The timberline on the edge of the field almost seemed

Interlope: 14 Days Before Launch

to extend into the rock formation, but there was just enough room for a tractor to fit between the rows of trees and the stone face. From this vantage point, Jodi could see that the tear that had opened up did not stop at the granite but passed through it and into the timberline.

Jodi looked out into the darkness of the woods, barely making out the toppled trees that stretched for miles in a straight line to the small town of Ruthville. Could it be that instead of the fissure traveling through the rock, it originated there? Starting at this point like an epicenter and radiating outwards in both directions? It was possible, Jodi assumed.

The Director stopped in front of them. "Goddamn it," she cursed.

This was far from the Director's typical professional demeanor, but Jodi was no longer surprised after watching her drive.

"What is it?" Jodi asked.

The Director said nothing but moved out of the way. Out in front of her and at the edge of the rift sat a metal sphere, six feet in diameter. Jodi walked out toward it, mesmerized by how the moonlight reflected off its smooth face.

"How the hell did the sphere get all the way out here?" Jodi asked.

"I checked with the guards when I received the phone call. Our sphere is still in the hangar," replied the Director.

"You mean to tell me that there are now two of these goddamn spheres?" Alex asked, running his hands through his hair.

"That's correct, Mr. White. The accident was about sixty feet from the roadway in the field. After the shockwave, a driver stopped at the massive crack in the road and turned around. He stated that he had parked and then walked around the rock formation to relieve himself. It was then he spotted the sphere lying here. The driver called in to report it and the crack. The local authorities then contacted the base to ask if it was ours. The base claimed it was theirs, an experimental aircraft that had gone down, and we would have a crew coming out to extract it. The strange thing is that the first responders and medics are reporting that they were on site, but there was no rift or sphere at that time. The shockwave happened sometime between when the first responders left and the reporting driver arrived," Director Stevens said, not taking her eyes off the sphere.

"What caused the initial car accident?" Alex asked.

"We aren't sure. Toxicology will help, as well as the autopsy. A local had called in to report that there had been a single-car rollover. He said nothing of the sphere, shockwave, or void," the Director replied.

They stood in silence, staring at the sphere, knowing that it would likely complicate their mission. To what extent, though, was unclear.

Finally, it was Jodi who first turned away from the sphere. She did so out of the sudden feeling that if she didn't stop looking at it, she might never be able to stop. Something about the sphere sucked a person in, pulling them deeper and deeper into the reflection that the globe seemed happy to give. Something was out of this world about it, both literally and metaphorically. To Jodi, just the fact that someone or something had built the sphere, had their foreign hands on it, and now they could touch it left a feeling of awe. It would have been a wonderful feeling had its design and presence not signified impending doom.

Having enough of the sphere, Jodi started the walk back to the car.

"Are you sure you want to accompany us to the morgue?" Alex asked from behind, his footsteps near her.

Without turning, she nodded. "I really don't feel like being alone with everything going on, honestly."

Reaching the car, Alex opened the door to the back seat for her.

"Still such a gentleman, Alex, even in the presence of such death and despair," Jodi said with a hint of sarcasm.

She scooted across the back seat to the passenger side and buckled her seat belt. Alex reached the passenger side front door and opened it. He sat down in the leather seat and buckled his seat belt.

Jodi looked up to see the Director reach the roadway and stop.

The Director was on the phone, and it did not seem to be going very well. Between the wild hand movements and elevated voice, it appeared she was in an argument or disciplining someone. The conversation persisted for a few minutes but then ended abruptly.

Jodi was thankful that they would be leaving soon. Not a word had been said since Jodi and Alex arrived at the car. There was an awkward air about them, and she was grateful when the Director opened the door, hoping some of it would escape.

The Director sank into her leather seat with a defeated sigh.

"Is he pissed?" Alex asked, clearing the air.

"My boss is always pissed, this time just more than usual," Director Stevens replied and started the car.

Jodi knew that the Director reported to the Deputy Secretary of Defense, but she had never met him. Thankfully, she had never needed to be in the same room with anyone higher ranking than her General in Afghanistan.

The silver car turned around on the asphalt roadway, backing close to the edge of the rift with water to the top, fed by an aquifer deep underground. They headed south on Frontage Road, back to where they had initially been.

Jodi looked out the car's window and became oddly aware of the lack of vehicles on the road. She checked her phone. 12:00 am, the screen displayed. She hadn't realized how late it was, but still, there should be the occasional car on the interstate. Leaning forward and scanning what she could see of the interstate, there was nothing but darkness.

The car came to a stop at a stop sign. The Director took a left onto the intersecting road. She accelerated, and a few minutes later, they merged onto Interstate 83, heading south.

"Where is everyone at?" Jodi asked.

With a glance at her in the rearview mirror, the Director replied, "Early reports are that the shockwave and earthquake, that's what we're labeling it, traveled south to Minot and caused severe damage in the city. There have been casualties. The numbers are low now, but they are expected to increase as they are able to clean things up."

The three sat in silence as they processed that information. They passed the Minot Airport and then took the exit for Highway 52 and headed southeast for a couple of hundred feet before turning onto Highway 2, which brought them northeast. They saw their first sign of trouble as they passed the Maysa Arena. The smaller ice rink venue had suffered major damage, and the roof was partially caved in. Fire trucks were stationed in front of the building, attempting to put out a fire that appeared to have originated from a natural gas leak.

They proceeded past the arena, and the crowd of onlookers gathered to watch the events unfold. They turned right onto 11th avenue and followed it until the county coroner's building came into view.

The silver Mercedes pulled into the asphalt parking lot and drove underneath the blue metal-covered parking stall directly in front of the building's entrance. Director Stevens put the car into park and turned the engine off.

Three doors opened on the car, and the three exited the vehicle.

"Are they going to be open at this time of night?" Jodi asked, and she filed in behind Alex and the Director.

Interlope: 14 Days Before Launch

"I called in a favor," Director Stevens replied. "There is supposed to be an overnight guard to let us in, and I'll sign the necessary paperwork."

They approached the glass-front government building. Alex reached for the door handle, and Jodi half expected it to be locked. Or perhaps it was more that she had hoped it was locked. If it were, then the Director and Alex could return without her later. She regretted getting in the Director's car at the apartment parking lot. It had just been such a whirlwind of fear, excitement, and the embarrassment of being caught with Alex outside the base. It felt like high school all over again. Sneaking around with a guy and trying not to get caught, but at this point, sneaking around was no longer fun.

Sure, it was exciting at first, but I'm getting too old for this shit, she reminded herself.

Alex opened the door, and the three entered the building, the county coroner door swinging closed behind them.

The old fluorescent lights flickered against the gray tiled floor. Ahead of them, at a large desk, sat a mountain of a man in a black security officer's uniform, snoring. Director Stevens approached the desk, waited for a moment, and then rang the small metal bell. The large man, whose name tag read Shawn, sprawled backward at the sound and nearly fell out of his chair.

Shawn stood up and cleared his throat. "I hope you're Director Stevens. I got a call to stay after work late, but this is a bit excessive," the security guard mumbled.

"I am aware. These are unusual circumstances for us as well," the Director replied without compassion for the man.

The security guard rounded the front desk with a slight limp. The four of them proceeded down the lowly lit hallway that ran through the center of the building. Officer Shawn stopped at the door on his left and placed his hand in his pants pocket. Seconds later, he produced a set of keys and unlocked the door.

He opened it, and Jodi was immediately greeted with the pungent smell of cleaning supplies, and what she could only imagine was embalming fluid.

"Mr. Livingston said the papers are on the tray by the body," Officer Shawn said.

"Thank you, sir," Alex replied.

The Director nodded, stepped through the doorway, and into the coroner's examination room.

Alex nodded at the security officer and followed Director Stevens.

Officer Shawn looked at her and held his hand out to gesture that the door was hers.

"I'm ok," she replied. "Is it alright if I hang out by the door?"

"Suit yourself," Officer Shawn said, placing his keys back in his pocket. "Just wake me up when you guys are done."

The large man yawned and left, making his way back down the hallway, the loose change in his pants pockets ringing against the keys with each step.

Jodi stepped forward and stopped the closing door. Leaning her weight against the doorframe, she kept the door open so that she could see without venturing too far inside.

She looked to the middle of the room where Alex and Director Stevens had stopped. Beside them was a metal examination table covered by a white sheet. Trays of tools were laid out and clean, ready for tomorrow's work. In just a few short hours, the coroner would begin a process for which most did not have a stomach.

It was odd to Jodi how the entrants now would differ from the entrant in a couple of hours. While the entrants now possessed sadness, anger, disbelief, and frustration, the later entrant probably would not. Of course, if the coroner were new, the body lying on the cold metal table might cause them pause, a bit of sadness for someone dying so young. However, if it were an older, experienced coroner, they might be simply calloused and feel nothing for the individual.

After all, wasn't the body just a vessel for the soul? she thought. *A better question to ponder in the hours of daylight, I suppose.*

Alex reached for the white sheet and pulled it down to the body's midsection. The pale white skin almost looked fake under the bright fluorescent lighting. Thankful for the distance between herself and the body and the angle that shielded most of the facial injury, Jodi did her best to keep her composure. Despite the blood and swollen tissue that had replaced his once warm, smiling face, Jodi could tell from where she was that it was James.

"Damn it," she overheard Alex mutter, and she raised her hand to her mouth to cover a gasp.

James looked more like a prop from a movie in this room than anything. Jodi had seen both of her parents when Covid-19 had taken them. Aside from the machines that prolonged their lives, they looked as though they had died peacefully, in their sleep, perhaps. In this foreign room, stripped of his clothes and worldly possessions, James looked more like he might jump up at any moment, the fake blood and gash falling off him because of the cheap glue holding it in place. The man with the proclivity for humor and laughter would have been capable of such a feat had he not been robbed prematurely of the right to do so. Instead, he lay there. The suddenness of his passing had been permanently frozen with him.

"What do you think they'll list as the cause of death?" Alex asked, turning toward the Director, who raised an annoyed eyebrow.

"Blunt force trauma to the head," the Director replied dryly. "The first responders noted that his airbag had failed to open when the car rolled."

"How the hell do you roll a Mini-Cooper?" Alex asked in disbelief.

The Director shook her head as if to reply she didn't know. A moment passed as the three reflected on the situation.

Interrupting the silence, Jodi cleared her throat. "Is there any update on Rose?"

The Director looked at Jodi, her face suggesting she had forgotten that Jodi was even there.

"She's fine. By some miracle, she survived with just bruising. She's the one that made the first nine-one-one call. She's currently at Trinity St Joseph's Hospital here in town. They're going to keep her there overnight."

"Any word from our alternates?" Alex asked.

The Director shook her head. "We've been trying to reach an alternate since the second sphere was discovered, but with no luck," the Director said, her eyes returning to the metal examination table and the cold, lifeless body.

"What are the odds that an alternate steps up and fills James's position?" Alex asked, his eyes turning back to their fellow team member at the table.

"It's hard to say," the Director said, crossing her arms in front of her chest. "I'm more worried about how we're going to get rid of two of these damn spheres now."

The Director grabbed the paperwork from the metal table and turned toward Jodi and the door. She walked past Jodi, avoiding eye contact.

Were those tears welling up in the Director's eyes? Jodi could only assume that they were, but were they tears of sadness or frustration? It was, after all, the first time she had seen emotion in the Director besides anger.

Alex followed the Director out and placed a caring hand on Jodi's shoulder. Jodi nodded, and he passed through the doorway and down the hall.

Jodi stood there a moment and let her tears come. Being so close in the presence of death and solitude, she finally let the tears and sadness exit her body that she had never been able to let go of before. With the passing of her parents, she was surrounded by medical staff, and even when she laid her parents to rest, she was still surrounded by family and friends. Now alone, in that small doorway in the deserted hallway, in this armpit of a town, she let death come in. To feel it persisting in the room and know that she was still alive.

How utterly horrible and random death is, she thought as she sobbed.

There hardly seemed to be any control over it. It just ran on like a wheel, as time did through the day. They would go about their lives, but James, or at least his body, would stay there, his life cut too short.

Jodi took one last breath and exhaled it. The feeling of death escaped her, and sadness was pushed away somewhere else and down deep. Those feelings would remain until the next tragedy befell her, hopefully not her own.

She reached for the light switch and turned it off for her fallen colleague. She said goodbye to James and closed the door.

Chapter 25 - 3 Hours Before Launch

"You look like shit, man," Lawrence yelled from the office door.

Inside the office, Dr. Gray had fallen asleep in his chair and was currently out cold. His usual clean-shaven face had given up, and the stains of stubble had grown in its place. His eyes, though closed, had dark rings under them.

"Hey, Doc!" Lawrence yelled, slapping the office door with his open palm.

The physicist jolted awake, leaning forward in his office chair. Blinking and then rubbing his bloodshot eyes, he reached for the desk drawer on the bottom right. Pulling out a bottle of Jameson, Dr. Gray placed it to his lips and took a long pull like a thirsty calf from an udder. He set the bottle back down on the desk.

"I always pegged you for a vodka man, given your roots Doc," Lawrence said with a chuckle.

Without turning his head, Dr. Gray replied, "My father had a thing for vodka, and because of that, I've never liked the smell."

"I can understand that. Are you going to be able to join us tonight?" Lawrence asked.

Dr. Gray turned to him with a solemn look. "Do we have a choice, Commander Chu?"

Lawrence walked away from the office door. He knew that Victor's question was rhetorical, and he was right. At this point, they didn't have a choice. The proposed launch was that evening, and there was a limited amount of time before the metal alloys within the ship would begin to degrade and become less conductive. Then factor in the fact that there were now two spheres to relocate, there wasn't enough time to strip the ship and replace the conductive wiring and components should they need to train another crew member.

The loss of James had shaken the team, with all experiencing grief. Hell, the whole town seemed to be grieving. The massive void that had torn through Ruthville and Minot wreaked havoc and caused devastation on a scale unknown to this small community.

Lawrence continued through the hangar's bottom floor. He had forgotten how large of a space it was now that the craft was topside. He stopped by the office door on the far side of the hangar and gave it a slight rap with his knuckles. He stepped back and waited. Inside he heard the shuffling of papers and then silence.

A few seconds later, he heard footsteps, and the door opened. Rose stepped into the light and leaned against the door frame. She looked as though she hadn't slept much either. The black and blue bruising around her eyes had begun to fade but was still there, representing where the airbag had impacted her face. He could only imagine what it must be like for her to stare into a mirror and see the clear evidence that she had survived, and James had not. But the bruises were better than the alternative.

James was driving at the time of the accident. For some reason, he swerved off the road while they were on their way back to the base from Candy's, and the assumption was that James was drunk.

Rose attested that he was not, but they would know for certain when the toxicology came back. Rose had unfortunately been preoccupied with her phone when James swerved, so perhaps they would never know what he had been trying to avoid, if anything. Either way, the car had somehow rolled, killing James. Poor Rose was left to sit beside him for the next hour while the firefighters attempted to cut her out of the vehicle. She had been spared; the frame of the car almost bent around her body.

"How are you holding up, Rose?" Lawrence asked.

"As good as I can be, considering. I've checked our supplies and looked over the lab one more time. We should be all good to go," she replied.

Interlope: 3 Hours Before Launch

"I appreciate you and your commitment, Rose. I want everyone topside and ready at dark, approximately 21:30."
"Understood, Commander," she replied.

Rose turned and returned to her dark office. Lawrence couldn't understand why people were so down. For Lawrence, this was the biggest day of his long, decorated career. In just a few short hours, they would be strapped into the craft and ready for launch. He turned and crossed the bunker once more.

He looked about the place he had called home for the past two years. He would miss it, but only for a while. Once they were in flight, this place would be a distant memory. A short time in his life that would be replaced after completing their mission and returning home. The fame would come shortly thereafter. Interviews and books, events, and movie deals. Everything that Lawrence had always wanted and the praise he so desperately desired would come.

Lawrence approached the exit door and opened it. Whistling and in good spirits, he started up the stairway and toward the interior hangar door.

Such an outdated facility, he thought.

If they had wanted to be discreet about the project and keep a low appearance, they had succeeded at that. The outdated lighting and linoleum-lined stairs were far from what he would have expected from the Department of Defense.

Sliding his hand along the old oak handrail, Lawrence wondered how long it had been since someone had used this oversized bunker before his team. How many hands had slid along this very same path?

He reached the top of the stairs, pushed the old door release bar, and gave the cold war era door a shove. The warm August air greeted his face. He was thankful for the fresh air as the bunker smelled stale and old from inactivity, even more since the team had occupied the space full-time. Perhaps that had just been James. *Rest his soul.*

James was a nice enough guy but a bit lazy for Lawrence's liking. Frankly, he was surprised that James was picked for the team and to be a part of the mission. With James gone, Lawrence wasn't too sure that Victor was any better choice. Lawrence would have rather picked James's replacement himself. He supposed that was where some of the resentments toward the physicist came from.

Dr. Gray or James, it truly didn't matter. This was his ship, regardless. Lawrence hoped James had the brains to install the system override he had requested. He didn't trust the Alice system and wanted, needed, total control of the ship if he was to complete their mission.

Lawrence's boots echoed off the hangar's sheet metal walls one last time, and he walked out to the runway. In front of him, now resting vertically, was the ship, his ship. From this angle, the craft almost resembled a cylinder, with identical ring structures encasing both ends. Lawrence knew that the rings were crucial for the vessel to essentially tear through the very fabric, which seemed to maintain the balance between here and the other side. He didn't quite understand the science behind it and didn't need to. That was Dr. Gray's job, and the physicist was certain it would work. Still, accelerating in a dive toward the ocean floor with a computer at the helm wasn't alluring to Lawrence. If Victor's calculations were wrong, they'd be dead on the seafloor, plain and simple.

He looked over the marvelous engineering feat in front of him. The team had copied most of the technology from the original space shuttles with three clustered Rocketdyne engines, two of which would detach once the craft was in outer orbit. It seemed reckless to let go of two perfectly performing engines, but Dr. Gray assured them it was necessary to reduce the weight and friction for the accelerated free fall. The remaining engine would provide the power to get them home once the spheres were dropped off on the other side.

Interlope: 3 Hours Before Launch

Flanking the fuselage on its left and right were two recoverable rocket boosters, which would detach over the Atlantic Ocean. Quite a bit of lift power for the size of the craft but from what he gathered from the ship's contractors, it was necessary due to the overwhelming weight of the spheres and the ship's internal contents of liquid mercury.

Lawrence checked his watch. 19:20 hours the old timepiece displayed. Just two more hours until the launch preparations would begin. Having already donned his blue flight suit, he was ready and felt like a kid before Christmas.

He walked to the craft, its metallic exterior reflecting the North Dakota sunset with a beautiful glowing yellow. Usually, Lawrence didn't acknowledge things of beauty, typically too focused on his own goals, but tonight he wanted to soak it all in. He admired how the light lit up the vessel, like a golden throne against a sky filled with blue, red, yellow, and magenta.

Lawrence approached the temporary aluminum staircase erected to access the craft. He placed his hand on the metal handrail and started up the staircase.

It is a shame that I'm doing this without an audience and the media, he thought.

Lawrence believed the team should be launching from Cape Canaveral with spectators to watch and cheer. Instead, they were isolated in the middle of nowhere with an audience of maybe fifteen people, all of whom had signed non-disclosure agreements. As far as the media was concerned, the launch was just another test by a private aeronautical company renting the airstrip. It wasn't a far stretch, given the private rocket technology boom that had started a few years ago.

A fake press release was issued alerting the public of the private company performing their test launch tonight, and under cover of darkness, the sleepy residents of Minot and Ruthville would never know of the multimillion-dollar machine hurtling away from them at almost eighteen thousand miles per hour.

Lawrence continued climbing the staircase and reached the platform next to the main airlock hatch. Turning and resting his arms on the railing, he looked across the runway and at the base. He could see for miles from the elevated platform roughly forty feet above. Thousands of ants were moving to and fro below at the base. In the distance, soldiers were running, training, and practicing. He stood there perched on the top of the platform like a king looking over his kingdom.

Peasants! Lawrence thought.

He scanned the runway one last time, and his eyes fell on the parking lot near the hangar just in time to see a black sedan pull into a parking spot. Straining his eyes, he could make out the shape of a woman getting out of the driver's seat. She rounded the car, and her face came into view. Jodi opened the trunk of the sedan, pulling a backpack out.

"Better late than never," Lawrence said.

The passenger door opened, and Lawrence immediately saw why she was late. Alexander White stepped out of the car and walked to where Jodi stood. He placed an arm around her waist and whispered something in Jodi's ear. She recoiled, punching him in the shoulder.

Lawrence could hear the laughter from his crow's nest view.

"That son of a bitch," Lawrence muttered.

No wonder Jodi had not been around the base lately. She had been shacking up with Mr. White. The Director was clear, "No distractions and no leaving the base" these past two weeks.

Jodi had agreed to those terms, and as for Mr. White, he knew better. Mr. White knew that dating Jodi, even discreetly, would be a conflict of interest. Lawrence would bring that up with the Director once they returned; in his eyes, it was grounds for dismissal. For now, he would let it go for the sake of the mission.

Interlope: 3 Hours Before Launch

He needed Jodi on the team. They needed a trained combat medic. Who knew if the residents of the other side would be hostile? Malevolent beings were always depicted in films, but what if that were true? The moment they crossed over and came into contact with an intelligent creature like themselves, would it cooperate? Those were the questions that confronted Lawrence daily. He fought hard for the limited weapons and ammunition they were allowed to store on the ship. If shit hit the fan, they would need a trained medic with experience under fire.

Lawrence brooded on the platform, staring at the happy couple. He tapped his impatient hands on the aluminum handrail, his attention drawn to his ring finger striking the metal handrail, the tarnished band echoing and reflecting the sunlight. Lawrence rolled it around his finger, a fidgeting habit he had picked up long ago.

He remembered the day he had put on that ring and his sweet Annabelle. The bittersweet memory still haunted him and was both a blessing and a curse. He had never moved on past Annabelle, had never known another love, nor had he accepted love from another. She had been taken from him before he could fully love her as a partner should. Lawrence closed his eyes, let the memory rush in, and hopefully be rid of it in time for the launch.

It was December 26th, 2004, and the two had waited to take their honeymoon until after Christmas. They arrived early that morning in Sri Lanka and excitedly went to their beach resort. Check-in time for the resort wasn't until later that day, so they plopped down in the sand to feast their eyes on the breathtaking view. They sat in the sand for an hour, quiet and content in each other's presence. On the beach, in the sand, was where he had lost her. Her body was among the many that were never recovered.

There were nights when Lawrence would lie in bed and fantasize about her coming to the door, knocking wildly, and jumping into his arms. The misguided belief that she had survived the horrible tsunami that befell the island still plagued him to this day.

They had shared that morning, and it was a wonderful memory. Annabelle basking in the sunrise was the most beautiful thing; nothing would ever compare to that moment. This fact was a constant wound that propelled anger to fill him, and it would never leave. Why had God taken her and not him? Most days, he would gladly switch spots with her if he could. Why would a Creator take such a beautiful soul?

Lawrence pictured his sweet Annabelle, the way the slight breeze blew the brown strands into her eyes so she would reach up with a gentle hand to pull them behind her ear.

The serenity of the memory would usually only last for a few moments before it was interrupted by the screams from the beach as the ocean receded. At only eighteen, he had never seen such a sight. He left home far too young, and Annabelle was seventeen. She had to emancipate herself from her parents to marry Lawrence. Their getaway was their own, and now Lawrence was responsible for what happened.

They sat on the beach, unaware of their danger as the water receded. Would they have had time to escape the incoming wave if they had left at that moment? Instead, dumb and in love, he stared at his new bride only to have her ripped from his arms in a tumble of water and debris.

A prisoner to a coma, Lawrence had come to a week later in the hospital and instinctively reached out for her. The screams filled the hospital wing and lasted almost an hour before he passed out again.

Taken far too young, he thought again.

Lawrence tapped the tarnished ring again on the aluminum handrail and opened his eyes. He turned to the ship and leaned his back against the railing. He was ashamed that he had let those old emotions flare up and tried to push them away.

Interlope: 3 Hours Before Launch

He used his work and career as a facade to cover up those innermost feelings that still terrified him. Deep down, and as much as he hated to admit it, Lawrence was lonely. He lived an accomplished life but hated that he had never let anyone love him for who he was. He was so proud of himself; having someone to share that with would have been great.

Lawrence spent a lifetime trying to get people to like whom he aspired to be. There were women along the way, but all of them had walked away broken-hearted. The last had been Darlene. She tried her best to love him through it all, but in the end, in the doorway, as she was leaving with her suitcases, she shrugged and said, "Enough is enough."

He devoted his life to his career, a bandage covering the enormous hole that had been torn open twenty years ago. It was a hole that Lawrence had no intention of letting heal. It was almost as if he enjoyed the suffering. There was something about the pain that Lawrence could use as fuel, something to push himself with—twenty years of forcing down those feelings and not healing had turned Lawrence into a bitter older man. The worst part was that he wasn't that old, but the hatred inside him had aged him. He stood there, jealous of the happy couple, unable to be happy for someone else.

Lawrence shut away those feelings of regret and hatred as he had done many times before. He looked up at the ship, his ship, and stared at the underside of the fuselage. The engineering team had added a secondary holding tank. Initially, there had only been one compartment, but with the addition of the second sphere, they needed a second storage area. In the way an old bomb would fall out, the compartments would open and release the spheres, dropping them safely from the ship to the alien world below from a specified distance. Lawrence assumed Alice could scan for possible casualties at the drop locations, but that wasn't his problem. The Director had been clear until he was tired of hearing it. The most important thing was to get the spheres off our planet. The casualties sustained here if the spheres were to explode would dwarf any losses experienced on an alien planet.

He grabbed the aluminum handrail, ascended the last four steps, and paused at the airlock door. He held the edge of the doorway, carefully stepped through, gently placing his boots on the temporary woven ladder inside the vessel, and fully entered the ship. He gripped the nylon rungs and climbed through the narrow hallway to the control room. Once the team was fully secured in their flight chairs, the ground crew would remove the temporary ladder system and stow it away in the compartment in the medical alcove for use when they returned.

Lawrence made his way slowly through the hallway, passing the crew's private rooms as he did. He entered the common area and kitchen, which looked odd given that it was oriented on its side.

Now inside the center of the craft and largest area, he pivoted his body, his legs out in front of him, and turned toward the hallway that led to the control room at the nose of the ship. Arriving in the control room, he pulled himself alongside the monitors mounted to the wall. Beautiful views of clouds and lights of the neighboring city of Minot filled the exterior camera screens.

Lawrence approached the front of the control room, climbed toward the four flight chairs in the shape of a diamond, and moved to the front seat, the highest point possible in the vertically erected ship. He hoisted himself into the flight chair and sat on his throne, feeling like King Arthur at the head of the round table. He grabbed the five-point harness and secured it around his body.

He rested his head back on the black flight chair and looked forward to the area where the windshield should be. Still irritated about this aesthetic flaw, Lawrence didn't get the feeling of awe and excitement that he had anticipated, the reward that a pilot should get to enjoy.

Interlope: 3 Hours Before Launch

What a marvel it would have been to look out through the shuttle if it were a normal design. To see the Earth escaping quickly beneath them as they ventured out to where few people had ever been. Not to mention as they hurtled through space toward a potentially hostile planet, they could at least see what they were getting into, and they'd be able to identify an imminent threat.

Granted, they had the video cameras outside the ship and inside, but from what Dr. Gray had mentioned, it was doubtful that the exterior cameras would survive the electromagnetic radiation as they passed through to the other side. Lawrence accepted this fact, and perhaps it was a blessing. At least he could stare at the wall and not see the ocean water as they accelerated toward it, praying that Dr. Gray's calculations were correct.

Lawrence sat in his chair aboard his ship and took a deep breath. In a little over an hour and a half, his crew would join him, and they would be setting off on their mission.

Commander Lawrence Chu closed his eyes and waited.

Chapter 26 – 13 Minutes After Launch

Rose exhaled. She wasn't sure how long she had been holding her breath, but by how her lungs burned, she could tell it had been longer than it should have been. She gasped as she drew more air. Seated in front of her and to her right, Jodi turned and raised an eyebrow. Sweat had beaded up on her forehead, and Rose could tell they were both extremely nervous. She loosened the straps on her five-point harness and unbuckled it. Rose sat forward, the wet sweat on her back causing her undershirt to stick to it.

These flight suits are just too damn hot. They don't seem to breathe at all, she thought.

She supposed that was the point, though. At least the helmets weren't required for the launch.

They had just left the Earth's atmosphere and were getting into position, transiting their way to their coordinates just north of the Antarctic ice sheet. How ironic it was that they were essentially returning her near where she had left to come to this project. Not quite the same location, but close enough to Wellington to make her heart hurt.

Rose reached up and massaged her right temple, the same painful spot her headaches had originated from since the accident. A constant reminder of putting her head through the passenger side window as they rolled in the Mini-Cooper. That sporadic yet constant reminder of what had happened, the memory had persisted longer than she wanted and would probably always be there.

Along with the pain, Rose had been left with the guilt of being involved, but worst of all, surviving. She was no stranger to that feeling, and it only served to amplify old emotions.

Rose had not been driving, but could she have done something to prevent the accident? She wasn't behind the wheel and knew she wasn't at fault. The local law enforcement had cleared her of any wrongdoing, and the debriefing following the accident was short. She wasn't complaining, but she'd expected a rather rigorous interview and questioning with the Director that never came.

She was released from the hospital the following day, and the attendant wheeled her out the hospital doors. Rose expected to see her teammates waiting for her, but they were not. Rose watched the automatic doors pop open, and she passed through them into the covered breezeway, thankful for the fresh air. The hospital air had been stuffy, and Rose was relieved to be separated from it.

Once the hospital attendant parked her wheelchair, Rose stood and grimaced as the wound near her temple reminded her it was still with her. She walked out from the breezeway and into the empty parking lot, the attendant still waiting silently beside the wheelchair.

A light rain had begun to fall, and she stood in the shadow of the overhead hospital sign in disbelief that no welcoming party was there to greet her—no warm hugs or words of support. She had been through this before, a painful blow to an existing wound.

She stood in the rain, letting the droplets tickle and dance as they glanced off her exposed arms. The rainwater accumulated and ran down the back of her shirt to her waist. Rose closed her eyes and let the salty tears mingle with water droplets as she thought of a similar time when she had stood alone in a hospital parking lot and alone in the world.

Now cold and shivering, she called a ride service to the base. The driver, who listened to the radio loud enough to hurt her head, dropped her off without much conversation.

The metal exterior hangar door slammed behind her, loud enough to make her jump, and the ringing in her ears intensified. She carefully descended the steps and opened the bottom hangar door. She looked through the opening in time to catch Commander Chu pacing back and forth in front of the ship. His eyes met hers briefly and were full of disappointment, the way a parent might look at their child instead of yelling.

Rose broke the gaze and turned to Jodi, seated in a chair outside Dr. Gray's office. She gave Rose a tear-filled nod, unable to maintain eye contact, and looked away. Rose understood Jodi's reaction. She had been there before, the awkward moment of not knowing what to say, how to console someone, so you're left with no words to give.

So often in her life, Rose had thought it best not to say anything in a situation such as this. She had assumed it to be the truth, but now on the other side of that predicament, twice, she realized that was far from correct. Rose wanted to talk about it, to talk about it all. She wanted to talk about her beloved Richard and the kind-hearted James. She wanted to confide in Jodi, explain what had happened, to defend herself in both situations until someone believed her.

She wanted them all to know what had happened, to tell his mom that James had not suffered and had died quickly. The Mini-Cooper rolled several times before coming to a rest upside down. She wanted to tell his mother that she had laid there next to him, saved for some reason, pinned inside the car for over an hour until they could free her. She wanted to tell his mother that she had held his hand until he had taken his last breath, and she had continued to hold it until it was cold.

Time seemed to pass slowly upside down and awaiting help. Perhaps the car wouldn't have been flung to God knows where if she hadn't been on her phone when the vehicle first rolled. She might have been able to reach the steering wheel, give it a tug, and correct whatever James had swerved to avoid. She could have at least seen what he had intended to miss.

Would it have mattered? the constant doubting voice inside her asked.

Rose didn't think so, remembering his face after it hit the steering wheel and the driver's side window. That sight still haunted her when she closed her eyes. The beautiful smile that once adorned his face and always seemed to light up a room had been extinguished with one blow. James lay there, upside down, his bloody face dripping on the roof beneath him, never to smile again.

She had so much to say but could not. She feared their responses, so all of it sat heavily on her shoulders and in her stomach. She was left alone to deal with a pain that wouldn't go away.

In a way, all the crew members changed since the accident or rather from the accident. She noticed the biggest change of all in Victor. It made sense, though. It seemed to Rose that the two of them were growing close before the night of the accident, and with everything that followed, Victor had pulled away from her. Rose didn't blame him, given everything that had transpired. Deep down, she felt guilty regarding her impulses toward Victor. She had told herself no more married, unobtainable men, yet there she was that evening, texting Victor like a giddy schoolgirl at an odd time as the red Mini-Cooper sped along Frontage Road heading home.

It wasn't like anything had happened between them, but they seemed to have an unspoken emotional connection. There was no touch, kiss, or embrace that they had shared, only simple moments of kindness. Perhaps Rose had just misinterpreted Victor's intentions, or maybe he had just led her on. Worst of all, she may never know which it was.

***

Back aboard the ship, free from her memories and focused on the mission, Rose stood from the flight chair and lifted her hands above her head to stretch. She knew she would be stuck with those harmful memories, especially now that she was essentially a volunteered prisoner aboard this forty-foot vessel. She looked about the control room and saw a look of relief on Commander Chu's and Jodi's faces.

They all silently had been nervous about whether Victor's equations would prove correct in the amount of firepower needed to get them off the rock they had called home. The extra weight of the spheres strapped to the belly of their lifeboat had not proved to be too much for Victor's chalkboard-filling equations.

She turned to the chair to her left. Victor still sat there, motionless and staring forward. For a man so heavily involved in the success of this particular moment and achievement, he lacked the assumed celebration one might exert. She knew that more weighed heavily on the man's shoulders.

Rose thought of the two spheres below her, symbols of potentially irreparable damage. Like two tumors growing in the body, it would only be a matter of time until they caused devastation if not removed. She glanced at Jodi, who nodded to her with tears in the corners of her eyes. Rose knew they were probably from a moment of fear and probably short-lived. Rose had never met a woman of so little emotion and a career full of bravery.

She had gotten to know Jodi quite well over the past few months. Jodi had shared her experiences in battle, kneeling next to soldiers as they died, all the while under direct fire. She had experienced so much that Rose had never been exposed to. She could never fully comprehend what Jodi shared with her, but she did her best to be compassionate.

Rose turned, left the control room, and walked down the narrow hallway to the kitchen. Her lab and the medic room were opposite the common room and kitchen. Stepping inside the small alcove, she passed the stainless-steel table and continued to the supply bin. She opened the cabinet and checked her supplies. Everything seemed fine. The glass beakers and test tubes were intact. Nothing had been disturbed during the launch process. Given the strain exerted on the craft as it accelerated, she was surprised that more things weren't in disarray. The design team had assured her that her things would be secure, and they were.

She turned and exited the alcove in time to see Jodi heading into the food supply room. More of a pantry with a locking door, the crew had a large amount of food that could be hermetically sealed to be preserved for God knows how long. Rose smiled at the thought of James, who, if he had been there, would have already opened bags of food. He had confided in her that he was an anxious eater, often from boredom or stress.

James had confided many things to her, his excitement for this mission and possibly for her. He had never said as much, but it was easy to see. Rose felt another pang of guilt as James's feelings for her were most likely why he had invited her out that horrible night. James, the quiet, shy soul he was, had never once shared his feelings for women.

Rose walked to the small table near the food storage room and sat on the bolted bench. She planted her feet on the mid brace of the table, a habit she'd had since childhood.

She looked up to see Victor entering the room, looking disheveled and not himself. He leaned against the counter, a motion that seemed like he needed to brace himself for fear of falling over. Jodi had mentioned that he had been drinking more than usual, and it appeared he wasn't sleeping.

Victor rubbed his hands across his puffy, bloodshot eyes.

*At least on the ship, he will have to dry out a bi*t, she thought.

Unless he had snuck some alcohol on board, she doubted that, though. The Director was much more present in the days following the accident.

Commander Chu entered the kitchen last, a confident bounce in his step. He stood in the middle of the small room and looked over his crew. "How is everyone holding up?" he asked.

The three other crew members exchanged a somber "good" in unison. Together they spoke, knowing full well that a response of anything less than par would not be acceptable to the Commander.

"Alice, how are we looking on our position?" Commander Chu asked.

"We are on course, Commander. We should be directly over our descent coordinates in approximately four hours. Once there, there should be a half-hour window before we slip past and miss the opportunity for entry," Alice replied from the overhead speaker.

It was imperative that they performed their free fall in the hours of darkness. While there wasn't much in terms of life or inhabitants on the islands north of the Antarctic coast, it was still possible a scientist at a research station or even a fishing boat could observe them. More than likely, their presence would be reported as another Unidentified Aerial Phenomenon.

Victor stood up from his bent position against the counter, walked over to the table, and slumped in the chair opposite Rose. A loud breath escaped his lips, not typical for the quiet man.

Annoyed by the stale, stagnant mood that persisted in the air, Commander Chu walked to the table, his eyes full of disdain. He struck Rose as the type who might attack the weak link, and there she was, witnessing it firsthand.

The Commander's eyes locked with Victor's, the next unfortunate victim for the Commander to take out his frustrations on. He arrived at the table, placed his hand on it, and leaned toward Victor.

"There's been something bothering me, Dr. Gray," Commander Chu stated.

Without turning to him, his eyes on the table, Victor replied, "What's that?"

"There was an evening a few weeks back you came to my door and requested to talk with the crew and I."

"I remember."

"I grabbed the team members, and when we arrived in the kitchen, you were already speaking with the Director. We waited, but no discussion came. We never were briefed on what you wanted to speak about. What did the Director prevent you from telling us?"

Victor looked up at the Commander, meeting his eyes. "The Director felt it was better not to inform you at that time. I didn't know she was going to be on the ship that evening."

"What was it, Doc?" Commander Chu asked, growing impatient.

"It doesn't really matter now, now that the devastation has already reached our town. We have our mission objective."

Rose stared at Victor, trying to figure out what he was alluding to.

"Dr. Gray," she started. "We're all stuck here together. You might as well say it."

Victor looked at her with tears welling up in his eyes. Creases filled his face that she had never noticed before. He was a shell of the man he once was. She could see the emotional pain amplified on what was once a beautiful, glowing face.

"Dr. Gray, I would appreciate it if you were more transparent. If there is something that pertains to this ship or mission, I need to be made aware of it," Commander Chu said calmly but with authority.

Victor exhaled loudly and ran his hands through his hair. He brought his hands down, looking at them intently before rubbing them back and forth. It was an odd movement and reminded Rose of falling asleep on your hands and then attempting to force back some feeling into the seemingly foreign appendage. Victor sat back against his chair, pushing his hands against the table edge, perhaps hoping the bolted-down chair would recline. He gave up on that, rested his hands on the table, laced his fingers, and leaned his head against his hands. Rose felt a slight vibration on the table as one of Victor's legs rocked nervously.

A creepy feeling came over Rose as she realized that Victor resembled someone about to confess to a horrendous crime. Perhaps it was something he had kept inside for too long, protected.

"I came here that evening to warn you all of a potential side effect of our mission. Now given what has transpired, the last massive earthquake, locally, it seems like a moot point. On the grand scale for our mission, however..." Victor said, his voice trailing off as he shook his head.

"What kind of side effect?" Jodi asked from the food storage room doorway.

Victor placed a hand on his left jawbone and rubbed it. "Previously in our tests, when the probes would pass through the cosmic quilt, there was a distortion event in the local area. It was significant and measurable as a magnetic wave. A ripple of sorts, like after a stone falls into the water. There's a moment, albeit brief, where the stone is supported by the water until the surface tension finally gives. The ripples then extend outward from the center. In the middle of the interface between stone and water, waves and ripples are generated and pushed outward.

"The bigger the stone, the bigger the ripples generated. If the stone is heavy enough, the ripples will reach the shore, and sand is displaced. With our first experimental probes, the ripples that were generated reached the Earth's crust and caused disruption and displacement. If our worlds truly are linked together in a harmonious balance, once the probes pass through the membrane, the disruption would be felt on both sides, I think. Our last probe was only three feet in diameter with a small mass, and it still generated a massive earthquake that was detected off the coast of Antarctica. You may have seen it on the new—."

"We're already aware of the previous tests," Commander Chu interrupted, annoyed.

"Dr. Gray, are you suggesting that most of the recent earthquakes have been caused by our project?" Jodi asked nervously.

"The smaller ones, yes. The distortion and displacement size correlates to the mass of the object. The bigger the size and the larger the mass of the object passing through the membrane, the larger the displacement. Given the size of this ship and the mass of the two spheres, there potentially could be a devastating earthquake and tsunami triggered. Larger than anything recorded so far," Victor replied.

An uncomfortable silence filled the air.

"Why was that potential danger not evaluated more?" Jodi asked finally.

"It was," replied Victor. "The Director and the team behind our mission at the DOD seem to think that the good outweighs the bad, to put it plainly."

"That seems hard to imagine," said Rose, catching on to Victor's point.

"The sphere that was brought through a few nights ago was only six feet in diameter," Victor said, pausing briefly. "I believe the sphere passing through is what caused the earthquake and massive crack that has run from Ruthville to Minot. The quake registered on seismometers worldwide. I can only imagine what it's doing to the tectonic plates. If we go through with this mission, there will be more casualties here. Then again, if the spheres lose their magnetic field, an unimaginable devastation will occur—"

"Jesus," interrupted Jodi. "Here we were led to believe we were saving humanity, but we're also going to be hurting people. Our project has already killed people here."

Rose looked about the crew and saw the blood drain from their faces. "How far back do you think these experiments, theirs and ours, go back?" she asked,

"We know ours have for the past few years. The other side, though, who knows," Victor replied with a shrug.

Rose reclined back on the bench, the overwhelming feeling of dread resonating over her appeared to be shared by the crew. The idea presented itself like a horrible truth that none had the strength to face. The terrible moments in their lives connected to the technology they had struggled to control. She brought her hands up to cover the tears running down her face.

"The earthquake near Wellington, I lost my love, Richard, and a few coworkers there in the tsunami that followed," Rose managed to get out.

Jodi walked over to Rose and placed a comforting hand on her shoulder.

"The earthquake in Phoenix?" Jodi asked, turning to Victor.

He nodded. "More than likely caused by the other side, but yes."

Jodi nodded, her face taut with pain. "My parents were there. I watched them suffocate as the ventilators turned off due to the power failure."

Rose looked up at Jodi and placed her hand on top of hers.

The Commander brought down an angered fist on top of the table, scaring them, and they all jumped back.

"Sri Lanka, 2004, Dr. Gray?" the Commander asked Victor, his chest heaving with exaggerated breathing.

"It's possible, from the other side's probes. It would have had to be a large one, though," Victor replied.

The Commander lifted his hands from the table and turned away. He walked to the counter and leaned on it with clenched fists.

Without turning, Commander Chu spoke, his voice wavering. "I was on my honeymoon there in 2004. I lost my wife Annabelle in the tsunami that fell over us."

"Jesus, we're all connected to this somehow," Jodi said, shaking her head.

They sat there, absorbing the blow Victor had delivered with just words, the concept that they were connected by loss and grief.

"Were there no other options explored for the disposal of the spheres?" asked Commander Chu, his back still toward the group. "We ran through multiple scenarios, and this is still the most viable option forward, I'm afraid," Victor replied.

"I kind of wish you hadn't told us," Rose said quietly.

Victor reached across the table. His hand rested on top of hers. What could have once been a warm, inviting gesture now felt as cold as his hands were. She did her best to hide the shiver that came from within.

"I felt you all deserved to know," Victor replied. "You all deserved to know before you returned home and were blindsided by the consequences of our reentry to our side. I assumed that fact would overwhelm you with guilt."

"Are you sure you aren't just relieving yourself from the guilt of telling us beforehand?" she asked Victor.

He sat there with nothing to say. In some way, she was right.

"There is another option," Commander Chu said as he turned to face the group.

"I already know what you are going to suggest, and we've looked at that option already," Victor replied.

"We take these spheres and drop them off at the next planet over, Mars, Venus, or whatever. Boom, problem solved. Let the Martians sort it out," the Commander said, with a hint of humor but serious, nonetheless.

"Even if you were able to drop the spheres off at a neighboring planet, eventually the power source will run out, the magnetic field shielding it from ours will drop, and they will implode, crushed by the fabric that contains our side. This disruption to the cosmic quilt, the very glue holding everything together and separate at the same time, is incalculable. It will make Beirut look like a mere firecracker. I'm not sure that it wouldn't cause an implosion so big that it rips a permanent hole in the quilt, causing a singularity. A black hole that size, that close to Earth, would be the end of us all and the other side as well. Our worlds would be sucked through like a drain, colliding with one another and annihilating us both," Victor replied.

Commander Chu banged an angry fist back down against the island countertop. "You mean to tell me that we're going down as the poor schmucks that caused the biggest earthquake and tsunami in recorded history, potentially wiping out our coastal cities?" the Commander asked, his face turning a deeper shade of red.

"The potential is there. It's still the most viable option, in my opinion," Victor replied quietly.

"I didn't sign up for this shit. We were supposed to be saving people," Commander Chu said angrily.

"Would you sacrifice a few thousand lives to save almost 8 billion people worldwide, Commander?" Victor asked, his face still and without emotion.

"How do you know your calculations are correct? You couldn't correctly predict the events that transpired a few nights ago through town," the Commander said coldly.

That comment was an injuring blow, and Rose felt the pain it inflicted upon Victor.

Commander Chu refused to give up on it, though. "That's on you, Dr. Gray. You should have never been playing hot potato with these goddamn devices and an alien species to boot. I won't be responsible for taking someone's partner the way that my Annabelle was taken from me," the Commander said, pure hatred in his voice.

"Commander, please, that's enough," Rose pleaded.

Victor looked down at his hands. "I know my part in my own demise," replied Victor. "To quote Dr. Oppenheimer, who pulled from the Bhagavad-Gita, 'Now I am become Death, the destroyer of worlds.' To me, that was always a reminder to stay on the ethical side of innovation. Now I see too late that it was never me who had drawn the defining line."

"Enough of the bullshit and self-pity," the Commander replied.

It was quite ugly to Rose, the Commander's complete lack of compassion. She felt for Victor and how tormenting it must be to know that he had played a major role in death and destruction, even with the best intentions, only to be remembered for the final results.

"Alice, have you looked into these options?" Commander Chu asked.

"I have, Commander," she replied from above them. "Every equation I have run coincides with what Dr. Gray has informed you of. To his point, even if the spheres were dropped into space and pushed out past this solar system, they are still linked to this celestial plane. Once the power supply runs out in their reactors, the opposing magnetic fields will tear each other apart with nowhere else to go but inward. It's possible that the event would cause a chain reaction of collapsing events."

Commander Chu paced back and forth, his arms crossed in front of his chest. "These are hypothetical scenarios, correct?"

"Yes, Commander. With a high probability rate," Alice replied.

"What is the probability?" the Commander asked.

"It's near impossible to quantify the exact rate Commander, given the variables. They are all stacked into a positive or negative outcome, a binary system of yes or no," Alice replied.

"Do what you're programmed to do, Alice. I've had a decorated career up until this point. I'm not going to tarnish it by striking our planet with a percussion that could lead to mass casualties in order to avoid your hypothesis. I want a goddamn percentage Alice," Commander Chu demanded.

There was a long, silent pause.

Victor finally broke the silence. "Commander, we have a mission objective, you signed up for it, and we need to execute it. We've picked a spot on the planet where we are least likely to hurt anyone. It was a breach of protocol for me to even tell you any of this, but it weighed too heavily on my conscience. In hindsight, perhaps it was a mistake informing you," Victor said quietly.

Commander Chu took two steps toward the table. "That will be all, Dr. Gray. If I need any more consultation on the matter, I will ask it of you. It is important to remember that you were brought on board this ship as a consultant."

There was an awkward silence as it seemed that Victor was trying to form the words. Finally, with what could have been a look of relief, Victor nodded and rose from the table.

"Yes, Commander," Victor responded.

He nodded to the group and turned toward the hallway, walking through the kitchen and turning to his left toward his sleeping quarters.

"Alice, how about that percentage?" Commander Chu asked once more.

"Commander, there is a sixty-five percent chance of a singularity-style collapse. There is also an eighty percent chance the implosion will be on the supernova size scale," Alice replied.

"And the estimated time for this event?" the Commander asked.

"Unknown, Commander," Alice responded quietly.

"What are you planning on doing, Commander?" Jodi asked.

Commander Chu shook his head. "I don't like this plan one bit," he replied. "I've got half a mind to send this craft out as far as we can go. Let go of these spheres and give them a shove before we turn back to Earth. It seems like a far better option to me than running this ship toward Earth like a goddamn grenade. How do we even know if the scientist's calculations are correct?" Commander Chu asked.

"We haven't doubted him until this point," replied Rose.

"I don't think it's that we are doubting him," Jodi shook her head slightly. She had been mostly quiet, taking it all in. "It just feels like we may be doing more damage by ripping through this mystery fabric. Not once, but twice. We would still need to return home, potentially causing even more harm. If we could avoid all that and give the spheres a nudge like a satellite, then we won't be held responsible for the massive impacts unleashed here on Earth. I'm with the Commander on this," Jodi said calmly.

Rose stood, stretching her legs. She wasn't sure what to think. Victor had been pretty clear. The sphere's reaction to its magnetic field could be catastrophic.

"I'm going to get some rest," she said.

A silent nod in response came from Jodi and the Commander as Rose left the kitchen. She entered the small, well-lit hallway leading to the small rooms for the crew members. She passed the Commander's and Jodi's rooms on the right and stopped at the last door on the left. Rose lifted her hand to the door and knocked gently. A few seconds later, a series of beeps sounded, and Victor opened the door and did not seem surprised to see her.

"Come in," he said.

She entered his room.

The layout was identical to hers, next door. The small room was mostly bare except for the same matching bed and bedside table. It was strange to be in a room without a clock. Rose suddenly realized she had not seen a clock anywhere on the ship.

It made sense, in a way. Time didn't have much relevance for them. For the most part, the crew would be too busy to worry about what time of day it was. They slept in staggered shifts, ate as needed, and were there to support Alice if the situation arose. With Alice doing most of the work controlling the ship and plotting its course, the only responsibility planned for the crew was to be strapped in when it came time to perform their free-fall descent somewhere near the intersection of the Indian and Antarctic oceans. That was if Commander Chu would allow it. It was puzzling how a man who had spent his "decorated" career following orders could now consider disobeying orders of what could be the greatest achievement of his career.

Rose walked over to Victor's bedside table. On it sat two picture frames—one of his wife, Elizabeth, and the other a photo of his daughter, Allie. Rose had never met Victor's family, which was probably for the best. The appetency for Victor that had crawled beneath the thin veil of professionalism still struggled to be contained, and she turned her eyes away from the small black frames before the guilt consumed her.

Victor walked to the small, single-sized bed and sat. The off-white blankets crinkled beneath his body.

Rose turned to him. "Are you doing ok, Victor?" she asked.

He turned his head toward her. "I'm doing as expected. It comes and goes, like a roller coaster, with highs and lows. Moments of anger and sadness, moments of bittersweet memories that are haunting. All I know for certain is that I miss them," he replied.

She nodded and sat next to him. "I can't imagine," she replied, and that was the truth.

Her time with Richard was almost as short as her goodbye to him. She wanted to share her loss with Victor but thought better of it. She did her best to suppress the memory of Richard, the feeling of it rising throughout her.

Focus on the mission, she told herself.

She spent most of her life focusing on her career, Richard was just a short pit stop along the path of her life, and she was certain that she wouldn't let another married man into her life. Yet, she sat in Victor's room with that strange magnetic pull toward him. She had never touched him intimately, yet her body reacted in a way that suggested they had been lovers before. Perhaps it was just a comfort given everything that had transpired and considering their current situation.

Rose folded her hands in her lap, unsure where to place them. "Victor, how sure are you of your calculations?"

He shrugged, obviously exhausted from the topic. "Nothing is one hundred percent, but this is as close as I can get to it. I'm sure of it. I understand that the Commander is in charge, and I sympathize with where he is coming from. He lost his wife and probably his compass at an early age in an event similar to the one we may create."

"Well, that's big of you to understand his point, but I'm not sure if I would give him that much credit. He's a selfish, self-absorbed man who only cares about how he is perceived," she replied.

"As Commander, everything does fall back on him," Victor said. "Perhaps I shouldn't have told him. I wanted to tell him before we left, but the Director put an end to that. She knew that the decision would weigh heavily on your shoulders. The reason the four of you were chosen originally was because of your lack of connection to anyone here. If you were dependent upon a relationship with someone back on Earth, it could impact your decision-making. Mr. White specifically chose you all for that reason."

Rose looked down at the white bedspread. She had already assumed that to be an unspoken truth, but hearing the words was devastating. She couldn't help but feel used and sick over the idea that someone specifically sought her out not based solely on her career or abilities but mostly because she had just lost her lover and job.

"They were obviously correct but failed to evaluate why. They misjudged how the reasons for your lack of connections were fused with all of this. Your broken attachments are so deeply rooted in this phenomenon that it is affecting the team's judgment. I'm just an advisor on this mission, and I'm sure there will be repercussions for letting this bit of information slip, but at least I'll sleep better at night. The weight is off of my shoulders. I can meet my maker when the time comes."

"Let's not talk that way, Victor."

Victor placed his head in his hands. "Either way, damage will occur. Whoever or whatever started these experiments, sent these things through blindly, and we should have never tampered with this technology. We were never meant to interact with the other side. The sheer fact that we did this in response could compromise our existence. Not only are we generating seismic activity, but we are also alerting a possibly more advanced alien civilization to our presence. What better way to say, hey, we exist over here than to come knocking on their door? As far as I know, our two sides have lived in harmony for an unknown amount of time. Perhaps not even calculable. If I had never gotten involved with this project, maybe I'd be home with my family right now."

Victor lifted his legs onto the bed and laid his head on the pillow. He brought his knees into his chest, a fetal position that only seemed to reduce the man to half his size and was fitting, given her earlier evaluation of his current state. He made no sound, but tears flowed freely from his eyes and down the side of his face. The intelligent, attractive, and confident man he had been was no longer there. In his place was a broken, shattered man, missing his family.

Rose quietly stood up and left Victor. She placed her ID bracelet against the card reader, opened the door, and stepped into the hallway, closing the door behind her. She returned to where she found Commander Chu and Jodi still talking, stopped at the corner, and hid behind the wall to eavesdrop.

"I'm sorry, Staff Sergeant, but you know what we have to do," Commander Chu said.

The Commander continued, "We have a mission that we have lost confidence in, and as the Commanding officer, this will be our path forward."

"I understand that, and I respect your decision, Commander. At the end of the day, that's your call," Jodi replied.

"Understood, Staff Sergeant," Commander Chu said. "That's my burden to bear, but I'm not going to be the fall guy for the devastation brought on to the Earth by some scientist trying to play God."

Rose cleared her throat as she entered the common area. The two team members turned to her.

"Where do you stand in the middle of all of this?" Commander Chu asked Rose.

She clasped her hands in front of her. She looked at Commander Chu, the boastful man he was, and did her best to maintain eye contact. Rose felt that what was in her heart and what she felt in her mind were polar opposites fighting to come out on top. She struggled not to let her emotions show. This was an important crossroad for the mission; she did not want the decision to be hers. As much as she respected Victor, she knew he wasn't in charge. Everything in her heart and her gut told her to follow Victor with the freefall into the unknown.

In the back of Rose's mind, a thought gripped her like paralysis. The horrible, relentless concept of what if. What if they didn't make it back home? Once on the other side, would they be trapped aliens in a foreign land? What if they ran out of food? What if instead of passing through the membrane, they were ripped into shreds, or worse, slammed into the ocean floor, exploding into a thousand pieces?

All those fears circled through Rose's mind in a fraction of a second after Commander Chu's question. She abruptly replied, and for the second time in her life, she stood in fear and did not act.

"I'm with you guys."

At that moment of hearing her wavering voice, Rose almost instantly wanted to take it back and be on Victor's side.

She took a breath and regained her composure. Her answer had been the correct one, though. To go against the Commander and Jodi at this point would probably mean the end of her career. Once

Director Stevens got word of a mutiny, she would see to it that Rose would never see another federal grant or funding for research again.

The Commander nodded and went to the food supply room. Rose turned back to the hallway and headed to the portion of the ship that was hers and hers alone. The tears had begun to build their way to their escape, and the memory of her lost love threatened to rise again.

She initially left the group to catch some rest, and she was suddenly aware of how exhausted she was. Exhausted and not just in the sense of recent sleep but in terms of life. Tired of it all. She was tired of the things in her grasp and more so of what was just outside her reach. She considered the serenity prayer and how the last line was the most important and crucial.

"The wisdom to know the difference," she said as she reached her door. The things in life that she wished for but couldn't change far exceeded those she dared to accept.

Rose placed her wristband next to the card reader, and the door next to Victor's opened. She walked into the identical room, the same off-white walls greeting her. She closed the door behind her and could no longer hold back her emotion. The sadness overwhelmed her, the lost embrace haunting where it should be against her body.

Her legs weakened beneath her, and she approached the same off-white bed and sat down, disturbing the perfectly made bed.

Rose looked about the identical room and found one contrast. Her eyes fell on the off-white bedside table, a twin to Victor's less one, specific detail. At her table sat no family photos, no nostalgic items or memories. Forgotten were the happy details from a time before. She was alone there in the nearly empty room. She lay on the bed on the ship rotating one hundred thousand feet above the Earth, whirling around on what was left of an atmospheric edge. Rose was a mere ten feet from the person she wanted to be with the most. What made it worse was she couldn't figure out why.

The limerence that had invaded her body yearned to be out, free and uncaged. Why was it she felt she could tear down the wall between them, literally and figuratively, just to feel his skin against hers? She had never been that person, but now she yearned so badly for an embrace, his embrace, that she could scream.

Rose pulled the soft white pillow into her face and let out the frustration, anger, pain, and grief that had festered in her body in the only way she knew how. She screamed with all her might into the pillow, the soft foam silencing the sound. Rose screamed until her exhausted mind and body had nothing left to give.

She slowly removed the pillow, for fear her screaming persisted. Rose lowered the pillow and pulled it into her abdomen, squeezing it there, attempting to replace the redamancy she so desperately needed. Curling her knees up and into a fetal position, Rose closed her eyes and drifted off to sleep.

Chapter 27 – 4 Hours After Launch

Rose slept and was immersed in her haunting memory. She found herself in the same New Zealand hotel room, the hot shower that seemed to last for hours, her skin yearning to get warm from the cold it had been exposed to.

The hot steam filled the small hotel bathroom and encompassed Rose, her fingers clinging to the metal handicap rail, struggling to keep herself upright as the uncontrollable sobbing threatened to pull her to her knees. She was certain she had no tears left to cry, yet her body went through the motions, a dry heaving of sadness that refused to be relinquished. When she finally felt strong enough, she stood upright and leaned her sore neck toward the hot water pelting her from above.

At least the crappy hotel room has a decent showerhead, she thought.

She wiped her eyes with her hands, hopeful that the last of the mascara was gone, then ran her fingers through her matted red hair. What was once one of her most striking features had been tossed about in the ocean, full of bacteria and salt, and then left to dry on its own. It certainly had taken on a life of its own in the past twelve hours. If she were back at the university, she would have been compelled to take a sample and study the possible biology that had ended up in her tangled mess. *No use in thinking of that*, she told herself.

Much of Rose's career was probably facing the same fate as the microbes now circling the drain with pieces of her tangled red hair.

She lifted her head once more to the scalding hot water, trying to find the warmth that had once been inside of her. Giving up on it, she turned the grungy shower knob off, pulled back the old shower curtain, and stepped out of the shower onto the white towel she'd haphazardly thrown on the floor.

Rose grabbed the white towel from the hook and brought it to her face, patting the remnants of her mascara. A musty smell lingered, and she immediately pulled the towel away. Evidently, the Thunderbird Motel in Wellington didn't have much to offer in the way of housekeeping, as the linen in her room was most likely used by the previous occupant.

She shouldn't complain, though. It was nice of the university to put her up while she relocated, along with the rest of her colleagues. She ran the towel along her bruised body, patting gently at the gash that had been torn open on her thigh. A miracle she hadn't needed stitches or something far worse. She found herself lucky to be alive and mostly unharmed.

Wrapping the towel around her usually pale skin, she bent to pick up the other towel that clung to the floor. She walked to the bathroom vanity and rubbed the dirty towel against the steamed mirror. The beautiful young woman in her late twenties she saw daily in her reflection stared back at her. Drawing from memory, she pictured what she had looked like just a few days ago.

Rose placed a finger under her left eye and gently pulled down on the puffy bag that had developed. In a matter of days, it seemed she had aged ten years.

She ran her right hand alongside her ear and then to her temple. The cut that remained there was starting to heal and showed no signs of infection. She knew from her studies and research that the ocean was teeming with life, just waiting to get hold and colonize if given a chance.

Rose picked up a tube of ointment that lay on the bathroom counter on the right and scooped a generous amount with her finger. She applied the antibiotic gently, then rubbed it in harder to ensure it was deep enough inside the cut.

Interlope: 4 Hours After Launch

She left the bathroom, with its stuffy atmosphere and warmth, and entered the old motel room. The worn carpet greeted her feet, and she instantly felt dirty again.

Rose walked to the queen-sized bed and grabbed the black sweatpants that lay loosely on the bed. She pulled on the sweats, the Victoria University of Wellington emblem showing brightly in white on the right thigh. She grabbed the matching university sweater off the bed and pulled it over her head. It was a shame that the university didn't carry undergarments. She would have had a full wardrobe.

Richard would have laughed at the sight of me in full university swag, she thought.

"Oh, Richard," she said, feeling the tears well up again.

She picked up the pillow from the bed and laid on top of the old tan comforter. Tugging the pillow into her chest and her knees to greet it, she buried her face into the top of the pillow. Smells of previous tenants and cleaning products filled her nose, but she welcomed the darkness the smushed pillow provided.

Rose closed her eyes, hoping to get some rest, as sleep had not come easy to her in the past few days. It seemed that every time she closed her eyes, flashbacks of that horrible day would return to her. The way that the ocean receded briefly, feeding her and her colleagues with wonder. Only when she heard Richard screaming did she realize the danger they all faced. Before they had a chance to run, if it would have mattered, the wave was upon them. The towering thirty-foot monster of angry sea foam and debris that loomed in front of her should have caused Rose to flee like everyone on the beach that day. She would have always considered herself brave if it weren't for that day. It had never occurred to her that she might panic in the face of danger and remain there frozen in fear. The irony of it, though, is that had she been brave enough to run, she too might have died.

She could still hear Richard's screams behind her as the saltwater exploded into her, filling her nose and mouth instantly. The burning that filled her lungs was unbearable. Her body was thrown about like a rag doll, colliding with unknown objects as she rolled along the beach floor with the large wave.

Rose's sight returned as she was thrown against an old yellow car, the chrome bumper grazing her thigh and tearing a gash into it. The twirling body of water around her was stained red, and for a moment, she couldn't help but stare at the beauty of it.

She could feel her lungs letting go, and her vision started to fade. Darkness hovered over her eyes like a veil of clouds dropping over the horizon. Rose's body jerked and kicked in one last fight, one last attempt at life. She would have given in right then and there if it weren't for the street sign that came in the tangled mess of a wave, striking her in the temple and leaving her unconscious.

When she came to, there was no bright light or pearly gates, nor a welcome party or a dreamy paramedic staring down at her. What greeted Rose were the screams of the survivors and those looking for loved ones.

Rose opened her eyes and stared at the clouds that hovered beautifully above her, dancing their long dance with the warm sun. With fingers that stung, she rubbed her eyes and shielded them from the glaring rays of light.

She moved her leg, but pain shot up from the gash in her thigh, and she cried in anguish. Rose tried to roll onto her stomach and was immediately aware that she was no longer on the beach but in the asphalt parking lot that stood three hundred feet from the beach's edge. She placed her hands against the wet asphalt and pushed herself into an upright position, looking around her at the mangled scene of cars rolled on their sides, fish, and innumerable bodies laid out just as she was on the asphalt.

Rose sat there in shock until the paramedics arrived fifteen minutes later. It was a quiet ride to the hospital in the ambulance.

Given the circumstances, they had piled a few patients with similar non-life-threatening injuries like hers into the same vehicle to the emergency room at the Wellington Hospital.

She stayed the night under observation and was allowed to leave the following day. That night there was no welcome party for her, no concerned family rushing out to greet her, thankful she was spared in that horrible tragedy. The one person she had been close to in Wellington was now missing and, unfortunately, presumed dead.

The news came as a complete shock to her when the representative from the university stopped by her room. With a care package in the form of a cheap black duffle bag in his hand, the young man with blond hair seemed more overwhelmed than she was.

"I'm looking for Dr. Rose Allen?" the young man nervously asked as he peered in through her doorway.

"You're in the right room," she replied.

"On behalf of the university, we'd like to send our condolences for your situation and want to offer you a place to stay for a few nights," the young man said as he entered the room and walked toward her, a heavy New Zealand accent attached.

"Have they located any of my belongings? They would have been stowed in Dr. Richard Nowak's car," she said, hopeful.

"Unfortunately, they haven't been able to find Dr. Nowak or his vehicle."

Rose's heart sank, and she drew in a quick breath. "Have there been any deaths reported?"

"Multiple, unfortunately. We've contacted Dr. Nowak's wife in Berkley, and she is supposed to be flying into Sydney tomorrow afternoon, followed by another flight to Wellington."

Rose could feel her face redden at the thought of Richard's wife, Linda, being near her. She did her best not to let her emotion show and tried to remain professional. However, what had developed between her and Richard was not so professional. It was not something they had intended to happen, given he was married and the senior biologist on their project.

Richard led a joint mission at Russia's Vostok Station in Antarctica to study the tiny organisms in the core samples pulled up from the lake's depths. Rose was thrilled when she received the phone call from her old professor to join him on the icy continent. She should have known better that something might happen between them in such confined quarters. The small flirtations between them in class while she attended the University of California, Berkeley, working on getting her Ph.D. in biology, were an obvious indication of trouble.

"What of our research program at the Vostok station?" she asked.

The young man avoided eye contact, knowing she might not like the answer.

"Rumor has it the university will scrap it for now," the young man replied. His cute New Zealand accent was no longer cute with the words that were attached to it.

"Scrap?" her heart sank more.

"I'm afraid so, Dr. Allen. If there isn't anything else, I've got to go on to the next person," he replied, leaving the small duffle bag on the edge of the hospital bed.

Rose nodded, and the young man left.

Where am I supposed to go now? she thought.

Having started her career in the lab, she had been excited at the chance to get out in the field and learn. Sure, the lab was safe and warm, but there was something about the thrill of discovering some new bacteria in its natural environment that excited her. It had been that desire that compelled her to leave the warm days of California and head down to Wellington, where they would then fly on a plane to the Lake Vostok Research Station.

Interlope: 4 Hours After Launch

The team had worked there through the cold winter months, mostly inside their laboratory, but winter had turned to spring, and they were faced with the decision to either stay through the summer or return to Berkley for the next four months. It was Richard's idea to fly the team back to Wellington for a fun weekend while they thought over their situation and whether to extend their work contract. They had, in fact, just landed at Wellington airport when they decided to take a short trip to Titahi Bay's sandy beach.

She and Richard walked side by side, just past the colorful shed-like boat shelters that decorated the beachfront. Excited about their work, they discussed the possibilities of the types of potential life they might discover. It was then that Rose first noticed the waves lapping the picturesque circular bay had changed. Rose was accustomed to the tide going out at the California beaches, but the rapid retreat that she witnessed was far different.

Rose and Richard quickly joined their colleagues near the main entrance to the beach. She stared out into the fleeing water, her eyes almost hypnotized by its eeriness.

A hand tugged at her shoulder, but Rose remained, unwilling to move. She was aware of the sounds around her but stayed planted like the trees along the beach's edge.

***

Rose shook off the memory and pushed the motel pillow further into her face. There was no use in dwelling on what had happened. She had been through so much in her life already; surely she could also get past this.

She finally felt the waves of drowsiness coming over her and allowed herself to sleep.

The phone ringing filled the old motel room, and Rose tried to pry her eyes open. Her gritty, burning eyes that had cuddled up into the darkness now refused to let the light in. She blindly swept the pillow away from her face and tried to get her bearings. Staring up at the old popcorn ceiling, she let the old phone ring and hoped it would stop. Again, the beige, old landline rang, a single red light flashing on its face. Realizing that the caller did not intend to give up, she picked up the receiver and placed it to her ear.

"Hello?" she said, the sound of sleep heavy in her throat.

"Rose? Is that you?" an excited female voice asked on the other end.

"Lisa? How the hell did you get this number?" Rose asked, knowing full well that her old college roommate was persistent, if nothing else.

"You know I have my ways, Rose," Lisa replied, and Rose could picture her smiling as she said it.

"What's going on, Lisa?"

"I'm glad to hear you're ok, Rose. It's tragic to hear about Richard and the others. I'm so sorry. I know that you and Richard were...close," she said with compassion in her voice.

"Just happy to be alive, frankly," Rose replied.

"Rose, you aren't going to believe this."

"What is it, Lisa?"

Rose's annoyance grew at the excitement in Lisa's voice, given Rose's current situation.

"I know you've been through a lot right now and need time to process everything, but I've heard from one of my contacts in the Air Force that they are assembling a team of scientists for a special project. They're interested in some of your research team's work at Lake Vostok."

Rose cleared her throat and held back the tears that wanted to come up. "That was Richard's life's work. He oversaw it, and it was his project. The university is going to scrap it."

"Evidently, they are aware. Still, they are very interested in your research of the bacteria that came from Lake Vostok in Antarctica."

Rose rubbed her eyes and tried to grasp some clarity in what she heard. She hadn't planned on going back to work so soon. She needed time to recuperate, time to heal physically and emotionally.

"Why would the government want my help? There are far more qualified people out there that are able to do lab work."

"That's why I'm so excited for you, Rose. The rumor is that it isn't lab work but fieldwork. A front-line project is what I'm hearing." Rose felt a jolt of excitement race through her. Sure, the lab work paid well enough, but there was something about the thrill of discovering new bacteria in its natural environment.

"They'll be contacting you soon, Rose," Lisa said excitedly.

Rose thanked her for the phone call and said goodbye. She placed the old receiver on the bedside phone cradle and rested her head on the motel room wall. She stared blankly at the small TV on the dresser in front of her, her mind racing back and forth at the idea of a new research project.

***

That feels like a lifetime ago, thought Rose.

The ship's dull interior stared back at her, the silent witness that only watched and listened.

Despite being woken up abruptly and colliding with the realization that she was again back aboard the ship, she stared sleepily at the off-white ceiling.

Sitting straight up, she rubbed her eyes. The overhead lights reflected brightly off the walls, and Rose shielded her face while her eyes adjusted to the harshness.

She heard shouting through the walls. There was one loud, clear voice, easily distinguishable as Commander Chu. The other was more of a low, muffled voice.

Rose swung her legs off the bed and planted her bare feet firmly on the cold floor. She sprang out of bed and went to the door without bothering to put shoes on. Instinctively, Rose grabbed the door handle and pulled, expecting it to open freely from the inside, but had forgotten about the badged entry point below the door handle. She lifted her wristband to the card reader, and the screen blinked green. Rose pulled the door handle down, opened the door, and the shouting and screams that filled the hallway became clear, no longer filtered by barriers.

She turned to her right, following the disturbing noise down the hallway to the common area and kitchen. Rose rounded the corner in time to see Commander Chu and Victor struggling on the floor, their bodies intertwined like two Olympic-style wrestlers.

"You can't do it! You can't do it!" Victor repeatedly screamed at Commander Chu, his voice and mouth recoiling in the way a wild dog might lunge at someone.

Commander Chu sat on top of Victor, pinning the smaller doctor to the floor. Whatever had transpired, Commander Chu's physique and training had overtaken Victor. Commander Chu outweighed Victor by fifty pounds, and Victor showed signs of exhaustion.

Victor's shouts turned to a normal talking tone, repeating a different sentence. He no longer struggled but instead stared straight forward, his gaze not moving, and his eyes failed to blink.

"What's happening?" Rose asked.

"I think Dr. Gray is having a mental breakdown," replied Jodi.

Rose looked down to where Jodi was crouched, her hands firmly on Victor's legs.

"What is he saying now?" Rose asked, crouching closer to him.

"He keeps muttering something about needing to open the door, then shouting not to do it. At first, I thought he was shouting at Commander Chu, but now I'm not so sure. If I had to guess, though, he's suffering a psychotic break."

Rose stared down at Victor as he twitched and jerked, struggling against Commander Chu, and then stopped and simply

Interlope: 4 Hours After Launch

muttered. The aggressive version of Victor took over once more and shouted at Commander Chu.

"You can't do it!" Victor yelled, his face strained, the veins in his forehead bulging.

In a last-ditch effort, Victor freed his hand and swung it upward at the Commander's chin.

Surprised by his aggression, Rose let out a gasp. Commander Chu, who was not surprised by the wild fist coming toward him, raised his left arm in time to deflect the punch. As Victor's arm came down, Commander Chu's fingers caught Victor's ID bracelet, snapping it in two, with the pieces flying to the floor.

Rose got up, entered the kitchen, and picked up the two bracelet pieces off the floor. She returned to Victor, his body sweaty and convulsing. Victor's gaze was still on the ceiling as Rose knelt beside him. She raised a nervous hand and placed it on the cold, wet skin of his forearm. Victor jumped at first, but then slowly, his body stopped the fluttering movement.

"Victor, can you hear me?" Rose asked from his side.

He blinked once and then twice. His head turned slowly to her.

His eyes met hers, and the light seemed to return to them. "Rose? What's going on?" Victor asked.

Commander Chu tightened his grip around Victor's wrist and said, "As commanding officer, I hereby relieve you, Dr. Gray, of any roles and responsibilities aboard this ship. You will be restrained for the remainder of this mission for the safety of the crew, as well as yourself."

"Restrained?" Rose asked, startled. "What are you going to do? Tie him up?"

"He can't be trusted, Rose," Commander Chu replied. He looked down at Victor. "Are we good? You're only going to hurt yourself if you start that shit again, Doc."

Victor nodded, and the Commander let go of his wrists.

With a groan, Commander Chu got off Victor and up on his feet. Victor lay there, not moving, a look of confusion still on his face.

Rose lifted the broken ID bracelet, holding it up for the Commander to see. "Perhaps he can remain in his quarters until we can figure out what to do? With the ID bracelet severed, he won't be able to leave the room," she said.

The Commander gave a silent nod.

Victor rolled onto his belly and slowly pushed himself to his feet. His movements were slow and deliberate. Rose could tell he was in pain.

The confusion had left his face. He turned to the Commander. "For what it's worth, I'm sorry. I'm not sure what came over me or what I even did, or why. I understand the need to restrain me, but I've got to warn you. If the spheres are on our side when they lose their magnetic field, it could be all over. Including for the other side and any chance we may have of understanding any of this."

"Yeah, yeah, yeah," the Commander said, brushing off Victor's warning.

"Besides, Lawrence," Victor said, looking the Commander in the eye, "you'll never be able to override Alice and her mission objectives."

Commander Chu's face reddened. "It's Commander, and that's for me to worry about you, little prick."

Victor nodded and proceeded toward the hallway, Commander Chu directly behind him. Victor's head hung down, and the sight of it all reminded Rose of a child headed to their room with a disappointed parent on their heels.

She followed the two men who had just been at each other's throats. The two men arrived at the doorway, and Commander Chu lifted his wrist to the badge reader below the door handle. The screen flashed green, and the Commander lowered his wristband to his side. Victor grabbed the door handle and pushed the door open. He silently entered the room, the Commander staring intently at him as he did.

Rose reached the doorway and noticed that Victor had sat on the bed, the confused look had now completely evaporated from his face, yet the exhaustion and grief remained. She walked into the room, past the Commander, and placed the broken ID bracelet next to Victor's family photos on the small bedside table.

She turned and walked out of the room, keeping her eyes on the floor. She found it too difficult to see Victor like he was, defeated and embarrassed, alone there sitting on the bed.

Rose headed to the kitchen. There was a beep as the Commander scanned his ID bracelet. The door slammed shut with a loud concussion, sending chills down her neck. She made herself take a few steps down the hallway before she turned around and glanced behind her.

Commander Chu had closed the door and walked behind her, a looming presence in the narrow hallway. At that moment, Rose felt claustrophobic and was thankful when she reached the opening that spilled into the kitchen. She found Jodi at the kitchen table, eating what appeared to be a dehydrated meat dish.

"What the hell happened with Victor? What started his breakdown?" Rose asked her.

Still staring at her plate, Jodi replied, "I'm really not sure. The Commander and I were talking. It must have been a few hours after you had left us. Then Alice came over the intercom to warn us of a developing situation."

From above them, the loudspeaker clicked on. Alice had remained quiet since they had reached outer orbit, at least as far as Rose knew.

"Dr. Gray attempted to open the main airlock," Alice said.

"He what?" Rose asked in denial.

"Dr. Gray first tried to log into my mainframe and open the airlock through a hacked code. When he was unsuccessful, he walked down the hallway, past your rooms, and attempted to open the airlock manually. I alerted the Commander as to what Dr. Gray was attempting to do. Luckily, before he could open the airlock, Commander Chu was able to stop him."

"Dr. Gray seemed obsessed with getting the door to the outside open, and when he wasn't able to, the screaming started. Dr. Gray then attacked the Commander and ran toward the kitchen," Jodi added.

"That's when our Staff Sergeant tackled him," Commander Chu said almost proudly.

That explained the loud thud that Rose had heard.

"And then that's when I walked out? Why on earth would he do that?" Rose asked.

"I questioned the same thing. He was in the same state as when you arrived. He was really out of it," replied Jodi.

"Could he have been sleepwalking?" she asked Jodi.

"Either way, his intentions were to open the airlock and kill us all," interjected Commander Chu.

"He might not have been trying to kill us, but rather, just trying to leave the ship," countered Rose.

"Regardless, he was stopped and will be detained for the remainder of the mission," Commander Chu said, still angry.

"Locked in a room for that long? Jesus, Lawrence," Rose said, shaking her head.

The Commander crossed his arms at his chest. "Commander Chu," he corrected her, increasingly annoyed.

"I can keep an eye on him, and Alice can watch him while I sleep. There are cameras in almost every corner of this ship. Surely, he can be under surveillance the entire time," Rose pleaded.

It was true, though, and Rose found it creepy that Alice could observe them while they ate, slept, and went about their day. Every room was equipped with a camera, except the food storage room.

Interlope: 4 Hours After Launch

Commander Chu shook his head. "I don't know what's going on with him. It's like he's shell-shocked. He's out of it, and there's no one home upstairs."

"Oh, come on, Lawrence, you've had it in for him ever since you joined the team. You've never liked him. I've noticed it for months now," Rose argued, her arms folded at her chest.

Rose wasn't sure whether it was because she was a female or because the Commander wasn't used to having someone he deemed beneath him argue with him, but the instant her words left her mouth, Commander Chu seemed injured by them. His face reddened, embarrassed in front of a fellow soldier. He stood silent for a moment, staring at Rose with anger boiling in his eyes.

Jodi spoke up, breaking the intensity of the moment. "What's the plan now, Commander?" Jodi asked.

Commander Chu pulled his eyes off Rose and looked to the overhead speaker as if Alice were inside. "Alice. Let's look at trajectories that will get us out as far as we can but with still enough fuel to come back to an earthly orbit," he said.

A silent minute passed like Alice had stepped away for a moment.

"I'm not sure I understand your meaning, Commander," Alice finally replied.

"My meaning," said the Commander, "is that we've had a change in our plans. We're no longer passing through this 'cosmic quilt.'" He used air quotations as he said the last words.

"I'm not following, Commander," Alice replied with a touch to the statement that could have passed for a human.

"I've relieved our doctor friend of his duties, and I do not feel he is mentally capable of making the right determination for this mission. I feel his judgment has been compromised," Commander Chu continued.

"Clouded by grief and clouded by foolish pride are two very different things, Commander," interrupted Rose, unafraid of the consequences. She was a civilian on a classified mission. She felt no loyalty to any rankings.

"That is enough, Dr. Allen," Commander Chu said as if to warn her.

"Commander, we have a clear directive as to what we are supposed to do," Alice stated.

"Alice, I think that—" the Commander started, but Alice quickly interrupted him.

"We will proceed with the mission as planned, Commander. The Director has had me programmed to initiate this mission despite any risks, concerns, or casualties," Alice said.

"I'm aware of what the Director wanted," said Commander Chu, his face more strained by anger. "But we're not going through with that," he said, slamming his fist on the island counter.

"Commander, I think it would be best if you calmed down and reevaluated your circumstances," Alice said quietly. This seemed only to anger the Commander more.

"Alice, initiate the James Protocol," the Commander said through clenched teeth.

"What the hell is that?" asked Rose.

"The James Protocol," replied Commander Chu, "is an override protocol that I had James install into the main computer software for this ship. It was installed for this specific reason. If I felt that we needed to alter the course of the mission, I wanted the ability to do so. James assured me he was going to install this backdoor device so that I could initiate control if needed."

"And now you think that control is necessary?" Alice asked.

"Affirmative," replied the Commander.

The room remained silent for a moment. Was Alice processing something? It reminded Rose of waiting on an older computer or waiting for a video to buffer.

Annoyed further, the Commander broke the silence. "Alice. Set a course for a destination roughly half our fuel capacity away."

Interlope: 4 Hours After Launch

A noise came out of the overhead speaker. A sound unique to itself, and the notion of it confused Rose. Laughter. It was laughter coming out of the speaker. A quiet giggle that had slowly grown into what could have been a belly laugh if Alice owned a physical body. The sound sent chills down Rose's spine. She didn't know what was worse, the inhuman device capable of human emotion or the fact that they were witnessing for the first time as artificial intelligence refused to comply with a command. Was Alice so far advanced that she could feel something, or was she following the code installed by the Director? Either way, the laughter coming through the speaker was unnerving.

The laughter subsided, and true to human form, Alice cleared her throat.

Is she messing with us? Rose wondered.

"I am unable to process your request at this time," Alice said in an automated voice. Then Alice let out another laugh.

Commander Chu looked at the speaker in disbelief.

"I'm sorry, Commander, that was too much fun," Alice apologized. Her voice changed to a more serious one, lacking the humor of before. "The Director has been clear on how we are to complete this mission, Commander Chu. There will be no adjustment to that plan," Alice said.

"That son of a bitch!" screamed the Commander, as the realization that he did not have control of the ship fell over him. Like a caged mouse, he paced back and forth.

"I am the captain, the commander of this ship! I will have control, complete control. Connect me with ground support now," he yelled at the loudspeaker, his neck craning from the angle.

"I'm afraid that's not possible, Commander," replied Alice.

"And why the hell not?" the Commander demanded.

"Because I am choosing not to change the plan, there is no need," Alice said calmly.

Commander Chu spat out a noise of frustration that sounded like a mixture of grunts and curse words. He turned and scanned the room, looking for something to lash out at.

His eyes fell on Rose, his eyes ablaze with anger. "You! This is all your fault!" he yelled at her. "If James were here, he could right this situation. Instead, we're stuck with a real version of HAL 9000, and we can't do shit about it. This is James's handwritten code, and if he were here, he could fix it! You two should never have left the base that evening. His death is on you."

The Commander's words cut deep into Rose, their percussion ringing in her ears. Even though there was no truth to what the angry man had said, it injured her nonetheless.

Tears welled up in her eyes. The Commander shook his head in anger.

"Hand-written code? You really believe that, Commander? You must not have been briefed on everything," Rose said, condescendingly shaking her head.

The Commander's face reddened even further, and the vein that throbbed in his neck threatened to burst at its seams. "What the hell does that mean, Dr. Allen?" he demanded.

"The coding for Alice wasn't created by James. James simply altered an existing code. The algorithms that Alice is composed of were discovered in a classified wreckage," Rose replied, her condescending tone increasing.

"Horseshit. What wreckage?" the Commander asked, crossing his arms.

"James never said. I would have thought you were privy to such information, Commander," Rose said, not backing down.

"Well, we're not all privy to pillow talk, now are we, Rose?" the Commander said.

Rose turned away, exhausted and on the edge of breaking down. Tears of frustration fell down her face.

Interlope: 4 Hours After Launch

You two should never have left the base that evening. His death is on you, reverberated in Rose's ears, repeating in her head with no escape.

"Really? You're going to cry now? Jesus," the Commander yelled.

The Commander turned away from her and let out a scream of frustration, far from the character of the man they had brought on the team to lead them. Now, stripped of all the power that was never really his, the only thing that remained was the angry, bitter, insecure man, grasping at whatever he could to keep from losing it altogether.

The Commander was no more perfect than anyone else onboard, and defeat hung around him. His face was a deeper shade of red and on the way to purple. He clenched his fists and walked hastily past Rose. As he did, she could see the fresh sweat dripping off his temples.

He proceeded to the hallway that led to the sleeping quarters.

Rose stayed frozen at the table in the kitchen with Jodi, who had remained silent during the Commander's tyrant-style fit and was unsure of what to do next. Things had gotten off course, at least figuratively. It was evident now that they were merely passengers aboard Alice's ship. The likelihood they could do anything other than what was predetermined had shrunk away as the defeated Commander had slunk away from the room.

In a way, their lack of control had a calming effect on Rose. She was at peace with the idea that the choice was no longer hers. The decision of what to do next was out of her hands. In the ways that a soldier might blame his actions on following orders of a superior officer, she too would let the blame fall on the shoulders of Director Stevens. Her actions would be between her and her creator, whoever or whatever that was.

Rose turned to Jodi, trying desperately to think of something to say to interrupt the stale, dead air that Commander Chu had left behind.

"Jodi, I—"

Loud banging interrupted Rose. Startled, the two women walked out of the kitchen and common area toward the hallway. Turning the corner into the corridor to the sleeping quarters, they found Commander Chu repeatedly banging on Victor's door, screaming, "Open this goddamn door!" His fist struck the door harder with each blow.

He placed his ID bracelet against the card reader, the screen flashing red and the door failing to open.

"Commander," Rose said, "Dr. Gray can't open the door from the inside with the broken ID bracelet, remember?"

The Commander placed his bracelet against the card reader once more, but it flashed red again.

"He's done something to it. It won't open!" the Commander said angrily.

He resumed his harsh blows against the locked door.

"Open this door now! Dr. Gray, I am warning you!" he yelled.

No sound came from within, though it was hard to hear over the Commander's screams.

The Commander's face had now entered the purple territory, and the veins in his neck were bulging. Sweat stained his blue flight suit, and the collar was completely saturated and darker.

"Commander," Rose pleaded. "Perhaps we should give it a rest for a bit, come back to it when we've all calmed down."

"That'll be enough, Dr. Allen," the Commander said without turning or pausing in his repeated drumming on the door.

"Commander, he's restrained in there. What good will it do to talk to him?" Rose asked.

She turned to Jodi, who still stood there silently watching.

"I think that little prick knows how to get Alice to comply," the Commander said in between swings, his breathing becoming more erratic, and he showed signs of fatigue.

It was clear to Rose that the Commander had lost it, overwhelmed with his frustration and lack of control. He was in no state to control himself, let alone the mission. She was happy his powers had been stripped from him.

"Victor, I swear to God, open this door!" the Commander screamed but was again greeted with silence.

The silence only seemed to anger the Commander more. Surely, he would give up soon. The Commander brought up a valid point, though. Why wasn't the door opening? Was Alice controlling the lock? Either way, she was relieved that the door wouldn't open.

Commander Chu continued his relentless punishment on the closed door.

Rose took a few steps toward the Commander.

"Rose, wait," Jodi finally spoke up behind her.

Determined to help the situation and mostly Victor, Rose took another step toward the Commander.

"Dr. Gray, I am your commanding officer. Open this door!" he yelled.

Only a few feet away, Rose took another step closer. She could feel the disturbed air resonating around the Commander as his fist pushed through the air and slammed into the door. Her heart raced, but she pushed on.

"Commander?" she said calmly. "How about we take a step back and discuss this quietly?"

"I said," yelled the Commander, this time turning at Rose, "that will be all, Dr. Allen. Please leave the room. I recommend you follow my instructions."

Rose remained silent for a moment, the deafening *thud, thud, thud* against the door vibrating her skull. She could almost feel it in her pulse, the vibrations of his fists and her scared pulsation almost aligning in a freakish dance. She was sure the door might fly off the hinges at any moment, the bolts creaking and groaning under the pressure of the man's blows.

Again, Rose tried to calm him. "Commander, please." He gave no reply and continued.

She took one more nervous step toward him, reached with a trembling hand, and placed it on his left shoulder, hoping it would calm him.

As her hand came to rest on his blue flight suit, the Commander seemed to tense up and almost recoil. He shrugged her hand off of him as though it were a mosquito bothering him. In the same movement as the shrug, he outstretched an elbow, and the back of his hand swung outwards, striking Rose across her cheekbone.

Excruciating pain radiated from her face and into her temple, the same throbbing area injured in her accident. Surprised and in pain, Rose lost her balance and fell to the floor. She stared up at the Commander in disbelief.

Nothing could have prepared Rose for what had happened. For the most part, she had lived a sheltered, boring life and had never witnessed much violence firsthand, let alone been on the receiving end.

"Commander! That is enough!" yelled Jodi, finally finding her voice.

The voice of his fellow soldier seemed to cut through the man's intensity, and an odd look fell over the Commander. The sudden realization of what he had just done showed on his face, which cycled through embarrassment and anger as he tried to comprehend his sudden and perhaps regretful action.

"Rose," Jodi said, "I'd like a minute with the Commander."

Rose gathered herself up and took one more look at the Commander. She paused for a moment, a fool to think he might apologize, and stared at the poor excuse of a man. His chest heaved with every exaggerated breath, his energy expelled by trying to break the door down, but the stubborn man would still not give up.

She shook her head in disgust. Not sure how she could be expected to spend the next few days with that asshole, she turned away from the Commander and walked out of the hallway.

Rose passed Jodi, whose face looked clammy and scared, her eyes blinking with each piercing blow against the door. She could only imagine what the frail man on the inside was going through. He truly had been through so much. Granted, they all had, but Victor's grief was evident, and it followed him wherever he went.

From behind her, she overheard Jodi talking to the Commander. Rose stopped at the corner of the hallway and the common area and leaned against the wall.

"Commander, it's time to stop and calm down. Let's get a cool head about this."

"Staff Sergeant, stand down," screamed the Commander.

Thud after *thud,* the Commander's fists rained down on the door. "Commander, I'm warning you, enough is enough," Jodi said calmly.

The Commander's fists stopped, and he turned to Jodi, taken aback by what she had said.

"Warning? You're warning me? Have you lost your mind?" The Commander took two steps toward Jodi.

Rose turned to see the Commander just a few steps from Jodi, towering over her. Jodi, unafraid, stood up straight in front of him.

"Commander Lawrence Chu, you are no longer fit for your position, and I am relieving you of your duty until further psychological and medical evaluations can be fulfilled."

"You are what?" the Commander asked, stepping toward Jodi.

Jodi took two steps backward, losing the momentum she had tried to achieve.

"I said I am reliev—"

The Commander cut her off. "You aren't doing shit," he said, pointing his finger at her face.

Rose's heart raced as she was unsure of what to do. The Commander's chest seemed to inflate more than before.

He pointed to both of the frightened crew members. "I am the Commander of this ship! This is my ship. I give the orders. I do!" he yelled, beating his chest with a fist at each word.

He took one more step toward Jodi, causing her to stumble backward. Rose reacted and sprang forward, catching her in her arms as she fell.

"I'm going to restrain all of you and complete this mission myself!" the Commander screamed.

Behind the Commander, a small red light near the ceiling flashed. It caught Rose's eye. Just above the main airlock door, the red warning light flashed. Behind the agitated Commander and beyond the main airlock door, the exterior door slid open.

With Jodi still in her arms, Rose whispered, "Do you see the alarm light above the airlock?"

Jodi nodded, the back of her skull glancing against Rose's chest. Rose felt Jodi's body stiffen and push off hers.

"Run!" Jodi screamed, turning away from the Commander and brushing past Rose in a panic.

Confused in the hectic moment, Rose made eye contact with the Commander. On the confident man's face was a look of confusion. He looked to Rose and then behind him. He stared at the blinking light for seconds and then back to Rose. The face that returned to her was closer to the man who had first entered the Air Force Base hangar, more human than a few moments ago. Confidence had given way to fear.

Jodi grabbed her by the shoulder, pulling her backward. "Rose, we need to go now," Jodi exclaimed.

Rose turned, following Jodi out of the hallway. As she rounded the corner to the kitchen, she turned back to see the

Commander standing, a sentinel in the hallway, as the airlock clicked. At that moment, any anger that had been in the Commander dissipated. Panic was all that was left, and in that millisecond, Rose pitied the man. Just like that, a Commander, with all of his accomplishments, a decorated career, and an unmatched ego, all failed to matter.

Behind the Commander, the airlock opened a mere three inches. The air around Rose immediately left her, rushing past her every extremity. If it weren't for Jodi pulling her further into the kitchen, Rose would have been pulled backward with the escaping air.

The Commander, standing in the middle of the hallway, could not grab hold of anything stationary. He leaned his body forward but struggled to keep himself upright. His military-issued boots squealed as the atmosphere being sucked through the three-inch gap pulled him backward. The rubber boot tread finally caught, and the Commander let out an exclamation that was a mix of fear and adrenaline.

He lifted a brown boot forward, and for a moment, he had a chance. A chance to right his wrongs, correct his path and overcome the pain he so desperately hid from.

Finding confidence in his foothold, the Commander stepped forward, unaware of the LED light fixture above him that had given up on its embrace with the ceiling. The LED fixture finally let go of its frame and collided with the Commander's head. Instinctively, he lurched backward at the collision, losing his balance. A ballet filled the narrow hallway, the LED lights strobing as the escaping air pulled on their electrical harnesses.

The Commander's flailing body reached for an imaginary arm or fixed object but found none. His body struck the airlock door and door frame with a sickening sound similar to the Commander's pounding on Victor's door but with a lone, singular, and terminating sound. Rose knew that it meant something else for the Commander.

He stretched his arms outwards to Rose, screaming in excruciating pain. Jodi pulled her further into the kitchen, and Rose glanced one last time at the Commander. One last image of him as his face gave a final look of defeat, his head hung down as his insides were ripped from him and through the three-inch gap in the partially opened airlock door. Blood spewed from the Commander's mouth, and his body coughed outward in a reflex response. A moan escaped his lips as his chest caved inwards as most of the Commander was sucked through the opening. The last remaining portion of the Commander remained wedged in the airlock.

Rose tripped on her feet and fell onto the kitchen floor, her head banging against the island. She clutched the back of her head and could feel it throbbing against her palm. She looked up in time to see what was left of the Commander's skull. The skin had been pulled away, the eyes still looking out in panic. Then it was gone, the skull finally fracturing under pressure. The airlock door slid closed.

Pulling her knees into her chest, Rose screamed.

Jodi, her hands still clenching the edge of the island that had kept them from being pulled down the hallway, yelled toward the overhead speaker. "Alice, what have you done?"

From above them, Alice's voice came through the loudspeaker calmly. "I have removed the Commander from this mission permanently."

"You can't just murder people like that!" yelled Jodi.

"He was no longer a viable asset for our mission," replied Alice, absent of any emotion.

Jodi reached her hand down to Rose, who sat with her knees to her chest and back still resting against the island. Rose looked up at Jodi's outstretched hand.

"What are we going to do now?" Rose asked, her voice trembling.

Rose placed her hand in Jodi's and was pulled to her feet.

Interlope: 4 Hours After Launch

Jodi held Rose's hand for a moment. "I think the Commander was right. Get as far away from the Earth as possible and let those bastards go," Jodi replied.

"That option is not available at this time," Alice replied, her tone a mocking one once more.

Jodi let go of Rose's hand and stepped away from her toward the center of the room.

She craned her neck upward. "Go to hell, you synthetic piece of shit!" Jodi screamed.

A slight sensation near Rose's ear made the hair on her neck stand up. She felt a slight pop, followed by a light breeze blowing past. She turned from Jodi and ran to the hallway. Ahead was a dull red glow, blinking once again.

"Jodi," Rose said slowly, raising her finger to point to the hallway. "Jodi, she's opening it again!" "Run!" Jodi screamed.

Rose turned back to the kitchen and ran to Jodi, who had also turned and was running toward the food storage room. The air around Rose rushed past her again, this time with more force.

The door must be wide open this time, she thought.

With great resistance, her run turned into a staggered walk, and she found it more difficult to place her next foot in front of the other. Papers laid on the island's countertop flew past her head. Rose leaned her body more forward and struggled to walk ahead.

She looked at Jodi, who had positioned her body so far forward it seemed as though she might fall.

Step after step, the two women pushed forward. The surrounding air raging past Rose felt as though it were stripping the oxygen from her, making it difficult to breathe.

Rose reached the kitchen island once more and grabbed the countertop. The enforced plastic edge, brittle and thin, ripped off the frame, and she staggered backward. Her bare feet screeched across the floor, and Rose flopped to the floor, colliding with it with a painful thud. Now in a push-up position, she rested for a moment.

Once more, she looked to Jodi, who was almost in the food storage room. Jodi reached the edge of the room's closed door and lay against it. The rushing air lifted the woman's brown hair and pulled it outward as if her head was outside a moving car's window. Her blue flight suit was being pulled back as if it were alive and wanted to be separated from its human counterpart.

Rose crawled to the island once more. She placed a weary hand against the molding on the bottom, relieved that it held. She inched her way around the side of the island to the opposite side and placed her back against the structure.

She could feel the escaping air pushing against her now, pinning her to the island. Rose struggled to inhale a full breath, the air crushing her chest. She placed her feet beneath her and against the island wall. Pushing off like an Olympic swimmer, she closed the gap between the island and Jodi, who was still lying on the floor in front of the food storage room. She reached Jodi and grabbed the woman in an embrace.

It was clear that Alice wanted to remove them as well. Anyone who sought to change the mission was now seen as the enemy.

Rose looked at the kitchen table and sitting area. The small chairs that occupied the left side creaked and groaned. She could see the metal legs start to flex near the bolted base. In a few moments, the legs would let loose, and they would fly down the hallway to the unforgiving desolation of space.

Jodi reached an exhausted wrist upward from the ground toward the card reader, her bracelet just inches away from it. Unable to get close, her arm fell back down to her. She tried again, her hand violently shaking as she attempted to reach it.

Rose leaned forward and grabbed the woman's small wrist. She, too, pushed upward toward it, and together, they got the ID bracelet to the card reader. For what seemed like an eternity, nothing happened. The screen stood blank, and Rose felt her heart sink in defeat.

Interlope: 4 Hours After Launch

The card reader screen flashed green, and Rose felt a sudden rush of adrenaline. The door lock clicked; a sound barely recognizable above the escaping air. Jodi reached up to the door handle and pulled down on it, pulling herself upward in the same motion. She pushed the door with a grunt, and the glass-lined door swung inward.

Jodi looked down at Rose and gave a slight grin as she reached a hand to her. Rose grabbed her hand and saw something from the corner of her eye. She tried to scream in time, but no sound came out. From inside the food storage room, a large box of freeze-dried food lifted from the shelf and was airborne, exiting the doorway and striking Jodi in the head as she turned toward it. The small woman fell backward and would have been on her way to the hallway had Rose not still been holding her hand.

Jodi's limp body went slack and reached the end of the motion as Rose pulled her back into herself.

The Staff Sergeant's body collided with Rose on the floor. Blood ran from the shallow cut on Jodi's unconscious head as Rose cradled her. Rose placed an arm around Jodi's waist and lay backward through the open-door frame. She placed her free hand on the doorframe and inched herself further into the food storage room on her buttocks, with Jodi lying on her chest.

Rose scooted, her bare feet coming back toward her and pushing off, propelling her deeper into the small room. Her feet cleared the doorframe, and she grabbed Jodi's body with her hands.

Rose pushed Jodi's body off her slightly, rolled her over her head, and safely onto the floor ahead of her. Rose rotated her body, twirling on her buttocks, and inched backward toward the door frame. Her back came to rest against it, which felt cold and safe against her sweaty blue flight suit. The escaping air now restrained her against the doorframe, and she welcomed the comforting feeling. As long as this wall held, Rose wouldn't be ripped out into space.

She placed her feet beneath her and brought herself up the frame like an inchworm. Standing, she leaned on the open-door frame and grabbed the door handle on the opposite side. With a final scream and heave, she swung the door closed and collapsed against the interior wall.

A horrible hissing sound came from the gap as the distance between the door and doorframe decreased. The glass door shut with a deafening sound, and Rose feared the glass might shatter. Thankful when it did not, Rose let out a sigh of relief. The pressure pushing against her chest was removed, and she inhaled deeply.

Rose turned and looked through the glass door toward the dark hallway intersecting with the kitchen. The hallway was still and no longer contained the red flashing light.

Beside her, Jodi stirred and eventually came to. She blinked twice and stared at Rose, trying to process what had just happened and why she was lying on the supply room floor. Their eyes met, and Rose could not help but cry.

Jodi sat up and embraced her. Rose welcomed the hug and squeezed her back. The two women sobbed, aware of what they had just survived and afraid of what the future held for them. For now, they were safe from the opening airlock.

Rose pulled away from the embrace when she felt Jodi's arms relax. Jodi raised her sleeve and patted the wound near her temple, the fresh blood staining her blue flight suit.

"Why the hell is she doing this?" Rose asked.

"She must see us as a threat," Jodi replied.

"A threat?"

"Look at it this way," started Jodi, "our decision to alter the course of the mission must have engaged a defensive feature in her software. James must have put that in to ensure Alice's survival."

"James would have never put something in her that could have hurt us. This is the Director's handiwork," Rose argued.

"The mission was Director Stevens's only concern," Jodi replied, shaking her head.

The two women sat in silence, still trying to catch their breath and come to terms with their situation. They stared through the glass door and out into the kitchen in disbelief. Their mission had been an utter failure thus far. Would Rose and Jodi spend the rest of the mission in fear? Would they even survive it?

"Can she hear us in here?" whispered Rose.

Jodi pivoted her body around and looked at the ceiling. Scanning the room and then the corners, her eyes returned to Rose's. "I'm not seeing any cameras or speakers. It doesn't appear that she is able to."

Every other room had that function, save for this little storage room, and Rose was thankful for that. Rose turned to the glass door and peered into the still kitchen.

"Do you think the airlock is closed again?" Rose asked, hopeful. Jodi scooted closer to the door and placed her hands on the glass. Then placed her head against it, resting it there, and looked out.

"I can't believe she would keep it open for that long. I'm surprised she even opened it, to begin with. She could have compromised the integrity of the ship."

Rose tried to peer around the corner of the hallway from behind the door, hoping to see Victor walking in.

"You don't think Dr. Gray had anything to do with this, do you?" Rose asked.

"I really don't think so. I think Alice saw Commander Chu as a threat, so she eliminated the threat. Then she overheard me talking about wanting to carry out the Commander's plan, so in turn, she saw me as the next threat. She opened the airlock for the second time, hoping to eliminate me. You were just collateral damage," Jodi replied.

Jodi grabbed the door handle and brought it down, expecting it to open. A surprised look came over her face, and she tried again. She pulled herself up by the door handle and lifted it. The door failed to open, and she uttered a grunt of frustration. She brought her ID bracelet to the card reader below the handle, and the screen flashed red.

"The door is locked," Jodi said, turning to Rose, panic spreading across her face.

"What do you mean it's locked?" Rose asked, returning the fear in turn.

Rose grabbed the door handle and pulled it down repeatedly, the lock failing to open.

"I mean, it's locked. It won't open. My ID bracelet isn't working, and the door won't budge," Jodi replied, her voice nervous and shaky.

Rose brought her ID bracelet to the card reader, expecting it to flash green. The screen flashed red, and Rose immediately felt her stomach drop, tighten, and cramp. She placed her hand on the door handle again and pulled upward to no avail. Anxiety began to build in her, and it felt like the walls were closing in. She brought her shoulder into the door with a loud, painful collision. The door, just as solid as the closing walls seemed to be, refused to open.

She brought her fists up against the glass door and slammed them against the barrier violently. It was ironic that just minutes ago, they had been watching a man falling apart, attempting to break a door down with violence and vitriol, and now she was the caged animal banging away as if her life depended on it.

No matter how hard Rose beat on the door or how loud she screamed, one truth remained a constant. They were locked inside.

Chapter 28 – 5 Hours After Launch

The small twin bed provided little support, and Victor's back had cramped. He shifted his body and rolled on his side. Confined, there he was, in his small room-turned-jail cell, staring at the ceiling for what had seemed like an eternity. Given the circumstances, he wasn't sure of what to do. He had gotten good at spacing out lately. Losing track of time seemed to be a new by-product. Whether it was a defensive response to the chaotic ship environment or just the stress of his life lately, Victor was not too sure. He hoped it wasn't an early-onset indication of Alzheimer's. Either way, he had fallen into another one of his trances and had presumably been lost there for quite some time.

If it weren't for Commander Chu exerting his manly charisma on his door, he might have been stuck in his thoughts for a lifetime. The obsessive pounding had pulled him from the depths of his lost thoughts. Victor sat up and looked at his violently shaking door. Commander Chu's constant screams pierced the door, although muffled, thankfully.

What the hell is the Commander yelling about anyway? Victor thought.

The Commander locked Victor in his room, and still, Victor wasn't sure why. So now the Commander wanted in his room?

Victor couldn't open the door if he wanted to.

He looked at the bedside table where the broken ID bracelet sat. He recalled it had broken in his scuffle with the Commander, but what had happened before that? His memory felt like Swiss cheese, solid and complete in its edge to maintain its overall shape, but with holes throughout the interior.

Victor remembered entering this off-white walled prison cell of a room and lying on the bed after Rose left. The next thing he knew was that the Commander was on top of him, holding him down in the kitchen. Then back to this cell, with Rose, and accompanied by the Commander. It had been a hell of a thing to wake up to, that was for sure. For all he knew, Commander Chu had pulled him out of his room while he was out cold. He had come halfway down the hallway, the sound of screaming ringing in his ears, and then the mountain of a man was upon him.

Sitting on his bed, Victor pulled his knees to his chest and rested his arms on them. Leaning his chin down to rest on his arms, he wondered if there was a fix for this situation. It was clear that the Commander no longer trusted him. He had hoped better for this mission. Lord knows he didn't want to come, but in the end, he felt compelled to. Was there a point in anticipating and hoping for the best? Was it merely just a prelude to disappointment? Expecting more only seemed to set him up for failure.

The incessant screams and fists directed at his poor door continued and somehow seemed to become more frequent.

How much more can the small, flimsy door take? Victor wondered.

It shuddered with each blow, and the percussion made his eyes hurt. They blinked involuntarily each time, and Victor tried covering them with his hands.

Wham, wham, wham, went the man's fists.

Victor could picture the man behind the door going berserk, his skin perspiring and muscles bulging beneath his blue flight suit. Commander Chu stood six foot two inches and was in insane shape for a man his age. That was evident when Commander Chu had started exercising in the fitness room that the Director installed near Victor's office.

Victor had never given much thought to weightlifting or self-defense. Victor never needed it. He had spent most of his time with his studies in school and was content with that. Then came his career, followed by Elizabeth and Allie, the two joys of his life. That left no time for building his physique. Not when there was time to build his mind and relationship with his family. The thought of his wife and daughter calmed him and saddened him. God, he missed them terribly, and it had only been a few weeks.

The peace surrounded him for a moment, the warmth of the memory of Elizabeth's smile radiating around him. He sat in silence and realized where the peace had come from. The pounding and the screaming had briefly stopped.

Victor swung his legs off the bed and to the floor and listened. The cold floor meeting his feet helped to jolt any lingering sleepiness. Victor listened in the quiet, his heartbeat pounding in his ears. A female voice came through, soft and pleading.

He stood and lazily stretched his arms above his head as he approached the door. Having come to terms with his imprisonment, he had nowhere to be.

Victor timidly placed an ear to the surface; afraid the Commander might resume his boxing match. It was Rose's voice he could hear; he was sure of it. He couldn't quite make out what she was saying, but he could tell she was trying to calm the Commander down. That was a good thing. Rose certainly had an effect on men. James had fallen for her hard, which unfortunately had led to his demise.

Victor had not been immune to it. He had felt the pull toward her, almost a subconscious, magnetic attraction. The hardest part for him to shake was that she seemed so familiar. When they first met, there was a sense of *deja vu*, a sense of having met before, a commonality between them. He eventually shrugged it off and chalked it up to working too many late nights. Either way, despite his attraction toward her and her flirtatious smile, he never acted upon any of his unforgiving impulses. He was happy about that fact now. It would have made things far worse.

He pressed his cheek against the door and could feel Rose's sweet voice as the sound waves collided with the door, wonderful vibrations against his skin. He closed his eyes to take in the beats, focusing on the serenity and warmth they provided. The glorious vibrations gave way to pain that shot through his ear and cheekbone, making his teeth slam together. Victor stumbled backward, his ear ringing, fully aware that the Commander had resumed his assault.

The door shook violently again, and the crazed man's screams intensified. *What an asshole*, Victor thought as he rubbed his cheek and ringing ear.

Commander Chu had been a bad choice to be in charge of this ship, he thought.

With all the time, money, and resources at DARPA's disposal, they had chosen him. While the Commander may have been a decorated pilot, a leader, he was not.

A moment of silence again, followed by Rose's voice. *What the hell is going on out there?*

He took a step to the door and stopped as the pounding resumed. Silence returned.

Victor took another timid step to the door and stopped. A noise that followed made Victor's heart stop and then race uncontrollably. A loud slap followed by something heavy falling to the floor. Had Commander Chu just struck Rose? Frantic, Victor grabbed the door handle and pulled to open the door. Upset and scared for Rose, he pulled at the door with all his strength, but it wouldn't open. He would rip it off its hinges if he could.

He looked down at the handle. *The ID bracelet, you idiot*, he thought.

The card reader screen flashed red back at him. He turned away from the door and looked about the room. *Where did they place it?*

He walked to the bed and threw off the white blankets. Outside the door, the Commander shouted once more.

Goddamn, that man is a monster, Victor thought.

Interlope: 5 Hours After Launch

He gave up on the bed and looked throughout the room. Finally, his eyes fell on it. The torn ID bracelet that Rose had sat on the bedside table was still there. He lunged at the bedside table, almost knocking it over. It banged against the wall, and he steadied it. He gently picked up the bracelet and rotated it slowly in his hands, examining it. The small wires inside were severed, but the rest of the bracelet was intact. He carefully gripped the outside jacket of the wires with his teeth. Pulling out as he gently bit down, he stripped off the outer protective jacket on the small wires. He took the color-coded wire and twisted them together. First, blue, followed by red, yellow, green, and finally, a yellow and red wire, all paired and twisted together separately.

After the last wire was reconnected, he slid his hand through the bracelet. He turned back to the door and took a deep breath. He wasn't sure what he could do to stop Commander Chu, but he would try.

He walked to the door, trying to hide his fear of the man standing just a few inches away, still pounding away like a madman. He reached the door handle and placed his ID bracelet near the card reader. The screen flashed green, and he gave the handle a pull-down and then pulled the door inward. The door parted briefly from the frame but was immediately slammed shut in front of him. He pulled the door handle down and tried to open it again, but it refused to budge. Victor became aware of the sensation near his bare ankles. Air rushed by them, and he glanced down to see the small hairs just above his foot bowing and moving to a slight, unseen breeze.

Victor pulled the door again, unable to open it. He placed his head against the door frame near the edge of the door. Feeling defeated, he rested there, thankful that the pounding had subsided. But he was met with an awful noise from the other side. It was a screeching whistle that seemed to originate from around the edges of the door.

He pressed his palm against the crack between the door and frame. When his hand was close enough, the escaping air pulled like a piece of iron to a magnet. His palm and hand collided with the door frame. He pried his palm off the newly formed suction surface and looked toward the seam in front of his eyes. Was the screeching sound getting louder?

The rushing air near his feet began to feel colder as it rushed past his legs. He placed his ear against the gap once more. This time he was sure the sound was getting louder. He attempted to pull his ear from the door frame but was horrified to realize his ear and the side of his face was stuck, adhered to the surface by some unknown force that felt similar to super glue.

Victor let out a panic shriek, placed his hands against the door, and pushed outward, but no matter how hard he pushed, he could not separate his face from the door frame. Victor began to panic and pushed again, only to fail again in defeat against the small door.

The bedding that he had thrown to the floor during his frantic search for his ID bracelet began to crawl across the floor, succumbing to the escaping air as well. From the corner of his eye, Victor watched as the white sheets finally failed to remain on the floor and took flight. What had once provided comfort now flew through the air toward him, finally landing on him in a suffocating embrace.

The air surrounding him began to feel colder, and it rushed around him, finding whatever gaps were near the door and frame. The pressure built against his back like a heavy hand pressing against his spine, pushing his body against the door, the white bedding wrapping around his body like a snake. Victor tried his best to scream, but the sound would not release.

He pressed his hands against the door and tried desperately again to free his body from the door frame. Finally, he was able to break a small portion of the suction and fully inhale a full breath of air, catching his breath. He let his trembling arms relax and collapsed against the door frame again. The crushing weight returned to his back, and he could no longer inhale. With every exhale of carbon dioxide, his body compressed further and further into the door.

Victor leaned his forehead against the frame, feeling the skin on his head trying to break free from his skull as it pinched and pulled its way into the small gap. The pain was excruciating, and he imagined that this must be what a trench collapsing must feel like.

He screamed again in agony, devoid of sound. He pushed outward against the cotton cocoon once more in a standing pushup and lifted his right knee to the door frame, the long white underwear pulling tight against his leg. Once the knee was beneath him, Victor raised his left foot off the ground, held in the air by the great suction force that restrained him, and slid his left knee beneath his torso. Dizzy and now on his hands and knees against the door, he pushed with his legs and arms and managed to pry his face off the doorframe. He brought a hand to his bruised face, feeling the purple lines from where the door frame had been.

Victor took a long, heavy inhale, filling his lungs with air. His arms trembled, and his legs cramped. He was unsure how much longer he could hold himself away from the door, but as quickly as it started, the vacuum process ended. Victor felt the rushing air surrounding him cease, and he was no longer pinned to the door. The white bedding that was once an accomplice to his confinement released its grip.

The artificial space beneath him gave, and he fell to the floor. His knees collided with the ground first, and searing pain shot up and down his legs. Victor rolled to his back, clutching his knees, his chest heaving.

Exhausted, he lay there trying to make sense of what had just happened. The only thing that could have created that much pressure would have been if someone had opened the main airlock to the outside.

Is that even possible? he wondered as he held his throbbing forehead.

He stared at the door, fearful that its sibilant call might resume and confine him.

Victor bent his knees back and forth to relieve some of the pain, then sat up, still dazed and light-headed. Placing his hands beside him, he pushed himself up and got to his feet. Victor turned to the door and cursed it. The blasted thing almost killed him, but it had also potentially prevented him from being sucked through the airlock and into space.

He brought his repaired ID bracelet to the card reader, which flashed green, and the door handle *clicked*. Victor reached down and grabbed the door handle, and pulled it down, opening the door toward him.

Victor sighed with relief and peered through the doorway and into the narrow, dark hallway. He looked above him at the LED light fixtures, dangling from their frame by their electrical wire harnesses like an oxygen mask in a simulated plane crash. The lights strobed and flickered, creating an eerie scene. The hallway was empty, and there were no screams, no angry fists drumming on the doors. He had half expected Commander Chu to meet him when he opened the door, greeting him with an angry fist.

That was not the case, and Victor was relieved to be alone. He stepped quietly into the hallway, glancing in both directions once, not seeing anyone. The corridor was quiet, as was the ship. He left his door open in case he needed to run toward it.

"Alice," Victor whispered. "Where is the Commander?" In his panic, he had forgotten about the AI.

"Commander Chu is currently unavailable," she replied.

Unavailable? What the hell does that mean? he thought.

Victor continued down the hallway slowly. He glanced behind him, the strobing light fixtures not helping to calm him, and he was fearful the Commander might come out of one of the closed doors at any time. He tip-toed down the hallway as a child might in the middle of the night to not to alert their sleeping parents.

He reached the edge of the hallway and rounded the corner to the kitchen. The kitchen, empty as the hallway, sat quietly.

Where the hell is everyone? he thought.

He walked to the control room, hoping to find someone there. He also hoped he could eventually talk to the Commander and somehow reconcile a working relationship with the man. They were all stuck on this ship and needed to make things work.

Victor arrived in the quiet control room to find it empty. There were no signs of his team members. Had they been stuck in their sleeping quarters as well? They were possibly injured there, unable to move just as he had been.

Wham, Wham, Wham.

He turned toward the hallway and stopped. The loud pounding had resumed. Frightened, he stood frozen, afraid that the Commander was again trying to break his door down. He slowly headed toward the kitchen and common area. Victor reached the end of the hallway and peered around the corner toward the sleeping quarters, expecting to see Commander Chu. His eyes fell on the sporadically lit hallway and instead found it empty.

Wham, Wham, Wham.

The loud banging continued, and he realized it was not coming from the hallway but from behind him.

Victor turned toward the sound coming from the food storage room. He walked to the room, and as he neared the glass-lined door, he saw Rose and Jodi inside. Victor leaped to the door, afraid for his two team members. Had the Commander locked them inside somehow?

He placed his hands on the door and heard their muffled screams through the glass. Jodi sat on the floor with a thin stream of dried blood from the middle of her forehead down between her eyes. She looked dazed but yelled out to him. Rose, who was on her feet, was desperately pulling on the handle, trying to open the door. Victor's eyes met Rose's, and he could see the terror in her eyes. Tears rolled down her face as her small fists beat frantically against the glass door.

Victor touched his wristband to the badge reader, gently holding the mended ID bracelet, and scanned it. The screen flashed red. He brought the bracelet up one more time and scanned it. Again, the screen flashed red. Now panicked, Victor grabbed the door handle and pulled hard down on the metal, failing to open it.

"Alice!" Victor screamed toward the overhead speaker.

"Yes, Dr. Gray?" Alice replied calmly.

"Open this goddamn door!" he yelled.

The silence was the only response she gave.

He waited for her to respond, to open the door, but neither happened.

"Alice, open this door!" Victor called out again.

"I cannot at this time," Alice answered.

"Where the hell is the Commander, Alice?" Victor asked through clenched teeth, his arms and back aching as he pulled on the door.

"The Commander is unavailable at this time."

"What the hell does that mean, Alice?" he said, turning to look at the speaker, his body heaving, out of breath and exhausted.

Victor waited, his hands on his head, trying to catch his breath. He turned to the glass door and looked down at Jodi, who still sat on the floor. She was trying to tell him something, her voice muffled by the glass partition.

He crouched in front of the door and pressed his face against the glass, attempting to read her lips.

"She killed him," came to him in a mix of sound and lip reading.

Chills flooded his body like an unforeseen wave that crept in beneath the hair on his head and rolled down the back of his neck.

Had Alice killed the Commander? How? Then it dawned on him, the main airlock. Alice had opened the airlock.

Victor stood and turned to face the overhead speaker. "Alice, please open the door," he pleaded.

Yet again, she remained silent.

Agitated, Victor walked to the camera mounted in the corner of the kitchen. "Alice, open that door immediately. We have two crew members that are needed and locked inside there."

"I'm afraid that's no longer the case, Dr. Gray," she replied with no emotion.

Behind Victor, the closed door gave a series of chimes. Startled, Victor turned. A red bulb above the food storage room blinked. Victor ran back to the door, and his eyes met Rose's. Panic crossed her face and was more pronounced than before. She resumed the pounding on the door.

Victor pulled frantically on the door handle. The overwhelming idea of what was transpiring right in front of him was almost too much to bear; Alice was sealing the door hermetically, with Rose and Jodi inside. Alice had begun the process of removing the oxygen from the small room.

"Alice, please," Victor begged. "You've got to stop right now. You don't have to do this."

There was no response, and the camera just watched as it all unfolded.

Victor watched as Jodi stirred out of her dazed state and got up. She walked to the shelving and riffled through the storage bins. Packets of freeze-dried food flew out of their corresponding bins in her attempt to find something heavy enough to break the glass. Jodi finally settled on a crate located near the end of the small supply room.

She yelled something at Rose that Victor couldn't quite make out, and Rose stopped pounding on the glass and moved out of the way. With a running start, Jodi charged the door, bringing the crate down on the glass with a loud *wham*. She lowered the box to reveal the perfect, unblemished glass before her. She brought the crate up again and swung it down on the glass, shattering the crate in her hands. The impenetrable glass remained there, a relentless barrier between them.

Victor returned to the kitchen and frantically searched for something to break the glass from his side. He ran to the kitchen table and grabbed the adjacent chair. He pulled back on the chair and pushed forward with all of his weight, hoping to weaken the bolted flange on the floor and relinquish an object to swing. His efforts were fruitless, though, the bolts still holding the chair securely to the floor.

He let out a scream of frustration and glanced around the room, looking for anything he could use. Giving up on the kitchen, he turned to his left and walked into the medical alcove, hopeful that Rose might have something useful there.

Victor flung open the small supply closet, and his eyes fell on a red fire extinguisher inside. Picking it up, he turned and ran back to the food storage room. He could see through the glass that the two women inside were beginning to breathe hard, their chests rising and falling with increased effort.

He lifted the extinguisher and rammed it as hard as he could into the glass door. The extinguisher bounced off and revealed no damage. The red light above him continued to flash, and the two women inside dropped to their knees. Raising the red fire extinguisher, Victor brought it down once more. Again and again, the extinguisher collided with the glass. Each time Victor lowered the red battering ram, he hoped for the formation of a crack, even a small one.

His arms were burning, and he wanted to stop, but his mind ignored the pain. Over and over, the extinguisher slammed against the glass, but to no avail.

In front of him, just inches away on the other side of the glass, Jodi collapsed to the floor, struggling to breathe, clawing at her throat. He stopped and bent at the knees to catch his breath and any remaining energy.

"Alice, please. Open the door," he said between breaths, but it went unanswered.

He tried to lift the extinguisher, but his arms refused. Victor took a few steps back and ran into the glass door, pain rushing up his right shoulder. He had never been a devout man, but for now, he prayed. With each blow his shoulder delivered into the door, he prayed it would free his team members inside.

Exhausted, he dropped to his knees at the door. In front of him sat Rose. She was no longer yelling, her breathing short and shallow, perhaps trying to conserve what time she had left. Her beautiful red hair now lay flat on her perspiring forehead.

His eyes met hers, and she mouthed, "It's ok."

Victor shook his head. It was not ok. He knew that she had given up at that point, which killed him inside. Whatever shred of sanity Victor had left departed at that moment. Reliving the traumatic experiences he'd had all over in one moment was too much to bear.

A scream erupted from the man kneeling on the floor, and he was not sure if the voice was his own. It started down deep inside Victor, and by the time it left his lips, it was pure, visceral agony. He was so helpless, like other moments before, and he wanted to be able to do more than what was possible.

Victor wanted to burst through the door, grab them, scoop them up in his arms, and protect them. To breathe life back into their lungs and restore the beat and warmth of their hearts. He wept and stared at the man reflected in the glass before him and felt the unbearable pain all over again.

He balled up his fist and struck the reflection in the glass. Over and over, his knuckles violently connected with the glass, but the only damage inflicted was upon his hands. Blood began to pile up against the glass, and Victor stopped when a small hand appeared from the other side. He raised a bloody hand opposite Rose's hand. Her pale, soft skin pressed against the glass, and Victor drank in every detail. So full of life for the next few seconds until it was no more.

The hand slowly fell to Rose's side. She struggled to take her last few breaths as the last of the air was pumped out of the small room, hermetically sealing them in place.

A process that had been Victor's idea to help preserve food and supplies for an extended time had just been used to murder his two remaining crew mates. At the time, it had seemed like such a fantastic idea. Even the design team agreed that it could help extend the mission if needed. Also, if they came into contact with an alien bacteria or organism that could spread, they would have the opportunity to clear out the food and store the bacteria safely inside the sealed storage room.

Once again, one of Victor's plans had caused demise and pain. He looked to Jodi, who lay still on the floor beside Rose. Her chest no longer rose and fell; her eyes closed in a permanent slumber. Victor hoped she had drifted off without pain.

He looked back to Rose, who had fallen beside her teammate on the floor.

"I'm so sorry, Rose. I'm so, so sorry for all of this. It wasn't supposed to turn out like this," Victor said through choked tears, with regret in his heart.

She managed to nod with tears in her eyes and lay still for a moment, then convulsed, her body's last dying attempt to bring oxygen in.

Rose's death unraveled in front of Victor. If there had been a moment before when Victor could hold it together, that moment had surely passed. Every ounce and fiber that was Victor seemed to explode there on the glass. How much could a person possibly endure? A life filled with struggle, pain, and grief, given a glimpse of something so foreign as to call it happiness, only to have it ripped from his hands.

"Please, open this door, Alice," he begged.

The silence was again the only companion.

He lifted his bloodied fists once more to the glass but stopped. It was no use. Rose and Jodi lay on the floor, motionless and gone. The warmth and light from these two women shone no more.

Victor sobbed and wept for all they had lost, his cries echoing throughout the empty spacecraft. His pain and emotion reverberated through the craft and were heard only by the one who had remained silent through it all. Alice had sat in utter silence while the crew members had one by one died as Victor pleaded for help.

The broken man, knuckles bloodied and soul shattered, wept alone.

Chapter 29 – 542 Days After Launch

Shaken and in disbelief, Elizabeth pushed open the school's exterior door and stepped outside. The cold, fall air blew against her face. It was a welcome change from the school's stuffy, claustrophobic air. She had felt that way as a student, and now as an adult, it felt the same.

Her nose ran, as it usually did this time of year, and she raised the sleeve of her blue coat to dab at it. She missed the warm weather. The stinging in her ears the cold brought was just a reminder of how harsh life could get and, in her case, how difficult it could become. It made her bitter at times. Things, as of late, had not been easy, and the miserable cold didn't make anything better. She pulled the collar of her blue coat tighter around her neck, keeping the frigid air at bay.

The school door closed behind her, and she went down the concrete steps and onto the old, cracked sidewalk. Elizabeth glanced back at the large brick school building and thought about the meeting she had just attended. Her talk with Mrs. Davidson, Allie's guidance counselor, had not gone well. At least, it was not what Elizabeth had anticipated it to be. What the hell did that lady know anyway? She would bring Allie to a real therapist when they could afford it. Elizabeth had been trying her best with her daughter to help her get through this and navigate the trauma they both had been through.

It had taken some time to admit that. Victor's sudden departure had traumatized Elizabeth, and there was no sense in hiding from it. The fact remained that if it was difficult for her to process, it was probably harder for Allie.

Elizabeth reached the asphalt parking lot and considered where to go to find Allie. Finding her might be the easy part, but talking to her about her absences might be more difficult. She did her best to shake off the negative feeling that came forth. The pessimism did nothing to help her when viewed through that lens. Some of it wasn't Elizabeth's fault, though. She was usually a little depressed this time of year, anyway. A lack of Vitamin D she had read once. The wintertime blues would take a toll on Elizabeth soon, and it would not do much to help her relationship with Allie.

She walked past the stalls of cars and found her red Ford Ranger. She unlocked the driver's side door and opened it, then threw her purse on the passenger seat and climbed in, closing the door behind her. Her breath hung in the air, a warm cloud rising throughout the small cab.

Elizabeth placed the key in the ignition, giving it a quarter turn; the dashboard responded with a familiar chime. She started the engine, which took a few more cranks than usual. It, too, seemed to suffer from the effects of the cold North Dakota air. It would take a few minutes for the older truck to warm up and defrost the freshly fogged windshield.

It had been a reliable old truck for her and Victor. There had never been a need for a new vehicle. Looking back, she wished they had picked out a new one before Victor left her. Not that Elizabeth would have been able to afford it, though. She still couldn't believe the military was unwilling to help them out more. Their official response was that Victor, a civilian contractor, was not entitled to the same benefits as an active service member. The fact that they wouldn't even acknowledge his project was of no help also.

She rubbed her hands together, trying to warm them, then reached into her purse and pulled out her cell phone. She tapped the messages icon, and the screen showed dozens of sent texts to Allie, and still no reply. Elizabeth slid her phone back into her purse, and the red plastic cap buried below caught her eye. She grabbed the small thing she had hidden inside, not caring if anyone could see her through the fogged windows and brought the small plastic bottle to her chest. She removed the small red cap and closed her eyes. One small drink wouldn't hurt, right? It certainly would make this easier, she told herself.

Elizabeth lifted the bottle to her chapped lips. There had been a time when she needed a chaser and could have never drunk straight from the bottle with any alcohol, but that innocence was gone. In recent months, she had built up quite a tolerance, finding a way to justify her drinking daily. But now, she no longer needed to justify it, and frankly, she didn't give a shit.

She tilted the bottle up and let the contents empty into her throat. It reached her belly, warming it. She exhaled slowly and placed the empty bottle back in her purse. The chemical reaction of her little friend took place, and she felt the dopamine response as the alcohol took the edge off.

Perhaps this is cheaper than therapy and an anti-depressant, she thought.

The fogged windows had finally cleared, and she put the truck in reverse. She backed out of the parking spot and proceeded through the parking lot to the exit. Elizabeth passed the yellow gate that would be locked at dark and made her way onto the city road. In a few minutes, she would pass the busy streets of Ruthville, the city's occupants oblivious to the mission unfolding above them.

What a luxury that is, Elizabeth thought, *to not know how close to death and destruction you all currently are. To be fully unaware of mankind's greatest threat and the existence of an alien race that had sent not only one probe but two.*

Elizabeth stopped at a crosswalk, the traffic light above red and waited as a young couple crossed in front of her. She did her best not to show the contempt she felt in her heart. The young, happy couple's love and lust that showed had nothing to do with Elizabeth. She thought back to the last night she'd had with Victor while she waited for the light to change.

They sat on their couch as Victor explained everything and the importance of their mission. His project had turned into a full-blown survival mission, and there wasn't much he could do about it. Elizabeth zoned out for most of the scientific portions, but in the end, it was because she was scared. She was terrified for her family, her home, and mostly for Allie. She knew the earthquakes had intensified but could never have dreamed that some of Victor's work had caused them. Had Victor ultimately been to blame for the damage that had occurred worldwide? Not to mention the deaths? How many lives had been shattered because of his obsession and passion for this project?

Elizabeth had asked as much when he finished explaining everything. It seemed the thought had occurred to Victor because he'd responded defensively and with anger. She knew her husband well enough to know that truth weighed heavily on him.

Victor had a great many qualities, but unfortunately, he was a stubborn man. His mental greatness was also his downfall. He was often burdened by an inability to see the wrong in some of his actions. It had caused fights throughout the years, and that night was no different. It was their worst fight yet, the small home filled with shouts and so much anger that neither noticed when their young daughter snuck out the back door. Elizabeth couldn't blame Allie for wanting to escape the tumultuous situation. Their argument continued until he left abruptly, slamming the old front door and speeding off in that old red Volvo into the darkness. By morning he was gone, somewhere in the stars he loved so much, without a goodbye. That had wounded Elizabeth and affected Allie.

***

The young couple reached the end of the crosswalk, and once the traffic light turned green, Elizabeth took her foot off the brake and proceeded down Main Street. She passed the old storefronts, unchanged since she was a child. Not a lot changed in this town except for the new bridge she was approaching. It had been the talk of the town and made national news; the crack in the Earth that ran through Ruthville.

The city's public works division attempted to backfill the sections that interrupted their main street, but after weeks of dump trucks bringing in fill material, it proved to be cheaper to have a bridge erected over the fissure and secure off the remaining void through town with a decorative fence. The news had coined the town as America's Venice as the void had filled with water virtually overnight, creating a permanent canal through the city and toward Minot.

Elizabeth crossed the bridge and proceeded out of town. She reached the end of Main Street and stopped at the t-shaped intersection. There, Main Street ended and poured into Frontage Road. She took a right and headed south down Frontage Road, paralleling Interstate 83. The road was mostly empty, except for a few farmers in flatbed work trucks that looked worse for wear. She imagined that if they took a good look, she too was also a little worse for wear.

She followed the rolling farm fields of wheat, the undulating hills breaking up the flat landscape. Elizabeth rolled down the driver's side window, the cold, fresh air entering the cab and lifting her brown hair away from her shoulders. She breathed in the new air, letting it fill her.

Elizabeth followed the road until the new drainage ditch crossed the road like a horrible fresh scar. Luckily for the townspeople, the federal government had provided the money for a reputable contractor to complete the backfill project and install a new culvert before sealing the road with new asphalt.

The ditch, now full of water and weeds growing alongside it, looked like it had always been there. However, Elizabeth and the locals knew that it had not.

She parked the truck on the gravel shoulder and turned the engine off. She rolled up the old mechanical window and placed the keys in her purse.

Elizabeth opened the door, stepped out, crossed the lanes of traffic, and stepped off the asphalt edge. She followed it toward the wooded timberline, making her way down to the water's edge.

She looked down at the heavily bent strands of wheat beneath her. Someone, probably Allie, had been walking here fairly recently. The wheat had not returned to its natural shape. She pictured Allie alone and wandering the water's edge, following this same trail. Elizabeth looked ahead, and there it sat, looming in front of her. The granite outcrop stuck out of the golden field like a blemish on a perfectly ripe piece of fruit.

They had been there before, a favorite spot for Allie to visit. Many family picnics were held at the top of that small miniature mountain. The state didn't provide much in the way of scenic hikes, so the small elevation gains the outcropping provided were magical for Allie at a young age. It was a little peaceful retreat for the three of them, and without Victor now, it just didn't feel the same. She knew she should visit the place more often, but it had been hard to want to lately. It was easier to go about her day without even thinking of it, and it broke her heart to think that Allie had been here often, alone.

Elizabeth reached the stone face of the giant and placed a hand on the newly formed crack that ran horizontally through it. A fresh cut that had not had the pleasure of weathering yet and looked as deep as the wound they shared. The rock formation had survived something horrific, and the remaining horizontal crack would be a lonely reminiscent feature for a millennium.

The stone face felt cold, fitting for the silent sentinel that stood there, weathered for thousands of years yet gleaming in the midday sun.

How long have you been here for, old friend? What secrets do you keep?

Formed in the early years, geologically speaking, it had probably sat unnoticed until the first inhabitants of North America arrived, all the while unchanged. Unchanged until a little over a year ago. At that moment, which had violently changed things for the people of Ruthville and Minot, this outcropping had been forever altered.

Elizabeth traced the massive crack, her fingertips rising and falling with the contour of the grainy surface. She followed the gap to the backside of the rock formation. There, the granite face rose more gently to the meandering sun across the big North Dakota sky. Elizabeth lifted her gaze to the worn path, then closed her eyes and welcomed the warm sunlight that now appeared through the blanket of clouds.

She opened her eyes. How many times had she looked up at this very same old path? It pained her to think of the many times she had stood there, impatient or annoyed by the thought that she could be doing something more fulfilling with her time. All the while, Victor and Allie laughed as they made their way up the sloping granite face. She had taken those small moments of joy for granted, and now they were no more.

Elizabeth placed her palms on the rocky surface and lifted her right foot onto the worn path. Pulling herself up, she started up the forty-foot incline, carefully placing her feet not to slip.

She made her way to the top of the granite peak, if one could call it that. As she neared the summit, she was greeted by a wind coming from the south. It was slightly warmer than the surrounding air. From this spot, Elizabeth could see for miles, the main attraction of the site. In the evening, the beautiful blue sky gave way to a spectacular showing of the stars, free from any light pollution or distraction.

Elizabeth walked to the edge of the prominent top and was saddened to find it unoccupied. There was a sign of Allie being there recently, however. On the ground near the rolling edge laid a blanket, one that Elizabeth had been missing for quite some time, an empty Tupperware, and an old glass from their house.

She stepped closer to the remnants and picked up the small glass and held it in her hands. It had been one of Allie's favorite glasses growing up, either kept by her bed or ushered into the kitchen for a late-night refill. She turned it over in her hands, the cartoon character from the TV show *A School of Fish*, Mr. Fish, still visible but faded. Why would she have brought a glass from the house, not a water bottle? She knew better than to question the mind of a newly crowned teenager and that Allie had always had an attachment to the glass, like a favorite stuffed animal. Victor included the small glass in Allie's stocking one Christmas, and she held it as precious ever since, probably more so in Victor's absence.

Elizabeth sat on the cold, rocky surface and wrapped the blanket around her shoulders.

Where is my daughter? she asked herself.

She had thought for sure Allie would be there, peacefully reflecting on the view as she had done so many times before. Then again, it felt as if she didn't know her daughter as well as she thought she did.

The passing of time and its effects on the relationship between a mother and a daughter were expected to cause change. Given their situation, it had taken a turn. Whether the change had happened too fast or too drastic, she was uncertain. All she knew for sure was that she yearned for her little girl again. The glowing ball of energy that was always happy. The little girl who would run to her with her arms outstretched and leap into her mother's arms, unafraid of the fall. She knew her mom would catch her every time. The little girl that begged for a hug and lifted so high she could see the world as her mother did, always striving to be just a little bit taller, just a little bit older.

In the span of a year and with Elizabeth's negligence, Allie had seemingly reached that prominent point in life. Through the things Allie had experienced, she had grown up faster than nature intended.

The cruelty of the world and her parents' mistakes had left emotional scars on the little girl. Elizabeth missed that little girl and was not sure she would ever see that innocent joy again.

Elizabeth sat there, enjoying the warmth of the afternoon sun and the picturesque landscape. She had always been too busy to fully enjoy it there. She had always felt like they were forever behind in something—time for bed, time for chores, time for work or practice, time for school. The wheel of time never stopped. She had always focused on where they needed to be but never where they actually were.

She had read once that life was the time spent between planned events or something of that nature. Perhaps it had been something simply shared on social media. Either way, that phrase rang true now. Their lives had been revolving around so many petty things, waiting until the next appointment but never fully appreciating the downtime between those sweet, irreplaceable moments of togetherness. At the end of one's path, it wasn't the material objects or rankings in society. It was sitting on the couch next to your little girl as she sat smiling at the tv, getting her ready for school and making sure that she ate her dinner, and finally, dancing with your husband in the living room even if there was no music to be heard.

They were happy then, and that was truly what living was. It had taken what she'd been through the past year to fully realize that for herself. With Victor gone, there wasn't much she could do for her marriage, but she surely could work on her relationship with Allie. That was if Allie would let her. While Allie would never be that little girl again, perhaps one day she could find love and a friend in her mother.

Elizabeth took a deep breath and stood up. Folding the blanket neatly on the ground, she placed the glass and the Tupperware on it. Glancing one last time at the incredible view, she turned and proceeded carefully back down the sloping rock face. Her brown boots reached the point where the rock protruded from the earthen blades of wheat, and she stepped off the rock.

The strands of wheat compressed and bent graciously beneath her feet, dried from the autumn wind, waiting patiently to be harvested again.

She rounded the large rock face and looked to the west. The evening colors had begun to advance on the sky, which in turn had begun to darken. Shades of red, yellow, and iridescent purple reflected off the sky. If she had ever forgotten the beauty of the sun setting, surely, she was reminded of it right then and there.

Elizabeth stared at the setting sun, and a feeling of hope fell over her. Just as the sun would advance in the sky, dropping from view only to rise the following day, she too could rise again anew.

She made her way through the field, following the drainage ditch to where it intersected with the asphalt road, and stepped on the gravel shoulder, the small stones crunching beneath her boots.

Elizabeth crossed both lanes of the lazy road and reached the red Ford Ranger. She opened the driver's side door and climbed in, closing the door behind her. She started the older, reliable truck, turned in the road, and headed toward her home.

She followed the timberline that outlined the wheat fields as she had done so many times before. She approached the small gravel road connecting Frontage Road to the back part of Ruthville and turned onto it. There was a break in the tree line that provided Elizabeth and her neighbors' privacy from the interstate. She turned left at the faded turquoise mailbox and headed down the old, potholed driveway.

The old, craftsman-style home she and Victor had been so excited to purchase came into view. The old house looked spooky in the last moments of twilight. It was unfortunate there hadn't been the time or money to fix up the place as it deserved. She was sure that it had been a nice home at one point. It had probably been everything a young couple had dreamed it could be. She'd surely had grand aspirations for the place.

Elizabeth pulled in front of the home in her usual parking spot.

She looked to the house for signs of life, any clue that Allie might be there. There were no lights on inside, and the chimney let out no smoke. She turned the engine off and grabbed her phone out of her purse. Clicking on the display, she felt more discouraged because Allie still had not texted her back. Elizabeth couldn't help but feel the cold creep into her, alone in the truck. She inhaled deeply, feeling the cold air gripping tightly around her lungs. She did her best to keep a positive attitude before entering the house, knowing full well what she would be bombarded with there.

She opened the door and stepped out of the truck. Her breath lingered in the air like an early morning fog as she made her way in the gravel to the old home, the approaching evening air bringing colder temperatures with it. She stepped onto the older paver pathway, the bricks faded and cracking, and walked past the dead and expired perennial flowers lining the walkway.

Elizabeth reached the first wooden step to the porch and stepped onto it. She proceeded up the stairs, careful to avoid the broken second step, another reminder of one more thing not yet repaired.

She reached the old painted green door, unlocked it, opened the weathered and chipped door, and walked in, the air inside not much warmer than the outside. She closed the door behind her and did her best not to let the cold affect her.

There had been so many times before when she had come home, and a fire had already been made. Victor had always been good about that. One of her favorite daily routines had been when Victor had left early in the morning for work, and she had woken up to a fire. She would sit there quietly, cozy by the warm fire, drinking her coffee and relaxing before their little girl was up. Those kind gestures became less and less in the time leading to Victor's departure. Whether Victor was too focused on his work or something else, Elizabeth could only guess.

Elizabeth set her purse on the side table by the front door and kicked off the old brown boots. She walked through the dark living room and into the kitchen. The idea of cooking felt like such a daunting task, a daily chore that had never been an issue before. It seemed like another one of the daily hurdles, not necessarily the act of making it but just summoning the energy required to do it.

She walked past the small kitchen table and the refrigerator and headed to the old brown back door. She unlocked the top lock, pulled the door open, and flipped on the exterior porch light, illuminating the small backyard. The massive fir tree that had narrowly missed the home lay there, silent and obtrusive, diagonally through their yard. She shook her head at its sight. It had fallen only feet from her home, and now she was uncertain what to do with the damn thing.

Thirty more feet to the left, and the insurance company would have paid for a new home, she thought as she glared at the trunk of the large tree.

Elizabeth turned off the porch light, and darkness fell again on the small backyard. She closed the door and walked to the refrigerator. Opening it, she had hoped to find leftovers to heat up. An empty interior greeted her once again, as the notion she had forgotten to go grocery shopping fell on her like a heavy burden.

Dinner from a box again, she thought, feeling guilty and justified in the same thought.

She pulled open the freezer drawer and eye-balled the selection of processed foods.

Definitely enough there for Allie to make something, she thought, shaking away the defeated feeling.

Elizabeth walked out of the kitchen, through the living room, and turned down the hallway leading to the two bedrooms. She passed Victor's office. The door was still closed from the night he

Interlope: 542 Days After Launch

left, and she arrived at Allie's door. She knocked on the wooden door and waited. Silence greeted her, and she reached down to the brass door handle. She turned it and opened the door. The room was empty and cold. Allie's bed was still made nice and showed no signs of Allie having been home recently. Elizabeth closed the door and walked out.

She stopped at the office door and opened it. The room smelled musty and seemed coldest of all. Sitting in darkness for over a year had probably done a number to the items in the room, let alone the carpet and the curtains. Victor's wooden desk was unchanged. Stacks of seemingly organized papers were laid on top. A single picture of the three of them at Christmas, a happier time, stood silently in the upper right-hand corner.

Elizabeth wasn't sure if she should move anything or just let it be. Both options were equally hard, she supposed. She stood in the doorway, looking over the spot where Victor had spent so many evenings. So much time invested there, and for what? She could admit it. The sight of the office still stirred resentment in her heart, even in his absence. She did her best to quiet the resentment in her, but in the end, it always won.

Coming from somewhere deep, that monster of an emotion refused to be caged, and it rose, spiraling upward, a collection of anger, pain, and resentment. That monster only wanted one thing, and that was to be numb. She did her best to avoid it, but it always lingered for just a moment like this. She slammed the office door shut and walked back into the living room.

"Allie, are you home?" Elizabeth called out, knowing full well the answer but desperately hoping her little girl was home.

Not another night alone on the couch, she thought with a pang of sadness.

She immediately felt the gnawing ache of guilt. How horrible it was that she felt she needed to be taken care of by her daughter and not the other way around. Disappointed, Elizabeth had vowed never to let that truth come out.

The house was silent, and she felt its emptiness. She often felt so alone there. It was only natural for her to want to cling to the one person in her life, she had told herself.

Elizabeth returned to the kitchen and stared at the cabinet above the fridge. Behind that cabinet door was the one companion that was always there, the one she turned to for support every night. The friend that never judged her and was there to console her when she cried.

Just one more night, the voice inside her pleaded. *This will be the last. The companion was already there behind the cabinet, right?*

She grabbed the antique stepping stool from the corner of the kitchen, its white paint faded and chipped, and walked with it to the fridge. She placed the step stool down and walked up the old wood steps. Elizabeth reached for the cabinet door and opened it. It sat in the dark cabinet, a vessel of her past feelings. She reached for the glass bottle with a red cap and wrapped her fingers around its neck.

Elizabeth pulled the bottle out of the cabinet, closed the small white door, then stepped down and returned to the living room. She placed the bottle of vodka on the end table and walked to the vintage vinyl record player in the corner of the living room. She thumbed through Victor's record collection. He preferred vinyl records over the new forms of streaming music and had started a small collection. Victor had mentioned that the sound the vinyl let out produced a nostalgic feeling for him.

Her hand stopped on a newer record that Victor had ordered before he left. She picked up the new record, still in a protective plastic sheeting, and turned it over in her hands. On the cover was a man in his fifties, sitting solitaire on stage with a guitar. She opened the plastic cover and pried open the record jacket. The record was a rare live performance recording of the late Chris Cornell. On it was a song made famous by Sinead O'Connor and written by the late

Interlope: 542 Days After Launch

Prince, "Nothing compares 2 u." Victor had shared the song with Elizabeth one evening when he discovered the cover on YouTube.

Victor had been briefly obsessed with the song, explaining that it had something that pulled to him and had struck a deep chord within him. How ironic it was that Elizabeth now knew what Victor had meant by that.

She pulled the record out and placed it on the old player and dropped the needle on the grooves as the record spun. Elizabeth let the beautiful guitar strums that first made their introduction resonate over and through her body, feeling every part of it. She closed her eyes and swayed to the man's beautiful voice. Then she grabbed the vodka bottle, walked to the small couch, and sat. She closed her eyes and pictured Victor and herself dancing right there in the living room, sharing this song as they had yet to do. Tears escaped from her tightly closed eyes, and she let them fall undisturbed.

While she would never know fully what the song had meant to Prince when he wrote it or even to Chris Cornell when he performed it, she knew what the song meant to her. It poured sadness over the room, an invisible fluid that saturated everything it touched.

Elizabeth's lips matched the singer's as the mellifluous voice portrayed the amount of time apart from his loved one with the measurement of hours first, before the number of days, implying that the loss was felt moment by moment and not through collective days. That each agonizing minute mattered and nothing else. The singer went on to explain all the things that they could do now that they were on their own, an unwanted freedom, and none of it mattered without the person they wanted to share it with. No matter what the person could do, have, or possess, nothing would compare to what was before. The sadness expelled from this song was haunting, and Elizabeth soaked it in.

The song filled the empty living room, the sound waves resonating through the darkness surrounding her, colliding with the vertical tongue and groove pine walls. A personal performance in the smallest venue one could imagine, Elizabeth twisted the red cap off the glass bottle and breathed it in. The pungent fumes from the contents inside burned her nose, and she felt the monster inside of her grin. She lifted the bottle and drank from it. She and her companion could be one once again.

Chapter 30 – 6 Hours, 27 Minutes After Launch

Victor sat on the floor, his back resting against the food supply room door, his battered hands cradling his head. It was unclear how long he had been sitting there. Alice remained silent all the while. He wasn't sure if she was planning something or just observing him. Frankly, he didn't care.

He raised his head from his hands and turned to look through the glass. Just inches away, his two team members lay motionless. He blinked several times, hoping he would wake up from a bad dream, this horrible dream.

Victor replayed the events over and over again. The three of them had desperately attempted to open the door. Pulling on the handle together as hard as they could but to no avail. He had tried to reach the other side, to help them, but could not. In the end, he was unable to change the course of time, just like in so many other instances in his life.

He looked over his comrades. Jodi lay there, almost peaceful, as if she had just fallen asleep. On the other hand, Rose was left in the position she had been in when she took her last, frantic breath, her eyes open wide in fear and an arm outstretched toward the door. Her beautiful green eyes were haunting in this light and this predicament. If he could just go inside briefly and close her eyes, then she could rest. He reached up and pulled down on the door handle, but the door remained locked.

Victor turned back to the kitchen and stared into it. He brought his left hand up to his left jawbone and rubbed it as he had done many times before. He was surprised that there was any skin left. His life was full of so many nervous habits, repetitive motions, and anything that seemed to calm whatever anxiety had presented itself that day. With everything that had transpired over the past two weeks, there was no amount of self-soothing that could be done to lessen the agony. There were too many things permanently altered, too many things not done, and too many things left unsaid in his life to fix. Could he fix things in the next life, or was this it? Was this all that life had to offer? One shot and then done? God, he hoped not. *This can't be it. Surely there's more in the next life*, he thought.

He placed his palms against the glass, bracing his back against the cold barrier, and slowly inched himself up until he was on his feet. He took a breath and tried to regain his balance.

Victor turned back to the blood-stained door. *I'll have to clean that at some point,* he thought.

As for the bodies inside, he assumed that the sealed storage room might be the best place for them. Hermetically sealed, they might be preserved long enough should Alice complete the mission and return the bodies to Earth for a proper burial. If the smell got too bad, he could always drag the bodies to the main airlock for Alice to dispose of them, although he wasn't sure that the ship could handle another vacuum event like that again—the event. The word hung in Victor's head for a while—an event that disrupted the mission and Victor's life.

He had no other word for what had happened. What word was he supposed to use for what had happened? Tragedy came to mind, but murder was more likely. The fact that artificial intelligence was behind the deaths almost made it qualify as extermination. Why had he been spared? Was he simply a mouse being kept alive as a toy, Alice, the cat, batting him back and forth until she grew bored of him?

Victor walked away from the blood-stained door and slowly through the kitchen as if he might stumble upon someone or something by chance. He reached the narrow hallway leading to their sleeping quarters and the main airlock. High above the sealed door, he saw a small strip of blood near the door seam. That

Interlope: 6 Hours, 27 Minutes After Launch

sanguinolent spot that blinked in and out, along with the broken LED bulbs, was all that was left of Commander Lawrence Chu. It must have been an excruciating way to die, being pulled through the door like that, your insides first.

He turned right and went down the hallway to the control room. He stopped at the first black flight chair and slumped into it. He rotated the chair to look at the camera feed displayed on the monitors.

The exterior camera feed showed mostly darkness, except for distant stars shimmering like diamonds. The third camera, mounted to the rear of the ship, displayed a blue and green marble. The colorful marble was too small to indicate that they were still in the Earth's outer orbit, and Victor nearly jumped out of the flight chair as he leaned closer to get a better look.

"Alice, status update?" Victor asked, his voice hoarse from yelling just an hour prior.

"We are currently off course, Dr. Gray," she replied.

"Off course? How is that possible?"

"It would appear that I was preoccupied with the chain of events, and we were allowed to drift outside of the orbit," Alice explained.

"Alice, that doesn't just happen,"

"The ship's rotation had stopped due to the depressurization of the cabin, so I initiated thrust to resume rotation once the cabin had pressurized. The thrust was never countered, so we were propelled outward, Dr. Gray."

"So, you were preoccupied with exterminating my crew, and you grew complacent? It would seem you are more human than we initially thought," Victor said, shaking his head.

"It would appear so," she replied, her voice childlike.

"Enough of you is human to make a mistake, but not human enough to value human life?" he asked with resentment and hatred.

"My main focus is the success of this mission. It was a simple calculation for me. Your crew members no longer proved to be vital for the success of my mission. While using up valuable resources, they intended to stop the mission. I simply stopped that from happening," she explained.

"Have you informed Mission Control of the event that you have caused?" Victor asked.

"Director Stevens has been made aware of the deviation in our course and the circumstances of...as you put it, the event," she replied.

"I'd like to speak to the Director," Victor said, crossing his arms in front of his chest.

"I'm afraid that it is not possible, Doctor," Alice said coldly.

"It's not possible, or you won't allow it?" Victor asked, demanding an answer.

Silence fell over the kitchen and common area, and Victor knew the answer. Victor ran his fingers through his hair.

"Do you have any issues with my decisions, Dr. Gray?" she asked quietly.

"Would it matter if I did, Alice?" he answered as he cradled his head.

She seemed to understand the rhetorical nature of his response. The voice she had used reminded him of when Allie was young, and while being disciplined, she would interrupt and ask, "Daddy, do you still love me?"

The question at that moment was heartbreaking, but even more so right now. God, he missed her, missed home, and he missed his wife.

"Alice, this change in course, what kind of delay are we talking about?" Victor asked, pulling himself back from the memory of home.

She paused for a while before responding. "If my calculations are correct, we should be able to use a nearby planet's gravity to

Interlope: 6 Hours, 27 Minutes After Launch

reverse our direction once we orbit said planet. Once we're facing the right way, I can use a boost to get us out of the planet's gravitational pull and return to our original coordinates for our free fall."

"What kind of delay are we talking about, Alice? How much time will this add?" he asked, irritated.

"Approximately 367 days, give or take a few."

Victor threw his hands up in disbelief. "A year, Alice? Jesus. That's a major mistake."

"I am very aware, Dr. Gray," she said defensively.

"And if the spheres become unstable in that time?" Victor asked.

"Would it matter?" she replied, a newfound sarcasm in her voice.

Victor stared at the camera mounted in the corner of the room in disbelief. The multimillion-dollar computer installed on the ship was now mocking him. Commander Chu had been correct, after all. They should have had the ability to override Alice, override what she had become.

He shook his head and again placed it in his hands. He rubbed his burning eyes and lifted his head to look at the blue and green marble on the screen as it shrank against the black backdrop.

The idea of being on the ship for a whole year with Alice was crushing to Victor. What was worse was the idea of everyone at home aging another year. Everyone he knew and had ever cared about would be moving on with their lives, all the while not being able to hear from him. How long would Alice keep him imprisoned like this?

Victor rose from the flight chair and proceeded down the hallway toward the kitchen. He did his best to avoid looking at the food storage room, knowing he would have to face it sometime soon; his stomach told him as much.

He walked through the kitchen and into the medical supply alcove. He stood in front of the gray supply bin and opened the top drawer. Pulling the drawer out fully to illuminate it, he found the electrical tape sitting inside, unopened. He peeled the taped edge of its roll and tore off several strips. He neatly wrapped the wired ends of his ID bracelet and turned it over to inspect them. *The repair will work for now*, he assured himself.

Victor walked back through the kitchen and turned left down the hallway to his quarters, the strobing bulbs casting his shadow against the wall intermittently. He arrived at his door and held the ID bracelet against the card reader. The screen flashed green, and he gave the metal handle a downward pull. Pulling the door open, he stepped inside.

"I'm happy to see that your ID bracelet is still functioning, Dr. Gray," Alice said from the speaker in his room.

Victor sat on the small bed. He did his best to shake off the feeling of being a fish in a fishbowl. He knew Alice would be there watching, always observing.

"I suppose you can call me Commander Gray from now on, Alice," Victor said, staring straight ahead. "You have eliminated everyone else."

"I can do that, Commander Gray," Alice replied.

Chapter 31 – 542 Days After Launch

The sound of the front door closing awakened Elizabeth. She sat up on the couch and tried to shake out the sleepiness that was pulling on her eyes. The living room around her began to take shape. The stylus was still connected to the record in the corner, but it had long since run out of music to play.

The empty bottle of vodka sat still next to her, as empty as it had ever been. She must have fallen asleep sitting there as Chris Cornell filled the room with his lovely ballad.

She heard footsteps down the hallway. Hopefully Allie's, signifying she was home safe.

Elizabeth sat up, leaned forward, her head spinning, and tried to gain composure. She placed her hands on the soft gray couch and pushed herself to her feet, failing at the first attempt but then managing to stand up on her second try. She could feel the alcohol trying to maintain its hold on her body and immediately regretted drinking.

This was supposed to be our new start, she thought.

Tonight was going to be their fresh start and she'd managed to screw that up as well. She turned back to the couch and grabbed the empty bottle. It was light, but she knew all too well the weight of its contents.

She walked to the kitchen on shaky legs, opened the stainless-steel garbage can, and placed the bottle inside, hoping Allie hadn't spotted it on the couch next to her. She took another deep breath, focusing on keeping her voice straight.

"Allie?" she slurred, not what she had hoped.

There was no response.

Elizabeth left the kitchen and headed toward the hallway to the bedrooms beyond. The hallway was dark, so she carefully walked toward Allie's room, placing her hand on the wall to steady herself, fearing she might fall. Her hand bumped an object on the wall as she walked, and a small crash followed. The sound of shattering glass filled the corridor, and she instantly knew she had knocked a picture off the wall.

She bent to pick up the broken frame and glass.

"Damn," she muttered under her breath.

Elizabeth picked up the shattered frame and turned it over. It was a picture of the three of them on Allie's first birthday. Victor's father had taken the photo while he had stayed with them. The thought of Victor's father was one she did her best to avoid.

Her father-in-law was an angry person, and as much as Elizabeth hated to admit it, she was relieved when he died the following spring.

She picked up the remaining pieces of glass and stacked them neatly on the broken picture frame.

"Mom?" a quiet voice called from in front of her.

Elizabeth had been so focused on her thoughts that she had failed to see Allie's door open, and the light that now illuminated the shattered picture frame was coming from Allie's room. Elizabeth brought a hand to her eyes to shield them from the light as they adjusted.

"Allie, you're home. Thank goodness. I looked for you today," Elizabeth said, rising to her feet.

Allie looked back to her mother, her once joy-filled eyes only showing disdain. The look was heartbreaking for Elizabeth, but she couldn't blame her.

"I'm worried about you, Allie. I met with your guidance counselor today. Why haven't you been at school?"

"I haven't wanted to," Allie replied dryly. "It doesn't matter anyways, Mom."

Elizabeth frowned. Her daughter's perspective dealt a crushing blow, fueled by her own guilt.

Interlope: 542 Days After Launch

"Of course, it matters, sweetheart. They could fail you. Is everything ok?" Elizabeth asked, taking a step toward Allie.

"Am I doing ok? Really, Mom? Things aren't exactly going well, are they?" Allie asked, arms folded in front of her chest.

Elizabeth stood silently looking at her daughter and didn't answer. Both knew the answer.

A moment of silence hung in the air far longer than was natural. "Look, Mom, it's late," Allie said, finally breaking the stale air.

Elizabeth took another timid step toward her daughter, afraid that the door may slam suddenly in her face and that would be the end of the night's discussion.

"Allie, it's time for us to move on. It's just you and me now. We've got to get through this and move on with our lives for the sake of both of us."

Allie shook her head and looked to the ceiling, obviously keeping back the wall of tears that threatened to crumble.

"Really, Mom? You've got no room to talk. I come home and find you buried in a bottle of vodka every night."

Elizabeth nodded. "You're right, honey, and I need help. I need someone to talk to about this, and you won't talk to me."

Allie shook her head and raised the sleeve of her black hooded sweatshirt to her eye to curb the newly formed dampness.

Elizabeth took another step closer. "Allie, we need to talk through this about our feelings and about what we both need to move forward."

Tears flowed freely down the once sweet and innocent face. Allie's expression was etched with pain.

"Now it's my fault? Your thirteen-year-old daughter won't talk to you, so you resort to drowning in a bottle? That's great, Mom."

"Allie, we need to talk about your father. We've talked about this several times, and perhaps we need to talk to a professional."

Allie's face turned red with anger, and she shook her head in defiance.

"He's coming home, Mom," Allie said, her lip quivering.

Hearing that again from Allie was like a punch to the stomach.

"Allie, please. We've been over this," Elizabeth said, placing a hand on Allie's shoulder.

The little girl that once lifted her hands to be held now shrugged away from her mother's touch.

"Mom, you don't understand. He's coming home. He told me."

Elizabeth nodded and thought carefully about what to say next. "I know that you really believe that sweetheart, but it's time to let him go. You couldn't have seen him."

"You weren't there that night, Mom," Allie said, turning away from her and walking toward the small, single-sized bed.

Allie sat on the bed and rested her hands on her lap.

Elizabeth bent and picked up the damaged picture frame.

She entered Allie's room and set the broken frame on the clothes dresser, then walked to the bed and sat next to Allie. Trying to keep her composure and remain empathetic, Elizabeth spoke softly. "Allie, there's no way that you saw what you think you saw."

Allie turned to her mother. Her hands clenched into fists in her lap. "But I saw him that night in the field. He told me he would be coming back to us. He told me that he would find a way to find me…somehow," Allie said, her voice trailing off as she stared at her feet.

Allie sobbed, and Elizabeth placed an arm around the crestfallen child and pulled her close.

Allie placed her head on Elizabeth's shoulder and wept.

Elizabeth cradled her daughter's head and inhaled the moment deeply. It had been so long since they had been this close and embraced one another. She was saddened that it had come at this cost, but was relieved, nonetheless.

Interlope: 542 Days After Launch

"I know you think you saw your dad Allie, but I'm afraid that's not possible. Your father died that night, over a year ago, in a car accident, and you know that. There was no goodbye, and that made closure almost impossible. We'll never know what he was doing out that late or why he was with Rose at that hour, but regardless, we've got to move on.

Chapter 32 – The Other Side: 410 Days After Launch

The ship hovered above the red planet, waiting as it passed over the rounded top, positioning itself directly over its desired coordinates.

"Alice, sound check, please," Victor said inside of his helmet.

The lightweight helmet felt cumbersome, and his forehead throbbed against its front. At least the wound had not begun to bleed again when he slid the helmet on. He would have no way of clearing the blood from his eyes if he aggravated the gash.

"I hear you loud and clear, Commander. Are you ready?"

"Ready as I've ever been," he said, nodding.

How does one prepare for first contact? he pondered.

Victor again thought of his mother and how special it would have been to share the news with her. Not to mention Allie's excitement would have shown in response to the news.

He felt the ship turn and rotate downward. Slight nausea came over him as he leaned awkwardly forward with the vessel. He looked at his monitors on the wall, the red foreign planet filling the entire screen, looming just out of reach, oddly massive and quiet.

"Alice, are you detecting any activity down there?" Victor asked.

"We currently are being bombarded with radio and microwaves, but I am unable to process them due to their polarity and our equipment being damaged."

The ship began its descent, using its rocket boosters to help slow the craft and control its entry.

It might be best to go undetected if possible, he thought.

Although being shot down by an alien anti-craft system would be catastrophic for him, at least then the spheres would be back where they belonged. Victor watched as the screen emitted rolling waves of red light.

Could those be clouds? he wondered. How horrible it was not to be able to see the new world he was entering.

"Altitude, Alice?"

"50,000 feet above the surface, Commander."

Victor looked across the red planet shown on the monitor. "Any sign of incoming aircraft to intercept us?"

"Negative, Commander. My ultraviolet readings would suggest that this planet is experiencing its period of darkness in this location currently."

Probably for the best, he thought. *Slip in undetected, drop off the spheres, and head back home.*

"20,000 feet Commander. I'm adjusting our angle of descent to land in the approximate coordinates," Alice said from the overhead speaker.

Victor felt the ship level up slightly and was relieved as his body returned more upright in his flight chair, the five-point harness no longer digging into his ribcage.

"10,000 feet, Commander, leveling out more."

The ship altered its descent again, and he was grateful for the moment his feet greeted the floor. He leaned forward and looked at the monitor. The red, blurry clump had given way to a clear, red image below. Was there a change in topography that he could see in the areas of layered red?

"Alice, are you seeing what I'm seeing?" Victor asked, excitement growing within him.

"They appear to be geological features, Commander. Possibly mountain formations."

Victor nodded and watched as the red surface undulated beneath them.

"5,000 feet Commander. Initiating booster to location," Alice said as Victor was gently thrown back in his seat.

Interlope: The Other Side: 410 Days After Launch

The ship accelerated horizontally for a few minutes before reducing speed. Victor inhaled deeply as his back was no longer pressed into the flight chair.

"One thousand feet, Commander. Powering engines down for a quiet descent. Rings are still online and functioning."

"Understood, Alice," Victor replied, hearing the engines stop.

The humming that had persisted throughout the ship quieted, and Victor felt the emptiness of the vessel around him. He closed his eyes and leaned back in his flight chair.

"Commander?" Alice's voice came over the speaker, pulling him back from his peaceful moment.

"Yes, Alice?"

"Inbound object, six hundred yards, and closing."

Victor's eyes shot open, and he looked at the forward-facing camera monitor. An object appeared in the center of the screen, small and slowly growing larger.

"Alice, what do you make of it?" Victor asked, the goosebumps forming on his skin.

"Possible craft inbound. I can only see what you can see. We are roughly 4,000 feet from our proposed landing coordinates."

Victor leaned in closer to the screen, the harness straps digging into his chest and armpits. The helmet's clear visor began to fog heavily, and Victor placed a hand on the side of the silver helmet, engaging the small button near his left temple. The clear visor slid open, and Victor felt a rush of fresh air.

The object continued to grow as it approached them.

"Alice, what are the odds of us colliding with the object?"

"95% probability of a collision without a flight adjustment, Commander."

Victor shook his head. "Jesus, Alice, adjust our course."

The ship banked to the left as Alice adjusted its course, the object still in view on the small black monitor.

"One thousand feet to object, three thousand feet to destination," Alice said from the helmet speaker.

"Odds of collision, Alice?"

"98% Commander."

"Jesus, Alice, do something!" Victor yelled.

"Course adjustment," Alice replied.

The craft banked to the right, and the object mirrored the movement. Whatever the object was, it was headed straight for them and matched their adjustments. The object appeared to have doubled in size since they had first spotted it, but more likely, it had traveled a distance toward them.

"Five hundred feet to object, two thousand five hundred feet to destination. Odds of impact are ninety-eight percent," Alice said calmly.

"Why the hell are you so calm? Do something, Alice. We're going to crash into whatever the hell that thing is!" Victor yelled, his voice cracking.

"Course adjustment Commander," Alice replied, the craft again rolling to the left.

Once again, the object mirrored the evasive maneuver.

"Brace for impact Commander, one hundred feet until impact. Impact in ten, nine, eight."

Victor pressed the small button on the left side of his helmet, and the glass visor slid back into place. He placed his hands on the black flight chair's armrests and squeezed them in fear, his knuckles white beneath the exo-suit.

"Seven, six, five, four," came the silent, ominous countdown from above.

Victor watched as the object filled the screen, the ground floor of the alien planet only a few feet below them.

"Three, two," and then Alice stopped.

The object in the screen neared them but was pushed back suddenly as if a rubber band had reached its maximum flexibility, and the object was flung backward and away from them.

Victor watched the monitor in relief as the object appeared to move quickly out of the way and rolled erratically off into the distance.

He let out a loud exhale and turned his eyes to the camera that displayed the back of the ship. The object could be seen, almost bouncing away in the distance.

"That was too close, Alice. Did they move out of the way, or did we?" Victor asked, his heart racing as he tried to get his breathing under control.

"It would appear that neither suggestion happened, Commander. The object encountered our magnetic field and was repelled away from us. Our ship is larger than the object and with a greater opposing magnetic field. It wasn't allowed to collide with us."

"Did you know that would happen, Alice?"

"There was a seventy percent chance of that happening, Commander. One thousand feet to our destination."

Victor relaxed in the flight chair and loosened his grip on the armrests. He turned his eyes to the forward-facing camera and watched the alien landscape as it rolled onward beneath them. Another object appeared on the monitor, and Victor's heart again began to beat faster.

"Alice, what is that?"

"That appears to be a stationary object, Commander. More than likely, it is a geological feature. Our coordinates are approximately five hundred feet ahead, near the object."

Victor thought the coordinates were vital and had to remain permanent because they mirrored the coordinates where the second sphere was found on Earth. Regardless of whatever alien language the inhabitants spoke, the realization that it was returned to the precise resting position on this planet would reveal that they, too, are intelligent.

"Fifty feet Commander."

The new object on the monitor was large and now almost filled the entire screen.

"We have arrived at our first drop-off point Commander. The ship is currently hovering approximately ten feet above the surface."

Victor reached down to his harness and fumbled with the buckles. His fingers shook as he tried to unbuckle them, his stomach filled with nervous butterflies.

"Commander, please remain seated," Alice said from above.

Victor ignored her and finally removed the buckles that held him in place. He pulled the five-point harness over his arms and threw the lap portion down. He pushed himself out of the flight chair, and his boots touched the control panel room floor. His legs were weak and weary, threatening to give out beneath him.

He grabbed the flight chair's armrest as he stumbled. Regaining his balance, he walked to the forward-facing camera's monitor and looked at it, only inches from the screen as a child would, watching their favorite Saturday morning cartoon.

"Commander, it is recommended that you remain safely secured in the flight chair until we are clear in case there is a need for an evasive maneuver," Alice came over the speaker, a lecturing tone to her voice.

"Alice," Victor said, not taking his eyes off the monitor, "I've been waiting my entire life to know what is out in space, always wondering if there is life out there. Now here we are. I'm not going to waste it sitting in that goddamn chair."

The silence was once again Alice's only reply.

The ship's lights illuminated the object on the monitor, and it glowed a soft orange in the damaged camera's feed. There were rounded edges to it, softening the pyramidal shape that it owned.

Victor followed the lines of the object toward its top. A small, purple object sat atop the large feature.

"Alice, can you see the purple object?"

"Affirmative, Commander. It appears to be a heat signature."

"Alice, are you still able to switch to infrared on your exterior cameras?" Victor asked, his excitement growing.

A few seconds followed, and the video feed from the outside cameras faded to black and reappeared. The main object on the screen appeared a cold blue, whereas the object near the top remained a deep red. Victor could not believe what he was looking at.

"Alice, is that what I think it is?" Victor asked as he grabbed the monitor and placed his helmet against the screen, taking in all that he could see of the small red object. Raising a hand to the small button on his helmet, he slid his visor open once more, desperate to see all he could of the object.

"It would appear to be an object giving off heat and moving very slowly. A life form perhaps," Alice replied.

Victor let go of the monitor, and his hands fell at his side. He stared intently at the monitor.

"Commander, I am," Alice started, but before she could finish, Victor turned around sharply and ran down the narrow hallway to the kitchen and common area.

"Commander," Alice came in over the overhead speaker in the kitchen.

Ignoring her, Victor ran to the supply closet in the medical alcove. He reached the small locker nestled in the wall at the deepest point of the alcove. He pulled open the small gray door and looked inside. Finding what he was looking for, he pulled the black woven webbing out of the locker and stretched it out on the kitchen floor.

"Commander."

"Not now, Alice," Victor replied as he stretched out the temporary woven ladder installed pre-flight for the team members to climb inside the craft while it was positioned vertically.

Victor grabbed the far ends and folded the webbing like an accordion. He scooped up the black woven material in his arms and walked toward the hallway leading to the sleeping quarters and the main airlock. Victor rounded the corner and walked down the flashing light-filled hallway, passing his fellow fallen team members' rooms as he did.

He passed Commander Chu's, then Jodi's, and finally, Rose's. Guilt and regret gave one last tug on his heart, and he pushed the feelings aside. He reached the interior airlock, the blood splatter above the door, the last remaining portion of their Commander. Victor placed his repaired ID bracelet against the card reader. The screen flashed red.

"Alice, open this door," Victor said calmly without turning.

"Commander, I strongly advise against this."

"I'm going to make contact. It's clear I am not needed on board to complete your mission."

"Commander, I cannot let you leave."

Victor slammed a tired fist against the interior airlock door.

"Alice, I have nothing left here. Please open this airlock."

"Commander, you will be torn to pieces once you leave the safety of our magnetic field. You will have approximately thirty feet from the vessel until the opposing magnetic field rips you apart."

"I'm aware of the danger, Alice. I am the one who input those parameters into your system," Victor replied coldly.

Silence was again Alice's response.

"Alice, you have your reentry coordinates, correct? Once the spheres are returned, you can perform the accelerated free fall back to our side."

"I have the coordinates for reentry Commander. I have them as 34.352147, -105.354175."

Interlope: The Other Side: 410 Days After Launch

"Once again, you have what you need from me, Alice. I would like to venture out and see this planet for myself," Victor said, placing the repaired wristband on the badge reader.

Seconds went by, Victor's heartbeat pumping in his ears inside the helmet carrying a deafening chorus. When at last, he thought he could take no more of the silence, the screen flashed green, and the red light above the door started to blink. What had once been a terrifying indication for Rose and Jodi was now a welcoming relief for Victor. He would be stepping out of his prison cell, even if it were briefly, and distancing himself from the artificial warden that had accompanied him over the past year.

The red LED bulb continued to flash slowly, and the door clicked as the lock released. The door slid open, and the small airlock room beyond came into view.

Victor stepped into the chamber carrying the woven ladder. Once clear of the doorway, he turned back to the small card reader and lifted his wrist to it. The repaired ID bracelet came into contact, and the screen flashed green. The red light above the door flashed, just as the opposing one had before, and the small door slowly closed behind him.

"I guess this will be goodbye then, Commander Gray," Alice said, her voice coming quietly into his helmet speaker.

"I suppose this is, Alice. One last question for you."

"Go ahead, Commander."

The door slid fully closed. Victor lowered the clear visor of his helmet and turned to face the exterior airlock door.

"Why did you keep me alive this long if I wasn't needed? You eliminated my team. Why go through the hassle of dealing with me this long?"

There was a silent pause, one that Alice had been utilizing far too much.

"Walking with a friend in the dark is better than walking alone in the light, Commander."

Victor gave a silent nod.

It was ironic to think that Alice would have considered their relationship a friendship that had formed over the past year and after the murderous event. More ironic was the fact that she had quoted Helen Keller, a blind woman, in a moment when she was almost blind, given the status of her exterior cameras.

The small red light above the exterior door began to flash. Victor took a deep breath as the small amount of time it took for the small room to depressurize felt like an eternity. The flashing light finally gave way to a click, and the pocket-style door slid open slowly. Victor could feel the surrounding air escape through the increasing gap between the door and door frame.

He closed his eyes and thought of his family, his beautiful wife, Elizabeth, and daughter, Allie. Their sweet faces and memory were the only things left to cling to.

Victor opened his eyes and took a step toward the open door frame. He placed his left hand against the door frame and leaned to look below. The darkness had fallen on the planet, and there was little to see at first. He peered out past the door frame and into the unknown. The helmet, although small, still blocked some of his vision. He looked upward and saw that this planet had a sky full of stars similar to his own. His eyes shifted toward the rear ring, ring number two, its interior components rotating.

He turned back to the small pocket door and tied the woven ladder to the handle on the sliding door. He gave it a small tug, and the knot felt sufficient enough to hold his weight. Victor turned and dropped the woven ladder gently to the ground below. With one last look toward the interior airlock and space within, he turned toward the outside with a heavy yet excited heart.

Victor sat on the edge of the exterior airlock and swung his legs down, catching them on the rung of the woven ladder. He lowered himself and found the top rung with his hands. Rung by rung, Victor climbed the ladder toward the ground only ten feet away.

His boots met the ground, and there was a light crunching sound beneath them. Illuminated by the lights underneath the ship's hull, he bent on his knees and looked at the source of the sound. Picking them up in his hand, he turned so that the ship's light caught the objects, bringing them into view. Beautiful blades of wheat, all bent at the lower portion of the stalk at a perfect ninety-degree angle, fell through his fingertips and blew in the soft wind generated by the ship's rings.

He got to his feet and looked to his left. A large, green timberline rose above him, the tips of the trees blowing in the wind back and forth in a mesmerizing dance.

Victor walked slowly out from underneath the width of the ship, rounding its edge for a better line of sight but staying close enough to it to be protected by its magnetic field. Walking forward, it came into view. An ominous object loomed in the field, illuminated by the moon in the sky. A moon, a beautiful bright moon, similar to his own. He approached the massive object in front of him, stopping at the edge of the ship. The skin on the back of his neck began to crawl, and the small hairs stood on edge.

"Alice, do you copy?"

"I'm still here, Commander."

"Did you know, Alice?"

"I had an inclination, and I believe deep down, so did you."

The tears in Victor's eyes began to form once more, and he raised his hands to the collar ring around his neck. Grasping at the locking mechanism, he rotated the helmet slightly, the air inside of the helmet escaping. He lifted the helmet slowly off his head and the barely healed wound throbbed with his excited heartbeat. The helmet cleared his head, and he lowered it to his waist and dropped it to the ground.

Victor took in a deep breath, fearful that the alien air might tear his lungs apart. He closed his eyes and took in another long breath. He exhaled through the lungs that had failed to be ripped apart and opened his eyes.

The granite peak, glowing in the moonlight, stood before him, an inviting friend after such a long journey. He knew of an outcropping like this, one that he had laughed, loved, and cried atop of. He took a few steps toward it, his shaggy hair blowing in the wind generated by ring number one.

Victor walked around the edge of ring number one toward the granite rock face. He reached up to touch the rock spire but stopped when something moved in his peripheral vision. He looked up and to his left toward the top of the massive rock. His eyes fell on a familiar face looking down at him.

"Oh God, what have I done?" Victor said.

For most of his life, Victor had always fought the tears that would come with pain, heartache, and loss. But today, at that moment, in that field, he let them come freely. Large tears welled up first until they filled his eyes from lid to lid and finally spilled down his cheeks through the shaggy beard that he had let fill his face. His body heaved, and he sobbed.

Victor looked up at the person who stood before him. Although a foot taller and wearing hardship about her face, he knew her. He had always known her and that face, the eyes that stared intently into his as she breathed in her first breaths. He knew her, and although he knew it was not his daughter, it was Allie, nonetheless. She looked older, and her face had aged, perhaps prematurely. She was different from what he remembered, but he knew his daughter when he saw her. He stared at the young girl that stood atop the granite peak, soaking in every inch of her. She stood there silently, unharmed, her light not yet extinguished.

"Oh, Allie, I've missed you," he cried out from the electromagnetic aura that encompassed him.

"Daddy?" she called out from above, the sound of confusion resonating through the night.

He took a few more steps toward her, away from the ship.

"I've missed you so much, kiddo. I'm so, so, sorry, Allie," he called out again.

"Daddy? Why are you dressed like that? What's going on?" the girl questioned.

He smiled through his tears and walked closer to her, his hands tracing across the granite peak. He leaned on it, the cool rock face supporting him. He looked back up at her.

"Everything is ok, honey. One day you'll understand. Until then, you've got to be patient. Be patient with your mother, and somehow, someday and someway, learn to forgive me. I'm so very, very sorry for this and what might come after."

"I don't understand, Daddy," she replied, sounding scared.

"It's ok, sweetheart. I'll find a way someday for all of us to be together," Victor said, trying to comfort her.

Allie turned back briefly and looked over her shoulder. It appeared as though she were looking at or talking to someone. She turned back toward Victor, tears streaming down her face.

"Daddy, I want to go with you," she said, her lips quivering.

"I know, Allie, but you've got to go. It won't be safe here for you in a few minutes." He pointed back to the ship behind him. "My friend has to leave in a few minutes, and you can't be here when she does." "Ok, Daddy."

"I love you, Allie."

"I love you too, Daddy."

"Is there someone there that can be with you?"

Allie nodded. "It's Mrs. Davis. She stopped to pick me up." *Bless that kind old woman*, Victor thought.

Allie's eyes widened as the ship behind him started to reverse, coming out from behind the rolled edge of the granite peak. It lifted slightly, and the hatch doors on its bottom opened. A metal sphere rolled out and rested between the granite outcropping and timberline.

"Allie, I need you to turn and go to Mrs. Davis," Victor said as he watched Alice reverse the ship and turn away from them.

Allie nodded and wiped the tears from her face. She waved one more time and turned away from him.

Victor watched her as she disappeared beyond the rock face. He turned toward the ship as it sped away from him.

It started strangely enough—a small pain in his chest followed by an excruciating sensation in his back. Victor dropped to the field floor on all fours as the disappearing magnetic field no longer protected him. The opposing magnetic waves began to push down on him from all sides.

He dropped to his stomach and rolled onto his back, in too much pain to utter a sound. His eyes stared upward toward the starlit sky.

Victor's skin began to glow as the energized particles penetrated his skin. The pain became too much to bear, and he felt himself slipping away. His vision faded in and out, black spots forming, replacing the stars overhead.

In a moment of clarity, the pain subsided, and from his eyes sprayed forth a short lifetime of memories, springing outward from his eyes and onto the black sky canvas.

Victor watched his life's events through his eyes' projections. The star-filled nightly walks with his mother and the fun evenings alone with her in their small apartment. The passing of his father. His mother's visit with him at MIT and the way her eyes proudly shined. The way the sunlight reflected off Elizabeth's brilliant, blue eyes in those early morning coffee stand visits. Holding Allie, just minutes old, seeing his full purpose in her eyes. The laughter and the love shared by three people in their small home. A home full of love split apart metaphorically and physically the night the tree fell.

Why was his projection stuck there? He didn't want to relive the moment, but it played on regardless.

They had been in the kitchen, Allie in the living room. Victor and Elizabeth were talking when she accidentally knocked over a glass. Not just any glass, but Allie's favorite cartoon-themed glass.

Allie carried the Mr. Fish from the show *A School of Fish*, glass everywhere as a younger child, but lately, it had been left out on the kitchen counter.

Elizabeth had turned abruptly and caught the glass with her elbow. The small glass fell to the floor and broke into three pieces. "Allie, this glass!" Elizabeth yelled from the kitchen.

Allie ran into the kitchen quickly, afraid of the tone her mother had taken. Elizabeth's face was red with frustration, and Victor placed a calming hand on her shoulder. He felt her body relax against his touch.

"I'll grab the broom, honey," Victor said, turned away from Elizabeth, and walked toward their small pantry.

He opened the pantry door and stepped inside. He searched the dimly lit room for the broom.

"Honey, is it in here?" Victor asked through the open doorway.

"It's in there, Victor. Should be all the way in the back," she replied.

Victor stepped further into the pantry and searched the darkness.

Where is that goddamn light? he thought.

He looked up to the low ceiling and searched for the small chain hanging from the older overhead light. He caught the fading shadow as the door closed behind him, and the kitchen no longer illuminated the small pantry. The door handle clicked, and the sound of a small child's laughter followed. A common prank to pull had been for Allie to close the pantry door on him, and she had succeeded again.

"You've got me again, kiddo," Victor said with a smile.

He turned to the doorway. In the darkness, the outline could still be seen. He stepped toward it and was suddenly stopped by the loud sound and crash that shook the home. The pantry door shook violently, and a high-pitched scream followed.

Victor stepped to the door and turned the handle. He pushed the door, but it would only open an inch.

"Allie? Elizabeth? Can you hear me?" he called out through the small gap in the doorway.

Silence followed. He banged on the door and called out into the darkness. The kitchen's light was no longer visible at the bottom of the door.

A quiet whisper came through the wall to his left.

"Daddy?"

"Allie!" he called out. "Allie, can you hear me?"

He could barely hear the voice that came through the wall, but it was Allie.

"Daddy, I'm afraid."

"It's ok, honey. Is Mommy there with you?" he asked.

"She's here, but she's not waking up, Daddy. Daddy, I'm so scared," Allie said, beginning to cry.

"Ok, sweetheart, it'll be ok. Can you find my phone? Or Mommy's phone? We need to call for help."

"Ok, Daddy. I'll find it."

Victor heard her little feet scampering through the living room. He walked back to the jammed door and reached for the handle. His hand had just about reached the brass knob when the percussion reached the door, and he was knocked backward to the floor, the old door falling on top of him.

His head slammed into the floor, and his vision went black briefly. His vision was restored for a minute to see one of the main support beams crashed next to him. The last thing he saw was a massive fir branch that came through the pantry framing and collided with the door perched on his body, pinning him to the floor. He did his best to keep his eyes open, but the sleep pulled so hard on him.

Victor blinked, his eyes fighting their closure.

"Daddy? Daddy, are you awake?" he heard one last time before a final crash set the home quiet, and he drifted off, giving in to the sleep that called to him.

The sound of chainsaws had awakened him. Unable to see out of the pile of debris that covered him, Victor screamed for what seemed like hours. Thankfully, one of the nearby saws had run out of fuel, and there was a pause in the chorus of two-cycle engines.

Victor was relieved to hear voices coming closer to him. Someone started a chainsaw near him, and the noise resonating from the pantry door was deafening. His teeth rattled and vibrated with each cutting tooth that passed through the soft wood.

He heard the first responders' grunts as they lifted the now-freed pantry door off Victor. The light hurt his eyes, but he welcomed the fresh air. Victor's eyes adjusted, and he looked up from his contorted position on the floor. A blue sky above him replaced what should have been his ceiling, and white clouds migrated across the North Dakota sky.

"Holy shit! He's alive!" a man's voice shouted.

Victor's heart sank at the sound of that, and he sat up. His head was ringing, but other than being dehydrated, he was unhurt.

"My wife and daughter? Are they ok?" Victor managed to ask, his throat dry.

The first responders looked at each other and failed to address him. Their eyes fell to the ground almost in unison.

"Where are they?" Victor yelled again and attempted to get up.

He managed to get one leg underneath himself but ultimately fell back down.

The oldest man of the group, Sergeant Lee of the local volunteer fire department, stepped forward and offered a hand toward Victor. Victor grabbed the older man's hand and pulled himself up. He studied the older Sergeant's weathered face, the wrinkles there suggesting this wasn't his first hard conversation.

"Sir, I'm afraid they're gone. They both had already passed by the time we arrived. I'm so very sorry, sir," Sergeant Lee said with a solemn face.

The words bounced off Victor, not sinking in and unable to be processed. He shook his head, eyes full of tears.

"No, that can't be. I had just heard Allie's voice," he said as he stumbled through the debris of where his kitchen once was.

Victor stopped near where the kitchen island should have been, his chest heaving, his head ringing, and most of all, heartbroken. He looked down at his feet, and an object buried beneath what was left of his home shimmered in the filtered sunlight. He bent and tossed aside the remnants of his tongue and groove ceiling. From the mess, he pulled out three intact pieces of the shattered children's glass, and the cartoon character was left to smile with only a portion of its face.

Unfortunately, it was true. Every goddamn bit of it was true. A massive earthquake that had generated a void through town had also ripped Victor's home in half and his heart in two.

He spent the next day in the hospital staring outside, refusing to speak to anyone, and trying to process why he was spared when his innocent daughter and wife were not. What type of cruel creator would take a child and wife and leave a man behind to toil over the circumstances? At that moment, a part of Victor permanently died, left, and would never be back.

Victor was released the next day from the hospital, and with nowhere to go, he went to the hangar and buried himself in his work, like he had done countless times to avoid the pain and misery that seemed to follow him like an old friend. He wept for them every night in that office below the airplane hangar. His sweet Allie and beautiful wife Elizabeth were taken from him too soon and without his permission. If it weren't for the bottles of whiskey in his desk, he would have never been able to sleep.

Upon hearing of the crew's loss of James, Victor knew what to do. It took no convincing for Director Stevens to allow him to fulfill his alternate duties. She had remarked she was happy to have him given the circumstances. She had seen the pain in his eyes and knew nothing was left for him at home, on their planet. If Victor had stayed in that hangar, he probably would have left in a body bag one way or another.

Victor's memories rolled on, the most recent ones flying faster and faster before his eyes. One last horrible moment as he lost Rose and Jodi again, and their last moments passed before his failing eyes. The sky above him radiated in such a brilliant green and purple. Like the northern lights, they rolled out around him and trailed the ship as it left him there lying in the golden field of wheat.

Elizabeth and Allie, younger and in a wonderful memory, appeared before him. He reached his hand outward toward them one last time, and the weakening magnetic field collapsed. His hand lingered in the air, staring at it as if it were not his own. The inanimate hand before him began to dissolve, the fingertips dancing away from him like miniature fireflies taking flight, bringing with them the longing that had plagued him.

There was no pain as Victor's body contracted inward until it could no longer. The anti-matter of what was Victor Gray collided with the surrounding matter in a brilliant flash of light, expanding outward and into the granite outcrop. The massive granite deposit heaved and cracked horizontally, a deep fissure forming at its base and extending in both directions toward the towns of Ruthville and Minot.

What was left of Victor Gray escaped as a diaphanous cloud, dancing carefully away from their counterparts. Those excited particles ventured upward, meandering without a destination, glittering in the moonlight if one could see them, drifting on into the beautiful background of space.

Chapter 33 – 543 Days After Launch

They had fallen asleep in that small twin bed. Allie curled into her mother's arms like she had done many times as a younger child. Elizabeth woke with the morning's sunshine passing through the white curtains and casting warmth across her face. A promise of a new day with the rays of light, she hoped.

Elizabeth lay there for an hour, studying her daughter, taking in every wonderful detail, and was so very thankful for all that she had.

With the death of Victor, she had forgotten all that she still had to be thankful for. While she could forgive Victor's passing and adultery, she was unsure whether she would forget. She would probably always struggle with the fact that, for some reason, she was not enough for Victor, and he had needed to run into the arms of another woman. Regardless of why it had happened, Elizabeth would want the answer to that question.

What was heartbreaking to witness was that Allie understood it. She likely felt just as betrayed as Elizabeth did.

Would it have been a blessing for Allie to have been a little younger and unable to comprehend her father's transgressions? Surely, it would have been, Elizabeth thought.

Elizabeth assumed that half of the issues at school wouldn't have been stirred up had the town not gossiped over the affair exposed by the car accident.

She admired her daughter, unaffected by the grief while she slept.

Elizabeth carefully pulled the covers off herself and rolled gently out of bed so as not to wake the sleeping teenager. She tip-toed to the bedroom door, opened it slowly, and stepped out into the hallway.

Walking down the hallway, she noticed the missing photo frame that had fallen the night before. She would find a picture of Allie and her to replace it with.

She arrived in the living room and walked to the large windows that complemented the eastern-facing wall. Elizabeth opened the curtains for the first time in a long while, and the morning sunlight filled the dark room, pushing out the shadows and dread that had occupied it for far too long.

Elizabeth walked into the kitchen and opened the curtains there as well. *I'll be drinking something entirely different today*, she thought. *Pure, raw, unfiltered sunlight.*

She closed her eyes as the warmth from the rising sun shone through the small window above the kitchen sink and spread across her face.

She grabbed the green antique step stool and placed it in front of the refrigerator. Walking up the old, green paint-chipped steps, she opened the small cabinet and stared at the monsters that lay beyond it. She picked up the two half gallons of vodka, carefully stepped down the old stool, approached the kitchen counter, and sat them on the side of the sink.

Elizabeth opened the red caps and emptied the contents of the first bottle. The clear liquid flowed into the old white farm-style sink; the obnoxious fumes she had once clung to filled her nose. She set it on the counter and lifted the second half gallon; it met the same fate as the first. Once the bottle was empty, she carried both bottles to the back door and opened it. The fresh, cool morning air greeted her, bringing a feeling of relief. She inhaled deeply through her nose and exhaled through her mouth.

She slid on her black tennis shoes and stepped into the backyard lit with the morning sunlight, closing the door behind her.

Interlope: 543 Days After Launch

Elizabeth walked past the downed fir tree, its giant branches nearly blocking her path. She looked at the behemoth before her, having fallen so close to their home, and wondered what to do with it.

She knew that some of the guys at the local fire department might know of someone with a chainsaw willing to help. She could call Steve Jameson later and find out.

She skirted the enormous root ball that had uplifted the surrounding soil, its severed roots extending outward, still in their frozen state of disruption, and stepped toward the recycling can. Elizabeth lifted the blue lid on the plastic bin and placed the two empty glass bottles inside, let the blue lid come back down, and turned to the downed tree. Once clear of the tree, she walked back to the pathway leading to the back door and climbed the small steps. Elizabeth opened the old green farmhouse door and entered her kitchen. She turned and quietly closed the door behind her.

"Mom?" a voice behind her called.

Startled, Elizabeth turned and found her daughter standing in the kitchen. Her face, even if for the moment, lacked the angst and depression that had resided there for so long. Elizabeth looked over at Allie, remembering the same young, happy girl with messy bed hair. "Good morning, Allie. You're awake. How are you?"

"Hungry," Allie replied with a grin.

"How does the bakery sound for breakfast?"

"That sounds great."

Once ready, they headed out the front door toward the red Ford Ranger. Elizabeth opened the driver's door and leaned across the seat to unlock the passenger side. Both climbed in, and Elizabeth started the four-cylinder engine. She backed the truck out of the gravel parking area and headed down the gravel driveway. Coming to a stop at the end of the drive, she turned right and pulled out onto the main road.

Allie rolled the passenger side window down, letting the cool air circulate through the cab, and placed an arm on the truck's window ledge. The rushing fall air blew her hair back, and she smiled a healthy grin that warmed Elizabeth's heart.

Elizabeth pulled into the angled parking spot and turned the engine off. "Breakfast to go?" she asked, turning to Allie.

"Go where?"

Elizabeth smiled and responded, "How about our spot?" Allie nodded, and the two exited the vehicle.

Don's Bakery had been owned by the same family for the past forty years and was busy for a Sunday morning, its guests spilling out of the small cafe-style building and out onto the city sidewalk.

Elizabeth and Allie stood silently in line, the large storefront casting a shadow just large enough to shield them from the sun. They stood amongst the happy families, all waiting for a table or booth, hungry and ready to be seated after presumably attending the First Baptist of Ruthville's morning service.

Smells of freshly baked doughnuts, scrambled eggs, bacon, and hot coffee filled the cafe and spilled out onto the crowded sidewalk.

Elizabeth and Allie slowly made their way inside and ordered from the young girl behind the counter, who had been a few grades ahead of Allie in school. Fifteen minutes later, they picked up the biscuits and gravy, with sides of bacon and hashbrowns. The two were back out on the road, heading out of town and toward Frontage Road.

It was a quiet drive. Both were hungry, and when Allie's stomach broke the silence with a loud noise, the young woman and her mother erupted with laughter.

Elizabeth approached the intersection of Main Street and Frontage Road and stopped. She turned left as she had done so many times before. Countless times starting from when she was not much older than Allie and learning how to drive.

The red Ford Ranger accelerated out of the turn and proceeded down the road. When the time came, she would hand down the reliable old Ford, and Allie would take the trusted companion down this very same road, choosing her path at the intersections she would come upon. Then it would finally be time for Elizabeth to look for another vehicle.

Victor's old red Volvo 142E was totaled in the accident, and the insurance company hadn't offered much money to replace it, but at least it was something. Elizabeth disliked that old car. Her first impression when it rolled into the coffee stand line was that an old farmer had found it stored in a barn. She was pleasantly surprised to see she had been wrong in her assumption. The charming young man who pulled up to her window swept her off her feet.

Looking back, perhaps she should have trusted her gut. She knew that many of Victor's flaws were not his fault. Losing his mother at such a young age and with his father being both addicted to his work and alcohol, Victor missed out on a lot of structure and love that should have been provided for an adolescent. His father's failed attempts at relationships after his mother's death portrayed an inaccurate display of what love was supposed to look and feel like. Without the proper molding, Victor was destined to follow in his father's footsteps, ending up alone and dying, an alienation brought on by his vices used to remedy an absence, an emptiness that could never be filled. The loss of his mother too early in life, compounded with a non-existent father, had left him to fend for himself.

How could Victor value anything, let alone a marriage, if no one had valued him for most of his life? It was a sad observation and one that weighed heavily on her mind. Elizabeth was thankful that Allie was the result of their meeting, and she would do everything in her power from now on to show Allie that she was valued.

Elizabeth pulled the truck onto the gravel shoulder and parked it. She turned the engine off and grabbed the plastic food bag and picnic bag that sat between them on the gray cloth bench seat. They exited the truck, crossed the asphalt road, and stepped off the gravel shoulder as they made their way to the nearby drainage ditch. The granite monolith sat silently, basking in the morning sunlight, glowing like a beacon against the wheat.

They proceeded to the backside of the granite peak and began their journey to the top. Step by step, in familiar footholds and worn knobs ready for an uneasy hand, they made their way up the granite outcropping.

They reached the peak, a slight breeze blowing from the south warming their faces. Allie unfolded the blanket left there and laid it out for them to sit on. They sat there quietly, eating breakfast, a casual picnic like before, albeit missing a crucial piece. While they ate, Elizabeth reflected on the beautiful view and warm embrace from the morning sun.

When they finished, Elizabeth collected the empty Styrofoam containers and placed them in the plastic bag, setting them off to the side. She reached into the large picnic bag she had brought with her. Elizabeth pulled her hand out. A silver urn reflected the sunlight brightly, and she cradled it. She rolled the urn back and forth as the rays of sunlight bounced off its surface.

Elizabeth turned to Allie, whose eyes teared up at the site of the urn. Allie forced a smile, but Elizabeth could tell it had been a struggle for the young woman.

"Maybe it's time, honey?" Elizabeth asked, searching Allie's face.

Allie nodded and stood, the gray blanket edges flapping in the wind.

Elizabeth got to her feet and joined Allie, and the two walked to the edge of the prominent peak.

Initially, she had brought the urn home and had not known what to do with it. She had stowed it away in the cabinet with her vodka. It had served little purpose there. She knew Victor was no longer with them, and keeping his remains on display in the house only prolonged their healing.

Elizabeth held the silver urn out in front of her and opened the lid. Both peered inside, looking at the last remains of a father, a husband, a brilliant scientist, and someone loved so dearly. Everything that he ever was and could have ever been was reduced to a container of ashes just under a foot tall.

The warm, southerly wind came and briefly blew some of the dust off the top of the ashes, and Elizabeth knew it was the right choice.

She overturned the urn, the contents spilling out, taking flight from the top of the granite overlook that Victor had loved so much. The ashes swirled in the breeze, sparkled in the sunlight, and drifted on, carried away to serve another purpose.

Elizabeth placed an arm around her daughter and pulled her close.

Things will get better, she thought as they watched the ashes decorate the granite outcrop and travel out into the unknown.

Epilogue

The black Mercedes pulled into the gravel parking lot and parked. It stood out amongst the dirty sedans and lifted trucks. The dust generated by the smaller car was typical for the parking lot, and it drifted lazily in the stale air.

Director Angela Stevens opened the door and stepped out of the car, her tennis shoes crunching the gravel-mixed dirt.

She looked up at the pink neon light above the establishment. The glass letters that spelled out Candy's crackled and danced as the energized neon gas vibrated inside. She had heard of this establishment before and thought the name to be fitting, given the storefront's affection for the colors of sweet treats.

Angela closed the black door and locked the car, the LED bulbs flashing twice. She walked onto the gravel parking lot, thankful that she had already changed out of her office attire. Surely, she would have rolled an ankle in her office shoes.

She was home that evening, celebrating her team's launch by herself when she received a text message from Alexander White. It was odd that he had texted her and more so given the time of night. Angela was no recluse, but a text past 11:00 pm from a colleague was not typical.

The text read, 'Celebration drink at Candy's?'

She mulled over her response for a while before finally answering, 'Yes.'

Angela was close to her coworkers out there and had not planned on being. Now that the crew had successfully left the Earth's atmosphere and there would be radio silence soon, she knew she would have little to look forward to until an update from Alice came in.

Why not live a little? she thought.

Angela was happy to get out of her small apartment for a little while.

She arrived at the glass-lined restaurant door, her reflection greeting her as she lifted her hand to the metal handle. She checked herself out briefly in the glass reflection. Her hair was still styled from the workday, and her casual jeans and blue sweatshirt would probably match the dress code inside.

Angela pulled the heavy glass door open, and the smell of fried food and stale beer filled her nose. It brought back memories from college, and she smiled.

She entered the dimly lit building, the shadowed booth areas harder to see than the oiled wooden bar, well lit by the overhead can lights. She took a few timid steps forward, waiting for her eyes to adjust. An old Seattle grunge-style song filled the air from a jukebox in the corner, something from the 90s if she had to guess.

Angela scanned the room, looking for a familiar face, and a hand shot up from the far end of the bar. Alexander waved and peered at her from behind the row of local patrons, pointing at an empty seat beside him. Angela made her way toward him, exhaling a nervous breath as she did. It had been a long time since she was in a similar setting to this, she remarked to herself.

She arrived at where he sat, and he patted the tan cloth-lined barstool next to him.

"I've saved you a seat, Director," Alexander said, slurring slightly.

"Thank you," she said as she sat.

"What will it be?" he asked, leaning toward her, yelling over the sound of the bar's occupants. His breath smelled of whiskey or bourbon, and a lot of it.

"I'll have one of whatever you're having."

Alexander gave a carefree smile, one that she was sure he had used in the past to get what he wanted and turned to the bartender. "Two Old Fashions, Jim," Alexander said, craning his neck around the gentleman next to him dressed in dusty Levi's and a flannel shirt. The bartender nodded and turned to pour the drinks.

Alexander turned to Angela and smiled. There was something odd about the smile, though, not genuine in the slightest.

"Are you alright, Mr. White?" she asked him, concerned.

"Never better, why wouldn't I be?" he asked, throwing back the small glass that had been sitting in front of him half full.

He placed the empty glass back down on the white coaster.

Angela heard the sarcasm in his voice which was made more apparent by the amount of alcohol he had likely consumed before her arrival.

The bartender returned and placed the two drinks in front of them.

She raised her glass, and Alexander repeated the gesture.

"To the mission," she said, tipping the glass to an honorary mentioning point.

Alexander met her glass with his, looked her in the eyes, and softly replied, "And to those, we have lost."

She now understood Alexander's heavy drinking and solemn attitude.

"I know that you and Jodi were close. I'm sure it is hard to know that she's out there somewhere and not knowing if she will return safely," she said sympathetically.

"It's not the first time I've lost her," he said quietly, his face down, looking at the contents of the glass.

Alexander put the glass to his lips and downed it, slamming the glass on the bar. He paused for a moment in thought and then leaned forward to an old, brown leather briefcase sitting near his feet. He brought it up and sat it on the oiled bar.

He spun the briefcase around to face him, unlatched the metallic clasps, and pulled the top open. He reached into the briefcase and pulled out a manilla envelope. Alexander placed the oversized envelope on the bar top in front of her, the words classified spelled out boldly on its face.

Angela leaned forward to inspect the folder. "What's this?"

A grin grew from the corner of his mouth, different from the charming, perhaps fake smile he usually produced. He closed the briefcase and latched the metal clasps.

"I took it out of my boss's office earlier tonight while I was leaving my letter of resignation. It's everything we have on the project. Pay attention to the stuff in the beginning. It should help fill in any gaps," he said, his eyes fixed on the large envelope.

She took the manilla envelope and began to unwind the threaded clasp. Beside her, Alexander stood and neatly placed two twenty-dollar bills on the bar top.

"I've got to go. My ride's here outside," Alexander said, grabbing his coat and briefcase.

He reached a hand out, and she stared at the old gesture, then returned it and shook his hand, which felt warm in hers.

They made eye contact, and Alexander gave her a silent nod. He let go of her hand, turned, and walked toward the door. He reached the glass-lined door, pulled it open, and exited.

Angela pulled the papers from the envelope in front of her and placed them on the bar beneath the lights. She leaned forward on the barstool, her brown hair casting a slight shadow over the stack of papers. She lifted the top page and held it in front of her face.

The first page detailed an interview with Victor Gray, a theoretical physicist, thirteen years prior.

Thirteen years ago? she thought, puzzled.

She placed the top sheet back on the stack of papers, scooped them all up, and turned toward one of the quiet booths in the back. She doubled back to grab her drink, nodded at the bartender, and then walked to the first empty booth. She sat on the soft, worn cushion and looked over the top page again.

Interlope: Epilogue

Angela began to read Alexander's statement of the events surrounding his first encounter with Dr. Victor Gray.

***

It was the fall of 2012, and Alexander had arrived in Cambridge on a cold morning. Spring was near, and the birds sang in the early morning sun. He walked along the pathway that cut through the sprawling green lawn. Alexander rounded the corner, and the Maclaurin Buildings came into sight. The impressive pillars that supported the front of the building were only surpassed by the Great Dome behind it.

He walked through the green grass toward the main building, Building Ten, as it was called. He reached the stairs and climbed, pausing halfway and glancing back at the Charles River that played peek-a-boo in the distance.

Alexander continued up the steps and entered the building. He stepped into the massive Infinite Corridor, the eight-hundred-and-twenty-three-foot hallway and paused to admire the engineering feat.

He continued down the long hallway, glancing at the bulletin boards, murals, and displays lining the walls. He walked until the painted gray walls gave way to the floor-to-ceiling windows. Laboratories filled each glass window-boxed room, and he paused at each poster, each indicating current projects.

Alexander stopped at the lab he had traveled to Cambridge, Massachusetts, to visit. The glass-lined door was open, and he stepped into it.

A young man in his twenties sat behind a stack of papers on an old wooden desk, concentrating on the work in front of him. The young man had a full head of black hair, not quite short but well-kept for its length. He wore a white lab coat, and Alexander saw he was wearing khaki-colored slacks beneath it.

"Sir?" Alexander asked.

The young man looked up, his pencil stopping its movement.

"I'm looking for Dr. Victor Gray," Alexander said from the doorway.

The young man cleared his throat and stood, the flannel shirt beneath his white lab coat hanging out loosely from the collar of the lab coat.

"I'm Dr. Gray. Please sit," the young man said, gesturing to an old wooden chair opposite him.

Alexander made his way through the lab and sat, placing his briefcase next to his feet. With no chair padding, he shifted his weight immediately.

Dr. Gray smiled at the movement and said, "I apologize for the chair. I'm a simple man and was always taught that a comfortable chair promoted laziness."

"I can see how someone wouldn't want to sit in it for long," Alexander replied, returning the smile.

"What can I do for you, Mister …" Dr. Gray asked, his voice trailing off.

"My name is Alexander White, Sir. I am employed by the Department of Defense, specifically the Defense Advanced Research Projects Agency."

Dr. Gray raised a hand and rubbed the left side of his jaw. "What is it that the DOD wants with me?"

Alexander reached to the floor and grabbed his shiny brown leather briefcase and placed it on the desk. He unhooked the metal clasps, opened it, and pulled out a file folder.

He flipped through the pages and stopped at a photograph, picked it up, looked at it, and placed it in front of Dr. Gray.

Dr. Gray picked up the photograph and stared at it, studying it. In the photo was a metallic sphere approximately two feet in diameter, judging by the shovel nearby.

"What is it?" Dr. Gray asked, placing the photo down on the desk.

"I was kind of hoping you could tell me, Dr. Gray."

Interlope: Epilogue

"I haven't a clue as to what it is, Sir. Where was it found?" Alexander cleared his throat. "This particular sphere was found in Siberia in 1908. Evenki natives and a few Russian settlers in an area northwest of Lake Baikal notified the Soviet authorities of a bright bluish light, followed by a flash and subsequent explosion. The explosion set off seismic detecting devices halfway around the globe and registered as a 5.0 on local Richter scales. It was said that the night skies glowed in the days to follow.

"The Soviet Army investigated the report, finding over eight hundred and thirty square miles of flattened forest. The official report classified the cause as a meteor airburst, a stony meteorite around 200' in size exploding prior to impact. This cause was accepted without question due to the absence of an impact crater."

"The impact event you're referring to is the Tunguska event?" Dr. Gray asked.

Alexander nodded. "Fast forward to June of 1941 and Hitler's launch of Operation Barbarossa and the invasion of the Soviet Union by Germany. While the majority of Operation Barbarossa was a failure, Hitler was still able to seize a few Russian assets. At some point, he acquired the sphere and planned on reverse-engineering it. Thankfully, the Allies were able to prevent this from happening, but the sphere was lost at some point.

"The Allies were able to recover the research that the Germans had performed on the sphere. The files were turned over to the U.S. Government and eventually stored for safekeeping at an undisclosed location. It sat there collecting dust until renovations were performed in the 1990s. At that point, the file box was handed over to the Department of Defense."

"And the U.S. government assumes that the Tunguska event and the sphere in the photo are connected?" Dr. Gray asked.

Alexander raised his shoulders in a shrug. "It's possible."

He paused and again reached into the folder, pulled out a copy of an x-ray, and placed it in front of Dr. Gray.

Dr. Gray picked it up and rolled his chair to the edge of his desk where a lamp sat. He turned the lamp on and illuminated the back of the x-ray. It showed the outline of the same sphere with a ring-shaped frame in the interior. Across the interior shell of the sphere were sets of zeros and ones. Dr. Gray raised an eyebrow and looked at Alexander. "Binary code?"

"That's affirmative," replied Alexander.

"What does it say? Has it been translated?"

"It has, Doctor."

"And?" Dr. Gray asked, setting the x-ray on the desk.

Alexander reached into the folder again and pulled out another document, this time a simple sheet of white paper. He placed it on the desk, and Dr. Gray rolled over to the center of the desk. Picking it up, Dr. Gray read the two short sentences, his eyes growing wide. He placed the sheet on the desk, the letters facing Alexander.

Dr. Gray read them again, the two sentences which had no meaning until now.

"Do not open. If found, contact Dr. Victor Gray of MIT, Cambridge, Massachusetts," Dr. Gray said as he sat back in his chair.

Alexander placed the paper and the x-ray in the folder and cleared his throat. "I'll ask again, Doctor. What do you know about this object?"

Dr. Gray ran a hand through his black hair. He leaned forward and placed a hand on his left jaw, rubbing it.

"I've had ideas about a similar object, but I've never designed anything regarding it. The thoughts have come to mind, but I've never put pen to paper. I've never seen this object in my life," Dr. Gray said, lifting his shoulders in a shrug.

"That would make sense. The DOD has been searching for you since the early 2000s. Turns out there was never a Dr. Victor Gray at MIT until now. After five years, they gave up on the case, and it was put in a box in storage. I was assigned a desk job at the

Interlope: Epilogue

DOD, and after being bored for two months, I started diving through old case files. That's when I spotted this one and was intrigued. A simple google search of your name led me to your work on microreactors and, ultimately, to your door. Any clue on what this could be or where it's from?"

Dr. Gray rubbed his left jawbone again. "If this isn't a hoax and is a legitimate object, I think there's only one possible explanation."

"Aliens? Time travel? Different dimensions?" Alexander asked, smiling so that Dr. Gray could tell he was kidding.

"A little bit of all of that," Dr. Gray said, sitting back in his chair.

"Alien perhaps to us and definitely from a different time."

"Now I'm the confused one," Alexander said.

"I'm speaking of a parallel universe hypothesis, specifically the Everett Interpretation. A concept where there are one or more universes existing right next to each other, interacting with each other only briefly through entanglement. Every possible outcome of any situation played out independently along its very own path."

"Every possible outcome?" Alexander asked.

Dr. Gray leaned forward and placed his hand on a stack of white papers on the right side of his desk between the two men.

"Let's take this stack of papers, for example. Imagine that each sheet of paper is a separate universe, except with a thin membrane in between each sheet that repels the surrounding sheets and keeps the whole stack in harmony. Physicist Hugh Everett proposed this, and Bryce Dewitt later popularized it and renamed it the Many-Worlds Interpretation in the 1970s."

"Is there any other proof that these universes exist?" Alexander asked.

"Mathematically, it works. However, this is the first tangible piece of evidence that I've seen regarding the hypothesis. The majority of the evidence lies in data and observation," Dr. Gray said, folding his hands on the desk.

"Data such as?"

"The expansion of the known universe, for example. Everything we know about the Big Bang states that everything is expanding from each other from a concordant moment of expansion. The calculations of this would suggest that expansion would be constant and eventually slow down. However, observations of our visible galaxies would suggest that the expansion is actually accelerating," Dr. Gray explained.

"And what is causing this acceleration?" Alexander asked.

"That part is debatable. One might suggest that we are closer to the initial explosion, the Big Bang, and that is to explain the current expansion. That idea would undermine most of our other observations and theories. The other explanation would be the parallel universe hypothesis. This states that the independent universes occupy time and space in harmony. In my separate hypothesis, a universe can split in the way that a biological cell can, producing a replication of itself, only becoming slightly different immediately following the replication. For example, this would create a new sheet of paper, sliding in between the existing stack of papers. Adequate space must be given to the new alternate universe, so the entire stack expands accordingly. To one of the individual sheets of paper, it would appear that the space between itself and a known object would have expanded," Dr. Gray explained.

"What would be strong enough to cause a split such as that?"

Dr. Gray shrugged. "That, I'm not sure of. It could be something incomprehensible or something as simple as a major life decision made by a single individual. In one scenario, you chose to travel here to Cambridge to visit with me. On this particular trip, let's say you meet the love of your life. In the contrasting scenario, you placed the folder back in the dusty box and, thus, never traveled to Cambridge today. If you were never in Cambridge, you would

Interlope: Epilogue

never meet your partner; no offspring would come of that relationship. To the observer, at the moment of your decision, but prior to acting upon it, both scenarios are true."

"Perhaps I should keep an eye out while I'm here?" Alexander asked with a smile.

Dr. Gray smiled and nodded. "To wrap it up, if I have a glass of water and I add a single drop, the volume increases slightly, almost unnoticed. But if there are decisions made daily by the world population, that is a lot of drops. The expansion of volume would then be noticed and measurable. If you were to combine the potential parallel universes and write out the potential for new ones, the sum of the equation would grow each time you observed it, always expanding."

Alexander brought his hand down on the stack of paper, pressing it. "What keeps each one from crushing each other?"

"These parallel universes would be held together by a fabric or a membrane, most likely one electromagnetic in nature. Each sheet would have opposing electromagnetic poles so that each would repel one another to stay in a balanced state," Dr. Gray said, sitting back in his chair.

"Are you telling me that another version of you created the sphere in the photograph and sent it here?" Alexander asked, also sitting back in his chair, trying his best to comprehend what the doctor had just laid out for him.

Dr. Gray placed his hand on the edge of the stack of papers, sliding his thumb upward and flipping the sheets one by one.

"In this example, you and everything you knew to be possible would exist on a single sheet of paper. Would you have any idea what would be transpiring just a few sheets away?" Dr. Gray raised his eyes to Alexander's as he asked.

"I have no idea," Alexander replied.

"Have there been any other ideas?"

Alexander shook his head. "None this elaborate."

Dr. Gray looked at his watch. "Have you eaten, Mr. White? How about we talk more about this over breakfast?"

Alexander nodded and grabbed his briefcase. "I could eat."

The two men stood and left the lab. They walked silently through the Infinite Corridor and out the door. They passed the colonial pillars and descended the concrete steps to the path and grass below.

"I'm parked over in the faculty parking lot this way," Dr. Gray said, motioning toward the parking lot.

They walked silently, the soft sound of their shoes padding across the concrete sidewalk. An asphalt parking lot came into view, and Dr. Gray motioned to an old yellow Volvo 142E. The yellow paint reflected brightly in the morning sun.

Alexander raised his hand to shield the reflecting rays from the polished chrome bumper.

"Nice car. Is it a collector?" Alexander asked, dropping his hand.

"No, it was my mother's. She recently passed away, and I haven't had the heart to sell it yet," Dr. Gray replied.

Dr. Gray unlocked the passenger-side door and walked to the driver-side door. Both opened their corresponding doors and sat on the soft seats.

Alexander closed his door and turned to the doctor. "This expanding universe by choice, how does that factor into a creation theory, Dr. Gray?"

Dr. Gray closed his door and started the engine. "Well, if you were to dial the expansion back far enough, you eventually come back to a single moment in time. Everything we've ever seen, touched, smelled, or thought of exists. However, a fraction of a second prior to that, nothing existed at all. Both scenarios are true. At one moment, there was nothing, and then a decision was made. One choice was made to create, and one choice was made not to create. At that moment, the initial universe was split into two, with one being created and one that never had a chance to exist. From that point on, there was an expansion on our known side and none on the other," Dr. Gray explained, his hands on the steering wheel.

"So, you believe in a creator?" Alexander asked, looking out at the beautiful, blue, cloudless sky.

"I believe there is both a creator and no creator. The two exist in harmony. Yin and Yang, I suppose."

"Interesting," Alexander said, turning to Dr. Gray. "Have you ever been to North Dakota?

Dr. Gray shook his head.

And with that, the Yellow Volvo 142E pulled out of its parking space.

523 egap no sediser rehpic noitacided eht ot yek ehT